SAIL AWAY

SAIL AWAY

CELIA IMRIE

B L O O M S B U R Y
LONDON · OXFORD · NEW YORK · NEW DELHI · SYDNEY

Bloomsbury Publishing
An imprint of Bloomsbury Publishing Plc

50 Bedford Square   1385 Broadway
London   New York
WC1B 3DP   NY 10018
UK   USA

www.bloomsbury.com

BLOOMSBURY and the Diana logo are trademarks of Bloomsbury Publishing Plc

First published in Great Britain 2018

British Library Cataloguing-in-Publication Data
A catalogue record for this book is available from the British Library.

ISBN: HB: 978-1-4088-8322-8
         TPB: 978-1-4088-8323-5
         EPUB: 978-1-4088-8321-1

2 4 6 8 10 9 7 5 3 1

Typeset by Integra Software Services Pvt. Ltd.
Printed and bound in Great Britain by CPI Group (UK) Ltd, Croydon CR0 4YY

To find out more about our authors and books visit www.bloomsbury.com.
Here you will find extracts, author interviews, details of forthcoming
events and the option to sign up for our newsletters.

PART ONE

Catalysts

S UZY MARSHALL's phone rang.
   It was her agent, Max. 'Interview, darling!'

Suzy sat down and took a deep breath. She'd not had a whisper of work now for months. She grabbed a pencil and notepad, ready to take down the details.

After twenty or more years working steadily in rep and TV, when Suzy hit her forties the job offers had started to dry up. Now that she had just turned sixty, even getting an audition seemed like a rare miracle.

Over the last few years Suzy, like most older actresses, had acted intermittently, and in between 'real' work, to make ends meet, she had taken small secretarial temp jobs.

Her savings had dwindled away. In fact, she had been unemployed for so many months now, she was no longer eligible to collect dole money, and at her age she was also put at the back of the line for the little jobs she had always depended on to fill the out-of-work days.

The last time she had turned up at the job centre, the man behind the counter laughed in her face.

'You're a pensioner,' he said. 'No one is going to employ a pensioner.'

Suzy had explained that even though she was just sixty she was not entitled to collect a pension for some years to come.

'Not my problem,' said the young man, slicking back his greasy hair.

'What am I going to live on? I'm broke. It's not fair.'

'That's life,' said the young man. 'Life's not fair, Ms Marshall. In another existence, I could have been a rich, sexy male model; instead I'm a clerk in a job centre.'

Suzy had no reply to this.

It was hard to believe now, but Suzy had once known a tempest of fame. For a good ten years, she had spent most of her train journeys and visits to the supermarket signing autographs for enthusiastic fans. She had played the principal role in the multi-award-winning mid-1980s TV drama series *Dahlias*, a show which had a regular audience of twenty million Brits who eagerly awaited Thursday evening's transmission. But, although at the time *Dahlias* had been a worldwide hit, now, more than thirty years later, everyone had forgotten both the series and Suzy.

From a professional point of view, it was no help either, for when *Dahlias* had been top of the TV ratings, the new wave of directors had not yet been born, so that *Dahlias* was now no more than a word printed on her CV.

'The interview is tomorrow at 10 a.m.,' said Max down the line.

Suzy wrote '10'.

'It's for two and a half weeks' rehearsal and a six-week run of *The Importance of Being Earnest*,' said Max.

Excited now, Suzy wrote the name of the classic play.

'You'll be reading for the role of …'

Suzy knew it would have to be Miss Prism …

'Lady Bracknell.'

Suzy's heart flipped with joy. Lady Bracknell was one of the best classic roles of all time.

While Max went on reading out the list of scene numbers that she would have to familiarise herself with, Suzy wondered where the production would be. She hoped it might be one of the larger reps in a big city like Liverpool, Leeds, Nottingham or Birmingham. Even a small theatre might be fun – a couple of months in a cottage in Wales or up in the wilds of Scotland would be a great adventure.

'The engagement is with the grandly named Zurich Regal International Theatre,' said Max. 'But rehearsals will be in London.'

'What's that?' asked Suzy. 'Zurich in Switzerland?'

'That's right, darling. One of the English-speaking theatre companies.'

Suzy's mood dipped. She knew that these little European troupes paid badly and had a very low, if not negative, value on the CV.

They played to tiny audiences consisting mainly of expats. No one back in England heard a squeak about the shows put on, which failed even to get a review in the *Stage*, a newspaper which reviewed every play, musical, pantomime and end-of-the-pier show from Land's End to John o'Groats.

The result was that, although an actor might be slogging away for weeks on end, as far as all the casting directors went, they might as well be dead.

In reality, to Suzy, an eight-week stint with the Zurich Regal International Theatre was another slide down the ladder (or in this case was it the snake?) of success.

But it was a great role, and it was at least a *little* money. And it would be a lot more fun to spend her time with other actors, keeping busy, rather than sitting at home alone gazing at the TV, waiting for the phone to ring.

Max gave Suzy the address of the audition.

'N13?' she asked. 'Where's that?'

'Palmers Green,' said Max. 'I believe it's the director's home.' He laughed. 'So, you can get to bellow out your "*handbag*" in his kitchen. Hope the neighbours don't mind.'

'Who is the director?' asked Suzy, hoping it might be someone she had worked with in her past.

'Reg Shoesmith. He does a lot of these sort of things – Hamburg, Vienna, Nairobi. Anyway, rehearsals start on Monday.'

Suzy finished the call with mixed feelings.

In the mirror she inspected the roots of her blonde hair. She had worn it in a Mary Quant page-boy style for probably over fifteen years now, she realised. She had kept her figure, and at five foot seven and a half inches, did she dare to admit she would make an imposing Lady B? Why not?

She had been in the game long enough to realise that she must be being seen for a last-minute replacement for the part. No sane person would keep the casting of Lady Bracknell back until a few days before rehearsals started. It would have been one of the first roles cast.

Therefore, the company was clearly desperate.

Suzy had never heard of either the theatre company or the director. But, looking on the positive side, she was really in with a chance. A company of such low prestige, which could only afford to hold auditions in the kitchen of the director's home in Palmers Green, should be so lucky to have an actress with such a strong CV auditioning for them!

They'd be mad not to have her.

The job would be a shoo-in.

Early next morning Suzy eagerly got on the Tube and made her way to the address in Palmers Green. For the whole journey she studied the play, familiarising herself with the lines, ready to deliver them with gusto.

But, once she was sitting in the director's living room, she realised that even this job was not yet in the bag. Far from it. She wished she wasn't lumbered with her rather cumbersome pink National Health reading glasses, but maybe she would use them to disdainful advantage when she was called in for her turn. Suzy recognised at least three of the other women sitting on the two sofas, swotting their scripts, silently mouthing the words. She surreptitiously studied them. They were all actresses, like herself, who had once been household names. One had spent years as the leading lady at the Royal Shakespeare Company, another played many major roles in every TV drama you could think of, while the other had even been nominated twenty years ago for a BAFTA (or was it an Oscar?) for a supporting role in a British film.

She hoped the others might be up for the part of Miss Prism, but no. Everyone was competing for the same role – Lady Bracknell in Wilde's *The Importance of Being Earnest*.

It was therefore a great surprise when, next morning, Saturday, Max phoned and told Suzy she'd got the job.

Rehearsals were to take place in a smelly church hall near Tottenham Cemetery. For Suzy this meant a little under two hours' travel at the beginning and end of each day. And, as actors tend to like arriving good and early, it meant that each morning Suzy had to be out of her front door at 7.30 a.m. sharp and she would be lucky if she was home by 9 p.m. But the journey, by Tube, train and bus, would give her time to fill in the wad of forms which always came with jobs away from home – tax information, passport numbers, bank account details – and also to look over her lines. Learning lines was much harder these days, and she certainly didn't want to be the last actor off the book.

She flopped on to the sofa and pulled her copy of *The Comedies of Oscar Wilde* from the bookshelf. As she flicked through the pages she thought back on her life.

Talk about starting at the top and working her way down that thing which the general public laughingly called 'the ladder of success'!

But here she was, still working. Not only that, she was going to a beautiful foreign city, to play one of the great roles in world drama with a group of actors. What was wrong with that? Far better than sitting in some suburban sitting room looking after noisy grandchildren, working for a pittance with all the part-time pensioners in B&Q, or commuting in from the suburbs each day to answer the phone in a call centre. Suzy knew that, although she could do that kind of thing now and then, for her, as a lifestyle choice, it would drive her to madness. As it was, bad luck and a succession of affairs with men who went off and married other people meant that she had no children and therefore also no grandchildren of her own. She lived alone, and, truthfully, was content with that. She detested the very thought of all those little domestic spats with the beloved other about who was in control of the TV and what they ate for dinner, or where they should go on holiday and when.

She had done the 'living together' thing a few times. But it had never really worked for her. In her own experience, once domesticity took a grip, romance went right out the window. Suzy was free, and, if she searched her soul, she had to admit that, deep down, she was happy. She was a born gypsy. She loved the never knowing where you'd be next week, and all the related unpredictability of the actor's life. She also enjoyed the camaraderie of other actors, who, though they could be catty, were rarely boring company.

Suzy kicked off her shoes, put her feet up and turned to Lady B's first scene.

"'You can take a seat, Mr Worthing,'" she read.

*

"'You can take a seat, Mr Worthing.'"

"'Thank you, Lady Bracknell. I prefer standing.'"

Two days into rehearsal and Suzy was about to block Lady Bracknell's famous 'handbag' scene.

She sat in the centre of the dusty rehearsal room, prop notebook and pencil poised, facing Jason Scott, a dark-haired boy with bright eyes and a glittering smile, who took the part of Jack Worthing.

'We'll stop there for the moment,' snapped Reg Shoesmith, the director, rising from his seat behind the stage manager's table and moving into the acting space. 'Time for lunch.'

Neither Suzy nor Jason could believe that a director would stop at this point in the script. But he was the director, so it was his call.

Suzy swapped a look with Barbara, the stage manager who sat at Reg's side. Barbara, a shrewd blonde woman who didn't speak much, had a very sharp way of expressing herself with almost imperceptible movements of the face. She rolled her eyes, and closed her script. It was clear she was in agreement with the actors on this.

'Half an hour, everyone,' Barbara called to the assembled company. 'Ready to pick up where we left off.'

Suzy took her bag of home-made sandwiches and went to sit out in the winter sunshine. The only green space nearby was the cemetery, so she found a bench between the grave-stones, and ate her lunch while thinking through the one and a half days they had done.

Although Lady Bracknell was a role Suzy had longed to play all her life, now that she was having a go it didn't seem quite as much fun as she had hoped.

She realised that getting a decent performance together was going to be quite a challenge in the mere two and a half weeks' rehearsal period. She was also frightened about the proposed single day set aside for the technical and dress rehearsal at the venue, before opening the same night in Zurich's Little Regal Theatre. It would be a real sprint, especially as Reg was messing around with the play in a way that would need a lot of technical work – with lighting, sound, and quick costume changes.

Suzy tried with all her might to give the director, Reg, the benefit of the doubt, but so far she found it hard to agree with anything he proposed.

'The play,' Reg had pronounced after yesterday's read-through, 'is a tiny bit creaky.' Nonetheless, he informed them all, he had some ideas which would 'freshen it up a bit'. The first of these ideas was that, between every act, the actors playing Algernon, Jack and the butlers, Lane and Merriman, should sing little ditties which Reg had written himself. They would all wear boaters and harmonise in the barbershop style, popping up and down from behind the furniture while they and the other actors put the tables and chairs into place to change the scene.

Reg's other 'fresh' ideas were equally grim. He had told Emily that Miss Prism would make her first entrance riding a bicycle on to the tiny stage, and, despite words in the text clearly indicating something quite formal, he expected Cecily and Gwendolen, during the famous cucumber sandwiches scene, to toast marshmallows over a barbecue he had positioned in the centre of a Japanese-style patio garden.

Suzy liked the rest of the cast enormously.

The young quartet – Jack, Algernon, Gwendolen and Cecily – were fresh-faced, keen and charming, excited to be playing their parts and looking forward to exploring Zurich. Jason Scott was exceptionally good in the role of Jack Worthing and his alter ego Earnest. Luckily enough, most of Suzy's time onstage was with him.

Lady Bracknell's daughter Gwendolen was played by India, a sharp-witted, well-heeled young lady with a nice line in tart remarks.

Suzy liked Emily, the actress playing Miss Prism, too. She was quiet but every now and then said something really droll. Suzy wondered what Emily was secretly making of the director's 'artistic vision'.

The only member of the cast who Suzy hadn't taken to was Stan Arbuthnot – the man who was playing Canon Chasuble. On only two days' experience, she already knew that he was a pompous bore, always sounding off about his escapades with famous actors, and delivering unfunny quips about everyone else's performance, going into sulks when he didn't get his own way. He also had an annoying habit of making remarks under his breath during other people's scenes. Suzy had not worked out whether he was going through his own lines, or making comments on the actors who were trying to work a few feet away. Whenever she was up in the acting space Suzy felt certain that Stan's mumbling was a running commentary on how bad she was.

But Stan/Chasuble was rarely onstage with Lady Bracknell. He stayed in the rehearsal room during lunch, sitting in the corner sucking up to Reg, while gorging on cold greasy bacon sandwiches which he had made at home that morning.

Suzy had been revolted when, during Monday's rehearsal, Stan had returned to the acting area after lunch with greasy shiny patches on his cheeks and little flecks of chewed-up sandwich on his double chin. She thanked her lucky stars that Lady Bracknell never had to go anywhere near Chasuble. She really pitied Emily, who had to have an onstage kiss with him, albeit a peck on the cheek.

Due to the short rehearsal period, lunch break was unusually only thirty minutes long.

Suzy made her way back to the rehearsal room. She grabbed her props – the notebook and a piece of stick representing her parasol – and took her place in the centre of the room, with Jason standing opposite her.

'"You can take a seat, Mr Worthing."'

'"Thank you, Lady Bracknell. I prefer standing."'

'Stop!' Reg advanced from the director's desk, rubbing his hands together with glee, the rosacea on his cheeks flaring, saying, 'We don't want any of that dusty old Dame Edith Evans stuff. Nor any of that subdued Dame Judi Dench version. This is a vibrant, living production, Suzy. Relevant. Hip. So, I'll let you into the secret now. When it comes to the iconic "handbag" bit I'm going to give it a modern twist.'

Suzy swallowed hard and reminded herself that they were opening in Zurich and consequently no one she knew was likely ever actually to *see* the show.

She really had to keep it stored away as a case of 'take the money and run'.

Reg eyed Jason then spun around and faced Suzy, his finger pointing towards her. He pursed his lips, raised his eyebrows and put on the face which he obviously thought made him look cute and naughty.

Suzy prepared for the worst.

Reg bent low and whispered in Suzy's ear. 'This is going to be soooo fabulous!' His breath smelled rank with tooth decay.

'Everyone's going to expect you to do an enormous swoopy *haaaaandbaaaag* thing,' he gave a pantomime rendition of Edith Evans's voice. 'Either that or they'll think you'll toss it away with the low-key-racing-through-it-as-if-it-didn't-matter thing. Sooooo …' He lowered his voice and said the words she feared most: 'I've had a brilliant idea.'

Suzy took a deep breath.

'I'm going to use the barbershop boys. They're going to do a kind of sliding-scale wah-wah-wah thing, after you deliver the line.'

Blinking, Suzy scrutinised the director's face to make sure he wasn't joking.

He wasn't.

'They're going to pop out from the wings, fluttering their boaters, and sing!' He turned to face Jason. 'Great idea, don't you think?'

'Ummmm,' said Jason, his voice only a tad above a whisper. 'Yeah?'

Suzy didn't want to be difficult, but … well … It was all right for these directors. They made these horrible errors of taste, and then, after the first night, they buggered off, never to be seen again. Meanwhile *you* were the one up there nightly onstage suffering the embarrassment, and the audiences' reactions. Not only that but the newspaper reviewers always plonked the director's awful ideas at the actor's door, making you look like a complete fool all over the press, and also, in these days of social media, all over Twitter and Facebook too.

She tapped her stick twice on the floor and said, 'Right ho! Let's get on with it then!'

However, by the end of the afternoon's rehearsal, Suzy could hold herself back no more and there was a heated stand-off. Jason took Suzy's side, but at that point Reg simply threw down the book and stormed out of the rehearsal room.

'Go home, both of you! Amateurs!' he yelled over his shoulder. 'I spent the whole of our precious half-hour lunchtime on the phone with the Swiss money man, so I've had quite enough of poncy prima donnas for one day, thank you. I'd like to work through the tea-party and the Chasuble/Prism scenes in fifteen minutes, if that's acceptable to the rest of the cast.'

Suzy and Jason rolled eyes at one another and silently gathered their things.

'We'll dodge round it,' Jason murmured, holding the door for her. 'Don't forget that, once we open, Reg will be back off to London. Then we can get together, change things and make it all work, our way.'

He winked. Suzy smiled back, feeling like a dangerous conspirator.

On the Tube home they decided to spend the rest of the afternoon going through their scenes in Suzy's flat.

Next morning, when they both arrived in the rehearsal room, Reg ignored them.

He was directing the opening scene of Act Two. This time Reg was picking on Emily. Stan Arbuthnot had had an idea about how he wanted to say a particular line, but this entailed Emily having to change the way she said her preceding line. Emily politely pointed out to Stan that acting was about listening to the other actor and replying, not planning gags on your own, which, to make them work, necessitated everyone else changing what they were doing.

'Just do it,' hissed Stan, spraying Emily with crummy spit.

'No,' replied Emily firmly, turning her back on him.

Stan sat down on the central banquette, folded his arms and squealed like a stuck pig. 'No! No! I will not give in!' He pattered his feet, as he sat, still shrieking in a high-pitched wail.

Suzy and Jason, sitting at the end of the rehearsal room, exchanged a look.

'Good lord, what a hellish noise,' whispered Suzy. 'It goes right through your bones.'

'It's like watching a four-year-old having a tantrum over broccoli,' Jason murmured. 'He really is the end.'

'I will not move or shut up until I am satisfied.' Stan's piercing scream was enough to shatter glass.

Reg moved on to the floor and addressed Emily. 'Just deliver the line the way Stan wants you to,' he said.

'Seriously?' Emily's lips tightened and her eyes flared. 'Fine. Whatever you like, Reg.' She shrugged her shoulders. 'You're the director.' Emily implied a slight query at the end of that sentence, as it was clear who was really in charge of the situation.

Reg nodded at Stan and he unfolded his arms and stood up, a grin spreading across his fat, glistening face.

Emily said the line. It sounded bizarre, and made her seem like an amateur actress. But Stan then made his well-practised reply, complete with eye-roll and tongue in cheek.

Suzy sighed, appalled to see something so cheap and end-of-the-pier in a play by Oscar Wilde, but then she remembered the use of the barbershop boys and realised that the whole show stank.

After the rehearsal for her scene ended Emily came across and sat next to Suzy.

'Poor you,' whispered Suzy.

Emily shrugged. 'I've worked with Stan before. When he doesn't get what he wants he turns into a real Violet Elizabeth Bott – you remember that temperamental girl in the *Just William* books. He throws a tantrum, complete with stamping feet, yelling in that really unpleasant tone until the other party gives in. It's very tiresome.'

'Why would Reg support behaviour like that?' asked Suzy.

'It's easier to give in to him!' She laughed. 'He will go on making that row until you agree to his whim of the moment. Honestly, it's just simpler to get it over and done with, give him what he wants and shut him up.'

'How pathetic. He must have been a very spoiled child.'

'He still is,' said Emily. 'But for us life goes on.'

Suzy was in awe of Emily's fortitude. 'I think it's really sad that such horrible conduct gets rewarded.'

By the end of the second week, when the company hit run-throughs, Suzy was crossing her fingers and toes, but ostensibly going along with everything Reg said. All the while Jason kept giving her surreptitious winks. Suzy winked back, gritted her teeth and smiled in Reg's direction.

She was not happy with herself, however. She was still grasping about for her lines. It didn't help to question matters in a production when you weren't confidently off the book. It was hard stuff to learn too. The major problem with Wilde is that the text simply couldn't take a paraphrase. One word out of place and the whole thing collapsed. The learning had to be precise. The words weren't going in and she knew part of that was because she was uncomfortable playing the role the way it had been directed.

On the last evening's rehearsal before their departure for Switzerland, Suzy was in an utter panic.

After taking a short tea-break, Reg announced that the final run-through was to have a small audience – not only the usual technical people like the lighting designer and stage management team, but also the backer and some of the director's friends. The Swiss backer, Reg told them, was new to theatre. He'd admitted to Reg that he'd never seen a play before. But he was rich, and had money to burn. Luckily the man had no idea how it all worked, Reg added, which in the long run he said could only be good for the company.

During the first act Suzy dried about four times and, at one point, even had the embarrassing moment of asking Barbara if she could look at the book before they continued.

'Don't worry,' said Jason in the interval break as he swigged from a sports water bottle. 'You'll be marvellous, Suze. Honestly, just stop worrying. It's a rubbish concept, but you're better than it.'

She felt tears prickle in her eye.

Jason put his arm around her shoulder.

'I'm not kidding,' he whispered. 'Head up, darling. You'll be great.'

'Jason! Suzy!' Reg shouted. 'Come here please.' He summoned them away in the direction of the gaggle of people at the other end of the room who were standing around whispering and sipping wine from plastic cups. 'Our principal backer wants to meet you.'

As she got closer she saw the man make a face and gesture which caused Reg to hold up his hand and say, 'Sorry, Suzy. Only Jason required.'

For a moment, Suzy felt really upset that the backer had appeared rather keen *not* to meet her. She got back to the row of chairs at the acting end of the room and dived into her script.

'Don't worry about that lot.' Emily patted her on the back. 'I've been in these European things before. That lot know nothing. They may have money but they're all "Am-Dram" experts, and feel quite free to shower you with reminiscences of how wonderful they were when they played the part with Scunthorpe Amateur Operatic Society in the eighties.'

Suzy laughed.

'I gather you've done these shows before.'

Emily nodded.

'What are the audiences like over there?'

'Much the same as the backers. They clap and cheer, then, at the mingle afterwards, zoom in on you to tell you how much better they were when they did it.' Emily stooped to retie her lace-up boot. 'And they're as old as we are. I remember you in *Dahlias*, darling. That was a very good show, and you were wonderful in it.' She leaned against the wall while she adjusted her petticoats. 'Chin up! Don't forget that the money people, especially small-scale ones like these, rarely have good taste in the arts. I'll bet you Mr Moneybags has only asked to see Jason because he fancies him.'

Suzy glanced across the rehearsal room and realised that Emily had hit it. The backer, a sleek-looking man in a very expensive suit, looked as though he had lewd designs on poor Jason.

'To be frank, when they offered me the job I was dreading it,' added Emily, 'but when I heard I'd be working with you I was rather excited! They told me the local people in Zurich went wild when they heard you were coming out to join the cast. Didn't Reg tell you that?'

Barbara, the stage manager, called the company to stand by and the second half started.

Suzy was puzzled. Reg had certainly not told her that. In fact, from the audition onwards, Reg really hadn't had a nice word to say to her.

But it was good to know that she had fans over in Switzerland.

For the second half of the play, Suzy was fine with her lines, and really enjoyed the rest of the run-through.

Afterwards, the actors gathered in the pub down the road from the rehearsal room to grab one last drink before leaving to pack for their flights the next day. As they compared notes they realised that, presumably in another ploy to save money, the producer had booked them on different flights with multiple airlines, all departing at different times.

'I don't think I've been given a ticket,' said Emily, panicked.

'Didn't you open your emails?' India, the young girl playing Gwendolen, held up a plane ticket. 'You had to click on the link, Emily. That takes you to the ticket. I printed mine out right away. Even though it's all here on my phone. Look!' India held up her mobile, displaying the flight ticket, with its QR-code square box. 'Give me your phone, Emily.'

Emily handed it over and let India click away.

'I printed mine out last night.' Suzy rooted about in her handbag and pulled out her ticket. 'We leave Heathrow at noon.'

'Not me,' said India. 'I go from City Airport at 2 p.m. What's going on?'

'This is no fun,' said the boy playing Algernon. 'I go from Luton at eleven fifty. What time is your flight, Jason?'

Jason shrugged and pulled out a slip of paper. 'And I've already checked in for my 10 a.m. flight from Gatwick.'

'Why have they done this?' asked Suzy. 'Whenever I've toured before the whole company always flew together.'

'Someone needed to keep us apart!' Jason laughed. 'We obviously have way too much fun when we're together.'

'Googled the last available seats, I should think,' said India. 'You can always get ridiculously cheap last-minute offers.' She handed Emily back the phone, displaying her ticket. 'There you are, Emily. You're also from City Airport. And I've checked you in.'

Suzy wondered what would have happened if there had been a massive rush for tickets to Zurich tomorrow – for a football match or something – and some of the cast couldn't get there. What would the company have done then? Would they have opened the show a day later, or simply missed out the dress rehearsal and expected the actors to get on with it?

'Wait a minute,' said India, displaying her ticket again. 'Are your tickets like mine? Exchangeable and refundable? I thought they cost more!'

Everyone took their tickets out and inspected them.

'Mine is too,' said Emily. 'Well, I suppose they think we're worth it.'

'Or they're hoping to extend the run?' suggested India. 'In case we're a wild success.'

'To us! And a bloody good show!' Jason stood up and raised his glass.

'Will we have supper together when we get there, on our last free evening?' asked Emily.

'I think I'd better bow out of that,' said Suzy. 'I'm still feeling a little shaky on my lines.'

'You're fine on your lines, Suzy,' said Jason. 'Not to mention "I hate people who are not serious about mealtimes ..."'

Everyone at the table finished the line: '"It is so shallow of them!"'

'That's decided then.' Jason finished his drink. 'We'll all meet at the Café Odeon down by the lake in Zurich, tomorrow night at 6 p.m. Deal?' He burst into one of his radiant grins. 'Come on, folks. Whatever happens, let's have fun out there.'

Suzy drained her glass and realised that she felt more excited and energised than she had for years.

'Viva tomorrow!' she cried. 'Viva us!'

2

Aᴀꜰᴛᴇʀ ᴀ ɴɪɢʜᴛ of heavy rain, the Clapham street was all puddles. Amanda Herbert's shoes were sodden and her clothes wet through from the steady drizzle which had continued throughout the whole time she and the men packed up the removal van.

Amanda helped the young man slam down the back door of the lorry, and then he ran to join his companion in the cab. All her things were safely stowed inside.

'See you tomorrow, Mrs Herbert,' the driver called, turning the steering wheel, ready to pull out. Shielding her brow from the rain, Amanda glanced over her shoulder to check for oncoming traffic, and signalled the driver the OK.

As her belongings sped away to spend a night in the lorry before being delivered to her new flat the following day, Amanda ran back along the street to her old home.

She felt her phone vibrate in her pocket. She had no intention of answering it now. She was too cold, too wet and too exhausted, having spent the last four hours helping the two removal men pack up her life's possessions and stack them inside the now departed lorry. She had to lock up and drop the key off with her solicitor, which meant she had only a few minutes left for one last walk through the empty building in which she and her family had lived for forty years.

It was in this house that she had brought up her two children and sent them off into their own married lives. Here she had played with her grandchildren, and stayed up late into the night talking and laughing with friends.

Now she hoped to give both children a little surprise, some of the money she was getting from the sale.

She started to hum 'So Long, Farewell' from *The Sound of Music*. The empty rooms now had a clanging resonance to them. Her voice rang out like a 1950s pop singer in an echo chamber. As she walked into the kitchen to take advantage of the acoustic she changed musicals. *Snow White* this time, 'I'm Wishing'. She sang the echo's little reply too.

She felt so happy that she was moving out, and was very excited, really looking forward to the new flat, and all the new beginnings it would bring.

She leaned against the kitchen counter and looked around her, remembering the birthday parties and dinners that had filled this room with laughter.

She walked over to the glass doors to the garden and turned the key one final time.

Normally Amanda wasn't of a nostalgic bent, but somehow today was different. She was allowed to have a little look back.

She and her late husband, Nigel, had moved into this house as newly-weds, straight after their return from their miserable honeymoon in soggy Devon. She had been twenty-two, her husband a few years older.

Not for the first time, Amanda wondered what on earth had persuaded her parents to give her, their only child, a wedding gift of a fortnight's bed and board in a creaky old hotel on windswept Dartmoor in the middle of November. Maybe it was because they disapproved of the marriage and had been trying to send her a warning? Perhaps they were having a last attempt at shutting the stable door after the horse had bolted. Maybe they hoped a grim honeymoon might put her off dashing young Nigel. If so their ploy had failed, for the wretched place and the bleak weather had, if anything, drawn them closer.

As Amanda walked up the stairs and along the corridor, peering into the echoing empty rooms, she laughed to think that her parents might have intended their honeymoon gift with malice. They were kind people. They had probably just read too much Daphne du Maurier.

But they had been right in their concern, of course. Nigel had not turned out to be the perfect husband she had hoped for. In fact he had turned out to be a total rotter. But then so had the husbands of so many of her friends ... especially once the children were safely away at college. She only had one friend who was still apparently happily married, and, coincidence or not, they had no children. Amanda and her other friends frequently debated whether that devoted husband was in fact secretly gay.

As Amanda closed her bedroom door, she thought about nights there with Nigel. He certainly wasn't gay – quite the opposite. The trouble wasn't the sex Nigel had with her. It was the sex he had with everyone else.

Unknown to her, during their marriage Nigel had shagged his way through quite a few women, some of them right under her nose. Looking back, Amanda couldn't see how she hadn't spotted it at the time. But the truth was she only found out that he was, well – unfaithful would be a polite way of putting it – when they were more than twenty years in. Only a week before the revelation he had even given her a bone-china tea set as a twentieth wedding-anniversary gift.

The fatal disclosure happened while Amanda was struggling with empty-nest syndrome, having first celebrated her daughter Patricia's graduation from teacher-training college and then seen her son Mark off to university.

It was during that autumn, when she was alone with him, that Nigel admitted he was in love with someone else. And within days of the confession he did the unthinkable and ran off to marry a girl more than half his age and younger than both of their children.

What made it much trickier was that Nigel was a dentist and the teenage girl was his patient. Sleeping with patients, especially those under twenty-one years, was the kind of behaviour which got you struck off the dental register. At the same time it would leave you disgraced and shamed, never to work professionally again. In those days you might even have ended up as a headline in the *News of the World*.

Amanda moved away from the marital bedroom and looked instead inside the bedroom which had once been Mark's lair. For the last ten years this had been her own study, the room where in the evenings she wrote the copy for her newspaper articles.

After Nigel left she had taken a job working in a twee little shop in Clapham's newly trendy Abbeville Road, laughingly referred to by locals as 'The Village'. The shop called itself a shabby-chic boutique and specialised in selling 'distressed' furniture. She often thought that the furniture could not be as shabby or distressed as she herself felt, but she needed the money both to exist and to make sure her kids would not go without. Shortly afterwards she had had a lucky break, getting a job writing a column for a local newspaper, which then got syndicated. Her secret joke was that she wrote about relationships, as a kind of up-market agony aunt, while feeling she was the least qualified person in the world to do so.

Amanda made for the stairs and stood on the landing, looking down at the windswept garden.

It was down there, one bright Indian summer's day, that Nigel had started a bonfire in the middle of the lawn. A neighbour phoned to complain about the smoke which was blowing into his bedroom window, and Amanda went to have a word with her husband and tell him to smother the fire. As she stepped out from the kitchen on to the patio a piece of singed paperwork flew towards her face. She caught it. She was surprised to see that it was part of a patient's dental record. She feared something highly illegal and so went towards him, waving it in the air and asking him what the hell he was playing at. Normally, when challenged, Nigel burst into a rage, but this time he simply blushed and looked down at the ground. It was only then that Amanda realised something more sinister was going on. Within a minute, Nigel was sobbing, blabbering on about how deeply in love he was with a girl who had been a patient and how he had decided that nothing or no one would stand in his way. He was determined to follow his dream, the dream of spending the rest of his life with Sharon.

So her husband had left her for Sharon! At that time the name was such a cliché it was comical.

In her misery and fury Amanda had been tempted to phone the Dental Board herself and report him, but, for the sake of their two children, she hadn't.

Now that the echoing rooms were empty, Amanda wondered why she had stayed here so long. She felt greatly relieved that she had finally decided to move. She was now sixty years old, the children had children of their own, and this place was far too big for a woman alone, so here she was, packing it all up and getting out.

As Amanda put her head around the living-room door, the phone in her pocket buzzed again. Again, she ignored it. She only had a few minutes till the taxi came to take her to the solicitors' office where she would sign the contract, ready to exchange on her new little flat not far from the river in Pimlico.

She stood in the living room thinking back on the good times she had spent with her kids here when Nigel was away 'in conference': playing board games with them; giving Mark a train set for Christmas and laying it out all over the carpet; dressing the tree with Patricia; evenings spent chewing pens, while helping both of them with their homework. Happy days. But nonetheless days passed. It was silly to keep looking back. The future was what mattered and she had much to look forward to. Amanda wanted to get the signing at the solicitors' over and done with then go to spend the night with Patricia at her home in Wandsworth. Tomorrow at noon she would move in to her new place. And simultaneously both her children should receive a lump sum which was left over from the sale of this old house.

She glanced out of the window. It was still drizzling. Her pre-booked taxi was already waiting, the driver fiddling with his mobile phone. She looked at her watch. There were five more minutes before the official time of the booking, but why just stand here for the sake of it?

She gave the taxi driver a wave, grabbed her coat and bag and left the house for ever.

As she locked the front door the rain came down in a sudden downpour. The phone rang again. She ran out to the taxi and flung herself into the back seat. Shaking the rain out of her hair, Amanda told the driver the solicitors' address. He said he already had it.

As the car drove off she decided not to turn back to take one last glance at the house.

Instead she took out her phone and prepared to deal with the missed calls.

Her lawyer's number.

Five times.

She rang, asking to be put through to her conveyancing solicitor.

'Mrs Herbert, thank goodness I caught you,' said the solicitor. 'Bad news, I'm afraid. The seller has decided to pull out.'

'I'm sorry?' Amanda thought she must have misheard.

The solicitor repeated herself. 'The vendor of your new flat has decided to pull out. You cannot buy the flat. He is not selling.'

'But he can't do that?' A raindrop rolled from Amanda's hair down the side of her cheek. 'Can he?'

'He can, I'm afraid. And he has. You haven't exchanged contracts yet, though technically you made an agreement when you paid the deposit.'

'But I … I've moved out of my home!'

'It is unusual, I admit. I have never dealt with a case of withdrawal of sale as late as this, but it does happen.'

'Can't you force him to sign?'

'He's a Swiss banker. In my experience men like him do not give in. Though, legally speaking, you do have one recourse.'

Amanda sat up. A glimmer of hope!

'You can sue him for breach of contract.'

Amanda's heart sank. She was in no position to sue anyone. She had already had quite enough of legal battles. She had neither the time, the money nor the constitution for another, especially with a Swiss banker.

'What about stalling the sale of my house?'

'Too late for that, Mrs Herbert. The monies are already being processed.'

'But where will I go?'

'I'm afraid that's up to you, Mrs Herbert. The proceeds from the sale of your house should reach you the day after tomorrow. So at least you'll have money in the bank. And, as a cash buyer, you're in the perfect position.'

Amanda told the driver that they were no longer going to the address on file and instead gave him Patricia's postcode. Closing her eyes, she sank back in the seat. She saw both of her children often, though not regularly, and had been looking forward to a catch-up and hearing all the news of the grandchildren.

Amanda had been due to spend only one night with Patricia. Now it would have to be two. Mother and daughter sat up late into the night, discussing what Amanda should do next.

At first, Amanda herself had been so shocked by the news that the purchase had fallen through that she'd forgotten to phone the removal company telling them not to take her lorryload of things to the new flat the next day. By the time it occurred to her, the company office was closed for the night. She and Patricia spent a long time trying to find an out-of-hours number, before, finally, doing the only thing they could do – dispatching an email through the firm's website. Amanda hoped that would work.

'You'll have to phone again in the morning, Mum, and arrange somewhere they can take all your stuff.'

Amanda suddenly realised that she had nowhere to put anything, and she was going to have to go down the self-storage route. It all looked so easy on the TV ads, all those bright young people walking you down shiny corridors, but Amanda felt sure it wasn't going to be quite such plain sailing as it seemed. Nothing ever was.

After having a bowl of hot soup, she and Patricia spent another few hours on the computer browsing all the storage firms in the area. The rates and terms were all so different. While Patricia went upstairs to check on her children, Amanda decided on a firm which had its office not far from her daughter's house and she printed out the details.

'Looks a bit low-key,' said Patricia, perusing the small print while Amanda settled on the sofa. 'What decided you on that particular one?'

'It's just around the corner from here. If I need to get anything out it won't be such a slog getting there.'

Patricia turned to her mother. 'What do you mean, "here"?'

'If I get somewhere near here to keep all my things, I can …'

'I'm sorry, Mum. I should have explained better. Of course, you can stay here *tonight*, as arranged. Perhaps tomorrow too, but on the sofa. From tomorrow I won't have the spare room any more. I've just started this new job, with no warning, no time for preparation, which is an immense responsibility. The new au pair arrives in the morning.'

'Why do you need an au pair?'

'To make sure the kids get off to school and have someone here in the evenings. He'll be in that room.'

'If I stayed I could do that,' said Amanda. 'The kids know me. It would be a fair exchange …'

'Mum, please stop!' Patricia put her face in her hands and growled. 'It's all organised now. Just because things have gone wrong for you, you can't expect everyone else to adapt to your problems. It's simply not how life works.'

'But …' Amanda felt alone and desolate. 'Where shall I go?' She had no idea that Patricia had such a hard streak. 'Please, Patricia, I was only …'

'God, Mother!' Patricia ran her fingers through her hair. 'This is all I need. You were the one who clung on to that stupid house for so long. You should have sold it years ago.'

'I kept it because of you two, and because of the memories …' Amanda thought back to the lonely days in that house, after the kids had left. Keeping their rooms ready, just in case they might some time want to come and stay.

'Neither of us wanted it. As usual you had to get all emotional about it. But whatever, you can't go on staying here. Look. Go on the web. There must be a nice B&B somewhere which won't cost you a bomb.' She stood up. 'Why don't you plan things better? Always such a drama queen. You and Dad were really well-suited.'

Amanda was so taken aback by this last barb she could barely speak, except to say: 'That's very unfair … Your father …'

'Was a selfish ingrate. Yes, I remember you saying, over and over. Now, I'm exhausted and I've got a lot on, so I'm off to bed. And when you go up, don't forget to turn the lights off.'

And with that she left Amanda to it.

Holding back the tears, Amanda stared at the computer screen. Patricia really had been unfair to compare her to Nigel. Perhaps she had been too young to remember the emotional ins and outs. But Nigel's carryings on had given Amanda years of hell, and she had fought for Mark and Patricia.

After the bonfire-side confession of his love for the young patient, Sharon, despite her own misery and burning desire for revenge, Amanda knew that, if her husband had been publicly reprimanded, both Patricia and Mark would be emotionally affected by their father's disgrace. Although the circumstances had been dire, Amanda recognised how important it was that she at least tried to keep his image as positive as it could be while the kids adapted to his departure.

Nonetheless, once Nigel told Mark and Patricia that he was divorcing their mother and, at the age of fifty, planning to marry a seventeen-year-old called Sharon, they both refused to see or talk to him again, and stuck to their promise. *They* were the ones who had overreacted, not her. Considering everything, Amanda had behaved with remarkable calm throughout the entire shambles.

Nigel had put in for a quickie divorce and started planning a huge wedding for himself and his blushing young patient. Amanda's own solicitor, not her husband, was the person who explained to her that things needed to move very fast because Sharon was already pregnant with Nigel's baby.

Amanda was still reeling from this information when, only a few months later, while the new wife-to-be was days away from giving birth, Nigel died of a heart attack.

All this would have been relatively fine if Nigel hadn't managed to die naked in the bed of Tracy, Sharon's best friend, and proposed maid of honour.

On top of it all, Nigel had left no will.

Amanda realised that she was simply staring at the computer through tear-filled eyes, and went into the kitchen to make a cup of tea.

She couldn't accept Patricia's remarks. She knew she had coped as well as anyone would have done under the circumstances.

A sizeable chunk of Nigel's estate had gone towards paying for the wedding-that-never-was, as no one had thought to cancel anything and the florists, photographers, caterers, venue and dressmakers all had to be recompensed in full.

The financial mess was further exacerbated when, during solicitors' searches, it turned out that Nigel had had yet another child, this one born while Amanda's own children were toddlers. The boy, Jean-Pierre, had been brought up in Paris by the child's mother, Ophélie, Nigel's former dental nurse. Amanda recalled how, all those years ago, Ophélie had, for apparently no reason, suddenly left her job and run back home to Paris – due, Nigel had said, to 'family commitments'.

While sorting out Nigel's estate the solicitor discovered that Nigel had bought Ophélie a house in Paris, which was still in his name, and for the previous fifteen years had also provided the woman with a regular income, which must still be paid, as he had signed a contract.

All the 'dental conferences' Nigel had gone to in Europe, Amanda came to realise, had been a cover for long visits to that other family of his in his Parisian love-nest.

The wrangling between the wives, girlfriends, lovers and his multiple children and the lawyers dealing with Nigel's estate went on for many years.

After running up a huge legal bill, Amanda and her two children had just managed to hold on to the house. That was all.

But Amanda did everything she could to keep them all on an even keel. She had gone out to work in that wretched shop, where she had been bossed about and patronised by a snooty woman half her age, simply to support them in something like the style to which they had become accustomed, and to pay for their further education.

She only ever wanted great things for Mark and Patricia.

How had it come to this?

Amanda had no intention of annoying Patricia, especially as her daughter had just started her new job, taking over as head teacher at incredibly short notice, mid-term. She faced quite a responsibility. The old head had had a near-deadly stroke and would not be returning to the position.

Amanda had meant no harm. Aching inside, with regret and awful old memories she would rather forget, she went back to the computer and continued her search for hotel rooms which were in range of the area where she wanted to buy. There was nothing she could find for under £90 a night, unless it was miles out of town. £630 a week! What happened if this went on for months? Every bit of money she spent now would decrease the amount she had for the new place. On top of that, if she stayed in a hotel she'd have nowhere to cook. She'd have to live on sandwiches and eating out which quickly added up.

She speedily closed the accommodation website and started browsing for available flats. There were places, but none looked as good as the flat that she had already decided on and lost. She got a paper and pencil and jotted down some possibilities to try and get viewings on tomorrow. When she had finished she realised it was well after 2 a.m. She climbed up the stairs leading to the spare room, lay down and, without undressing, was asleep in seconds.

Next day, by lunch, Amanda had trudged around five flats in the Victoria area. Some were so small and poky she knew she could never live in them, while others were so updated and shiny, in the neutral style, that all the character had been smoothed out of them, and they had all the ambience of an operating theatre.

She was astonished at the difference between so many flats which were all much the same price. Who decided that a grubby low-ceilinged two-room flat, on the sixth floor with no lift, opposite a night shelter, should be worth the same as an airy high-ceilinged first-floor flat with a small roof terrace in a wide quiet street, like the one she had just been thwarted on?

Amanda sat in a sandwich bar taking lunch, while waiting for another estate agent who had just bumped their appointment forward an hour. She flicked through the other estate agent details, then looked back on the brochures for the places she had seen this morning. Whoever had a job writing these things should try for a job in politics. They certainly knew how to spin silk purses from sows' ears.

Once that was done, Amanda took a moment to phone her son Mark on his mobile. She knew that she couldn't stay on at Patricia's after tonight, when she would be on the sofa, so perhaps he might be able to give her a few nights in the living room on his sofa-bed in Islington. Amanda didn't feel one hundred per cent enthusiastic about this as, although she got on very well with her grandchildren and with her own son, she couldn't say the same about his wife, Ingrid, who was very pretty, but had a sharp tongue on her, and made no disguise of the fact that she thought Mark could have achieved more both in life and the Mother stakes.

'Hello, Ma!' said Mark breezily down the line. 'How's tricks?'

Amanda told him about the trouble she had had with the flat she had been hoping to buy, and explained that unexpectedly she now needed somewhere to stay.

'I wouldn't want to impose, but I'm desperate ...' She hung on for a response but Mark was silent. She could hear him breathing down the line.

'What was that, Ma?'

She told him again.

She heard female giggling in the background.

What was going on?

She dreaded to think.

'I'd love to have you over, Ma, really I would. But, you see, at present I'm rather in the doghouse myself.'

Amanda waited for him to continue. She knew there was about to be a revelation.

'I'm actually staying at a friend's place just now, you see, Ma. Beginning and end of it is – Ingrid has thrown me out.'

Amanda's mind span. He was definitely with a woman now. So the giggling was not Ingrid.

'How are the children, Mark?'

'Oh, they're fine. But you know Ingrid. She's always so hardline about things. No doubt it'll all settle down in time, Ma. But, as I say, I'm crashing with Jasmine now, so I'm in no position to offer you a bed.' There was an awkward, too long a pause. 'I'm ever so sorry.'

'Mark, please don't turn into your father.'

More giggling. Then Mark let out a loud sigh. 'For fuck's sake, Mother. You sound just like ruddy Ingrid. Got to go.'

He hung up.

She regretted mentioning Nigel, but, at the same time, knew she had to say something. She felt awful. Now she had managed to alienate both children.

Amanda thought through all her friends and wondered whether any of them might have a spare room she could borrow. But when she went through her address book she realised that no one really had spare rooms any more. One pal was now living in a granny flat with her family, another lived hours out of town, up in the Midlands, where, although she could lay her head, it would be impossible for her to continue house-hunting. All of her other friends lived in one-bedroom flats and studios.

So, this afternoon, between flat viewings, Amanda would have to patrol the B&B-type hotels in the area and see if she could find one with a vacancy which might give her a good deal for at least a week.

Her phone rang.

The solicitor.

'Your seller has phoned.'

Amanda sat up.

'He thinks he's on the verge of changing his mind again. Whatever that might mean. But I gather that it all depends on the sale of somewhere he is after himself.'

'I thought he was chain free.'

'So he told us, but actually it appears that he is not.'

'What does this mean for me, exactly?'

'He is saying that he may still sell to you.'

'May? That doesn't sound too bad.'

'It does. I've been on to his solicitor and they cannot affirm anything. We're trying to get something final out of him. My advice would be to keep on looking, Mrs Herbert. Who knows, you might just find somewhere better.'

Amanda wandered out of the sandwich bar and along Belgrave Road where she knew, from bus rides into town, that there were many small hotels and B&Bs. The first one she entered, which didn't look all that salubrious, quoted her £2,000 a week. She moved down the road into hotel after hotel, and the lowest she found, that was not actually a doss-house, would charge her £725 for the week.

'But we only have the one room left, I'm afraid.'

While Amanda was pondering whether to take up the offer her mobile rang.

'Mrs Herbert? About your stuff ...'

The removal company. She had forgotten all about them.

'Yes. I'm so sorry. You did get my message about the flat falling through?'

'Yes, we did. But you haven't told us where to go instead.'

The signal was bad so she waved to the hotel reception-ist then walked out through the front door and stood on the hotel step.

'I'm just getting somewhere to stay organised now. Can I phone you back?'

'We need the lorry, I'm afraid. It's currently full of your things. If you don't give us somewhere to take the stuff, we'll just have to dump it.'

'Of course.' Amanda felt her spit dry up. She realised that after last night's difficult conversation with her daughter she had forgotten to go any further with the storage problem. 'Do you know any good storage places?'

'Lots. But it's up to you, madam. Also, as you've gone over the noon deadline, we have to charge you a double fee. It is in the terms and conditions.'

'I wasn't expecting …' Amanda felt panic rising. Rarely had she felt so out of control of her own life. 'I didn't know the flat would fall through.'

'I understand, madam, but you have to see that that is your problem. Not ours. Look. You've got an hour to get back to us.'

He hung up.

Amanda sat at the bus stop in front of the hotel and googled 'self-storage'. This was hopeless. There were too many companies to inspect on the tiny screen of a phone. All the prices seemed so variable, depending on how long you needed it and whether you wanted access, and she could see from the amount of unreadable small print that there were also all kinds of hidden charges, like insurance and late fees. She phoned the first company on the list, the idiotically named Aardvark Storage, and was greeted by a cheery Australian girl who offered her all kinds of special deals if she wanted a six-month rental.

'I don't know how long I need.'

'Oh, everyone says that,' said the girl. 'We find that most people need them for five months.'

'But you just offered me six months.'

'No worries. It costs more for five months. Even more month by month or week by week. If you do month by month or week by week you'd end up paying more than twice the amount for five months. Better to take the six-month deal.'

Amanda felt a dark fog descend on her brain as the girl continued talking balderdash in her bright cheery tone. All

Amanda knew was that she needed to find somewhere right now. 'Can I move my stuff in today?'

'No worries.'

'I'll phone the removal men right away and tell them to come over with it.'

'No.' The girl coughed. 'No can do, sorry.'

'What do you mean, "no can do"?'

'We cannot confirm that you have the space until you have completed all the relevant paperwork and provided us with original copies of your ID. You'll need to come in person to sign, pay up and get the key. Only then can you ask the removal men to bring your stuff.'

'Where are you?'

'Near Wandsworth Bridge.'

'When do you close?'

'Well, the place is open 24/7 but the office shuts at five and we don't allow new deliveries in after that. The whole signing-up procedure shouldn't take more than an hour.'

Amanda looked at her watch. There was no way she'd get all this done in time if she went by public transport.

'I'm on my way.'

'No worries,' said the girl once more, clearly ignorant of how many worries Amanda was having.

Amanda hailed a passing cab, jumped inside, then leaned back in the seat, mentally counting all her hard-earned cash as it evaporated into thin air.

It was only as the taxi turned into Wandsworth Bridge Road that she realised she had not gone back into the hotel to confirm her booking.

Now that she was away from Belgrave Road she couldn't remember the name of the hotel either, so there was no chance to phone them.

After completing yards of forms, Amanda and the removal men spent a good hour stacking all her belongings in the tiny-looking tin room at the end of a long bright shiny orange corridor. Once they had finished, they walked back to the front office, which was now closed.

As the men headed off Amanda searched around in her bag for a tip and pulled out her last tenner. The removal men nodded brusquely and climbed up into the lorry.

It was only once they had pulled out of the car-park gates and turned into the main road that Amanda realised she was now standing in the middle of an unfamiliar industrial estate with no cash. To make things worse the rain had started up again while they packed and now it was positively biblical.

As she looked back towards the offices, she half expected to see Noah and his Ark appear around the corner, with two giraffe necks sticking out of the top. Everything at the storage facility was shuttered up now, and the only access was by using her key code. She got inside but all that was there was the labyrinth of long silent corridors lined with other people's storage spaces.

She would call another taxi and hope it took credit cards.

She pulled out her phone.

It was dead.

With a shudder, she suddenly also realised that her phone charger was in a box somewhere at the back of that storage room. When she had packed it yesterday at home, she had only thought it was going into storage for one night.

Damn.

She turned up her collar as she left the unit and ran for it. Trouble was she had no idea which direction to run. The place was lined with two-storey buildings which all seemed deserted. Offices, garages, the Iranian Bazaar, lots of places called so-and-so 'property services', something-or-other 'supplies' or such-and-such 'imports'.

She rounded another corner.

Dead end.

She tracked back the way she had come and this time, at the crossroads, took another direction.

More supplies, services and imports joined by an exotic sauce company. There was even the workshop of an 'ice sculptor'. She tried pressing a few bells, but no one was at home, anywhere. She trudged onwards, in the middle of it all wishing she could lose that three-quarters of a stone she'd been promising herself to, then maybe all this might not seem quite so uphill. She was now desperate to reach a main road, preferably with a nearby bus stop.

When she did eventually climb on to a bus, as she pressed her pass on to the scanner, feeling like a drenched lost dog, the driver actually laughed at the state of her.

The bus took for ever but it did get her back to Victoria railway station. From there she walked briskly down to Belgrave Road and went back into the hotel she had chosen to spend the week from tomorrow night.

A different girl was on reception.

She saw the girl smirk.

Amanda was still dripping wet, and knew she must look a sight.

'I was in here before,' she said.

The girl stared up at her blankly.

'And?'

'I had arranged a deal on a room for the week starting tomorrow night ...'

'One moment ...' The girl looked down at the screen of her mobile phone and laughed. Then the hotel phone rang. She picked it up. 'Good evening, Starbreak Hotel, can I help you?' While she talked on the office phone she was tapping something into her mobile and smiling to herself.

Amanda sighed. She hated the new priorities. Surely a human being standing two feet away from you merited first service, and Facebook messages and phone calls came after that.

The girl was talking brightly into the receiver for quite a few minutes, while glancing down at her mobile phone.

When at last she finished the call, without acknowledging Amanda once, the receptionist got up and went back into some behind-the-scenes room. At least six minutes afterwards she reappeared.

'So, let me know what can I do for you?'

Amanda started up the whole story again.

'I see. This afternoon. That must have been Pixie. She lives in a dream.' The girl flicked through the register. 'You said £725? That seems very low for us.'

She looked up again at Amanda. 'No. I see it. Room 503. Top-floor attic. I realise now that I just gave that room away on the phone a few minutes ago.'

'You mean while I was standing here?' Amanda wanted to slap the grinning girl.

'Yes. Seems so.' She spoke in a cheery sing-songy voice which brought out deep rumblings of anger in Amanda. 'Sorry about that. We've nothing left. Soz.'

'But you have to …'

'Nothing left now.'

'You can't do this to me …' Amanda was torn between fury and tears. 'Where will I go?'

'I'm afraid that's up to you,' the girl said, as though Amanda had really posed her a question. 'I can't help you with what you do with your life. Now I'm sorry but I have to get on.'

She picked up her mobile phone, swiped her finger and laughed again.

Amanda went out into the street.

It was still raining.

She trudged from door to door, trying a few more hotels. They were all fully booked.

She turned a corner and saw, on a block of wood hanging in a window, the magical word: 'Vacancies'.

Amanda went in through the front door of a rather jolly-looking pub.

This would be nice, sitting by the fire, then buying herself a nice glass of Brouilly and taking it up to bed. Amanda had struck gold.

She went over to the side counter which had a row of keys behind it.

'I wonder what your rates are. I'm looking to stay a week, maybe longer. Starting tomorrow night.'

'A hundred and eighty pounds,' said the young bearded man behind the counter.

'I see.' Amanda tried to do the sum in her head. This was way over what she had been expecting. 'Might you have anything cheaper?'

'I just thought ...' The young man looked her up and down and shrugged. 'Well we do have a couple of places left at £120.'

'Nothing cheaper?'

The young man laughed and said 'No' in that upwardly inflected, sarcastic way which Amanda felt sure meant he thought she was slightly deranged.

'Of course. I'm sorry. I'll take it.' She didn't want to lose this. She'd seen how few and far between were the rooms to let around here. She took out her wallet. 'Should I put down a deposit?'

'At this late stage of the day that would be usual,' said the bearded man. 'Deposit in advance. You have till midnight tonight to cancel. After that if you cancel we have the right to withdraw the whole cost for one night.'

Amanda handed him her credit card.

3

Suzy got off the plane at Zurich Airport and took the train into the city centre. The sun was shining and she was glad to be out of dismal London. The sight of the Alps, glistening in their snow-draped splendour as the flight came in to land, had raised her spirits and she felt better than she had done in weeks.

Her digs weren't as bad as she feared either. She'd had trouble finding the street at first because she had remembered it as Hermesstrasse, whereas in fact it was Mercurstrasse – same god, different language! The landlady's husband had died in a car crash and she let rooms to make ends meet. She had a young family and was helping her kids to learn English, so always invited British actors to stay because they were sociable and talkative. She gave Suzy a map of the city centre with directions to the theatre and marked out some decent cafés and bars along the way.

Suzy wrapped up and took a stroll through the cobbled Old Town and down to the lake. Frost glistened on the roofs and passers-by were muffled up in woollen pom-pom hats and chunky scarves.

Despite being the biggest city in Switzerland, Zurich had a villagey feel.

It didn't take her long to find the theatre. It had a small but messy front, which still had faded posters up for the last show, a comedy by Tom Stoppard. She noted that it had finished over three months ago – so hopefully the audience would be keen for something new. She peered down through some dusty low windows at the side of the building, but, through the grime and cobwebs, couldn't see a thing. Suzy knew that this part of the theatre was bound to be the dressing-room area. On her way to the front again she looked through the grille by the entrance. There was an old-fashioned arch-style box-office compartment, and next to that the locked doors which must lead to the foyer. She took a walk around the block, searching for a stage door, but found nothing. She'd worked in other theatres like this, with no separate entrance for the artists. She remembered the same thing somewhere she had worked years ago. Was it Perth Rep? Even at the Donmar, in London, actors came in and out the same way as the audience. It looked to be similar here.

Suzy walked down to the lake and sat on a bench, gazing out over the water, which twinkled in the winter sun.

It was a beautiful day today. And yet she felt uneasy. She had no idea why.

She was happy to be here in Zurich, which was much more stunning than she had ever imagined it might be. She was with a charming group of people, playing a fantastic role in a great play. What was there to worry about?

A tram rattled past.

Suzy looked up, holding her face to the sun, and then in the distance she saw Reg. He was crossing the bridge, heading towards her. She didn't think he'd seen her. He was talking earnestly into his mobile phone. He looked very agitated. He was flailing his arms about, dripping sweat, purple in the face, his wisps of grey hair stuck in straight lines over his bald head.

As he drew closer to where she was sitting, Suzy looked down and fumbled around in her handbag. She didn't want him to see her.

As he passed by she could hear Reg ranting.

'I know you didn't want her, but, as you know, we were badly let down at the last minute …'

When Reg was safely out of sight Suzy got up and walked briskly in the opposite direction. Could it have been her that he meant? Was he explaining that they didn't want her for Lady Bracknell? She was certainly a last-minute choice. If someone else had been taken ill or offered a better job and dropped out it would certainly explain why she had auditioned only two days before rehearsals started.

So, someone was still going on to Reg about how he didn't want her for the part of Lady Bracknell.

Suzy felt quite sick. Ahead she saw a café with a red awning. A coffee was certainly in order, if not something stronger.

It was only as she entered that she realised this was the famous Café Odeon, where the company had arranged to meet later.

She took a seat in a small alcove by the window and ordered a strong espresso.

Her phone rang.

Her agent, Max.

She pulled herself together. The one thing an agent didn't want to hear on her first day here was that she was upset and depressed. Especially as she might be imagining the whole thing.

'Max!' she said brightly. 'To what do I owe the pleasure?'

'Suzy, darling, how are the gnomes of Zurich?'

Suzy looked around her. She wasn't sure whether this kind of phrase was in the lexicon of language you were currently permitted to use.

'Can you say that?'

'Say what?'

'That word starting with a G?'

'I haven't said a word which starts with G. Have I?'

Suzy cupped her hands around the phone before whispering 'Gnome!'

Max laughed. 'I was only tricking you into saying it aloud, Suze. But according to many of my clients, who had starring roles in *The Lord of the Rings* and all those sub-Terry Pratchett

TV series, I'm pretty sure the word "gnome" is currently not only permissible but all the rage, along with goblins, dwarves, orcs and elves. But to business … How's it all going?'

'Who knows? I've only just arrived. The company are meeting tonight for a drink, then tomorrow we have the tech-dress, and open.'

'Well, good luck, darling, and keep in touch.' Max paused then said, 'Just one little thing …'

Suzy knew that this was a phrase to be feared. Something bad would inevitably follow:

'… Have they given you your per diems in cash?'

'Not yet. I imagined we'd get them tomorrow at the theatre.'

Max left another heavy pause before asking, 'They haven't paid you your rehearsal wages direct, have they? I know we had to give your bank details and I wasn't quite sure why.'

'No. They haven't paid us anything.' Suzy felt a flutter of fear. 'Why? Is there a problem?'

'And you've received no hard cash in hand?'

'No.'

'I'm sure it's nothing,' said Max. Suzy couldn't help but worry that Max sounded slightly cagey. 'We haven't had anything in, either. Just so you don't think that we're holding on to the money.'

'Oh God,' sighed Suzy. She had dipped into her savings account over the last weeks, certain that she would get it all back soon enough.

'Don't worry, darling.' Max turned on his best breezy agent voice. 'I'm sure it'll all be fine. These things happen. Good luck tomorrow. Call me if you get any money.'

During the conversation, the waiter had placed a coffee and the bill on Suzy's table.

She raised the cup to her lips and took a sip.

'Can I join you?' Emily's neat figure stood before her. 'Us oldies are always the first to arrive. Over-keen really, aren't we? Seize the day and all that!'

Suzy wasn't sure whether to tell Emily about the call from her agent concerning pay. Talking about money with the other actors was just not done. But once Emily's order of hot chocolate arrived Suzy couldn't stop herself.

'I wouldn't worry about it, darling.' Emily fanned the frothy cup and tried to take a sip. 'These tin-pot outfits don't behave the same way as the RSC, you know. We'll be OK. Just you see.'

The rest of the cast soon rolled in and they all spent a few hours comparing notes on their digs and journeys, their prospects and some moments in the show which were on their minds. The girls tried a bottle of local wine, while Jason and the boys sampled the fancy Swiss beers. Splitting the bill, they moved off to share a fondue at a famous Swiss restaurant up the road.

Suzy was about to pull out of going, worrying about cash, but Jason pointed out that, while they were here in Zurich, none of them would get another chance to visit the hallowed home of the fondue, as the place was closed on Sundays – the company's only night off. So, if she wanted to try a genuine version of the famous local delicacy, it was now or never.

Suzy noticed that when Stan took his leave from the Café Odeon, no one attempted to persuade him to join them for supper.

'I have a prior engagement of a sensual nature,' he said in a lascivious voice. 'Just call me Mr Good Time.' His top lip was greased in sweat.

When Stan had gone, as she reached for her coat, hat and scarf, Suzy turned to Emily.

'Doesn't Stan like being part of a company?'

'Don't ask. I dread to think where he's off to. Cottaging or something, I expect.' Emily wound her scarf round her neck. 'No doubt tomorrow I'll have to endure a lot of wink, wink, nudge, nudge while he hints at having been up to unspeakable things all night.'

Suzy tried to get the image of a sexual Stan out of her mind.

The dinner was not only delicious but everyone was charming and brimming with enthusiasm about their six weeks in Switzerland. She listened to the younger members of the company planning Sunday skiing trips, while she and Barbara talked about taking a boat trip on the lake, and visiting the famous Zurich Kunsthalle.

'Is it good?' asked Suzy.

'They've got Fuseli's *Bottom*,' said Barbara.

'You might need to rephrase that one,' said Suzy.

The company agreed to order a large communal fondue and again share the bill. Happy to be with such a cheery ensemble, Suzy dug in with gusto to the delicious pot of steaming hot cheese.

Towards the end of the meal, she noticed Jason go outside to take a call. He came back inside, bent down and, in a low voice, spoke into Suzy's ear.

'That was Reg. The producer bloke wants me to go up to his hotel suite tonight.'

'A kind of money-pleasing mingle?' asked Suzy. 'Bit late in the evening for that kind of thing, isn't it? Do you want to go?'

'Not at all.' Jason grabbed his jacket from the back of the chair. 'But Reg made it quite clear that it would be "better for us all" if I did go.'

'What on earth does that mean?'

'You tell me. It seems that something has upset Mr Moneybags and that he needs charming.'

'Will Reg be there?' Suzy thought of the phone call she had part-heard that afternoon.

'He's on his way there. So's Stan, apparently.'

'Some charm offensive that'll be,' joked Suzy. 'An all-male affair then?'

'A private invitation from the producer bloke. To be frank, I didn't like him when he came to the rehearsal, I have to say. Slimy type.'

'If you don't want to go, just don't. It's not a pimping shop, Jason. It's a theatre company. Surely people know this. If I were you I'd cry off and go back to your digs.'

'It'll just be drinks and chat, I imagine. And Reg has been on my back all day, phoning me. Nag, nag, nag.' Jason shrugged. Nonetheless, he looked very concerned. 'If I don't go now, no doubt the barrage will continue until I do go. Best get it over with.'

'So why not pop in for one drink, just for a few minutes, Jason, then make your getaway? You have a perfectly good excuse: we open tomorrow night!'

'That's it.' Jason swigged back the dregs of his espresso. 'That's what I'll do. Ta-ra. See you in the morning.' He looked across at Barbara, the stage manager. 'What time do you want us?'

'Everyone in full costume and make-up, ready to go at 8 a.m.' Barbara drank the remnants of her wine. 'I reckon that really means the tech-dress starts on the dot of eight thirty, after a costume and make-up line-up, and maybe going through a few odd technical bits. I leave it to you to decide how long you need to get made up and ready.'

India laughed. 'It's getting nearer to a nine o'clock start with every phrase you utter, Barbara!'

'It better not be,' she replied.

'What time will the theatre be open?' asked Emily. 'I need at least an hour; better still, longer.'

'According to my information, everything opens up at seven,' said Barbara. 'Reg and I will be there then, as we'll be doing the lighting while you make up.'

'*Bon soir à tous!*' Jason pulled his hat down. '*À demain!*' He gave everyone a wave and left the restaurant.

Suzy decided to get there for seven too. It was always important to leave extra time in a new venue to find your bearings. It was also important to allow for potential make-up disasters. There was always something time-consuming to sort out – like there being no plug sockets or adapters in the dressing room for the hair curlers, or the wardrobe department forgetting to buy spare tights.

Soon after the end of dinner, Suzy returned to her digs, had a quick go-through her lines, and then went to bed, and dreamed of bearded gnomes in boaters serenading her in the barbershop style.

4

THAT EVENING Amanda was given short shrift by Patricia. But Amanda understood why.

She tried to make things better. 'Obviously, you'll be up to your neck for the next few weeks, darling, so why don't I look after the kids for you?'

'No, Mum. Do you not listen? I have a new au pair, Sofian, just arrived from France.'

'Is she nice, this Sophie Anne?'

'He, Mother. HE. Sofian is a man.'

'Why's he got a woman's name? Is he cross-gender, or whatever it's called?'

'It's a French thing. And right now Sofian's upstairs, unpacking. So, I am up to my eyeballs. I need to show him around the house, detail the children's schedule, explain where everything is and how it all works. It's incredibly difficult here tonight. So why don't you just sit quietly in the corner and watch telly or something.'

Amanda felt completely embarrassed, and now wished she had moved into the hotel right there and then, instead of taking up Patricia's offer of one extra night, this time on the sofa.

It didn't take a genius to see that, to her daughter, Amanda was nothing but an annoying inconvenience. She would be better out of the way.

So, next morning, Amanda got up early, tidied up the sofa, and was in the kitchen preparing breakfast for everyone, when Patricia came in.

'Stop!' she shouted. 'Mum! Please don't interfere. I need to show Sofian what to do in here, so that tomorrow morning he can do it all alone. Now go and wait in the living room.'

Feeling like a naughty child, being told off by her headmistress daughter, Amanda made her way back to the sofa where she sat, hands in her lap, contrite, waiting for instructions. She wouldn't have been in the slightest bit surprised if Patricia set her a detention or made her write out one hundred times 'I must not interfere in my daughter's well-regulated life'.

If everything had gone to plan this would not have happened. Bloody vacillating banker. She cursed the wretched man who had withdrawn his flat from sale, the swine who had effectively put her in this awkward position.

She glanced at her watch. It was still before 7 a.m. She could not move in to her hotel room until this afternoon at three.

She used her phone – now luckily rejuiced overnight on one of her daughter's spare chargers – to check out a few more estate agents and left messages to see if she could spend the day doing viewings.

After breakfast was over, Amanda thanked her daughter for the use of her sofa and slipped out quietly, gripping her overnight wheelie case.

She caught a bus across the river and walked the streets, noting down the addresses on 'For Sale' notices.

As soon as offices started opening, she called on the first estate agent she came upon, which was in a bright glass-fronted office.

She took a seat at a desk and started setting out her requirements.

'I'm sorry,' said the blonde girl behind the desk. 'I think you've made a mistake.'

'Don't you do apartments?'

'Sort of,' said the girl in a breezy way. 'But not the kind of apartments you are looking for. This is a travel agent. We do holiday lets.'

Amanda looked around again.

How had she been so stupid?

There were certainly apartment signs around the shop, but they all had ravishing sea views or swimming pools.

She stood up. 'I am so sorry,' she said to the girl. 'It's just one of those weeks.'

'You look as though you need a break,' the girl replied.

Amanda wished she had a mirror.

Did she look so bad? She pushed her hair out of her eyes, reminding her that her last attempt at a stylish cut had long since grown out. And although she hadn't had to regularly dye her chestnut-brown hair, she felt at that moment many more specks of grey must be showing.

So that she wouldn't look as though she had made such a stupid mistake, as she left Amanda grabbed a few random brochures, and crammed them in the side pocket of her over-night case.

After she walked out of the shop Amanda realised that the girl was probably only saying that she needed a break to try and lure her into buying a holiday.

Amanda spent the rest of the morning visiting dreary flat after dreary flat. They were all roughly the same price as the one she thought up till yesterday that she had bought. She couldn't picture herself living in any of them with their low ceilings, stale smell, vertiginous staircases and lack of light. She went on doing viewings through lunch until it was after three. Then, with a handful of new details from other estate agents, she went to find her hotel room and have some time to herself.

The pub door was open, and the sun had come out, and crowds of cheery young people huddled around the tables on the pavement. Amanda decided to have lunch here too. She checked in, leaving her case by the desk, then went out and ordered herself a bowl of soup and a large glass of red wine.

As she put the spoon to her mouth her phone rang.

Her solicitor.

'He really will sign, he says. As soon as you like.'

'I'm sorry?' said Amanda. 'You mean my banker friend?'

'That's right. He now wants rid of the London flat, asap, but if you agree, you need to sign today, and so will he. Then you can move in in two to three weeks.'

'Two to three weeks!' said Amanda.

'Those are the terms he's offering. If you want that flat, I suggest you get here today, then, hopefully, by tomorrow the place will almost be yours.'

'Could he pull out again?'

'Who knows with such a loose cannon? But we will move in tandem with his people, who say they plan to hold on to the signed documents.'

Amanda looked at her watch. It was coming up to four.

'What time do you close?'

'Five.'

'I'll be there.'

Amanda, relieved, practically drank the soup from the bowl, then threw the wine down after it, before hailing a cab over to the City where her solicitors had their office.

Phone calls went back and forth between her solicitors and the vendor's agents, until it was finally agreed that the owner had in fact signed and that the flat would really be hers in around a fortnight. No more changes.

The solicitor opened a bottle and offered her another glass of wine, which she happily accepted before leaving in a taxi and heading back to the hotel.

It was too early for bed when she got there, so she settled down for supper in the main part of the pub.

The place seemed to be such a buzzy hub for young people. Amanda could hear Australian and American accents, as well as some young adults talking French, Italian and German. She loved central London and its wonderful cosmopolitan air. She ordered an omelette and chips, along with another glass of wine, and watched a documentary on the television hung in the corner of the room.

It was about ten o'clock when Amanda decided to turn in. It had been such a strangely tiring day, considering she had done nothing much.

She went to the desk and asked for her key and suitcase.

'Dropping off one of the kids, eh?' said the young concierge.

'No,' she said. 'It's for me.'

He pulled an inexplicable face and said, 'OMG. LMFAO,' followed by Amanda's room number – 6. 'Top of the stairs, turn right. First door on the left. Bathroom at the end of the corridor. Two bed.'

'I'll never remember all that,' said Amanda. 'OMGLM what?'

'You only have to remember six, two.' The concierge smirked and gave Amanda a thumbs-up before exploding with laughter.

As Amanda hauled her case up the rickety stairs she felt bewildered that, for this price, the bathroom was not en suite, but decided against saying anything as the young, hip staff were already looking at her as though she was something of a joke.

She dragged her bag to the end of the hall and opened the door to Room 6.

Four girls were sitting on the floor, playing cards.

'I'm sorry,' said Amanda. 'I thought this was Room 6.'

'It is,' said one of the girls. 'You must be Bed 2. Like a beer?'

Amanda looked around. She could see four pairs of bunk beds, every bed but one stacked with rucksacks and bedrolls.

Panic was setting in. An eight-bed room sharing with seven strangers!

And Amanda had reserved for the whole week.

She was too old for this, and too exhausted.

Not to mention all that money …

'You pay £120 a night for this?' Amanda said before she could filter her thoughts into two departments: those in her head and those which came out of her mouth.

The girls laughed, rocking back and forth from their cross-legged yoga positions on the floor.

'No!' said one girl. 'Not for a night! It's £120 a week, silly!'

Torn somewhere between laughing and crying, Amanda rolled her case into the room and tried to lift it on to her upper bunk, which was clearly marked Bed 2.

'Let me help!' Another of the girls leaped up. 'Look, lady, I'm going to swap your bed with one of the boys. They can climb the damned ladder. You're way too old for it.' The girl took Amanda's suitcase and flung it on to the bottom bunk, while grabbing the rucksack which was already there and hauling it on to the bunk above. 'Now, if I were you, lady, I'd get into bed now. Then, when the blokes come back, you pretend to be asleep. Leave me to tell them.'

'Blokes!' said Amanda. 'You mean we share with men too?'

The girls looked at her with varying degrees of pity.

'Of course,' said one. 'You're from that old generation which was all prim about sex, aren't you?'

Amanda wanted to reply that no, she was in fact a child of the 'swinging sixties and the sexy seventies' but, as the evidence was against her, decided to keep quiet.

While the girls on the floor continued their noisy card game, Amanda shyly undressed, put on her nightie and climbed into bed.

PART TWO

Getting Aboard

WHEN SUZY AWOKE and glanced at her watch she was happy to see that she had almost an hour in hand before she had to leave for the theatre.

She pottered around for about half an hour, filling her wheelie case with her make-up box and the usual dressing-room stuff: hairdryer, electric curlers, mini-kettle, towels, tissues, cotton wool and her raggy silk dressing gown which she had always used for every show since she was at drama school. She needed to restock on mascara and a few other items, but she hoped she could find a pharmacy open on her way into the theatre; otherwise she'd nip out during one of the scenes she wasn't in.

When the case was ready, Suzy strolled along towards the shower room.

Her landlady was hoovering the landing. She expressed surprise that Suzy was still there as she had left a note saying that she wouldn't need breakfast because she was leaving for the theatre at a quarter to seven.

'I've got a bit of time,' explained Suzy.

The landlady shook her head and pointed at the hall clock. It was already seven thirty. Suzy looked again at her watch. She was an hour behind. She realised that, after getting off the plane yesterday, she had failed to adjust to European time.

She was already late.

Forgetting the shower, Suzy hurriedly dressed, grabbed her tote bag, plonked it on top of her wheelie case, and ran along the cobbled streets. She glanced up at church clocks as though, by checking them, she could somehow make time stand still.

As she scrambled down the steep lane leading to the theatre, her case clacking loudly on the cobbles, she could see a small crowd gathered outside. She hoped it was not a gaggle of photographers. She must look a wreck.

But as she drew closer, she realised it was the cast and crew of *The Importance of Being Earnest*. They all looked agitated and cross.

'What a nightmare.' Suzy was panting like a dog. She had not run so fast in many years. 'I forgot to change my watch.'

'Don't worry. No one noticed you weren't here.' Emily took her elbow and said quietly, 'Reg has obviously overslept as well, and no one seems to have the key to the theatre.'

Suzy looked around. The boy who played Algernon was stabbing urgently at his mobile phone, while India was scouring the peeling posters and signs outside the theatre, and reciting the phone numbers to him.

Barbara looked close to tears. 'I've tried every number they gave me. Every single one on answerphone. London office is just ringing out. But of course over there it's only 6.50 a.m.'

'What should we do?' asked Emily.

'There's no point everyone standing here.' Barbara looked around her. 'Just keep together, could you? How about everyone going into that little sandwich bar and having a coffee.' She moved away and started rounding up the cast, along with the lighting designer and assistant stage manager, a strange silent girl with long Pre-Raphaelite hair.

'Give me half an hour,' said Barbara. 'Then, later, perhaps, we should call Equity.'

Suzy was startled by that news. If Barbara was flummoxed enough to be calling in the union, then things really must be bad.

'Who's the Equity deputy?' asked Suzy.

'Me,' said Emily. 'But their office won't be open for hours yet.'

'Early days, early days,' said the ASM, hauling a tapestry bag over her shoulder and smiling blithely.

Suzy lost her cool with the girl. 'What do you mean, "early days"? We tech-dress-rehearse today and open before an audience tonight. Even if things were going really smoothly this whole shambles would be nothing but lunacy.'

The ASM gave a slightly sarcastic shrug and went back to join the younger actors.

'You don't think they've done a moonlight flit, do you?' asked Emily as she joined Suzy crossing the road, heading for the café. 'It wouldn't be the first time.'

Suzy looked at her. This thought had not occurred to her. She had just imagined that the person who kept the key had overslept.

Suzy thought back to her agent's phone call about the pay – or, rather, the lack of it. She decided to broach the subject again.

'Emily? Out of interest, have you checked your bank? I haven't got any money yet.'

'Not a bean.' Emily pushed into the café. 'But as I said, these foreign operations are frequently chaotic. I was only thinking yesterday how well ordered this one was looking.'

As they settled at a table by the window Suzy looked up to see a man in a two-tone blue blouson and navy woollen hat arrive at the theatre and hammer on the door.

'Is that one of ours?' asked Emily, pointing.

India peered out of the window. 'That, my dear, is a Swiss policeman. I've had enough brushes with them while on skiing holidays with my parents up in Klosters and St Moritz to recognise the uniform a mile away.'

'What are the police doing here?' asked Emily.

Barbara came around the corner to the theatre front doors and spoke to him.

While Suzy was trying to lip-read their conversation, her phone buzzed. An unknown English mobile number. A man's voice.

'Suzy? Are you alone? It's Jason.'

She touched Emily's arm and signalled that she would take the call outside.

'What's happening?' Jason asked. 'Are you inside the theatre?'

'No,' she replied. 'We're all locked out.'

'Oh no!' Jason groaned down the line. 'He cannot be serious.'

'You knew?'

'I didn't think he meant it.'

'Who?'

'What a total bastard.'

'You *know* what caused this?'

Jason was silent.

'You obviously do.'

'I did.' Jason spoke quietly. 'I caused it.'

Suzy felt her temper rising. How had this chit of a boy managed to get them locked out of the theatre?

'How did you do that, Jason?'

Jason paused. Then spoke in a hesitant voice. 'I had an enormous row with Reg and the money bloke.'

'Where is Reg?' she asked.

'I've no idea. And, just to warn you, as far as I know the show is cancelled.'

'Tonight's show?'

'No,' said Jason. 'The whole run. *The Importance of Being Earnest* is cancelled.'

*

Amanda awoke with a start and looked at her watch. It was 5.30 a.m. She had no idea where she was, but suddenly remembered that she was in a bunk in a dormitory above a pub.

She was surrounded by deep breathing, muffled snores and snorts. The air was acrid and slightly damp.

She felt utterly trapped. She tried to go back to sleep, but, after an hour, she realised this was not going to happen. As her eyes became accustomed to the dark she could see the switch for a small individual reading light and was about to turn it on, but realised that this would illuminate her and she didn't want to draw attention to herself. She reached out and felt for her suitcase which was beside her, standing upright on the floor by the edge of her pillow. She pondered for quite a while how she could get dressed without waking anyone. Eventually she decided to grab her clothes from around her feet, then, still in her nightie, go out into the corridor, which she could see from the gap under the door was well lit. Once out there she could dress easily, and creep downstairs.

As she swung round and put her foot on the floor, a board creaked and one of the men snorted in response. She froze for a second and then continued her furtive exit.

Safely in the corridor she sighed with relief and hastily dressed.

She wasn't quite sure what she was going to do next. Obviously at this time of the morning there would be no cafés open. Maybe she'd just sit in an armchair in the bar downstairs and read. If she nodded off, that would be fine.

She gripped her case and tiptoed down the creaky stairs.

At the bottom of the staircase she tried the bar door. It was locked. There was a tiny vestibule and an emergency push-bar exit.

She sat on the painted wooden steps.

Now that she was here she realised that she didn't have a book with her, so what did she think she was going to read?

She fumbled around in her suitcase and pulled out the estate agents' details of the places she had seen yesterday. She was glad she didn't need them any more. With nothing else to do, she glanced through them one by one. They were all horrible, dark and depressing, and wouldn't have been right for her at all. With some relief she lay them aside.

Then she came upon one of the brochures she had only picked up to cover her embarrassment when she had mistaken the travel agent for an estate agent.

Mermaid Cruises.

Now there was something she never had the slightest desire to do. Go on a cruise.

She flicked through the sunny pictures of cheery bright older couples, dining and dancing onboard, alongside glossy photos of pretty harbours like Porto Fino and Venice.

She flicked to the back of the pamphlet and was about to put it in the bin with the estate agents' brochures, when she came to the price list.

She had never before even thought about what such things cost. A fortune probably. She had read articles about people saving up for their 'cruise of a lifetime'. That surely meant loads of money.

'Inside cabins from £1,900 for seventeen nights, full board.'

That couldn't be right, could it?

She looked again, and did a little mental arithmetic. Seventeen nights. That was about £112 a day. The same price as a poxy room in a hotel on Belgrave Road, but, onboard the ship, all food and entertainment was thrown in.

Amanda started enthusiastically poring over the pages. At prices like that she would be mad not to try to get on a ship as soon as possible and stay on it till the time came to move in to the new place.

She flicked through page after page.

Looking at the cabins, and noting their floorplans, she quickly saw that a balcony room was worth the extra couple of hundred as it not only got you a view, and some outside space, but lots of other extras, like a welcome bottle of sparkling wine and £40 to spend in the onboard shops and casino.

She was now really excited.

What if she could get on a ship somewhere today? She'd wave goodbye to the payment for a bunk bed for the remaining six days, but so what? She had no intention of ever going back to that bed anyway.

Amanda looked at her watch.

She had a few hours before the travel agent opened. She decided there and then that she would go out, catch a cab and return to her storage room. She'd pack a few evening gowns – she had noticed that formal wear was a necessity onboard – grab her laptop and a few other useful things – underwear, shoes – then she would book herself on any ship which she could embark tonight. Hopefully a ship which would bring her back to the UK just in time to move straight in to the new flat. Even if it arrived back a few days later that would be OK. She just hoped the cruises weren't all sold out.

6

A LONG WITH everyone else, Suzy was talking into her mobile phone. They were all calling their agents, trying to work out what they should do next.

Jason had been short on detail and had sworn Suzy to secrecy. He told her not to mention that he'd phoned, and promised to contact her very soon. She said she would phone if she got any further news. But the truth is that she was furious with him. She wanted to know everything, to hear the whole story from someone – be it Reg or Jason. Anybody who might explain how an after-dinner argument led to a show closing before it had opened. She wondered whether Jason had been rude to the backer. But as she barely knew the boy after only two weeks' rehearsal, all she could hope was for him to ring back later.

Coming into the café, Barbara explained that the policeman's arrival was nothing to do with them. They were apparently looking for someone called Herr Appenzell. Meanwhile, although it wasn't yet 8 a.m., she had managed to rouse the owner of the theatre who, after a few more phone calls, called back to tell her that *The Importance of Being Earnest* was indeed cancelled. The reason he gave was that the major backer had withdrawn all the finances from the production and that the police were looking for the said backer, but he had no idea why. He had no address for the backer.

She had told the theatre owner that, under the terms of their contract, it was illegal for the theatre to lock them out.

He reminded her that his only contract was with the production company, who had just pulled out of the show. Their individual contracts were English and that meant, as they were now in Switzerland, the whole affair had nothing to do with him. When Barbara tried to argue this one out he told her to shut up. He simply owned the damned building, he shouted, and now he was going to be seriously out of pocket. People paid him rent to use it. Their gripe was not with him. He was as much a victim as they were.

Barbara made one last attempt at finding a solution from the theatre owner. Any quarrels should be picked with Mr Reg Shoesmith, he told her. Reg Shoesmith had called the owner in the early hours to ask whether he could still hold on to the use of the building, even though, at this moment, he had no money to put down a deposit. The theatre owner had laughed at Reg and hung up. It was nothing to do with him, he told Barbara, who then tried Reg's phone. It went straight to voicemail.

When the company started murmuring between themselves, Barbara suggested that they all go and talk to their agents again and to Equity, but most importantly cancel their digs, change their flights and get home, pronto.

There was no show.

Oddly, after weeks dreading and fearing the job, now that it had evaporated before it even started, Suzy felt desolate.

'Will we get paid?' asked India. 'The money would be incredibly useful.'

'As I told you,' shouted Barbara, waving her arms to try and get everyone together, 'call your agents. For your information, I've not been paid rehearsal money either, which is why I hold out no hope and I am heading straight to the airport. I need to get home and get another job asap.'

'Stan's not here,' called India. 'Someone should tell him. And Jason.'

'Stan only ever arrives at the last minute. He'll not arrive till nine on the dot.'

'He knows he's not on till Act Two,' India grunted. 'Like some other people, including me. But I can manage it.'

'Men always turn up at the last minute for techs,' said Emily.

'They'll phone me quick enough when they find we're locked out,' said Barbara, still practical. 'And I'll leave a note pinned to the theatre door.'

Suzy found the whole saga hard to swallow. She thought of all the money she had laid out already – the fares back and forth to rehearsal, the sandwich lunches, the drinks and meal last night. Over the last few weeks she had run her credit cards up near their limit. And now she also had to find the money she owed to pay the Zurich landlady. She hoped the woman would let her off lightly; after all she had been expecting Suzy to be in the room for the next six weeks. She wondered how much notice she would want.

Suzy looked around. She could see the same panicked expression on everyone's face.

'Someone better call Jason,' said India, turning to Suzy.

Suzy nodded. Rage boiled inside her towards the young actor. What on earth could he have done to cause this fiasco?

'Let's go to our digs, pack our things and get to the airport,' she said. 'I'll phone Jason. See you all there.'

Once out of earshot she called Jason and told him they were all on their way to the airport.

'Please don't be cross, Suzy. How could I know this would happen? Look, we'd all better get a move on and get on our planes home. I can't stay here.'

He hung up. He sounded utterly anxious and forlorn, but Suzy was too stressed about finding a way to get home to think about his problems now. After all, once back in London, she might never meet him again.

Suzy found her landlady on the doorstep, just going out with her kids. When Suzy told her what had happened the woman was clearly upset to lose her rent, but agreed to charge for only one week.

Suzy went to pay with her card, but the landlady said it had to be cash.

She rushed up the road to find an ATM, and, while she was there, she checked her balance. After paying for the digs she would have just under £200 credit left. And that was it. No other tappable funds.

While she was returning with the cash, Jason phoned again.

'Don't speak to me now, Jason. I'm too upset.'

Suzy pressed the button to end the call, swept inside and handed her landlady the money. She then gathered her bags and headed for the station.

For the third time, Jason rang. 'We can meet up at the airport,' he said.

'I know that!' yelled Suzy. 'First you might explain how the hell this has happened to us all?'

'Look, I'm on my way to the airport,' he said. 'I'll see you there and tell you all.'

Suzy dragged her cases across the tram lines and a busy, very confusing junction, opposite the railway station.

Using her credit card again – she was quite out of Swiss francs now – she bought a ticket to the airport, which she realised, only after she'd entered her PIN, was in fact a weekly pass. Another few pounds down the drain.

The airport departures concourse was bright and busy. Suzy saw a small group from her company and headed towards them. They appeared to be arguing amongst themselves. Emily was waving her hands in that pacifying way, while India was shouting 'Perr-lease!' at the top of her already rather strident voice.

Suzy asked India, who was now typing into her mobile phone, what was happening.

'We can't use our return plane tickets.' She looked up briefly then went back to the phone.

'But I thought you said that they were refundable and exchangeable.'

'Exactly!' said India. 'They were. Only somebody exchanged them, got them refunded, and left us with duds. We're stranded.'

'We've no tickets? How will we get home?'

'That's what we're all asking ourselves.'

Suzy looked around. She noticed that Stan Arbuthnot was missing.

'Oh, he's all right, Jack,' said India. 'Loaded, apparently. He's already out of here.'

'Did you see him?'

'No. Barbara saw his name on the list when she was checking her own dud ticket. He was already through security and away. She called his mobile, but he wasn't picking up.'

'Probably too busy loading up in Duty Free,' said Suzy. 'He wasn't at the theatre this morning, so he must have known that all this was happening before we did.'

'Apparently so.'

'Stan's close to Reg, isn't he?'

'Sorry, Suzy, I really have to concentrate. I'm trying to get myself a ticket by amassing all the points I have on every credit or hotel card anywhere, anyhow.'

Suzy went to the desk and asked how much was the cheapest flight to London this morning. She was told prices started at 500 Swiss francs.

'But that's ...' She tried to convert it in her head.

'Around £400,' said the desk clerk. 'There's a big expo on this week. Many people are trying to get back to London.' He looked up at Suzy and smiled. 'Prices will be very much cheaper next week.'

Suzy wanted to cry. What could she do next? If she stayed here in Zurich, simply eating out for a week would cost her the same as buying a ticket today. And she'd given up the room and also had nowhere to lay her hands on any funds.

She moved over to a quieter corner of the departures concourse and phoned her agent's mobile. Though it was out of office hours, he picked up. She told him what had happened and that she was now stuck in Zurich. She asked if he could wire her some money or a ticket or something. Anything! As long as she could get home.

He told her to hang on. He'd phone her back.

Suddenly someone touched her elbow. She swung around thinking a thief was going for her purse. But it was Jason. He looked wrecked, his clothes ruffled, his eyes heavy.

'Let me tell you what happened,' he said.

Suzy turned to face him. She was close to hitting him.

'No, Jason, let me tell *you* what has happened. We've no job and we are stranded. They've cancelled our return tickets.'

'He's a bastard. A bastard!' Jason momentarily put his head in his hands then looked at Suzy. 'I'll pay your fare. How much do you need?'

'Four hundred pounds.'

Jason's eyes opened wide. 'Four hundred pounds? For a flight to London? That's daylight robbery.'

'Exactly.'

'Sorry. I couldn't do that. I thought it would be less than £100. So, we're trapped here.'

'Unless we have private funds, or can fly out next week, yes. Greasy Stan, the Chasuble, by the way, is already en route to London.'

'Oh really!' Jason's lips tightened. 'I'll bet he is.'

Suzy was amazed that Jason was not more apologetic, if indeed his actions had caused this awful upheaval.

Her rage and fear left her shaking. It was difficult to refrain from slapping his pretty-boy face.

'So tell me, Jason, exactly what *did* you do to bring on this catastrophe for us all?'

Jason looked Suzy in the eye. 'Do you know an actress called April McNaughten?'

'I've heard of her, of course, she's a star, but what has this …?'

Jason bit his lip, as though deciding whether or not to confide something with her.

'She's on tour here in Zurich. She's playing the lead in *The King and I.*'

'But Jason … what has April McNaughten to do with this?'

Suzy wondered why he was changing the subject. She could see Jason putting on the brakes and rewinding the story he was about to tell. Whatever had happened last night, Suzy knew she was in for a highly edited version.

'Nothing. Look. As you know, while we were at the fondue place last night, Reg called me. He wanted me to go to some swanky apartment suite in the centre of town. So I went. It turned out to be a party thrown by that man who was at the mingle.'

'The backer?'

'That's him.' Jason swallowed hard. 'But Reg had set me up.'

'In what way?'

'The bloke, whose name is Appenzell, was … Look, does it really matter what happened?'

'It really does, actually, Jason. Are you going to tell me?'

'I didn't like him and I didn't like what he was up to.'

'Which was?'

Suzy could see that Jason was holding something back.

'Reg is obviously some kind of pimp. Boys like me must be how he raises money for his poxy little shows. Mr Appenzell has never produced a show before. He just has the cash and thought it would get him some favours.'

'Don't be so silly, and tell me exactly why he pulled out.'

'Appenzell is a crook and Reg has a desire to protect him.'

'Fancying young men isn't a crime any more.'

'It is when …' Jason paused. He took a breath then continued. 'Look. He … made a pass at me, so I lashed out at him, then I panicked. I hadn't noticed on the way but there was now an oriental rug over the front door and I couldn't find my way out. Somehow I managed to escape into the street, only to find Reg there, ringing on the night bell, about to come in. He was saying, "I know he's … not on the straight and narrow. But he's our paymaster, so just turn a blind eye." I'm afraid I laid into Reg. I told him I was going to the police.'

'You laid into him? What the hell is going on?' said Suzy. 'Did anyone see you?'

'What do you mean by that?' Jason had indignation in his tone.

'I just wondered if there were witnesses. People from the hotel, perhaps?'

'It wasn't a hotel. It was a kind of block of service apartments.'

'What happened next?'

Jason hesitated then said, 'I don't remember. Reg will probably have a black eye. And no doubt he'll blame it all on me.'

Suzy knew that Jason was only telling a quarter of the story.

'The police are looking for Appenzell,' she said. 'They were hanging around outside the theatre this morning.'

'Oh God, Suzy! We have to get out of here. I don't know what to do.' Jason now appeared to be on the verge of tears. 'I phoned my agent on the way here. It turns out he also represents Reg. They go way back. I told him what had happened, and he said I'd let the side down and then he fired me.'

'He can't do that.'

'He just did.'

'You'll have to report him. And Reg.'

'Can you imagine the awful publicity that would get me. I'd never work again.'

Suzy's phone rang. It was her own agent, Max.

'Now, Suzy, concentrate. If you can get yourself to Genoa by five thirty this afternoon …'

'To where?'

'Genoa, Italy. It's straight down from Zurich. On the coast. Look, I've got you a job. Not only that – it's a passage home, free lodgings and food – and they pay you! Peanuts, I'm afraid, but better than the nothing you got for Zurich. Only thing is you've got to get a move on. If you're late, this ship will have sailed. Literally.'

*

Amanda found that getting through her things in the storage room wasn't quite as easy as she had hoped it was going to be. For a start, all the boxes stacked up on one another were identical. The removal men had unloaded everything so neatly and now most of the boxes and suit-cases she wanted, it seemed, were either right at the back, behind everything else, or at the bottom and underneath. She scrabbled through the few accessible boxes and got herself a risible set of outfits. She also threw in her laptop for good measure. Perhaps she could get some mileage out of the trip itself, write it up as a travelogue and try to sell it somewhere.

From the brochure pictures, Amanda had set her heart on a cruise which was heading out through the Suez Canal and to various South Sea Islands, so she packed lots of silk and flimsy summer clothes.

By the time she locked up her storage booth and climbed into a taxi heading back to the travel agent's in Victoria, it was already 9 a.m. and she was elated.

The girl who had previously served her was not there; instead Amanda sat down at the desk of a spotty youth with a wispy attempt at a beard.

'I would like to get on a cruise today,' said Amanda, fumbling in her bag for the brochure. 'It's going to the Suez Canal, leaving from Southampton this afternoon.'

'Oh, yes. Mermaid Cruises,' said the boy, tapping into his keyboard and gazing lazily at the screen. 'Yes,' he smiled. 'The *Pink Mermaid*. Sold out, I'm afraid.'

'You mean there's not one solitary cabin left for me?' Amanda was amazed at how disappointed she felt.

'Not even a tarpaulin left in a lifeboat for a stowaway on that one,' he replied. 'Sorry.'

'There's nothing else leaving today, is there?'

'To the Suez Canal?'

'Something leaving today.'

'I do have a short break from Spain, fly to Gaudí old Barcelona and come back via Gibraltar – home to the Pillars of Hercules, the rock, the monkeys, and fish-and-chip-loving Brits. Onwards, across bumpy old Biscay, to Santander – not the bank, the town, birthplace of famed golfer Seve Ballesteros, then home.'

The boy bit the side of his cheek, proud of his descriptions.

'How long would that take?'

'A week.'

'That's no good. I want two weeks, minimum. Maybe three.'

'And where would you like to visit?'

'Anywhere.'

'When you say anywhere,' the boy peered at her around the side of his computer screen, 'do you actually mean "anywhere"?'

'That's right.' Amanda realised that what she was just about to say probably sounded slightly preposterous, but she said it anyway. 'I simply want to get on a boat, today, and not have to get off it until three weeks have passed, perhaps even longer.'

'A single cabin?' asked the boy, looking her up and down.

Amanda was getting used to people looking at her as though she was barking mad. In fact, she was beginning to enjoy it.

Yes, I'm batty! An old mad cow. So what! Who cares?

'You aren't wanted by the police or something, are you, madam? I wouldn't want to be guilty of aiding and abetting a bullion robber.'

'Let's start again,' said Amanda. 'Do you have any cruise, leaving for anywhere, but leaving today, and not bringing me back for three weeks?'

The boy gave her a mischievous smile and set to work.

'How much would you like to spend?'

'Do you have a calculator?'

The boy gave her an old-fashioned look.

'Let's say three weeks' worth of £150 a day. How much would that be?'

He tapped at the computer, all the while murmuring to himself.

At one point, he glanced up at her and said, 'You do realise that you are giving me the travel agent's equivalent of the taxi driver's "Follow that car!"?'

For some minutes he went utterly silent, scrolling the mouse, making clicking sounds with his tongue against the back of his teeth.

Suddenly he leaped from his seat, shouting 'Eureka!' Then bent low and spun the computer monitor around to face Amanda.

'Would you be prepared to fly?'

Amanda's heart sank.

'I had got used to the idea of a cruise,' she said.

'I understand that,' said the boy. 'You have to see, Mrs …?'

'Herbert.'

'You have to see, Mrs Herbert, that this is a wonderful challenge for me. Such a difference from the usual people who come in here wanting a family fortnight in Fuerteventura or a minibreak B&B in Benidorm.'

He picked up a pen and pointed to the top corner of the computer screen. It showed a map of the Mediterranean. 'You see this cruise. It's not full, so they're offering rock-bottom prices for people getting on today.'

'Where will it take me?'

'You fly out and get on there.' He wafted his pen towards the north of Italy. 'Then you head back to Southampton.'

How boring, thought Amanda as she said aloud: 'That can't take three weeks.'

'No,' he said, 'it doesn't. But if, after docking at Southampton, you remain onboard and transit through, then you can go across the Atlantic …'

'The Atlantic Ocean? Isn't that a bit dull?'

'People love the Atlantic because it gives you days and days of non-stop nothing. Absolute rest. It's totally relaxing, you see, cos no one can get you by phone, and the internet is way too expensive to waste your days scanning your mobile for things to annoy you on Twitter. Therefore, the Atlantic gives you a genuine break from the hustle and bustle of home. It's just you, the fabulousness of the ship and the ocean.' Closing his eyes, he leaned back and took a deep breath. Refreshed, he eagerly swiped his finger across his computer screen. 'And then, when you're fully rested after those seven days at sea, dawn comes up as the ship pulls in to New York Harbour, squeaks under the Verrazano-Narrows Bridge into the Hudson River, passes near the Statue of Liberty, then you have nine hours to explore the city, grab a bagel and fries. After that the *Blue Mermaid* whisks you up to Boston, Cape Cod, Newfoundland and then home again. Interested?'

Amanda felt her heart skip a beat as she prepared to say the fateful words. It was like deciding to lay a pile of chips on a roulette board, and then waiting for the ball to drop. 'I'll take it.'

The boy seemed almost to pop with joy as he said efficiently, 'I hope you have your passport on you.'

Amanda pulled it from her handbag and laid it open on the desk.

The boy flicked through it, noting down her name and number. He handed it back and said solemnly, 'There are only two hitches.'

Amanda's mood deflated.

She knew all this sounded too good to be true. The boy was now going to tell her it was for Under-25s only, or some other thing which ruled her out.

'If you want to get off the ship in the USA you'll need to apply for an ESTA, but you've got ten days to do that. I'd put the request in today as they'll probably ask whether you have one before you sail out from Southampton.'

Amanda had done this before. Now that she had her laptop with her it would be easy enough to fill in the ESTA forms while waiting in the airport departure lounge.

'And the other hitch?'

'You'll need to get to Victoria Station, Platform 3, within fifteen minutes. You could easily do it in five.'

He presented her with the contract, hot from the printer. 'Sign here.' He made a cross near a box at the bottom of the page, then handed it to her.

Amanda pulled out her credit card and stuck it into the card apparatus, while the boy stood at the printer.

'I've issued you a train ticket too.' He held up a large envelope. 'Train, flight and cruise tickets. Your plane leaves Gatwick Airport at eleven thirty.'

'Leaves Gatwick for where?' said Amanda, almost breathless with excitement.

The boy leaned in and whispered, 'La Superba. The largest, most important seaport in Italy.'

'That's where I go aboard?' asked Amanda. 'I don't know Italy awfully well. Which city is that?'

'The city of Christopher Columbus,' said the boy, throwing her a feverish glance. 'The magnificent naval centre which the French call Gênes, the Italians call Genova and we Brits call Genoa, as in the cherry cake.'

*

When Suzy enquired at the airport about the cost of a flight to Genoa she was given much the same price as a flight to London, 514 Swiss francs.

That's when Jason grabbed her arm. 'Come with me.'

'I need to get to Genoa, Jason. Now.'

'I know. I heard. Trust me, Suzy. I can get you there for much less than a hundred quid. I know how to travel cheaply. Say your farewells.'

'How?'

'Train of course. No one ever thinks of it. I'm going to help you. It's the least I can do. Come on. We've no time to lose so I'm going to look up the timetables, see if I can buy the tickets on my phone. See you at the entrance to the train station.'

Suzy went across to the little huddle of actors who remained. They said they had all managed to raise the money for their flights home and were checking in their bags, awaiting departures to London.

'My agent bought my ticket,' said India. 'He's got me an interview for a movie tomorrow morning, so I'm rather happy this all happened, cos it's freed me up for something which could be so much better.'

Emily said she was looking forward to getting home too. 'I'm thinking of this experience as a one-day holiday in Switzerland,' she said. 'I would never have come here normally, and now that I've done it I don't need to do it again. And I've made some lovely new friends.'

Suzy didn't want to tell them that she had no way of finding the money so said, 'My agent is sending me on a little adventure. Only first I have to catch a train from Zurich Hauptbahnhof.'

'We've only just come from there!' shrieked India.

'I know.' Suzy tapped her nose. 'Must rush. See you back home one day, folks,' she added. 'Good luck everyone.'

Suzy met Jason as arranged at the airport station and together they hopped on to a shuttle back into the central station. Jason explained that he had been a lifelong railway enthusiast and that he knew trains from Zurich ran regularly through to Genoa and cost a lot less than a flight.

'I'd never have thought of that,' she said.

'No one ever does,' said Jason. 'Remember when that Icelandic volcano went off and people were on TV saying that they were trapped in Madrid or Copenhagen and couldn't get home for a week and that the hotel bills were crippling them. I was yelling at the TV: "Take the train, you fools! You'll be home tomorrow."'

'Won't it take days?'

'No. There's a train leaving Zurich for Milan in less than half an hour, and if we make it, we'll be in Genoa at a quarter to five. And it'll cost us less than a hundred quid each. Ninety-seven euros in fact.'

'You don't have to come ...'

'I've nothing better to do, have I? Might as well escort you down to the coast then perhaps I'll stay there, earn myself a few euros waiting on tables on the Côte d'Azur. It's only just along the coast from Genoa. No job, no agent. Got to do something.'

Suzy looked at Jason and, however angry she felt about him starting the catastrophic termination of their job in Zurich, she couldn't help herself liking him. And he would hardly have done whatever it was he had done in order to hurt her. After all, he too was out of work and broke as a result of whatever had happened last night.

En route to Zurich Hauptbahnhof, Suzy had phoned her agent again to tell him what she was doing. He then gave her the details of the job in Genoa.

'Don't laugh – it's on a cruise ship. They've been left high and dry after the social hostess ran off with a ghost in Rome.'

'Max dear, please don't talk in riddles.'

'I'm not,' said Max, laughing down the line. 'You can dance, can't you?'

'I'm a bit rusty …'

'Don't say that. What they're going to need is five days of you teaching people the foxtrot and the cha-cha-cha, and going to all the balls and things like that. And in return you get free bed and board, plus the journey home, and a very modest fee.'

'What's the catch?'

'There is no catch. It's a regular job.'

'Max?'

'Yes.'

'What did you mean by she ran off with a ghost? Is there something weird about this job? I don't think I could take two bizarre engagements on the trot.'

'No – a ghost. A ghost! It's cruise lingo for what is essentially a charming gigolo. They wear smart clothes and dance with solo ladies. Officially known as gentlemen hosts. But you see what happens once that gets abbreviated on the call sheets – G. Hosts equals ghosts. They're men with a bit of charm who can sweep a lonely lady off her feet.'

Suzy flashed a look at Jason, sitting opposite her. Surely it would be more fun to have an ally onboard, someone to talk out the events with?

'Does this mean that they also need a replacement ghost?' Suzy cupped the phone and whispered to Jason, 'Can you dance?'

He nodded.

'Ballroom?'

'Natch,' said Jason. 'Great *Strictly* fan!'

'I've got just the man for you.' Suzy spoke again into the phone. 'A lovely actor called Jason Scott. He played Jack Worthing.'

'His own agent should deal with that.'

'He doesn't have one.'

'I'm on it.'

7

Amanda had dragged her suitcase into Victoria Station, boarded the train to Gatwick and flown into Genoa without a snag.

On the Genoa Airport concourse there was a woman holding a sign with a blue mermaid on it, and Amanda had asked her if she was anything to do with the Blue Mermaid cruise.

'Exactly,' she said, pointing to the picture of the fish-tailed woman. 'The bus is waiting outside.'

The luxury coach took Amanda right up to the doors of the embarkation building. While she was waiting for her suitcase to be unloaded from the coach's luggage compartment, she looked up at the ship. The curved white prow, reflecting the water's ripples, seemed to twinkle against the cerulean sea. What a magnificent sight. She was thinking 'just like the *Titanic*', but realised that was not quite the thought she wanted to have before boarding.

As she took her suitcase from the collection of luggage on the pavement, a man rushed over and snatched it away from her. For a moment she imagined she was being robbed, but when she reached out to grab the case back he said, 'It a-wait for you in cabin, Madame.'

Thus, clutching only her handbag, Amanda moved into the check-in area, and within half an hour was through security, walking up the gangway and on to the boat.

As she stepped into the central lobby, a small chamber orchestra was playing 'The Blue Danube'. She so wanted to swoop into a waltz right there and then. Amanda passed along a wall of bellboys and officers – or at least men and women in the ship's uniform – and into an area carpeted in royal blue with little yellow mermaids. There was a sweeping staircase leading up to a gallery and, at the far end, a large counter with a sign which said 'Purser's Office'.

Amanda remembered when she was a child travelling on cross-Channel ferries that her mother was always going off to do important things at the purser's office. At the time she had not understood what these were, but vaguely recalled it was things like exchanging money and getting her visa stamped. She also remembered her mother saying that the purser's office was always in the centre of the ship, and wondered whether that snippet of useful information was still true. If so she would use the purser's office as her compass.

With the help of many smiling bellboys and porters, Amanda found her way to her cabin, which was amazingly luxurious, especially when compared with the dingy hotel bunk-room she had been in last night, or, indeed, her daughter's sofa.

On the table there was a bottle of sparkling wine in an ice bucket and an elegant vase of fresh flowers with a card bearing her name. Amanda slid open the glass doors and went out on to the balcony. She looked out at the bustling harbour and took a few deep breaths of sea air.

Why had she never done this before? she wondered. It was fabulous.

The only way to travel.

Coming back inside, she popped open the bottle and poured herself a drink, then, taking the shiny brochure called *Daily Programme*, she went out again and lay on one of the sunloungers, basking in the warm Ligurian winter sunshine to read. According to the brochure, tonight was 'Informal'. Fine, thought Amanda, I can stay as I am. Then she read on and discovered that the ship had a very different definition of informal than she did: 'Cocktail dress or stylish separates; no denim, shorts, trainers or sandals.'

She went back into the cabin and unpacked her suitcase. Amanda realised that for this trip she had grabbed quite the wrong pieces of clothing from the storage facility. She could dress for an evening in the heat of Egypt but not for the cold of Europe. Tonight she would have to let the side down a little, but tomorrow she would force herself to a clothes-buying spree in the onboard shops.

She made a quick phone call to her solicitors' office back in London and told the very talkative secretary that she was going on a cruise, which would call in briefly at Southampton in a few days, and would then take her to New York, up the coast and back again. Therefore, any messages would be best done by email, as her phone would be out of signal. The girl was a bubble of excitement, telling Amanda it had always been her 'dream come true' to go on a cruise and that she fancied going on one round the Far East. She was interested in which cruise line Amanda was on, and whether the cabin was 'comfy'. Sometimes they had famous people, the girl told Amanda. People like Sting, Rod Stewart or Alesha Dixon. Were there any stars on Amanda's cruise? She wondered whether Amanda had tried the food yet. 'You can eat as much as you like, all day and all night,' the girl informed her. 'So you need to be careful with the exercise regime.' Amanda thought she would never get the girl off the line and when, finally, the call ended she worried that the receptionist had been so excited by the information about cruising that she would never pass on her actual message. So Amanda fired a quick text message off on her phone, then did the only thing she could – trusted that all would be OK, and went and lay outside again to make the most of the December sun, shining low in the sky, sinking down into a rose-red sea.

When she awoke some time later it was cold and dark. She could hear a bleeping noise, which was followed by an announcement over the speakers that passengers who had embarked today at Genoa must take their life jackets from their wardrobes and go immediately to their muster stations.

Amanda had no idea what a muster station was, but felt sure someone would tell her.

Once she left the cabin there were crew everywhere, all wearing life jackets and waving their arms about, ushering her towards the stairs down to Deck 7.

After the drill was over, still carrying her life jacket, Amanda took a stroll around the ship. She noted the cinema, which was showing a film she would like to see. She passed any number of cafés and restaurants, a casino and an indoor pool. There was a row of shops too, selling everything from cameras and binoculars, to bags of sweets and toothbrushes.

Near the purser's office the string quartet had now been replaced by a harpist in a green velvet evening gown.

Amanda flopped down on to one of the large sofas and enjoyed the music.

She suddenly felt the ship move, and the ship's whistle blew a growling low blast.

They were off.

Amanda took the lift up to the boat deck. There was a distinguished-looking man inside already. He was obviously crew.

'Boarded today?' he asked.

'Yes. It's all very exciting. My first time on a cruise ship, in fact.'

They both stood in awkward silence for a few seconds as the lift went up, then, simply to make conversation, Amanda said, 'I have to say you all have very attractive costumes.'

The man made a little grunt and said, 'It's a uniform, actually.' He held out his hand. 'I'm the Captain, by the way, heading for the bridge.'

'The bridge? A kind of gangplank? You're not getting off, are you?'

'No,' said the Captain, as though speaking to an idiot, which Amanda was starting to think she was. 'The bridge is like the driver's seat, except that it's a large room in the bow – the front of the ship, to you. If we were all pirates we'd put on a Devonian accent and call it the fo'c'sle.' The lift door opened with a ping, and the recorded sing-song woman's voice announced Deck 7. 'And if you're looking for the boat deck, otherwise known as "outside", you get off on this floor, oh, I mean this deck!'

Amanda left the lift. She turned to smile at the Captain who winked and, as the doors closed behind her, she was sure he said 'Aaaargh! Avast and belay!' in a piratey voice.

Rather embarrassed, she pushed the door open and walked out on to the open deck. Leaning against a wooden rail, feeling the chill evening breeze against her face, she watched the sparkling lights of the Italian coastline vanish into the black.

How much more fun this was than trudging around London, looking at flats, or sitting in a lonely hotel room watching *The Great British Bake Off*.

At dinner Amanda treated herself to a glass of wine. She had been placed at a table with a lone elderly lady and two rather camp young men who talked about art-deco concrete work and antiques. As she adored knocking around boot sales and second-hand markets, she couldn't have had a more interesting conversation, complemented by her vast knowledge of the shabby-chic and distressed furniture with which she had spent many an afternoon trying to tempt her Clapham clientele.

After dinner Amanda explored the rest of the ship, strolling through the miles and miles of corridors lined with slightly naff artwork. There was even a replica of an Olde Englishe Pubbe, inside which a big crowd was gathered to partake in the ubiquitous pub quiz. She picked up the menu and was happy to see the place served typical pub fare – fish and chips, hotpots and ploughman's.

Eventually, after yet more corridors lined with spectacu-larly populist paintings and *objets d'art*, Amanda found herself approaching the ballroom.

As she got nearer, the thrill of an echoing live dance band hit her. She loved that sound. It made you feel as though you were in a film – all very exciting, all very romantic.

She strolled through the open ballroom doors. The place was decorated with Italian flags, presumably as they had just set sail from Italy.

The dance floor was heaving with couples, swaying on the parquet to the slow waltz which played. She took a seat quite near the front, and before she could get her bearings a waiter was at her side asking what she'd like to drink.

'A glass of champagne,' Amanda replied. Drinks and sundries she presumed would all get charged to a bill which she wouldn't get till the end of the voyage, so why not live now and worry later? After all, she felt that, having survived the last few troublesome days, she deserved a drink.

She looked around and noticed quite a few women of her age sitting it out. Were they all here alone too? she wondered. Widowed perhaps, or simply dumped for the younger model. Was this ship a posh version of the ladies' over-sixties singles club?

While she waited for her drink she watched the danc-ers. She was relieved to see that the ballroom wasn't only populated with old people. The age groups were quite well balanced; a few couples looked as though they were barely out of their teens. She was very impressed by the dancers' technique and the ease with which they twirled around the floor. Of course, *Strictly* had gone a long way to suddenly encouraging young people's interest in ballroom dancing.

Amanda wished she had someone to dance with.

Feeling as though she had inadvertently rubbed some enchanted lamp before making the wish, she thought she heard the phrase: 'May I have the pleasure?'

She looked up to see a stout man of about her own age, with a little military-style moustache, holding out his hand.

What the hell! thought Amanda. These ships are like magic. All you have to do is think of something and it appears!

She stood, taking the proffered hand. The tempo had changed now to a brisk foxtrot, and she enjoyed having a go. It was years since she had had such fun.

After the first dance, to her delight, she was approached during the evening by any number of men and she danced for about half an hour without a break.

She was amazed that she could still do it. It was a long time since she had taken a spin around a ballroom floor, yet she remembered all the steps.

After a particularly exhilarating quickstep she collapsed into her seat. She certainly wanted a few more sips of her champagne and to get her breath back.

To think that this time last night she had been on the brink of despair, lying in a bunk bed in a smelly rucksackers' hostel!

Her mind wandered to thoughts of her new flat. She hoped that while she was away there would be no more complications. The solicitors had assured her that everything was fine, but after so many twists Amanda still felt nervous. Meanwhile in a few days they would put in at and then leave Southampton to sail across the Atlantic. A great adventure lay ahead. She'd been lonely for too long. Who knew – she might meet someone aboard, and the solo flat for one would become history.

She raised her glass, and mentally proposed a toast to the mix-up which had landed her here.

*

Suzy lay on her bed, in an echoing little cabin with a small porthole to one side. She was exhausted, having spent the best part of the six-hour train journey from Zurich to Genoa in the corridor practising the waltz, the foxtrot and the tango with Jason. He was a good dancer, but they both knew he needed to arrive seeming like an expert rather than an actor who had just learned to dance at drama school some years back. They were happy to use the first part of the journey as a rehearsal, with a break for a genuine Italian espresso when they changed trains at Milan.

On the second train, they took their seats and caught up with some sleep. When Suzy tried once more to broach the subject of what had happened the night before, and find the reason the show had been cancelled, Jason clammed up.

'I'm tired,' he moaned, 'I didn't sleep at all last night.' He shut his eyes and leaned his head against the window.

Suzy knew that there was much more to his story than he had so far told her.

But like in all acting work, once one job came to an end, it was straight on to the next. It was too late now to do anything about Zurich's English Theatre. Once they were on the ship, she'd have all the time she needed to get an explanation out of him.

The train arrived in Genoa with only a quarter of an hour to spare before the ship's latest boarding time of 5 p.m. so they grabbed a taxi for the short ride from the railway station and went straight down to the Stazioni Maritime, even though they could easily have walked it in five minutes.

They were hastily checked in, ushered through security and brought on to the ship via a lower gangway, reserved for staff and crew only. Jason said that it reminded him of those places where you get your tyres changed. Wheeling their suitcases, together they found their way into the main part of the ship, and up to the entertainment quarters, an unmarked corridor where the luscious carpeting suddenly stopped and was replaced by a squidgy lino which smelled of swimming pools. Once through the secret door, they were in a practical working world of gloss-painted metal walls, where the cabins were rather basic. They peered into their respective rooms. Suzy's was tiny but at least she was lucky to be alone. Poor Jason had to share with a stranger, a fellow gentleman host named George.

They parted company and went to their rooms to settle in. They had agreed to meet in forty minutes for a snack. Neither had eaten anything for hours.

Suzy was just dozing off when there was a rap on the cabin door. She yelled 'One minute' and got up, taking a quick glance in the mirror before opening.

In the doorway stood a small man in steward's uniform, a slimline jacket buttoned up the front and pillbox hat which he wore at a jaunty angle. He was holding out a large letter.

'Hello, Miss Marshall. I am Ong, your steward.'

'Hello … there!' Suzy wasn't quite sure she had caught his forename so omitted using it.

'I will be looking after you on the voyage. If there's anything you need, you can ask me. I will be making up your bed in the morning, so please don't forget to put out the sign, when you go to breakfast. Here is your information package. Good evening. And welcome to the *Blue Mermaid*.'

Thanking him and ripping open the envelope, Suzy went back to lie on the bed.

Among the useful things inside the packet were a number of introductory letters, a call sheet and a pull-out pocket map of the decks of the ship, marking areas like swimming pools, restaurants, shops and theatres. There was also a kind of block-coloured roster for the few days between Genoa and Southampton, showing events onboard at which her attendance was necessary. Finally, there was a list of cabin and phone numbers of the other entertainers and entertainment staff.

She pulled up the call sheet.

Entertainment division lecturers' meeting, at 18.10 somewhere on the ship called Interact. She looked at her watch: 18.12.

She leaped up, checked to see her make-up wasn't smudged and dashed out of the door, slamming it behind her. It was only when she reached the lifts that she thought about the map of the ship, which she had left lying on her bed.

Never mind, she thought, no time to go back. A boat couldn't be that big.

But, after ten minutes walking briskly, with no certainty that she was actually going in the right direction, she realised her error. She had hoped there would be signposts everywhere, but no.

She noticed a man in uniform and stopped him to ask her way to Interact. He pointed her back in the direction she had come and down three decks.

'It's aft,' he said, pointing. 'Stern.'

Suzy's face betrayed the fact that he might as well be speaking Chinese.

'Right at the other end,' he said. 'At the back of the ship.'

Suzy marvelled that anyone could possibly know the front from the back in a stationary ship.

She arrived, breathless, a few minutes later to find an area in which two sofas were placed facing one another in a long corridor. Two men were sitting, chatting; another stood between them with a clipboard. He turned and smiled at Suzy. 'Hi, I'm Andy, the production manager.'

'So, so sorry,' said Suzy. 'I got totally lost.'

'Don't worry. Newbies are always disoriented on the first day.'

'Andy, can I go now? I have things to do.' One of the seated men had stood up. As he squeezed past Suzy, he turned and shook her hand. 'Dr Tony Hanson, lecturer on History of Shipping in the Med and on the Atlantic Ocean.'

The other man looked up from his papers and said, 'I'm Mike Turner. "Diet and Health". And you are?'

Suzy smiled and gave her name as she took a seat beside him.

'So, Suzy,' said Andy, poising his pen over his clipboard. 'Will you be needing PowerPoint and/or sound clips? Movies?'

Suzy had no idea what he was talking about.

'For your lectures?'

'I thought I was giving dancing lessons and things?' said Suzy, feeling a rising fear.

'No. That would be the social hostess's job.'

'But I thought …?'

'Between here and Southampton you have to give two 45-minute lectures.'

'Lectures?' Suzy started to panic. 'On what?'

'That's what you're here to tell me,' said Andy.

'Oh God,' drawled Mike Turner. 'Not another B-list thespian amateur.'

'I am not an amateur,' said Suzy, feeling desperate. 'But ten hours ago I didn't even know I would be here.'

'I think the whole point of hiring people at the last minute is that they are usually well-prepared and previously experienced,' said Mike Turner. 'Told a few porkies, did you, to get the engagement?'

At this moment, Jason turned the corner and appeared behind Andy's shoulder. He winked at Suzy, and made a gesture meaning to stay calm.

Mike smirked and scanned a list which lay on top of the folder on his lap. 'So, Ms Marshall, we can presume you have nothing prepared for your talk …' His finger ran up and down the paper then flicked the edge as he peered up, glaring at her over the top of his spectacles. 'Which – as it happens – is tonight. Just over an hour from now, in fact.'

'I … I …' Suzy had no idea what to say. She wanted to kill her agent, who, by giving her incorrect information about the engagement, had left her utterly vulnerable. She'd wasted that whole train journey dancing when she could have used the time to get herself prepared to give a talk.

'So, Andy, I suppose you would like me to step in?' Mike gave a dramatic sigh as he slid the papers back into his folder and rose from the sofa. 'Clearly they picked a dud with this one.'

Suzy wanted the sofa she was sitting on to open up and swallow her alive. The humiliation!

'Suzy's first talk is on Oscar Wilde, including extracts from *The Importance of Being Earnest*,' said Jason. 'I've just been putting the final touches to her notes, as we've only come aboard an hour ago, and she had to come straight down here to get to the meeting in time, while I've been trying to locate a printer.'

'It's through that door there.' Andy pointed over his shoulder as he jotted down the name Oscar Wilde.

Jason sidled towards Suzy, then bent down and whispered in her ear. 'What else have you done lately?' he asked.

'Nothing,' she replied.

'Come on – tell me a play you know about?'

She twigged what Jason was suggesting and turned to Andy, saying with some authority, 'And my second talk will be on Shakespeare's *Twelfth Night*.'

'And your talk-to session?' said Andy.

'My what?'

'It's a kind of interview, Q and A.'

Jason laughed. 'Isn't that obvious, Andy? Suzy is going to talk about her fabulous life with the stars, in TV and theatre. For many years she was the most popular actress in the UK and I feel sure many people onboard will remember her brilliant series *Dahlias* in which she played a lady barrister at the Old Bailey. Her third talk is called "Hey Diddle Dee Dee – The Actor's Life For Me". And, if I may, Andy, I will pose the questions.'

After the meeting, as Jason steered Suzy towards the lifts, heading back up to their cabins, Suzy thanked him profusely and told him how lucky it was that he had magically appeared just when she thought it couldn't get worse.

'No magic, involved, Suze,' he said as they got into the lift. 'I was lying on my bed reading the reams of paperwork we'd been sent and I saw that you were down for tonight's mystery talk. Our agent clearly made a little slip-up with the info. Realising, I dashed along, so you didn't make a gaffe.'

'Ours? Is that all kosher now with Max? You've spoken.'

'Mmmn-hmm,' Jason nodded. His eyes sparkled. 'From now on, Max will officially get twelve per cent of my earnings.'

'Thank you so much for saving me, Jason.'

'No. Thank *you*, Suze. You got me the gig onboard. It was the least I could do to help you out. Max is in trouble, though.'

'Max? Why?'

'I'm apparently aged between forty and sixty-eight.'

'I'm sorry?'

'Those are the requirements for my job as a gentleman host. Male, presentable, able to dance, aged between forty and sixty-eight, as my room-mate, George, never stops telling me. He's very disgruntled about my presence.'

'Oh lord. I never said you were young. What's going to happen to you?'

'They can hardly throw me overboard and get an elderly gent to swim out to the ship and take my job, so they're stuck with me, at least till Southampton.'

'Agents!' said Suzy. 'Well, at least Max got us a passage home, even if neither of us fits the bill. I'm hardly qualified as a lecturer either. How am I going to give those talks? I don't know nearly enough.' She looked at her watch. 'Oh God! We've got less than an hour to cobble something together.'

'Darling, this is not Oxford University. It's a cruise ship. They don't want dusty old footnotes. They'll want something light and amusing. It's easy. You blether on for a bit about the sad old genius and gay icon, Oscar Wilde. Tell them about the trial and read some "Reading Gaol".'

'You're right. There's tons I could squeeze in. I don't suppose you could give your Jack Worthing and I can reprise my "handbag"?'

'Sans barbershop!'

The lift pinged and came to a stop.

'Why not, Suze?' he said. 'We can do it. But, seriously, first we need to get some grub. My stomach is howling. I don't want us passing out onstage.'

They whirled through the cafeteria, talking in Wildean phrases and swapping ideas for the lecture, while grabbing things to make a dressing-room snack – a chunk of cheese, some bread, a few small tomatoes, two cakes – then returned to Suzy's room in entertainment quarters to write up their notes.

'Your cabin is *charmant*!' said Jason, looking around Suzy's new home and flopping down on her desk chair. 'I'm in bunks. My cabin partner is a seedy old chap who must be an ex-sergeant major, straight out of Joe Orton. Luckily he's into keep-fit, so I'm hoping he'll be spending hours in the gym, or jogging round the decks, rather than sounding off all day in the cabin with me. I think he thinks boys of my age should all be doing National Service.'

'Yes. OK. OK. Later, darling,' said Suzy, pulling out pens and paper. 'We have to get on with this.'

Jason took the pen and started noting down all the subjects they had discussed, while Suzy laid out the plates on the bed, assembling the tomatoes, the salad and the cheeses between buttered baps.

'Open with the handbag scene ...' Jason grabbed a new piece of paper. 'Then facts – birth, success, green carnations, Bosie, the trial and doom ...'

'We'd be in the middle of Act Two now,' said Suzy, handing Jason a cheese-salad roll. 'Opening night. Imagine that! It already feels a lifetime away.'

'This is so frustrating,' said Jason, scratching away on headed ship's notepaper with one hand while tearing his teeth into the roll with the other.

Suzy's mobile phone rang. 'Damn.' She looked at the screen. 'It's Reg!'

'You're kidding!' Jason leaped across the cabin and perched beside her on the bed. 'Take it!'

Suzy slid her finger across the screen and started the call.

'Suzy!' Reg's voice was bright but oily. 'Just touching base, darling, after the catastrophe yesterday. Did you manage to get home all right?'

Jason had put his head close to hers and was listening in.

'No, actually, Reg. I didn't get home yet. Did you?'

Jason made plane wings, and tapped his watch.

'I'm still in Zurich,' she lied.

'Ah.' There was a pause. 'I don't suppose you've seen or heard from Jason Scott?'

Jason shook his head.

'Not since this morning, no.'

'He managed to get a flight out, then?'

'Not as far as I know. Reg, did you not hear every one of our return flight tickets was voided. What on earth was all that about?

'Ah.' Another pause. 'Not my department, unfortunately. I am only the director.' Reg sighed. 'Listen, sweetie, when you get back to town I think we should all meet up. Just because we lost the venue in Zurich doesn't mean the show's over.'

Suzy pulled a horror face at Jason, but said nothing.

'Well, anyhow, Suzy, just give me a bell when you get to London. And, if you see that boy Jason, please ask him to phone me. It's very important.'

'I presume this means you're at home already, Reg.'

'That's right. Luckily I got an early flight.'

'No question of the captain going down with the ship then?'

By way of reply Reg cleared his throat.

'You flew home with Stan?'

'Whatever makes you think that?' Reg's voice betrayed outrage. 'In fact, I haven't heard from Stan since dinner last night. Have you spoken to him? I've been trying to reach him but his phone is going straight to answer.'

'As far as I know, Stan was on the first flight out of Zurich this morning.'

'I doubt that,' said Reg. 'How would Stan have known the show was called off? I hadn't told him, neither had Barbara.'

Jason did a mime of fighting. Suzy got the hint.

'Barbara seemed to think you weren't well, Reg?'

'Walked into a kitchen cupboard. Bit of a black eye. Nothing serious. But if you hear from Jason ...'

Jason's face was filled with anger.

'Must go now, Reg.' Suzy was about to cut him off when she thought of something. 'Oh, just one other thing. You talked about putting the show on in town. Is your Swiss backer still going ahead, then?'

'That's not what I meant. I was thinking that one of those little fringe venues might take us in. There'd be no pay, of course. But at least we wouldn't have wasted our time.'

'So, the producer, what was his name ...' Suzy snapped her fingers at Jason who scribbled on the *Blue Mermaid* notepad on the bedside table. He held up the paper. Suzy read aloud: 'Mr Appenzell. He's not taking up the show if we open in London?'

'Uuuummmm,' said Reg. 'I don't think so. It was the first time I'd used him for a producer. A bit of a mistake. He didn't really know his way round "theatre land". I mean ... He's used to big business. Finance, stock markets and that stuff. For him we thespians are a bit of a joke – small fry. I won't be using him again.'

'That doesn't mean he can get away with this, Reg. Even though the show was cancelled we're still owed money.' As she spoke Suzy felt a rush of justified bravery. 'Anyway, if we can't go after him for the money we're owed, perhaps we'll come after you.'

'Now, hold on, Suzy.' Reg's voice registered panic. 'Look. I'll chase him up. I know he was set to see a solicitor about selling his London flat. He's due off for business in LA or somewhere. You know these jet-setters. Touch down at their various international *pied-à-terres* then within twenty-four hours they're off again.'

'Oh, by the way, Reg. If I bump into Jason should I ask him what happened last night?' asked Suzy.

'No. No. Don't mention anything to Jason.'

She knew that she had touched a nerve because Reg was now trying to get off the line. Why would Reg not want her to talk to Jason? She hoped Jason might explain this to her later.

'As I said. Call me when you're back in the UK, Suzy dear. Must rush.' And he was gone.

Suzy flung her mobile on to the bed and grabbed the notes for her lecture.

'We'll never get any of that money, will we?' she said as she ran her finger down the list of subjects.

'No.' Jason spoke definitively.

'We could go down the path of law.' Suzy put her hands up. 'But I've seen what happens to people who have fought their corner in this business. Twenty years of legal hell. Eventually they win some pitiful amount. But during those twenty years, no one will employ them. Life ruined. No, thanks.'

'I have a feeling Mr Appenzell is going to be well out of touch with the law.'

Suzy looked at Jason, who was doodling on the desk pad. She could see that his thoughts were running. Whatever had really happened last night, it wasn't what he had told her. There was something more. Something he was clearly reluctant to admit.

'What was the name of Bosie's father, Jason, the one Oscar sued for libel?'

'The Marquess of Queensbury.'

As Suzy scribbled down the name, she looked up at the wall clock.

'Hell! Jason! Look at the time. We've got to be backstage in fifteen minutes!'

She edged herself on to the desk seat so that she could face the mirror, while Jason continued writing. 'I've got to get my slap on.'

'You could talk about Oscar Wilde's tomb in Paris.'

'Isn't that a bit morbid?'

'No – fabulous anecdotes. Once part of it was a statue with enormous testicles – until they got stolen …'

'I can't tell a story like that on a cruise ship!'

'All right. How about the fact that so many people put on lipstick and then kissed the tomb that the stone started to rot away, so they had to erect a kind of plastic shield round it?'

'How do you know all of this?'

'I was brought up in a flat just up the road from Père Lachaise Cemetery. I used to hang out there with my friends.'

'I just don't think it's right to talk about tombs.' Suzy licked her kohl pencil and started on her eyes.

'He died in a hotel on the Rue des Beaux-Arts, you know,' said Jason. 'And he was going under another name.'

'Really?'

'Sebastian Melmoth.'

'I think I'd prefer to concentrate on his mother, his upbringing in Ireland, and his success,' said Suzy. 'Rather than disaster and failure. So … we start with the handbag scene …'

Quarter of an hour later, Suzy stood in the wings of the ship's theatre, Jason at her side. She took deep breaths. Through the curtain, she could hear the buzz of the audience. It was a full house.

'This is terrifying,' she whispered, taking a sniff of her Olbas inhaler stick.

One of the stage hands swept past her. 'It's packed out there. We'll probably have to wait another couple of minutes while they get them all seated.'

Suzy glanced down at the folder which she and Jason had assembled.

'I hope I can read this in the lights.'

The stage hand waved them to the gap in the middle of the curtains. 'You're on.'

The curtains pulled open a few feet and Suzy walked out into the spotlit stage.

'Good evening, ladies and gentlemen. My name is Suzy Marshall and tonight I'm going to talk to you about Oscar Wilde.'

The audience applauded politely. She scanned their faces, and, sitting in the centre of the stalls, near the front, was Mike Turner. He was not clapping; his arms were defiantly crossed.

Suzy turned and introduced Jason. 'This is my friend, Jason Scott. And tonight we are going to start with probably Oscar Wilde's most famous scene. It's from *The Importance of Being Earnest*.'

Suzy stood in the glare of the spotlight and looked down. She could see her own shadow shaking. She didn't think she had ever been this nervous on any stage in her life. But then neither had she ever been this unrehearsed.

When the scene was over, Jason took a bow, and left the stage through the red curtains.

Suzy walked down towards the audience.

'Oscar Wilde famously said "I have nothing to declare but my genius", and that genius led him to become the most cele-brated man in London, but at the height of his success, events took such a terrible turn that he died in exile, shunned by the society which had once worshipped him, existing in abject poverty, his famous name so toxic that he chose to live under an alias.' She looked down at the script in the folder, grasping for the name he had gone under. The pages were in the wrong order. If that wasn't bad enough, the lights were dazzlingly bright and Jason's handwriting so spidery she could barely make out one in three words.

'Erm …' She paused, flipping the pages, trying to find the bit about Wilde's mother and early life. 'It's in here some-where …'

She looked up to smile and caught eyes with Mike. A smug smirk was playing on his lips.

Suzy walked towards the wings. She decided to dump the script on the lectern and make up as much as she could remember, from now on, not relying on the notes at all.

She took centre stage again.

'Jane Francesca Agnes, Lady Wilde, went under the fanciful nom de plume, Speranza. But Lady Wilde was no flibbertigibbet. A renowned supporter of women's rights and Irish nationalism, her life in many ways predicted her son's. She too was involved in a sex scandal, and sued for libel by a girl who accused her husband, Oscar's father, Sir William Wilde, of seducing her. After the libel suit, when Sir William died, they discovered that he had squandered all the family money and they were left broke.'

Suzy wasn't sure why, but the audience seemed to be growing uncomfortable. She could hear people rustling and murmuring.

While she continued about Lady Wilde's career, how she wrote and sold folk tales to make ends meet, someone in the audience edged out of their row, ran up the aisle and left. Two others followed.

Her talk was obviously a disaster.

Panicked, Suzy moved downstage to talk about the reception of Oscar's first plays. '*A Woman of No Importance* ...' Suddenly she could not remember the names of any other plays. She went back to the lectern and flicked frantically through the pages. She could hear the audience getting more and more edgy. People were talking now, standing up and leaving – they seemed not to be strolling up the aisles, but running.

As she stammered more truisms about Wilde, the lights changed and behind her she heard a commotion. Suzy turned and saw a man wearing a velvet jacket holding a microphone walking out on to the stage. He held up his hand, requesting Suzy to stop talking.

She couldn't believe this was happening to her.

The audience must think that she was so bad she was being taken off.

The man, a kind of compère, walked past her to the front of the stage.

'Can we have houselights right up, now, Andy!'

As the lights in the auditorium came up Suzy saw that nearly all the audience was standing, many people shuffling along the rows, trying to get out.

'Thank you, Suzy. Sorry to stop your talk, but we have a bit of a medical emergency on our hands.' The man turned to the audience. 'I know you'll bear with me when I ask you to clear some space.' He then waved to the medical team who were heading down the aisles, with large bags and a stretcher.

'I'm afraid tonight's show is over, folks. Suzy's talk was fascinating but right now we need to give the sick gentleman urgent care. Could you please leave as briskly as possible through the doors to the right so that the medical team can make full use of the left aisle.'

As everyone made their way out, the man with the microphone came over to Suzy and whispered in her ear. 'It looks like a heart attack. So sorry to interrupt. I'm Blake, by the way. The entertainment manager.'

One of the medics looked up to the stage and shook his head.

Blake lifted his microphone again, calling out to the stragglers who were lingering in the aisle trying to look back to see what was going on. 'That's it, ladies and gentlemen. Show over. Plenty of other things to do – there's the casino, the cinema, dancing in the ballroom. You'll have another chance to hear Suzy's brilliant talk soon. Just read your *Daily Programme*. We'll reschedule.'

As the last of the audience left the auditorium, Suzy looked down at the medical team. They had laid the person out in the aisle and were giving him mouth to mouth.

It was only then that she realised the man whose heart they were pumping was Mike Turner.

Taking Suzy by the arm, Blake walked her from the stage.

'What happens now?' she asked.

'I need to get down to the office and get the schedule reordered. There's nothing we can do here. He'll be taken down to the infirmary.'

'Poor man,' said Suzy.

'Not really,' said Blake. 'He's a bitter man who makes life hell for everyone onboard. I wonder how many people will believe his lectures on living a healthy lifestyle now?'

Despite herself, Suzy laughed.

'I don't think you've much reason to laugh, Miss Marshall. That man saved your bacon,' said Blake. 'You were floundering up there. Not enough preparation, I fear.'

Backstage, while she had her microphone removed, Suzy stayed silent. What could she say after that slap in the face? She felt like a naughty schoolgirl waiting to be given a black mark.

'As for Mike,' Blake continued, 'the Medical Centre will take good care of him. We've a first-rate team onboard. Proper medicine, unlike the silly guff in his talks.' Blake laid his hand-held microphone in a basket on the stage manager's console and walked Suzy out of the stage door. 'Andy tells me that Mike went for you earlier at the tech meeting.'

'He was just being tough on the newbie.' As they strolled together along the red-carpeted corridors, Suzy was afraid to admit how much Mike had terrified her. 'And as it turns out, he was right. What will happen to him now?'

'Depends how it goes. We may chopper him to the mainland, or if he's well enough to keep going a few days he'll be offloaded when we get to Southampton. Are you finishing your stint in Southampton too?'

Suzy nodded.

'Heading off to do some glamorous film job, I suppose.'

'Hardly!' Suzy laughed. 'I'll be getting off to sit at home and wait for the phone to ring. The usual actor's life.'

Blake peeled off and opened an unmarked door, just behind the purser's office. 'Go and enjoy yourself,' he said. 'What happened tonight is unfortunate, but not your responsibility. But before you get back on to one of our stages, Miss Marshall, please make sure you know what you're doing.'

She returned to her cabin to gather her thoughts. She felt like an idiot. Had she been that awful? She knew that Blake was right when he said she was unprepared but how could she prepare when she hadn't even known that she was doing the bloody thing?

She flopped down on the bed, feeling utterly depressed.

Now that she was onboard doing this job, she really wanted to make it work, and yet it appeared by the end of day one she had already failed.

How come she spent her life yearning for work and now that it had arrived everything had gone so wrong? *The Importance* should have been good for her, in one way or another. Either because the audiences enjoyed it and she'd have the thrill of the laughs and the applause, or at the very worst she'd have some money coming in.

But neither had happened.

And now this further failure.

She was bewildered.

Her mind went back to Zurich.

Why would a producer cancel a whole show simply because one of the actors resisted his advances? And Reg seemed to have taken the whole business too calmly, as though it was normal for a show to rehearse, go to Zurich and get cancelled, while no one got paid, and all their return flights got annulled, leaving the actors to get themselves home.

She wondered if she was right to trust Jason.

Something huge was missing in this equation. She had not been told the whole story. Whichever way you looked at it, the individual pieces didn't add up at all.

Suzy decided she should phone Barbara. She felt that, with the insouciance she had shown in Zurich, the stage manager must have a sane outlook; plus, by now, she might know more of the facts. Perhaps she even knew the truth. In which case, her opinions might help Suzy to stop having these panics.

Suzy picked up her mobile phone but then saw that there was no signal.

As she touched up her make-up she looked into her eyes in the mirror. Her face still showed the anxiety of the last twenty-four hours. What a day! Still, at least she was on her way home. And she felt that, once she was safely in London, this whole escapade would take on the same properties as a dream – it would become an anecdote, she hoped, a conversation to have with fellow actors, another disaster story about a job which went wrong, something to laugh about.

Nonetheless, as Suzy fastened her necklace, brushed herself down and left her cabin, she still felt a dark niggling worry, a worry which was not going to go away.

She wanted to talk to Jason, to have a debrief.

She looked at her watch and realised that now he would be at work, strutting his stuff as a dance host. She left the cabin and made her way to the ballroom.

As she walked down the central corridor, a couple in evening dress strolled past her.

'Such a pity your talk was cut short,' said the lady. 'We were really enjoying it.'

Suzy smiled, astonished. After Blake's acerbic response she could only remember the audience's disturbance, so she couldn't imagine that anyone had found it entertaining.

'I look forward to the repeat event,' said the gentleman. 'I gather the poor man in the audience had a heart attack.'

'I'm afraid so,' said Suzy.

'Life goes on,' said the lady. 'We need to make the most of it, you know. These moments are a sharp reminder.'

'We'll look out for you in the *Programme* tomorrow.' The gentleman took his partner's arm and they drifted away.

Suzy found the ballroom with ease. You could hear the dance band reverberating along the corridors leading to it.

She found a table near the back of the room and ordered a stiff drink. Once her eyes became accustomed to the light she could make out Jason working on the dance floor. He was in the centre of the room, waltzing, smiling, charming the pants off some middle-aged woman.

He looked so at ease, and yet, this time last night, he had apparently been in the middle of some drama terrible enough to get the whole run of a show cancelled. Apart from the forty winks they'd both taken on the train journey, Jason couldn't have got much sleep in the last twenty-four hours, yet he still looked so fresh.

Suzy felt her mobile phone vibrating in her handbag. She was confused that suddenly there was magically a signal when she had assumed there was no hope of one onboard. She fumbled about and answered. It was her agent.

Holding a finger to one ear to drown out the dance music, Suzy scurried to the entrance so that she might hear better.

'Are you sitting comfortably?' he said. 'Good news. Lecturer on health dropped out at the last minute. So, anyway, they've offered to extend your trip, if you'd fancy it.'

Suzy thought he must have been mistaken. The entertainment manager had all but told her she was rubbish, and, on top of that, having a heart attack wasn't exactly what she would call "dropping out".

'I was there, Max. It was horrible.'

'It wasn't your fault … or was it?' Max laughed again. 'A Miss Marple plot.'

'Stop kidding about it all, Max. Please.'

'I'm sorry. Insensitive. But how about it, Suze? Sail on to New York and back? Or if you like you can do to New York and then fly back. They have a vacancy. What do you think?'

Suzy was tempted, but after Blake's comments she felt terrified and, anyway, lecturing was not really her métier.

'Oh, I don't know, Max. Wouldn't I be better off back in town, hanging out for a TV role?'

'It's dead over here, darling. Not a squeak of work anywhere. We're all fingering prayer beads, pleading for the phones to ring. Absolutely nothing new is starting up now till Christmas is over. You'd only be coming back to nothing.'

Suzy was torn.

'I don't think the entertainment manager likes me. It could be difficult.'

'Well someone onboard called Blake was just on the blower, raving about you to me. Truly, Suze,' said Max in his best persuasive manner, 'I can think of worse places to be employed in December than a luxury cruise ship.'

Suzy couldn't take this in.

'Blake?'

'Yes, it was Blake who just phoned me.'

Suzy was mystified but always willing to take her agent's advice.

'What would I have to do, though, Max? I don't know that I can come up with many more lectures.'

'Morning acting classes four days of the transatlantic crossing, plus two talks, and they can be the same ones you're doing on this leg.'

In the adjacent ballroom, the band struck up a quickstep tempo version of 'Let's Do It'.

It was a sign.

'You're on, Max darling,' she said. 'Let's do it.'

As she re-entered the ballroom, Suzy found herself doing steps from the charleston, which she remembered from playing

Maisie in a production of *The Boyfriend* in her younger days, at Worthing Rep.

She noticed that the woman who Jason had been dancing with was back at the table now, swigging champagne and smiling.

It certainly was the life, here onboard. Like being in a bouncing bubble of Fairyland.

And if Suzy worked this Atlantic trip it would give her a little money in time for Christmas.

She took a seat at the empty table beside Jason's recent dance partner, waved down a waiter and ordered another glass of whisky.

Jason swept off the floor and stood before a flamboyant elderly lady wearing a tangerine frou-frou top and huge gathered 1950s-style skirt. He held out one hand, offering her a turn at the Gay Gordons. The lady gave a coy smile and went with him. As he marched past her, Jason gave Suzy a surreptitious wink.

She was certain he was not telling her the truth about what happened last night in Zurich.

But now that she was here doing another job, did Zurich really matter?

She had not been paid for the weeks of rehearsal and had lost the money she had spent on lodgings in Zurich. But Max would chase all that up as best he could and, now that she was set up here onboard the *Blue Mermaid*, surely it would be better to forget the whole escapade and put it down to experience. 'Cancel and continue', as one of her favourite actresses had once said, after a particularly bad onstage experience. Cancel and continue. That was the way forward.

Jason would be getting off the ship in two days and the entire business would be old news.

Suzy realised she must still be looking worried. She lifted her head and put on a smile. How did that song go? Something about wearing your frown upside down.

And another old adage: if you look forward instead of looking back, things will start looking up.

She sipped her whisky.

Simultaneously the woman at the next table raised her champagne glass and smiled at Suzy.

The current dance ended and Jason prowled the tables scanning for lonely females. He stopped in front of Suzy, held out his hand and whispered in her ear. 'What are you doing here? Is your talk over already?'

'Long story,' she said. 'But I won't dance just now.'

'Guess what?' Jason pressed his face closer to her ear. 'They've asked me to stay on.'

'I thought you were in trouble for being the wrong age.'

'Max is in trouble for dissembling. But the man who was going to replace me at Southampton has just taken a tumble and broken a hip. They may want mature men, but these old geezers come with their liabilities. Anyhow, now they need me as far as New York.'

He spun away from her and asked the elderly lady behind him if she'd like to dance.

Suzy watched as the boy led her to the dance floor.

Now that Jason was staying on, Suzy knew that she couldn't let the whole Zurich saga drop. If she did it would always hang in the air between the two of them.

'Are you travelling alone too?' asked the woman at the next table, leaning over the side of her chair.

'Kind of,' Suzy replied.

'He's a right little charmer, that boy. I danced with him earlier. I've only just realised they are all employees of the ship. At first I thought my luck was in!' The woman scrutinised Suzy's face and added, 'Have we met before?'

'I don't think so,' said Suzy.

'Oh wait! I know! You're an actress. Sorry if I'm wrong, but weren't you in that wonderful old legal TV series, *Dahlias*?'

'That's me!' Suzy took another sip of her drink. 'Suzy Marshall.' She extended a hand.

'Amanda Herbert.' Amanda lifted her glass. 'They should bring that show back. I loved it.'

'Fashions change, I'm afraid, Amanda. It was a little too gentle for today's taste. Plus, we're all a bit past it now.'

'I always forget that.' Amanda laughed. 'I feel as though I'm still twenty-six.'

'Do you cruise a lot?'

'No,' said Amanda. 'It's all a fluke. My first time. I got on at Genoa. But I'm heading to New York.'

'Me too,' said Suzy.

They both turned to watch the dancers.

Two women of an age, sitting at adjacent tables, simultaneously raising a toast. Two passing strangers, on a ship in the night.

Little did these two women know that, thanks to the eventful turns of the last few days, they had something in common.

And, not realising that they had anything in common, they could not know that that factor was a person.

Nor did they realise that, when the *Blue Mermaid* sailed out into the vast and lonely Atlantic Ocean, this person would unite their lives in a most unexpected and chilling way.

PART THREE

Southampton to the Porcupine
Abyssal Plain

8

O N T H E N I G H T the *Blue Mermaid* sailed out of Southampton, Amanda took her place at the dinner table, and saw that she had a completely new set of companions.

'Myriam La-Grande-Motte. That's Myriam with a Y,' announced a large lady in a frilly top which exposed slightly too much bust. Her accent was a bright Californian. 'And this is my darling nephew, Tyger. He's also a Tyger with a Y. We're all Ys in this family.' She burst into song: '"Y y y the beat is crazy!"'

Tyger gave a quiet groan.

'He's very shy,' said Myriam with a Y, running her plump fingers through her bright orange hair. 'Quite the blushing violet. Don't worry. He'll groan out of it.' She gave a throaty laugh.

Amanda glanced at the very striking boy, who must be around thirteen. He had long auburn hair, a fancy quiff and the most piercing green eyes.

'Good evening, Myriam.' Amanda unfurled her napkin and placed it on her knee. 'Good evening Tyger!'

The boy grunted and disappeared behind the menu.

'I'm Amanda, by the way.'

'Oh my! English!' sighed Myriam, laying her chubby hand on her wrinkled décolletage. 'How darling. That accent! I'm going to insist that you talk and talk and talk.'

'I always think it's you Americans who have the accent,' said Amanda with a smile.

'Really?' Myriam threw her head back and laughed loudly. 'So, my deary, from which part of the old country do you hail?' she asked.

It took Amanda a few seconds to realise that Myriam was asking where she lived. Naturally she replied: 'London.'

'London.' Myriam elongated the word as though it was a ravishing poem to everything heavenly. 'Tyger and I did a day trip this time round. Actually, I used to live there for a little while in my youth. So many happy memories.'

'Which part of London?' asked Amanda.

'Hertfordshire,' beamed Myriam. 'Do you know it?'

Amanda shrugged. Without appearing rude, what could she respond? So instead she busied herself, flicking through the menu.

'Tyger and I adored London, didn't we? We saw all the sights, Bucking-ham Palace, Piccalilli Circus, the Grenadine Guards. We had a marvellous time!'

Myriam grinned at the dark-haired lady on her other side. 'What a table we have here – with Amanda and her "oh so English" accent, and the lovely Liliane here talking her divine Francaisies, I shall be in parody each and every mealtime. Not to mention the ravenous food. La fooda divina! Ooh la la la!' Myriam reached down for her evening bag, a small drawstring pouch heavily studded with multicoloured jewels. She pulled out a smart leather notebook and sparkly pen. 'Why don't we all swap ship addresses now? Day one.' Myriam beamed. 'Then, if ever we need each other on the rest of the voyage, we'll know which locale of cabin to direct our messages.'

'Why would we need zem? We see each other at meal-times.' Liliane, the epitome of French style, elegant, beautifully coiffed and dressed, with pale, fine skin, a red slash of a mouth and heavily kohled eyes, gave an enigmatic smile and took a sip from her water glass.

'Ah but sometimes things pop up suddenly – we might fancy being part of a quiz team or want to invite one another to a party, or whatever. Which reminds me, were any of you invited to Dorothy's party?'

'I don't know Dorothy, I'm afraid,' said Amanda.

'Nor me,' added Liliane.

'Me either,' said Myriam. 'I just saw it in tomorrow's newsletter and wondered. Oh, my dears, there are always so many enchanting things happening onboard. And you know this ship is so big – Tyger has found out it's longer than four blocks in New York City. Imagine! It's possible never to meet someone at all on a week-long cruise. It happened to me once before.'

Amanda took a pen and pad from her handbag, scrawled notes and handed the two ladies her cabin number. Myriam ripped two pages from her notebook and passed them over. Amanda offered her pen to Liliane, but, before she received it, they were interrupted.

'Chris McConaughy,' said a lank-haired highly-tanned man, who pulled out a chair next to Amanda. There was no doubting where he came from, as he spoke with a strident Australian accent. 'And this here to my right is the lady-wife, Jennie.'

Amanda wondered whether it was possible to have a gentleman-wife. She smiled at Jennie, who took her place beside her husband, gave a timid nod and immediately looked down at her lap.

'Me and the little lady are new to cruising,' Chris added proudly, whipping his table napkin out as though it was a matador's red cloth. 'Cruise novices, as it were. Are you lot cruise virgins too?'

'*Au contraire*, Chris,' said Myriam with a chuckle. 'When it comes to cruises, I'm practically a lady of the night. *La Dame aux Croisières*! In fact I've twice circumvented the globe.'

'It's my first time too, Chris,' said Amanda. She noticed that Jennie did nothing but nod in agreement with her husband. 'The little lady' certainly knew her place.

'I absolutely adore the ocean, dear. Don't you?' said Myriam, wafting the menu so widely she narrowly avoided clipping Jennie across the head. 'Are you, Amanda, like me, a lone traveller?'

Amanda looked quizzically at Tyger.

'Oh, the boy doesn't count. He's a mere child. But don't he brush up swell in his Little Lord Fauntleroy suit? We bought it yesterday at Harrods. I guess that, wearing that dinky blue velvet, he could pass for a real Lord of the manners.'

'Zis room is so beautiful,' said Liliane. 'I add-mire zis ceiling, don't you? It reminds me of Paris – *les grands magasins*, Du Printemps, Galeries Lafayette.'

They all looked up at the domed stained glass above them.

'A bit too reminiscent of *The Poseidon Adventure* for me,' said Chris. 'Let's hope that glass ceiling doesn't end up being the floor, eh?' He crossed his fingers and winced. 'Shouldn't have said that,' he added. 'It's one of those "don't mention the war" things, I expect, on a boat …'

'Ship,' murmured Tyger just loud enough for Amanda to hear.

'And no talk of that *other* film …' Chris bowled on as though he had not heard the correction, and maybe he really had not. 'As you know, I'm talking about the one starting with a T followed by an I and rhyming with Hispanic.'

'I loff zat film,' said Liliane. 'I have seen it many times. He is exquisite, zat man, Leonardo DiCaprio.'

'You call that little squit a man?' Chris had a way of cutting the end of people's sentences while topping the volume of the previous speaker, and thus seeming to make his own comments more important. 'When I first saw a photo of him, I took him for a lesbian … Excuse my French.'

'I have to admit it right now, Amanda …' Myriam lowered her head and peered at Amanda through her heavily pencilled-on eyebrows. 'I'm here onboard this beautiful vessel looking for love. It's romance, romance, romance all the way to the U.S. of A. You too?'

Amanda realised that romance was the last thing on her agenda. She hadn't considered such a thing for years. But, here she was, for the first time in her life, on a ship. Perhaps that was the point of sea travel. She thought back to pregnant afternoons lying on the sofa watching *The Love Boat* on TV and felt her blood pressure lurch. She certainly hoped that the *Blue Mermaid* wasn't just a glorified version of *The Dating Game*. Finding a man during these few days afloat was certainly not her goal. She just wanted a bit of peace and quiet before moving into her lovely new London flat.

*

Suzy spent the day that the ship was docked at the port of Southampton in her cabin, working at her computer. She was making notes for the morning acting classes and perfecting the talks she had already given.

Today's work marathon she knew would not be in vain. If she planned things out now, her workload for the voyage would be much easier, less frightening, and she would have some relaxed time to enjoy the facilities of the ship and to socialise, meet new people. Also, having landed the job, she couldn't afford to get another telling off from Blake.

Since Genoa, Suzy had spent most of her time either in the ship's library, doing research, or in her cabin writing it all up and shaping it into proper talks.

There was serious pressure too, as she had been warned by Andy that, once they left the shores of England, internet and phone prices would be ferociously high, so she needed the Southampton day to look up all the things she wanted online, especially if it involved downloading.

There was a knock on the door and Ong came in, bearing a Hoover.

'Do you mind, madam? Or would you prefer me to come back?' he asked, heading for the corner to plug in the vacuum cleaner.

'Should I put your phone on the bedside table?' He had had to unplug Suzy's mobile, which lay on the floor, charging.

All day it had been bleeping. Suzy decided not to pick up. She knew how distracting it could be once you got sucked into the world of messaging, Facebook or Twitter. Once hooked in, the hours vanished into the social-media black hole, so Suzy was strict with herself, ignored it and kept on working at her desk. There would be time enough later to catch up with the trends and friends.

Ong laid her phone on the desk top, and turned on the Hoover.

'You are enjoying your time on the ship?' he asked, raising his voice over the noise of the machine.

'I love it,' she replied.

'Too much working,' said Ong. 'You should treat yourself to some happy time in the spa.'

'Do you get happy time onboard, Ong? You and your fellow stewards?'

Ong nodded. 'We have a crew bar and cafeteria. We often stay up late, drinking, singing. It's good company.'

'Do you have family?'

'My parents are still in the Philippines. I send them money. But my wife is onboard, so we have a cabin together.'

Suzy hadn't even imagined this – family life below the decks. 'Is your wife a stewardess?'

Ong laughed. 'No, Miss Marshall. She is a beautician in the spa.' He unplugged the Hoover, gave the tops a quick wipe around and made his way to the door. 'Don't forget, if there's anything you need, simply ask me!'

And he was gone.

Though it had been only a couple of days ago, Zurich now seemed like a dream or a long-lost, shadowy memory. Suzy still wanted to get to the bottom of what had really happened between Jason, Reg and the backer, but the quest now felt much less urgent than it once had. She and Jason had seen little of one another for the last few days. Their schedules were in direct opposition. Suzy worked in the day, while Jason started dancing at teatime and was still at it in the early hours. Every time they met, colliding in the entertainment corridor or the entertainment office, Jason had kept up his cheeky-young-man act. It was starting to disturb Suzy. Why was he showing no sign of worry or upset about what he had brought about in Zurich? Either he didn't give a damn that his actions had put a whole load of people out of work or he was a psychopath or sociopath or whatever the terminology was these days for those who didn't care about others and their feelings. Perhaps if she had been a young man in Jason's place, she might have behaved the same way. She herself might be over the whole episode and stuck into the next job, but she still wanted to know what had happened, and in what way Jason had been involved.

As Suzy typed she could hear all kinds of announcements coming from the speakers in the corridor. The new America-bound passengers had been welcomed aboard, told about the events on offer this evening and been summoned to life-boat drill. The hooters had gone off and the ship was already moving serenely down Southampton Water.

Suzy looked at her watch. Only five minutes till she was due at dinner, and here she was looking like a right scruff. She saved her documents and grabbed her make-up pack, then started pulling smart clothes from the wardrobe and throwing them on to the bed.

It was amazing how a life in the theatre meant you could tart yourself up in minutes. All those hasty costume changes in the wings finally had a practical use in the real world.

She dressed, made-up, plumped up her hair, gave herself the once-over and left the cabin.

'My word, Miss Marshall!' It was Blake. 'You've scrubbed up well.' He held out his arm. 'May I lead you to the lifts!'

Suzy wasn't sure whether this was a compliment or an insult, but smiled anyway.

'Are you bearing up OK?' he asked. 'Properly prepared for the next informative offering?'

'Thank you for the job,' Suzy replied. 'I'm presuming it was you who kept me aboard to New York?'

'Oh, better the devil you know …' Blake pressed the call button for the lift. 'It was easier to use someone who was already aboard. Have you met the new magician?'

Suzy shook her head.

'Arturo. He's quite a hoot. I believe he'll be at your dinner table tonight. Prepare yourself. He's something of a character. Stiff competition for you.'

And with that, the lift arrived and Suzy stepped inside, leaving Blake turning to stroll off in the other direction.

Suzy had no idea how to read Blake. Did he really think she was terrible, or was he one of those people who kept you in control by being contrary? Whichever, she knew she had to keep on her toes. She simply could not afford to let Blake think she was hopeless one more time, otherwise he could make her life very difficult for the remaining weeks of her contract. And on a ship there was nowhere to run!

While she was in the lift, Suzy took the minute to inspect her phone. She'd been called by both India and Emily. No doubt Reg was coming up with all kinds of plans to transfer the show to some dreary room above a pub in Croydon or Penge.

She slipped the phone back inside her rather-too-tiny evening bag.

As she strolled the length of the ship, Suzy sensed a whole new atmosphere. In the couple of days coming back from the Mediterranean she had thought the entire enterprise tacky, though fun. But now there was a sense of excitement. The new set of passengers were more smartly dressed, and the open areas buzzed with animated conversation. It was electric.

In the dining room too the difference was palpable. The previous assembly had chomped their dinner as though it was something of an ordeal to be got through, attempting to cram as much of your money's-worth into your mouth as fast as possible. Consequently, any conversation was dull and sporadic. Now laughter and a keen hubbub surrounded Suzy as she edged her way to her new table, very near the centre of the room. There was so much animated chatter that it sounded more like a glittering aviary than a dining room. Even the lighting seemed to be different; each separate table looked more intimate and sophisticated.

'Good evening,' she called to her dining companions as she took her place.

'Good evening,' replied an elegant grey-haired man opposite. 'It is smooth so far, no?'

'Like a millpond.' Suzy picked up the menu. 'But it's pretty cold outside.'

'What do you expect for December?' The man, a sleek silver fox, shrugged.

'We met before, didn't we?' Suzy knew the man was familiar but could not place him.

'Yes. We met, for a second or two, on your first day onboard in Genoa. Tony Hanson. I'm lecturing on the Atlantic Ocean.'

It all rushed back – the first meeting in the Interact lounge, when the ship was still moored, where Mike Turner had been so rude to her. She couldn't believe she had not recognised him, but a man slumped down in a rumpled old sweater and corduroy slacks looked quite different when sitting up in an impeccable dark green velvet jacket and matching silk dicky bow.

'Forgive me. Of course, Tony. I remember now.'

'So – it seems Blake's got a thing about you.'

Suzy was so shocked by this statement she couldn't think of a suitable reply. She rewound all her meetings with Blake in her head and couldn't imagine why Tony should say this.

'Are you sleeping with him?' Nursing his wine glass in one hand, Tony leaned back in his chair, looking her in the eye. 'Bit of rumpy-pumpy in the Ents Office?'

'Certainly not. I have only ever encountered him in corridors and lifts!'

'A lot you can do in a lift. Didn't you see *Fatal Attraction*?'

'I did, but absolutely not.' Having said this in such an explosive manner, Suzy realised she needed to wind back. 'Blake is nothing more than a colleague.'

'So you don't like Blake, then? You one of the sisterhood, perhaps?'

'I didn't say that, Tony. But I am simply shocked that you would think such a thing.'

'There must be some explanation why someone with no experience of this world of maritime entertainment, whose only presentation was cancelled halfway through, should land the plum job of delivering the star lectures on the transatlantic crossing.'

'My first one was only cancelled because someone was taken ill.' Suzy was desperate with desire to put things straight and to defend herself. 'I didn't even ask for the job. He got on to my agent ...'

'There, there! Calm down, dear!' Tony smirked and poured himself another glass of wine. 'No need to get het up about it.'

Thankfully at this point another man arrived at the empty chair. He had a look of the mad professor about him. His hair seemed to be modelled on Albert Einstein's, his bow tie was askew and the top button of his shirt undone. '*Allora! Finalemente!*' He threw his arms up, patted his pockets then sat. 'Arturo,' he announced, holding his hand out in the direction of Suzy. But before she could reach it, he clapped his hands and a bunch of flowers appeared in the centre of the table. 'I think it's nice to have a decorated table, don't you?'

Arturo made a great fuss of flapping his napkin open, forming it into a bird and then a hat before laying it flat on his lap.

'Yes, lovely, thank you, Arturo,' said Suzy, trying anything to avert further conversation with Tony. 'Have you sailed before?'

'It's my job,' he said, tucking the napkin under his chin. 'I drive the ship.'

'You're on the crew?' Suzy wondered if something had been lost in translation. 'I thought you were the magician.'

'Don't be frightened. When I say I drive it, I mean I control the vessel with my mind. I steer us to safety. But this is my first time on the Atlantic Ocean, which they tell me can get very ... what was the word? ... chopful.'

'Choppy,' said Suzy.

'I think choppy is a very kind word for what we're due to run into.' Tony picked up the menu. 'But this ship is a sturdy old girl.'

'Tony is with us, lecturing on the vagaries of this ocean, Arturo, so he should know.'

'Hmmmmm?' went Arturo. Suzy wasn't sure whether the sound he made was associated with his perusal of the menu or his doubts about Tony's expertise.

'I presume you are, like us, working on the ship, Arturo. Not just enjoying the elegance of the crossing?'

'I perform,' he said. 'I am Arturo the Luminoso – the greatest magician of the age.'

Now it was Tony's turn to make an ambiguous sound. His face still in the menu, he let out a muffled groan. 'So you'll be expecting us to believe in a lot of hocus-pocus,' he sighed.

Suzy looked down at her own menu, squirming with embarrassment. This table was going to be wearing. A disagreeable scientist and a mad magician were obviously never going to see eye to eye. And Muggins would be left to act as referee.

'We'd better choose what we want,' she said, trying to lighten the tone. 'I see a waiter bearing down on us.'

The ship rocked a little – probably going through the passing wake from another vessel.

While Suzy and Tony placed their orders, Arturo started breathing very heavily. He patted his pockets and then plunged his hands into them. He pulled out a rosary and laid it on the table.

Suzy looked down at the string of pearl stones ending in a tiny silver crucifix and wondered how, if he was so scared of a tiny wave, Arturo would cope with the rest of the voyage.

With his other hand, Arturo placed a rabbit's foot on his place setting, then a piece of salmon-pink coral and a little mother-of-pearl horn. These were followed by a one-inch piece of black rope, a holy picture, a charm bracelet and a pebble of lapis lazuli on a golden chain. Finally, out came a St Christopher medal, a wrinkled chestnut and a clove of garlic.

'Pardon me,' said Arturo, holding up the garlic between his thumb and forefinger. 'I believe I have been given the evil eye.' He tilted his head towards the corner of the dining room, leaned in to Suzy and whispered, 'You cannot be too careful.'

Suzy glanced in the direction that Arturo had indicated.

'No, madam! Do not look. I stood beside him as we queued for security. He emanated danger. He will hurt you too. He is the Devil. I have seen Satan before, many times. But I did not expect that Lucifer himself would be aboard this vessel.' He crossed himself before picking up the menu. 'But he is. And he's just walked past.'

Suzy nodded, peering about her trying to see if she could see to whom Arturo was referring, then smiled at the waiter who was hovering at her side. She placed her order and took a deep breath.

'I am sensitive to the malevolent vibrations. Beware of demons,' Arturo whispered into her ear. 'And beware the evil eye!'

Ah well, thought Suzy. Whatever was going to happen, this trip looked as though it would be far from boring.

*

After dinner, as Amanda left the dining room, Chris caught up with her. Jennie took care to stand a few steps behind.

'Hey there, Amanda,' he said. 'Might I have a little word in your shell-like?' He put his hand on her shoulder. She dared barely breathe in the miasma of his very pungent aftershave. 'Jennie and I don't think it's quite right that we should have to share our table with that nasty little teenaged lout. What do you say about it?'

'I'm sorry?' Amanda couldn't believe what she was hearing. 'I don't understand.'

'It's clear from his manner that the lad called Tyger is no more than a little hooligan and far too young to appreciate the finesse of fine conversation at an adults' table. And what with you being a woman of *a certain age*, we thought you might come with us to the purser's office to make an official complaint and get him chucked out of the adults' dining room.'

Before Chris had made the comment about her own age, Amanda was already bristling. Now she was fuming.

'The boy has a perfect right to sit with his aunt, doesn't he?' She spoke quietly, calmly, though she felt far from calm. 'They have paid for their cabin, just as you have.'

'Tyger with a Y! Whoever heard of such nonsense?' said Chris. 'Why not Jim or Pete or some sensible proper bloke's name?'

'It's after the poem by William Blake, I presume. I think it's rather romantic.'

'William Blake? Who he?' To Amanda's ear, everything Chris said sounded as though it was set within inverted commas. 'The absent father, I suppose.'

Amanda realised there would be no point explaining to Chris that William Blake was a major figure in world literature who had been dead for almost two hundred years so instead she looked to his wife for some sense.

'And what do you think, Jennie? Tyger seems a nice boy, doesn't he?'

Jennie cowered beneath her fringe and simpered, 'It's not my place to contradict Chris.'

'Maybe if you don't like the company at our table you should ask to be moved to another table where you can sit by yourselves. There certainly are tables for two,' said Amanda and as she spoke the phone in her evening bag buzzed. Merciful release! 'I'm sorry, Chris, I really can't talk about this now. I'm expecting an urgent call.' In fact, Amanda wasn't expecting any calls, and was amazed to be getting a signal, but the phone excuse was as good a way to escape as any.

'I'd watch out if you're using a phone onboard ship,' Chris called after her. 'The charges can be astronomical, you know.'

Mind your own business, thought Amanda, pulling the phone from her bag. 'We're still just near enough the English coast for it to get a local signal,' she said, pushing through a double door and out on to the open deck. In the distance, across the black water, the lights of the Cornish coast twinkled.

'Hello!'

'Mum?'

'Patricia! How's it going?'

Patricia's voice was near hysterical.

'This French boy is hopeless. Absolutely hopeless. Stupid name – Sofian. With a name like that I should have known he'd be useless. You're right. It does sound like a girl, doesn't it? Anyhow, Mum, he left … well, actually, I've sacked him. I suppose you couldn't come over right now?'

Amanda suppressed a huge laugh.

'I'm afraid not, darling.'

'What do you mean, afraid not?' Amanda could pick up the tension in her daughter's voice. 'Look, Mummy. I know it's almost bedtime for you. But just this once … Look … I really need you here, right now.'

'I'm sorry, darling, but it's out of the question.'

'I'll pay for the taxi, Mum. A real one, not an Uber. I'll prepay if needs be. A proper black cab. I'll phone now and order it. That would be a perfect solution. You need somewhere to stay, after all. I want you here. We're doing one another a favour.'

'I'm so sorry …'

'Look! What's the problem, Mum? Just come over. Now!'

Patricia left a pause.

Amanda broke it, speaking softly and calmly.

'I'm so sorry, darling, but I genuinely can't do that.'

Patricia continued in a cooing tone, 'You'll have a lovely room, Mummy – the spare room … all to yourself. I can bring you breakfast in bed. Anything …'

Another uncomfortable pause.

'And, if it's money, I could pay you what I was paying Sofian. I'll put a TV in your room, with satellite channels. Anything you want.'

Amanda braced herself.

'I'm sorry, Patricia, but, you see, darling, I'm about to go out of range any minute now.'

'Out of range? Mummy! What on earth are you talking about?'

'I'm on a cruise ship bound for America, sweetheart. And we're just about to pass Land's End.'

'Mother! Are you feeling quite well?'

'I'm serious, Patricia. I'm on a ship and in a short while we'll be entering the Atlantic Ocean.'

'Mummy, please! Enough joking …'

'I hear that Mark needs somewhere to stay. Perhaps you could try him …'

'Mother … You're being ridiculous. This is too much …'

The phone signal cut off. Amanda felt she should call back but when she looked down at the screen she saw at the corner the words 'No signal'.

A gust of wind rippled through her hair. She looked up from the phone. Ahead now she could see only a vast expanse of black – the sea and sky merged into one dark chasm. She looked down the side of the ship at the water, reflections from the lights, green and white, dancing on the ripples, as they ploughed onwards into the darkness.

Amanda felt a mixture of guilt and euphoria.

From now on it would be 'no signal' all the way to New York.

Seven days of peace and quiet.

The wind was whipping up, and, standing on the open deck in her cocktail dress, Amanda was chilled to the bone.

*

After dinner Suzy left the dining room, and went to the entertainment office to print out her script. She hoped that Blake would not be there. She knew she would be at a loss for words. Tony's insinuations would be at the front of her mind when they next met, and she would blush needlessly. But first thing tomorrow she was due to take her first class and she wanted to prepare her costume and make-up ready to go. On top of that she knew that this time she had to really get it right.

After giving a tentative knock she entered. The office was empty, though one of the desk lights was on, so someone had obviously just gone off to the loo or something. She quickly printed out her lecture and returned to her cabin.

As she walked the long corridors, she glanced through the script. There were still typos which needed correcting, and some bits she knew she'd muddle if she didn't use a highlighter and mark up.

The cabin was a welcome refuge, a bit like the dressing room in a theatre. Out in the ship she knew she always had to be on duty. She could never let the smile drop or next morning some know-all, who didn't realise or care that the charges for using a mobile onboard were astronomical, would be savaging her all over Twitter or dropping messages into the ship's Suggestion Box saying that in real life Suzy Marshall was a right bitch.

She got into her pyjamas and started laying out the clothes for her morning class. She felt quite ill at ease about both Tony and Blake, who were in a way her team while onboard. Once the first lecture was done with she would have to dedicate some time trying to work out a way to make things better with them.

As she chose her shoes, the phone in her evening bag buzzed. She opened up.

Three messages in the voicemail. She clicked the answering app and listened, all the while looking out of the porthole. There were still a few yellow lights twinkling on the coast. Land was still in sight. It must be the Lizard – a name she recalled from geography classes at school. The most southerly point of England. After this there would be no coast to see till they neared North America.

First message: India. 'Darling! Have you checked your bank? Call me back.'

Hoorah, thought Suzy. Perhaps they had finally been paid – the rehearsal money, at least, and the per diem and expenses for Zurich.

Second message: Emily. 'Hello, Suze. It's all a bit worrying, isn't it? Not sure whether the others have contacted you. But we should talk soon. We need a united front on this one. I've got Equity on to it. Phone me when you get a chance.'

India: 'Really, Suzy, what's happening? You must contact me … NOW. I don't care if it's late. It's India, by the way. And it's URGENT.'

Suzy rapidly shut down the answerphone app and rang India. She glanced at her watch. It was after half past eleven. She hoped India really meant what she had said about phoning late.

India picked up.

'India? It's Suzy!'

'Oh Gaaaaaaaahhdd! Isn't it terrible? What are we going to do?'

'I'm in the dark, India. What has happened, exactly?'

'We've all had our bank accounts cleared out. Identity scam. Haven't you seen?'

Suzy shuddered. She had very little in her bank but she couldn't risk losing it.

'When you say "we've all", I presume you mean the *Importance* company.'

'Exactly. My parents have talked to their lawyer about it. The bastards have taken my allowance, my dividends, everything.'

'Have you spoken to Reg? Has he suffered too?'

'I told him about it. He got off the phone to check out his bank. He was going on about Jason for some reason. He says it's all his fault.'

'Jason?'

'Yes.'

'Did you speak to Stan?'

'No one can track him down. Like Jason, he's vanished from the face of the planet. Even their agents don't know where they are. I hate to think that they might have run off together, especially if they've taken our money.'

Suzy tried to interject but India was fired up.

'At first I thought it was just me, but then Barbara called and she said practically everyone else had been in contact. My bank told me that some of the money had gone into a Swiss account under the name J. Scott. So you see it must have been him. What a bastard! And he seemed so nice too.'

India's voice was dipping in and out.

'India. I'm on a ship and I'm just going out of signal – but let's be in touch by email.' Heart pounding, she gave India her email address and added that she knew where Jason was and that she would corner him, but when she looked down at the phone she saw that there were no rungs at all on the signal bar. The phone had already gone out of range. Suzy had no idea how much or how little India had heard.

She hurried to the laptop and signed up for an internet package then went straight online to her bank. Both her savings and current accounts were empty.

Suzy wrote an email to the bank, warning them that her accounts had been accessed illegally. She suggested they open a new account for her to put her wages into and explained that there should be no withdrawals for the next week and to stop *any* money going out apart from her usual standing orders, adding that if they needed to get in touch they should only use email.

She quickly did a Send and Receive, picked up a bundle of emails, then went offline.

Was she nurturing a serpent to her bosom? Could Jason really have faked his friendship with her while bleeding her dry? She felt sick to her stomach.

Slowly Suzy worked through the inbox, her mind racing. She'd received mainly the usual junk – shops and restaurants advertising deals, energy companies asking for meter readings. But there was one message from Barbara, who wrote, in a very matter-of-fact way, explaining that members of *The Importance of Being Earnest* company should check their banks and, wherever possible, change their passwords, put blocks on their accounts, do anything to protect themselves. The police had been informed. She would keep in touch with everyone and tell of further developments and if anyone had any information they should contact her.

Suzy closed the computer. Could Jason really be at the bottom of this?

She looked at her watch. Midnight. She really should look at her script then go to bed, but she felt so disturbed by this new development that she knew she would never sleep, especially if she was aiding and abetting the very criminal who had robbed her and the rest of the company.

Suzy wondered what happened if you discovered a crook onboard a ship while in the Atlantic Ocean and nowhere near a port. She didn't think they'd have bilboes, like in pirate days of old. Did they have an onboard prison cell? Did they lock suspects in their cabin? Or did police arrive ... by fast ship or helicopter? Were there police already onboard, or marshals? Or did the Captain act as a de facto police chief?

She wanted to ask Jason point-blank whether he had bled all their accounts and watch his response.

It was late.

He must be coming off duty around now.

She had to find Jason.

*

Back in her stateroom, Amanda decided to write a letter of apology to Patricia. She felt bad at having let her down but couldn't help also feeling a sneaking touch of *Schadenfreude*, or at least tit for tat; after all, just a few days ago Patricia had not had that much sympathy for her own situation. But Amanda hoped to write and make it all better.

As she opened her email she saw one there from her lawyer. No! Surely not another U-turn by the seller.

She hastily clicked on it.

Dear Mrs Herbert,
All change! The vendor has yet again changed his mind about the sale.

Oh no! Amanda took a deep breath and continued reading. Please God the man could not have withdrawn it from sale yet again. Only a few days ago the solicitor had assured her that the whole process was watertight and that all she needed to do was be patient.

> The vendor has today left the keys with his solicitor, who assures me they will be with me tomorrow morning at 9 a.m. The monies are all exchanged, and should have reached the vendor's bank account this afternoon. Therefore the sale is complete. So this note is to let you know that, legally, from midnight tonight, but technically (due to the key!) from tomorrow when the office opens at 10, the flat is available for you to move in. I did try phoning your mobile a few times today, but with no luck. I hope you received the messages. Congratulations on your purchase and I hope you have many happy years in your new flat.
> Etcetera.

Amanda wondered what was wrong with them that they had understood neither the phone message she had left with the garrulous girl on the switchboard, nor the email she had sent from her phone. Did they think she could just jump off the side of a ship and swim back to the shore?

She looked out of the sliding glass door at the black space beyond her balcony. No sign of coastal lights now. She opened the door and stepped out. The only sound was the slosh of water as the ship cut through the wine-dark sea. All she could see was the pale blue peaks of the wake radiating from the ship's prow.

Amanda knew that after the ship passed by the tip of Land's End there were only the pancake-flat Scilly Isles and then straight on to the USA, with no nearby coast until they approached Newfoundland in five days' time.

Could she get off? Was there any way she might reach land now?

If she went down now to the purser's office and asked, perhaps the ship could lay on a small tender which could speed her to land on the Scillies.

But it would have to be prepared now, in the black of night. And the poor boat driver would have to go all the way there and then motor all the way back to the ship before it had travelled miles and miles onwards into the ocean. And for that to happen the ship would have to stop and drop anchor, or whatever they did, to wait for his return.

No.

What a fuss!

It was a ridiculous idea. And, even if it were possible to accomplish, who knew how much that kind of thing would cost? If she abandoned ship now, Amanda would certainly get no refund for her trip from the cruise company. It wasn't as though they could resell her cabin!

She looked down at the waves, crashing into the white hull.

How amazing the sea was. If those waves looked so big from up here, just imagine how big they'd seem from a tiny open boat.

No. Ploughing through the black sea at night in a small open motorboat was not her idea of fun, even if it were possible.

Ah well. Just accept it. She needed a relaxing break, and the new flat would still be there when she got back in a few weeks, by which time she would be refreshed and energised from the voyage.

Amanda came inside and sat at her desk to write emails to Patricia, then to Mark, explaining where she was and when she would arrive back in England. When she set it out in black and white, her voyage seemed so extravagant. But why couldn't she spend her money on herself? Especially when she'd have spent the same amount of money, if not more, if she'd remained in England, sleeping in a dingy hotel, eating sandwiches on her grubby candlewick bedspread while watching a tiny TV dangling from a bracket from the dreary papered wall.

It was strange to Amanda to think that her children might take it badly that she had done something so spontaneous, while they didn't give a damn that only a few days ago she had been practically camping and sleeping in a student dormitory.

That ruddy banker and his flat! If it had been a woman, changing her mind every couple of days about selling or not selling, then about exchanging, and finally actually completing so suddenly and unexpectedly, it would be called dithering. Amanda supposed there was some nice businessman's phrase to cover up all this annoying coming and going: 'paradigm shifts' or 'keeping your options fluid'.

To Amanda's mind it was just bloody infuriating.

So, here she was, trapped on a ship, with all her worldly goods stacked up in a storage unit and her flat now sitting there empty, but ready to move in to.

The best thing to do, she knew, was put the whole subject out of her mind and get on with enjoying life onboard this luxurious ship.

She lay on her bed, and read the *Daily Programme* for tomorrow.

On the cover she recognised the small black and white photo portrait of the woman doing the ten o'clock class. It was Suzy from *Dahlias*, the woman she had seen in the ballroom a few days ago. Amanda marked the event. The acting workshops took place in the ballroom every morning, the *Programme* said. Suzy Marshall was also giving lectures.

That should be interesting.

Amanda had always fancied a try at the performing arts.

This was fun, living on a floating hotel with all kinds of entertainment thrown in.

She wondered how Myriam and Tyger were getting on. She hoped she could protect them both from the casual insults of those grisly self-righteous ghouls, Chris and Jennie.

It was important always to ignore bullies but, somehow, as she grew older, Amanda had stopped being able to do that. She wondered how long she would last before giving Chris a piece of her mind. Obviously, it was best to bite your lip and, if Chris drove her too mad, Amanda herself might be goaded into using the alternative dining facilities. Eschewing a beautifully served meal in a delightful room for a buffet snack in the cafeteria would be no problem if it meant she could escape that man's vile bigotry.

Amanda curled up, turned off the lights and lay gazing out into the night.

The sky was so black, and the stars sparkled.

*

Suzy sat at the back of the ballroom, where a few determined dancers still held the floor. The band had announced their last number and told the revellers that once they'd packed up anyone who fancied it could carry on dancing till the early hours at the disco next door.

Suzy hoped the gentleman hosts weren't expected to go on bopping till dawn. She looked at the couples whirling round the dance floor. They looked so happy. It was difficult to pick out which were real couples and which were hosts with random women. Jason was proving a great success. With his movie-star looks and his flashing smile, he was making some elderly lady swoon. He was such a baby-faced young man, his features radiating charm. It was difficult to think of him as a crook.

But then some serial killers were good-lookers too, weren't they? Suzy thought of Ted Bundy and Jeffrey Dahmer. Being handsome did not necessarily equate with being innocent.

Perhaps Jason saw her because she was looking at him. For, as he swirled the old dear around in his arms, he glanced over her shoulder and gave Suzy a knowing grin.

Suzy tried not to smile back too widely. She was about to have a very serious conversation with him.

A waiter arrived at her side. She waved him away.

The band played the final chord, bowed to the dancers, then started packing up their instruments as the lights came up.

Jason led the old lady back to her seat then made a beeline over to Suzy.

'Didn't think you'd be up so late, Suze, my dear. Aren't you on first thing tomorrow?'

Suzy didn't want to have such an important discussion here, in such a public place, especially as the cleaning staff were coming in, turning the working lights full on. Meanwhile, she didn't want to give Jason time to come up with a plausible excuse.

'I'd like some help, please, Jason. I know you must be tired, but could you come to my cabin for just a half hour?'

'Sure!' Jason smiled and waved at various women as he strolled at Suzy's side on their way through the main hall. 'Is something wrong?'

'What makes you think that?'

'Something about you.' Again Jason inclined his head towards a woman in full evening dress, cradling a cup of hot tea, heading for her cabin. 'Weather's going to pick up over the next few days. Did you hear? The Captain's going to advise people who don't have sea legs to go to the Medical Centre before we hit the gale.'

'Gale?'

'Remnants of a hurricane, apparently. In a couple of days.'

Suzy had no idea whether or not she had sea legs. Her only memories of travelling by ship were as a teenager on ferries to Ireland, and she'd been all right then.

As they entered her cabin, Jason commented on the piles of paperwork lying all over the floor.

'My word, Suze, you have been busy! It looks like the cabin of a mad professor.'

'Sit down, Jason.'

'Oooh-errr, missus.' Jason winced, and pulled a childlike face imagining trouble afoot. 'That voice sounds very serious indeed.'

'I've heard from Emily and India.'

Jason's face brightened.

'Great! How are they? Got home safely, I hope.'

'They're at home all right … but they've both had their bank accounts cleaned out.'

Jason's mouth opened in astonishment. Suzy wondered if he was a really great actor. He appeared genuinely shocked and was certainly betraying no signs of a guilty conscience.

'Here's the thing, Jason. All the money, it seems, was siphoned off into a Swiss bank account in your name.'

She peered at his face, watching for tics betraying his involvement.

'A Swiss account? What do you mean? You think I have a Swiss bank account?'

'A bank account under the name of J. Scott.' She didn't take her eyes from him. 'Our friends' money has been stolen. My money has been stolen. I haven't told them where you are – but only because the signal was cut off. But they all know you did it, and they're all looking for you. And, lucky for you, at this moment, no one knows where you are.'

As she said this Suzy realised she had made a big mistake.

'Except you.' Jason smiled. A truly plausible smile. '*You* know where I am, Suzy.'

Suzy watched him slowly rise from the bed.

'I hope that you know I wouldn't be capable of stealing, Suzy. Least of all from you.' Jason moved towards the door. 'Whatever has gone on, this crime had nothing to do with me. Nothing.' He gripped the door handle. Suzy could see his knuckles showing white. 'Obviously, I will do everything I can to clear my name. Meanwhile, if you don't mind, I'm going to return to my cabin to check my Swiss bank account, to see how flush I have become with all these ill-gotten gains. Though I have to admit, I have been frightfully stupid using my own name when I could have taken a numbered account to commit my criminal activities.'

'Jason!' Suzy watched his back as he pulled open the door.

'I'm disappointed in you, Suzy,' he said, without turning. 'I thought you knew me. I believed that we were friends.'

And he was gone.

Suzy flopped down on the end of her bed. She realised she had been very clumsy in the way she'd handled the whole thing. She was tempted to follow him and knock on his door to ask to finish the conversation, but she knew that he shared the cabin with George, another ghost, and she didn't want to drag anyone else into this mess until she was sure.

She slowly started putting the papers from the floor into neat piles, one for each class or lecture. She consulted the lists and arranged them in order of when each one would be necessary, leaving tomorrow's class notes on the top, ready for her to grab in the morning.

Could Jason be innocent? All the evidence pointed against it. Innocent? If tomorrow he showed her online bank state-ments, who was to say he didn't have two separate accounts – one straight, the other crooked? She found herself humming the tune of the 1950s song 'The Great Pretender'. Was Jason stringing her along?

Guilt is easy enough to prove, if you're in the police and have rights and warrants to look everywhere. But how could she prove anything? An actress, alone on a ship in the middle of the Atlantic Ocean?

Comically, Suzy remembered TV's amateur sleuths, Miss Marple and Jessica Fletcher.

How would they nail Jason, and get him bang to rights?

It was after 1 a.m. She knew she had to be up before eight, to reread her notes, grab breakfast and get to the other end of the ship to be ready to go for nine forty-five.

She climbed into bed, but sleep did not come for a long time, and when it did it was a tiring dream in which she kept losing her way while being chased along the ship's corridors. She was scared and knew she had to keep running. But when she looked forward there was someone waiting at the far end of the corridor, and it was Jason. Except that it wasn't – it was the Joker, from *Batman*.

9

A MANDA GOT UP slowly, luxuriating in the shower, then carefully laying out her clothes for the day. She had never been to an acting workshop before. Was it the same as going to the gym? Should she put on sporty gear – not that she had any, but she could easily get a leotard in the little shop outside the onboard fitness centre. Oh no, wait, miles too revealing. Amanda gave an involuntary shudder.

She opted for a casual pair of jeans with a T-shirt and train-ers. She remembered seeing TV shows and musicals about acting, where the students always seemed to wear something like bunched-up socks around their ankles. But she wasn't a pro so she would do without.

In the café she collected herself a very healthy bowl of muesli and some fruit and sat in a window bay.

Myriam, walking through, stopped at her table with a swoop.

'Amanda, darling! I hope you're going to the theatre-arts workshop. I adore expressing myself, don't you? I love to feel completely uninhabited!'

Amanda gulped down her mouthful and thought she might choke on a nut which got stuck in her throat. She coughed until tears filled her eyes.

'Are you OK, Amanda? Should I give you the Himmler Manoeuvre?'

Amanda really regretted the healthy breakfast choice which looked as though, rather than extending her life, it could finish her off.

'Why on earth do people eat this stuff? It should only be served in a nosebag. I am going to the drama class, yes,' she said in a tiny voice, all that was left of her vocals while the grains and nut remained unswallowed. 'Will Tyger be going too?'

'No, no, no, no!' said Myriam. 'Still asleep, I suspect. You know these youngsters. No stamina.' She perched on the edge of the table while Amanda tried to finish her breakfast. 'I do hope we do some Shakespeare. I simply worship the Beard of Avon. "Oh that this too, too sullied flesh would melt, thaw and resolve itself into a doo." Sounds like someone needs to go on a diet!'

Amanda wondered whether Myriam was having a dig at her.

'*Hamlet*,' Myriam continued. 'The Great Dane himself.'

Amanda had now given up on the muesli and wished she had got herself toast and marmalade instead of an apple.

'According to the little daily newspaper,' Myriam's voice bubbled with excitement, 'this woman giving the class is a well-known actress. But I've never heard of her. Perhaps she's very famous in England. But not in the States. When I think of famous actresses I only think of Bette Davis, Gina Lollabrigadier and Gretna Garbo.' Myriam stretched out her arm then looked busily at her watch. 'Come along, Amanda my dear – we're going to be late, late, late. I shall go ahead and save us both a place near the front.' She glanced down at Amanda's bowl. 'You should have got yourself something more substantial, deary! Muffins or pancakes. At this rate you'll fade away. That's not enough to feed a tit.' Myriam pulled a face of horror and moved off. She made an abrupt turn and swung back to whisper in Amanda's ear. 'Did you see in the *Programme*, that Dorothy woman is throwing *another* of her sore-eyes this afternoon? I really must find out how you get yourself invited.'

As she swigged down the rest of her coffee, Amanda watched Myriam bustle off. Before leaving the café herself Amanda grabbed a couple of chocolate biscuits and nibbled one as she walked. The other she dropped into her pocket for later.

By the time she arrived in the ballroom, the seating area around the dance floor was very crowded. The room looked quite different by day. The curtains were all open, and huge picture windows reflected the light from the sea and sky. It was bright, echoey and airy.

Myriam was sitting at a table in the corner. She caught sight of Amanda and waved her chubby be-ringed hands in the air. Amanda moved in her direction but, before she could get there, Suzy Marshall had stepped into the middle of the dance floor and clapped her hands for silence.

Amanda slumped down into the nearest empty seat.

'First,' said Suzy, rolling up the sleeves of her loose cardigan, 'we're going to play some games.' She surveyed the crowd. 'Everyone up on their feet, and on to the dance floor.'

As Amanda stepped forward she heard Myriam calling aloud: 'Tyger! Tyger! Come join us! We'll be an ensemble together.'

Amanda turned to see the poor boy resting on a window seat, shaking his head and hunching up his shoulders.

Suzy produced a stripy, blow-up beach ball, the kind which seals usually balance on their noses on old-fashioned greetings cards.

'I am going to throw this ball, and when I throw it I will say my name. Each person who catches the ball must throw it on, randomly, while saying their name aloud.'

Amanda wondered what on earth this game could have to do with acting, but stood up, ready to play.

*

As Suzy set the players off, she prepared herself for the next game, a deep-breathing exercise. She looked around at the participants of the class – such a jumble of people, but seemingly much more keen than your usual gang of actors on a first day of rehearsal.

While the ball passed round the circle, and names were called aloud, Suzy noticed Jason come softly in and watched him as he perched on one of the window seats, adjacent to a young boy with long auburn hair and startlingly green eyes.

Why was Jason here? Had he come to taunt her? Was he actually holding everyone's money in his bank? Had he lied to them and cheated them all out of their savings? Should she report him to the Captain, or write emails to Barbara, India and Emily and tell them that he was here onboard? Or should she interrogate Jason first and make sure everyone was right in their supposition before turning him in?

'Suzy?'

Suzy snapped her attention back to the class. Everybody stood patiently in the circle, staring at her.

'What do we do with the ball now that we've reached the end of the group?'

Suzy took the ball and applied her mind to the session. She got everyone to find a space for themselves and then pulled out all the relaxation exercises she remembered from drama school and from working with tired old rep directors who used them to prove that they were being relevant.

'We'll start by shaking our feet. Then our hands.'

When she looked back at the window seat, both Jason and the young man were gone.

'Right … now I'll need you to shake your heads till your faces are relaxed.'

While the class did this, with Suzy joining in to show them, she tried to snap her mind away from Jason and the money scam.

'Tomorrow, when we know one another a little better, I am going to start work on getting into character – becoming someone else. But for today we're going to do some things regarding basic stagecraft.'

Suzy moved forward into the middle of the gaggle of people and raised her arms.

'OK! Now let's split into two groups. Everyone to my left go and sit behind me. The others remain on the stage.'

The passengers dithered about until they were sorted into two groups. Suzy recognised Amanda, who had sat near her a few nights ago when the ship was leaving Genoa.

'Now. All of you sitting will be the audience.'

The sitting people let out a suppressed groan.

'Don't worry, you'll get your turn next. But this exercise is about being seen, something which you would have to learn both onstage and especially onscreen. I want everyone onstage to mill around until I call "stop!". Then you will freeze, but be aware of whether the audience has a clear view of your face. If they don't, use whatever method you can to put yourself in a better position. You'll only have one second to do this. It might mean taking a step forward, or kneeling or leaning. And you'll have to sense instinctively what your fellows are doing. OK. Here we go!'

She turned and addressed the audience group. 'You'll have to watch out to make sure you can see everyone. Eagle eyes, please.'

She sat among the class.

'This should be fun!' She winked in the direction of Amanda, who was part of the observers' team. 'Eyes peeled, everyone! Now, actors – move around. Let's see how easily you can adjust to keep yourselves from being hidden from the audience.'

*

After the class was over Amanda went up to the cafeteria for a coffee and a bun. It had been great fun, and she had laughed a lot. She was so stirred up by taking part in a group activity, something she had not done for years, that she had decided, once she was back in London and settled in, to sign up for evening classes, in order to keep her hand in, mix with strangers, do something different. It was all too easy to fall into a lonely life and fester in your solitude.

In the other section of the café she could see Tyger, sitting with the handsome young gentleman dancer from the ballroom. She wanted to call them gigolos, but that seemed too loaded a word for men who were simply paid to give lone women a chance on the dance floor. Liliane was with them. They were all laughing.

Amanda felt stupid as she realised she experienced a tiny tinge of jealousy. That man was her own personal private dance partner – hands off!

Cradling her coffee cup, Amanda sat back in her little alcove and looked out, watching the waves rippling and sparkling as far as the bright horizon. Up here in the café you could see for ever – miles and miles of nothing but water. No birds, no other ships, just glittering sea, crowned with sky.

As she watched the wake spread out, creating new waves, which crashed into the teal-coloured swell, she noticed the spume riffling, forming something on the surface which looked like a wide span of lace, spread over the water in ever-increasing circles. It resembled a huge mystical doily.

Behind her there was a sudden commotion: people standing, rushing to the window, murmuring with excitement.

'Dolphins!' cried a young woman nearby, as she collected her children and thrust them towards the window. 'Look! Look, children! Dolphins!'

Amanda, with the best seat in the house, remained where she was, as people gathered around her table, leaning forward, battling for space with their tablets and iPhones pressed against the glass, trying to get a glimpse of the creatures as they leaped from the water, forming wonderful patterns of black semicircles, diving in and out of the blue.

Amanda wanted to knock all their wretched camera equipment on to the floor.

She marvelled at their stupidity as they missed the actual moments happening – while focusing and fiddling about behind a lens, and blocking the windows from people who just wanted to see.

'*J'aime beaucoup les dauphins*,' said Liliane, moving forward, gripping Tyger's shoulders. '*Ravissantes!*'

'*La plus captivante créature de la mer*,' replied Jason.

'Hey, you guys,' said Tyger, shaking away Liliane's hands. 'Stop speaking in code.'

Liliane and Jason exchanged a wince, at the same moment that the dolphins took a unanimous dive and disappeared again beneath the surface.

Now that the spectacle was over the gaggle of people and their phones and tablets dispersed.

Amanda saw that Tyger was holding an ice-cream cornet.

'How lovely,' she said. 'Ice cream.'

'Over there.' He pointed to the corner near the tea bar. 'You can serve yourself all day and all night, if you like.' He took a long lick. 'Did you know that onboard this ship the customers devour eight thousand gallons of ice cream a week? Eight thousand! That's enough ice cream to fill a 24-foot swimming pool!'

Amanda had no reply to this, and Tyger moved off, leaving her sitting alone again with a half-drunk cup of cold coffee and the crumbs of her fruit bun. She would have loved to have gone and got an ice-cream cone but she felt suddenly tired, depressed and lumpen.

She decided to return to her stateroom and have half an hour on the laptop catching up with events at home.

Her cabin was fresh and recently cleaned.

She briefly checked the *Daily Programme*. If she ate an early lunch, something salad-ish, there was a film on this afternoon which she remembered loving when it first came out. She had forgotten the salient point of the plot but recalled that it was about a French Resistance heroine and an orphaned boy, in France before D-day. She marked it.

While the laptop software opened up Amanda stood on the balcony looking out at the row of lifeboats hanging, sturdy and orange, from their davits just below her cabin. She wondered what they would be like on the inside. Then decided that she didn't really want to know, as there would only be one reason she'd ever get a chance to see – if the ship sank – and she certainly didn't want that to happen! She noticed that some lifeboats had windows and looked like quite pleasant boats on which you might take a trip, while others had only a few slits for light. If the worst ever came to the worst she hoped that she would be in one with windows. The very thought of bouncing about on giant waves in one of those orange windowless pods made her feel quite seasick.

She came back inside, signed into her internet account and picked up her emails. She was halfway through reading one from Mark when she remembered that she should quickly cut off the pay-connection, rather than waste the precious minutes simply checking her inbox.

Mark's letter depressed her. Not content with his wife throwing him out of their home, he had been now chucked out of his new girlfriend's place. He had spent the night on Patricia's sofa. It had been a nightmare, he said. The girl-friend, Jasmine, had been a nutter, he told her, and he was glad to have escaped her poisonous claws, but Patricia's kids were running wild, almost encouraged by some teenage girl who Patricia had got through an agency.

Amanda felt a surge of guilt. If she had stayed in London … But, as there was simply nothing she could do to wind back the clock, she read on, trying not to take on the implied blame.

Mark was now down to begging all his friends for a place to stay, but 'their grasping wives don't like me', he explained.

He now feared that he would end up wandering, night by night, 'like a needy whore'. Amanda couldn't help feeling that Mark could easily make everything better simply by being a little bit less selfish, by thinking of women as human beings and by trying to patch things up with his wife.

But then she remembered how she herself had felt after Nigel left her and knew that those spousal wounds weren't quite so easy to heal. Ingrid was probably deeply injured emotionally, but at the same time happy to see the back of him and his sexist diatribes.

The next email was from the storage company with a receipt for yet another wasted week's storage.

Then a message from the solicitors, asking if she had a firm date for when she would pick up the key.

Oh damn. When you were away from home, and out of phone contact, it was so pressurising when the real world kept on nagging at you like this.

She kicked off her shoes and lay on the bed.

When she awoke it was lunchtime.

She hastily washed her face and put on a bit of make-up then strode along to the restaurant. She had decided that she would definitely go to see the movie, so she only had time to have one course and hoped it might not be in the tiresome company of Chris.

*

After the morning session was over, Suzy found herself surrounded by a few of the quieter members of the class, who, one by one, wanted to bombard her with questions. 'My niece wants to be an actress, could you give her some advice?'; 'When we did the emotional exercise I disagree with you over the meaning of the term winsome ...'; 'Could you tell me the names of the best drama schools?'; 'I just wanted to tell you about my aunt who was an actress for a while. She had a regular part in *Crossroads*, but gave up the business to have a baby. Do you think I should encourage her to get back into the profession?'

In comparison with this tricky string of questions the class itself had been a doddle. Suzy had to walk on eggshells, particularly as she realised that none of these people really wanted to hear an honest answer; they wanted her to make their dreams come true.

And the world of showbiz really was not like that. It was hard, lonely and filled with disappointment.

It may have been only noon when she had done, an hour after the official end of her class, but Suzy felt in need of a stiff drink. She went back to the cabin, showered again then slipped into some smarter clothes rather than the deliberate sporty workshop-style look she had gone for earlier.

She decided against visiting the posh restaurant for lunch and went down to the pub instead and tucked into fish and chips, while the others sitting around her took part in a quiz.

The players all laughed aloud. The quizmaster had announced that the correct answer to his question 'How many lifeboats are aboard the *Blue Mermaid*?' was twenty-two, not, as someone had written, 35,750,000.

'We thought you said lightbulbs!' cried the team leader, getting another laugh from the room.

Suzy wished she knew where Jason was, and why he had popped into her class. Perhaps he had wanted to talk to her, but realised he was too late as the session had already begun.

En route to her own cabin she had knocked on his door, but there was no reply.

He might be in there, hiding, but Suzy somehow doubted that.

If Jason was guilty, he was playing a brazen, wide-open game.

After lunch she wandered to the theatre end of the ship. All the time she scanned for Jason but on a ship this size there was little hope of bumping into him. She had read yesterday that the onboard population was the size of a small town, like Cricklade or Jedburgh, and that the *Blue Mermaid*'s surface area was three acres, which was then multiplied by fifteen decks. If you were seriously searching for someone who lived in Cricklade you wouldn't just stroll randomly around the town, would you? Wandering about looking for Jason wasn't worth thinking about.

She was tired and didn't feel like talking to anyone, but didn't want to go back to her cabin and waste her time while she was on this wonderful ship.

She saw a sign saying 'No Entry – Rehearsal in Progress'. She slipped past it and stood at the back of the shadowy theatre watching the troupe of show dancers rehearsing in the stage's working lights. She loved to sit alone in the dark, watching other entertainers practising their craft. This lot certainly had some complex routines to learn, and the troupe leader was very strict. The sequence she watched was spectacular.

While the troupe was going over one of the many costume changes, Suzy slipped out of the auditorium and took the corridor leading behind it.

A poster displayed on a digital screen announced the afternoon performance of a film entitled *The Dangerous Season*. This was the first time Suzy had realised there was a cinema onboard. She wasn't sure whether or not the film had started but who cared? If it was already on when she went in, it would feel like the old days, when she was a kid with her parents, at those news theatres, or even the real cinema. Whenever you arrived you'd go in and, if you'd missed the beginning, you'd stay on after the end and the titles had scrolled past, then watch the opening scenes. It sounded mad now, but in those days no one seemed to mind.

She pulled open the door, and realised from the shimmering light within that the film had indeed already started. She shuffled into the small room.

There were plenty of empty seats so she took a place on an aisle, near the back.

Onscreen a battle scene was in progress. It appeared to be Second World War, Normandy, with British and American soldiers fighting Nazis in the dusty remnants of a typical French village. So far, she didn't think she had seen this movie before, but in her head all war films blended into one.

While bombs exploded and machine-gun fire rattled onscreen, Suzy's mind returned again to the troubled subject of Jason and the stolen money.

She shook her head, furious that she could not even for a moment escape her own thoughts. She tried once more to concentrate on the film. After all there was nothing she could do about Jason until they were face to face.

The screen scene changed to the shattered fragments of a bar, where a woman, covered in dirt and pieces of plaster, sheltered behind the counter. A massive explosion, a direct hit, shook the building behind her, blowing the wall away, revealing what remained of a wooden staircase, suspended in daylight.

The actress playing the woman was familiar, but for the moment Suzy couldn't place her.

'Damnation!' said the woman, crawling out into the rubble-strewn bar. Suzy immediately recognised the distinctive voice of April McNaughten, an Oscar-winning, much-loved British actress now mainly based in Hollywood.

April McNaughten? Hadn't she been in Zurich, playing *The King and I* at the same time as *The Importance* cast were there? There were posters everywhere and Suzy remembered that, out of the blue, Jason had changed the subject to talk about April's show when she was trying to quiz him about the inexplicable events of the night before their own show was cancelled.

Damn!

Here she was thinking about Jason again.

She directed her attention once more to the movie.

As the dust settled on the bombed-out building, the under-stairs cupboard door creaked open. April McNaughten crept forward, perceiving a small child, white with ash and debris, crouching inside. Keeping a lookout, April reached out to touch the child, offering her hand, but he recoiled. Stealing towards him on her haunches, April grabbed the boy and hauled him from the cupboard. Once outside she cradled him in her arms. Moments later the entire house collapsed.

Suzy laughed to herself. These war films!

The scene changed to a copse by a river, where April washed the child and shared bread with him. Once the dust and grime was cleared away from his face and hair, the little boy was beautiful, with his dark hair and cheeky smile. His sparse dialogue was in English, spoken with a French accent. April's character spoke back to him in perfect English.

Suzy was puzzled, as always, with these mainly English-speaking films where every now and then people spoke different languages and accents. Was April's character really an English member of the French Resistance? After all, the Nazis in this film were speaking in German, with English subtitles, and the boy had a heavy French lilt. Or was every-one, except the Nazis, supposed to be French?

Whichever, the French child was a very good little actor, although he didn't have much to say.

He had a natural presence.

He reminded her of Jason.

Suzy began to think she was becoming obsessed with Jason. She was seeing him in everything.

By the end of the film, in a dramatic scene where the child escaped, running through a cornfield, while April sacrificed herself to keep the Nazis from reaching the fleeing boy, Suzy had become so convinced that the child in the film really was a very young Jason that, even though the house lights came up before the titles rolled, she waited behind to check the cast list.

The rest of the audience was up, pushing along the aisles, heading for the exits.

'Hello!' Amanda stood in the row in front of Suzy. 'That was great, wasn't it?'

Suzy didn't want to be rude, but Amanda was blocking the screen. She tried to twist her body away so that she could talk and read at the same time, but to no avail. Short of shoving the woman out of the way, she could not see the cast list.

'I really enjoyed the class this morning,' Amanda continued. 'Very inspiring. I shall be coming again. Thank you.'

Suzy gave her a wide smile, and a feeble thank you, wishing Amanda would shove off. But by the time she had moved away, the cast list was down to best boys, foley artists and dolly grips. After these rolled up there would be no more actor credits.

Suzy came out of the cinema and decided on taking a circuit of the deck before heading back to the cabin. She was craving fresh air and a little exercise. She hoped too that if she moved around in the public areas she might bump into Jason.

She ran up the stairs to the boat deck, then pushed through the double doors leading outside. She jogged along, under the lifeboats, stopping occasionally to grip the rails and survey the navy-blue horizon. The wide breadth of water was scattered with rolling white peaks. The wind was moderate, making Suzy's hair flutter about, whipping against her cheek. She turned and ran. As she speeded up to a trot she took deep breaths. She wished she had gone to her cabin first and put on a jacket, but the cold would make her run faster, so she persevered. When she had done one lap she went inside to the café to pick up a hot cup of tea to help thaw her out.

In an hour's time, Jason would be gearing up to put on his eveningwear, ready to grab supper before taking on the ballroom dancers. Suzy hoped to catch him then.

Back in the cabin, sipping her tea, she opened the laptop and picked up her emails. Another from Emily.

It really looks as though Jason is responsible for this banking thing. Not only that, but he's in it with Stan. No one has heard a squeak out of either of them since we left Zurich. I even had Reg on the blower asking if *I'd* been in touch with Stan. Me! Why would I stay in touch with that odious glutton? What is it with people that they think because you play a double-act with someone that that means you knock about with them in real life? You'd expect that kind of cliché from a member of the public, but not a professional director. Mind you, I suppose we *are* talking about the charlatan that is Reg Shoesmith!

Stan and Jason? Suzy baulked at the idea. It seemed an unlikely partnership. But hadn't Jason said that Stan was also at that disastrous backer's party? Maybe this was a bluff too. Perhaps Jason and Stan were in cahoots.

While the computer was still online Suzy moved over to IMDb to look up the afternoon movie's cast list. She typed in the film's name: *The Dangerous Season*. She couldn't remember the boy character's name. So she scrolled down the cast list and reached the end. No actor called Jason. At the bottom there was a note saying that April McNaughten had won a BAFTA for her performance as French Resistance heroine Yveline Lenval. Suzy started again at the top of the list. No Jason, no Scott. She was wrong: the child actor wasn't Jason at all.

A rap on her door. She went to answer it.

Standing there, grinning, holding out a plate full of chocolate cake, was Jason.

'Can I come in?'

'Sure.' Suzy tried to remain cool. This was not at all how she expected their encounter to be. She had planned to corner him, catch him off-guard, but here he was presenting himself to her.

'I don't know how I can convince you, Suze, that I had nothing to do with this bank business. Nothing at all. The only thing I can say is that in the few weeks you have known me, you must know that that's not the kind of person I am.'

'I didn't take you for a man who'd get into punch-ups with the director, either. But that happened. And, as a result, we're all out of a job.'

Suzy pulled out the desk chair for him, and perched herself on the end of the bed.

'We really need a cup of tea with this,' said Jason, taking a second plate out and splitting the cakes between the two. 'But I didn't have enough hands.'

Suzy took a breath and went in on the attack.

'Did you scam your friends out of their money, Jason? I really need you to tell me the truth.'

'I don't know how many times I have to say it, Suze, but it wasn't me. Honestly, I had nothing to do with it.'

'Was your own bank account cleaned out?'

She realised that a good alibi would be for him to say yes, but instead he said, 'As far as I can see, no.'

He held out a plate of cake.

Suzy refused.

She thought it might choke her.

'You don't mind if I do? I'm famished.' He took a huge bite of cake, leaving a brown clown-smile of chocolate on his cheeks. 'Sorry about that.' He helped himself to a tissue on her desk. 'You do realise your internet counter is still logging up minutes?'

Suzy reached out for the laptop, panicked. What a waste of money!

'No problem.' Jason swivelled on the seat. 'I'll log you off.'

Suzy didn't want him touching her computer. Maybe he'd have some trick to get her passwords or something. She grabbed the laptop.

'Don't be silly, Suze. I know how to do it.' He stopped suddenly and handed it over to her. 'Oh. I see.' He spoke slowly and deliberately. 'You didn't want me to see that you've been checking up on me.'

Suzy quickly tapped herself out of internet time.

'Oh Suzy, Suzy, Suzy! You can go on checking me out for ever.' Jason shook his head. 'You're not going to find that I am a serial killer in disguise, or even a high-grade embezzler with a Swiss bank account. I'm just an actor, like yourself.'

'Why would you think that?' Suzy looked him in the eye. 'I wasn't checking you out.'

'So why were you looking up my past?'

Suzy had no idea what Jason was talking about.

'*The Dangerous Season*?' he said. 'It's there on your screen. Don't try to deny it.'

'So, it *was* you? I saw it this afternoon. Why are you not on the cast list?'

'I am.' Jason flipped back the laptop screen. 'Right there in black and white.' He pointed to the character called Henri. 'Jacques Berry. That's me.'

Suzy peered at the screen through his fingers. 'So where does the Jason Scott come from?'

'I moved to England. I needed a British name. I tried Jacques Berry, but there already was a Jack Barry, and Equity wouldn't have it. Not that I really would have wanted to use my father's surname, even if I could have. There was a Jack Scott, too. So professionally I became Jason, because it was more memorable than Jack, which I wasn't allowed, and Scott for my mother's maiden name.'

Suzy decided that while he was in confessional mode she would put another question to him.

'What is your relationship with Stan Arbuthnot?'

'I'm sorry?'

'What is your relationship with Stan Arbuthnot?'

Jason gasped.

'Stan, and you. In league.' Suzy eyed him carefully. 'Aren't you in touch with him?'

'What is wrong with you, Suzy? You know very well I cannot stand the man.'

'It's only that, from the facts I've been told, it looks as though you two were running this criminal scam together.'

'Are you kidding me?' Jason plonked down his plate of cake heavily on the desk, stood, and backed towards the door. 'Seriously, Suze? Are you bloody kidding me?'

He turned and strutted through the door, slamming it behind him.

Suzy leaped to her feet, knew it was too late and realised that once again she had mishandled the whole thing. Instead of coaxing information out of Jason she had managed to put up an even higher wall between them. Or was it that whenever she touched on to a sensitive subject he got away, slippery fish, evading his need to answer her? Whichever, for all her detective work, she had got no further in finding out whether or not Jason was responsible for the thefts …

10

THE WIND, WHICH had been howling round the decks, whistling through the davits bearing the lifeboats, vibrating through the slats of the wooden sunloungers on Amanda's balcony, had died down.

It was already dark enough to need to put the cabin lights on and evening loomed, with its dress code and formal dinner. Tonight, Amanda saw from her *Programme*, was the Ascot Ball. Presumably this somehow meant wearing a huge hat. She wondered whether all the other passengers had come aboard with a Stephen Jones model.

That couldn't be true! When she boarded, she would have noticed a spate of hatboxes lining up to go through the scanner. And that must mean that one had to improvise. Hmmm. She left the cabin to see what she could scavenge in the shops to make up a 'creation'.

There were a few hats in the gift shop, but they were sun hats and baseball caps bearing the ship's logo. Next door in the fashion store there were no hats at all.

'I suppose you ran out of hats because of the ball tonight,' said Amanda to the girl behind the counter.

'Not at all,' replied the girl, with a smile. 'We never stock hats, with the exception of the odd fascinator for onboard weddings and things.'

'So where does everyone get their hats for the ball? Or have I got it wrong? The Ascot Ball – I presumed it had to be hats.'

Amanda pulled out the day's *Programme* and presented it to the girl, who laughed.

'Of course! Look down here. There's a competition for best hat. Plus, if you rush down to the art studio on Deck 2, it looks as though there's a hat-making workshop happening right now.'

Thanking her, Amanda left the shop and made her way down to the studio. It was in the lower parts of the ship, where the echoing walls were unapologetic iron, painted in cream gloss. The hat-making studio was definitely happening here. Amanda could hear the bustle and laughter resonating along the metal gangway.

She turned into the crowded room, where a hubbub of earnest people crouched over tables laden with coloured paper, tissue, cardboard, rolls of net, glue guns, tinsel, glitter and all kinds of ribbons and streamers. Some were giggling as they modelled their creations, others were solemnly stapling swathes of glittering net to long pieces of card.

'Amanda! Darling! Come and help me pin.' Across the room, Myriam La-Grande-Motte was waving with one hand while pressing a strip of tangerine card, covered in glittering sequins, up to her forehead. 'Tyger has of course made the most divine creation. I predict he'll be the new Philippe Tracy. Look at that hat!'

Tyger stood in the corner, regarding himself in the mirror. On his head was a black and white top hat with a huge satin bow and an adornment like a paper feather, which resembled the keys of a piano. Amanda could see it might well pass for a Philip Treacy!

She leaned in to whisper to Myriam. 'I am hopeless with my hands. Never could do all that *Blue Peter* stuff with Fairy Liquid bottles and sticky-backed plastic.'

'Who's blue Peter? He sounds like a very naughty boy!' Myriam gave a throaty laugh. 'Tyger will help you. He may not be blue, but he's very gifted.' She presented the back of her head to Amanda. 'Sweetie, could you just fix that clip so that I can staple it together?'

Amanda fiddled with the clip then gingerly removed the orange hat from Myriam's head. 'There you go. Now for me to start. What colour do you think would suit?'

'What are you planning to wear with it?' asked Tyger, gathering pieces of grey card from the table.

Amanda mentally ran through her wardrobe, and decided on the long red evening dress.

'There are many shades of red, Amanda,' said Tyger. 'Scarlet? Crimson? China red?'

'What is China red?' asked Amanda.

'In the UK I think it might be postbox red,' said Tyger, his fingers manipulating the card into fantastic shapes. 'Or maybe phonebox red. Or doubledecker-bus red to you.'

'Yes. That would be the one. China red.' Amanda felt awkward asking this boy for help, but could see that he was excited by the prospect of making another hat.

'Do I assist you?' she asked him. 'Or do I just stand here and watch?'

'Choose your favourite sparkly things or some point of interest for me to use,' he said, wrapping the grey card around her head. 'While I create the base.'

'I've always adored balls, haven't you, deary?' asked Myriam, snatching a piece of flame-coloured velvet from the table and stabbing it on to her orange card with a safety pin. 'Can never get enough balls. The bigger the better.'

Amanda wondered whether Myriam really knew the things she said were ambiguous or if she maybe did it for effect. It certainly got the people around the table giggling into their chins.

'I'm hoping to get another exhilarating tango with that charming boy, Jason.' Myriam's laugh pierced the intense concentration of the others gathered in the room. 'Phwoar! He's actually a professional, you know, working for the ship, but he's a great little mover, and when you shimmy with a handsome young blade like him you can't help feeling as though you're Ginger Rogers.'

'As opposed to ginger-vitis,' said Tyger, stabbing a pair of plastic cherries on to Amanda's hat.

*

Suzy went down to the entertainment office. A quizmaster was consulting some huge books and hastily writing out a page of questions. Nearby, the social and German language hostesses were bent over the photocopier, fitting a new ink cartridge.

'*Scheisse!*' called out the German secretary, as the ink cartridge tumbled on to the floor. 'Pardon my French!'

In the corner, Blake was concentrating on a computer screen where the next day's *Programme* was displayed.

'Hi, Suzy!' he called over his shoulder. 'Everything OK?'

'Just coming to print out some notes for tomorrow morning's class. The students wanted to have some exercises to take away with them.'

'We used to hand them useless diplomas in acting!' Blake laughed. 'Some people even got them framed at the photo shop.'

'Diplomas?' asked Suzy.

'Bits of fancily printed paper which said they had successfully attended six classes and were therefore proficient in acting, blah-blah-blah. Meaningless. But people like make-believe things like that. Stuff they can put in their cases and show people back home. Bits of fakery.'

'You don't think people actually try to use them to get jobs, do you?'

'Who knows?' said Blake, pressing return on tomorrow's newsletter and sending it off to the print queue. He twirled round in his seat and faced Suzy. 'Got any ideas for awards or things like that you could give out during your classes?'

The two women at the photocopier let out a yelp as the machine lurched into action.

'Who needs technicians?' laughed Melanie, the social hostess. 'Do you have your document ready to go into the queue, Suzy?'

Suzy handed it over.

'There's about a five-minute wait, I think, if you want to go off and come back later to pick them up.'

Suzy perched against the long counter, littered with lists, books and clipboards. She preferred to stay, to let Blake know she was serious about the job.

'Don't you go dizzy having to balance all this stuff?' She waved her hands at the paperwork. 'And dealing with the public too.'

Melanie laughed. 'It's only a problem when you get whiners.'

'There's always at least one,' said Blake, rising and stretching. '"You call this cabin luxury? My dog's kennel is bigger." Or "Why do they always play country music for the line-dancing class, I prefer classical." You wonder if some people don't spend their whole life trying to find something to complain about.'

Near to Suzy a phone rang.

Melanie picked up.

'Good evening, social hostess speaking.' She rolled her eyes. 'Yes, that's right, sir. It's the Ascot Ball, as it says in your *Daily Programme*.' She cupped her hand over the receiver and shook the phone as though she would break it. 'Yes. That's right. Hats … It is customary to wear a hat, but it is not compulsory.' She gritted her teeth while the man spoke. 'Certainly, sir. It's more usual for a woman to wear a hat, but there are many men who like to join in. It's entirely up to you, sir. I'm sure no one will mind whether you choose to wear a hat or if you don't. Thank you. No. No problem at all, sir. Enjoy your evening!' She hung up and stuck her tongue out at the phone.

She swung round to face Suzy. 'That's one of the annoying ones. Instead of simply reading his *Daily Programme* like everyone else, he phones up to check on every detail of what is "usual".'

'Makes me wonder why I bother to write the bloody things if people don't read them,' said Blake, pulling a stack of papers from the copier. 'Instead of sweating over a hot computer every evening, I could be propping up the bar in the Digbeth Road.'

'Digbeth?' asked Suzy. 'In Birmingham?'

Blake laughed.

'No, it's our name for the lower portions of the ship. The private crew-only quarters. Has no one taken you down there?'

'No.' Suzy loved the idea.

'Canteen for the waiters, and chefs. Bar for officers and crew. It keeps you sane when you can escape from the passengers now and then – go off duty. It's not as though the crew could pop home for the evening, and as you've probably noticed, once you are out of your cabin you are always on duty.'

The copier beeped.

'That'll be your document starting.' Melanie strolled across and whipped out a stack of paperwork. 'Tomorrow's class! Napkin folding. Care to come, Suzy?'

'What time?'

'Ten o'clock.'

'Exact clash with mine, I'm afraid.' Suzy wasn't sure whether she was relieved or disappointed. 'Pity. I've always wanted to make one of those water lilies, or even a cardinal's hat.'

'Here you are then.' Melanie laughed and handed Suzy one of the illustrated pages, still warm from the copier. 'With that, as they say, you can work 'em up at home.'

*

Amanda whooped it up as everyone in the ballroom marched around to the Ascot Gavotte.

She and Tyger walked hand in hand, while, behind them, Myriam danced along with a gentleman host, also wearing a fetching hat. Chris and Jennie sat stolidly in the front row, arms crossed, neither wearing hats, both looking glum.

'Some people!' said Amanda, nodding and smiling as she passed them. 'They seem determined to be miserable. Don't ever be like those two, Tyger. Whenever something gets you down try to find the sunshine. And don't create your own gloom when everything is absolutely fine. Just look at them!'

'They're awful people,' Tyger muttered, as though scared he would be overheard, although by now the dance had moved them to the other side of the floor. 'They think that only the things that they believe are right.'

'Desperate to be ordinary.'

'That sounds like a book.' Tyger slid slightly and gripped Amanda's hand. 'Perhaps one day I'll write it.'

'Do you want to be a writer, Tyger?'

'I'm not sure what I want, yet. But I know that if I do write I'll have to experience everything, to know what it's like for real before I set it down.'

'Not quite everything. I think you'll find that Shakespeare and Dickens used quite a lot of imagination.'

'But those were people living in the olden days,' said Tyger. 'Now everyone wants veracity. They want to think what you write is the truth, not just rubbish you made up.'

Fiction is the word, rather than rubbish. But Amanda decided not to argue.

The music came to an end, and, along with everyone else, Tyger and Amanda shuffled back to their ringside table.

As they walked past Chris and Jennie, Amanda leaned down and asked, 'No hats?'

Chris snorted. 'We think hat-wearing is a pretty juvenile idea. Paper hats are for children. Suitable only for kids, like the ankle-biter on your arm, for instance.'

'And for wearing at Christmas dinner, Chris,' said Jennie in the voice of a mouse. 'Paper hats from the crackers, remember. You always wear one.'

Luckily enough the band started up again and further conversation was impossible.

As Tyger and Amanda arrived back at their table a slightly scruffy man wearing a black and gold velvet fez appeared at Amanda's side.

'While you wear a formidable hat like that, Signora, I feel obliged to ask you for a dance.'

He opened his eyes wide, flaring his nostrils as he proffered his arm.

Amanda took a step back. Was this man mad?

He lifted both arms and wafted them around in the air, while Amanda flinched, thinking he might at any moment pull out a knife, but instead he extracted a pink silk rose from his sleeve and presented it to her. 'My name is Arturo the Luminoso.'

Amanda flooded with relief. He might look out of place here, but she had seen his name in tomorrow's *Programme*. He was the big act in the theatre, a stage conjuror.

As they stepped on to the floor for a foxtrot, Amanda told him her name, but all hopes of a quiet conversation while dancing were dashed. Arturo was a proficient, though silent, dance partner. Amanda smiled. To think that now she could add to the list of new experiences: dancing a mazurka with a magician. She couldn't imagine anything madder, especially in comparison to the dismal days she had spent trudging around London before she came onboard.

'I've seen your profile in tomorrow's *Programme*,' said Amanda, hoping to end the silence. 'I plan to come to your evening performance.'

Arturo smiled. 'You will not be disappointed.'

He looked over her shoulder then she felt the muscles in his body contract. He pulled away from her, and took a few steps back.

At first Amanda thought she must have trodden on his foot. But he continued walking backwards, his eyes fixed, while his hands fumbled in his pockets. She wondered whether he might be ill – perhaps he was asthmatic, and reaching for an inhaler, or maybe suffering from angina and needing to take a pill. She moved towards him. But then he suddenly took a pose like a fighter, pulled something from his pocket and thrust it forward. Thinking it must be a gun, Amanda automatically threw herself to the floor, and crawled away from him towards the tables and chairs, while several men leaped forward and grabbed hold of Arturo, who started howling.

They struggled with him for some moments then he landed on the dance floor with a thump. The item he had been holding fell from his hands and rolled towards Amanda.

It was something like a furry toy. As it slid closer she realised it was one of those lucky rabbit's feet that people once won at fairground stalls.

She sat up and wiped herself down.

Arturo lay in the centre of the dance floor, crossing himself and murmuring into a string of beads which he held to his lips.

Two of the gentlemen hosts helped him up, then led Arturo out of the ballroom.

'You took quite a fall there, madam. May I assist you?' A sleek silver-haired man bent down and held out a hand. 'I'm Tony, by the way. Poor Arturo. He's harmless. Just a bit eccentric. I work alongside him, and we dine at the same table, so I know his little foibles. He keeps telling me that the Devil is onboard! Perhaps he just had a visitation.'

Amanda clambered awkwardly to her feet. She felt quite wobbly from the double shock.

'It's strange how your imagination takes over,' said Amanda, taking Tony's arm as they crossed the floor. 'I thought he had a gun.'

'A gun? Remember going through all the security scanners before you came aboard? I don't think anyone could get a gun on to this ship.' Tony smiled and asked: 'Would you care to continue the dance?'

Amanda had been winded by the shock of the fall. She needed a little time to pull herself together.

'Do you know, I'll pass for now. But you're very kind.'

Instead of going to the table, she decided to take a stroll, get her breath back. She would go to her cabin for a few minutes – to powder her nose, as they used to put it. Then she would return and start afresh. After all the night was yet young – on a floating pleasure palace like this, anyhow.

For no real reason, when she got to the cabin, and saw the neatly turned-down bed, the chocolate on her pillow, the ship's newspapers and *Daily Programme*s spread out like a fan on the coverlet, Amanda was overtaken by an overwhelming feeling of loneliness.

Tears welled up. She felt stupid and forlorn. Here she was in a floating hotel with thousands of strangers, when she could be at home with people who really loved her.

She opened up the laptop and collected her emails.

Three came in. She opened the one from her daughter first.

Patricia's was rather a snide message informing Amanda that she had at last found a solution to her childcare problem and 'a wonderful new nanny' had just moved in. It wasn't hard to see the implied subtext – 'no thanks to you'. The nanny was Norland-trained and would cost a fortune, but at least, said Patricia, it meant that the children would have 'the best possible care'. Better than Granny, thought Amanda, wishing she had let the computer be. She suppressed the stab of her daughter's subliminal accusation and opened the next message.

This one was from her lawyers. A PDF receipt for the bill for the conveyancing of the sale of the house and the purchase of the new flat was attached. Amanda noted that the solicitors had removed the money from the sale of her old house, so there was no actual bill to pay. They had helped themselves.

The email came with a PS. From the end of business hours tomorrow, all personal enquiries, signatures, meetings etc., would need to be done from their head office in Leicester. This was due to a long-planned refurbishment of the building, which would also necessitate all phone lines and electricity cables to be replaced. They hoped it would not be too much of an inconvenience to their clients. Once completed, the bright new office with state-of-the-art technology would result in a far better service for everyone.

Amanda couldn't imagine why that was of any interest to her, here in the middle of the Atlantic. Then she remembered that she still had to pick up the key of the new flat. So now, when she did get home, that would entail a day trip to Leicester.

She opened the last email, from Aardvark Storage, reminding their 'dear client Amanda' that, as she had failed to renew the contract but her stuff was still there, she would be put on to the premium daily rate. She could renew right now on the cheaper monthly or even cheaper six-monthly basis, but in the meanwhile they would continue taking those extortionate daily payments from her credit card … blah-blah-blah.

Now totally depressed, Amanda tried to get on to the Aardvark website and make an automatic renewal, but there was something wrong with the site and the links wouldn't connect to the payments section.

Another email pinged in. Her son Mark. He must be live online at this moment.

Amanda had prayed for good news from him, but instead got another sob story. After 'that bloody Jasmine' had dumped him, Patricia had grudgingly let him stay on the sofa-bed for a night, but then she had come down for a glass of water at dawn and caught him canoodling with the au pair, who she promptly sacked – rather unfairly, Mark thought. Patricia had now found a new live-in agency nanny and, without so much as a thank you, had thrown him out on his ear. He couldn't help it if the silly girl had decided to snuggle up with him on the sofa-bed, and so wasn't there in the nanny's room when one of Patricia's wretched children had started crying in the night. Mark was 'at the end of his tether', after spending the day looking at hotels. But he found them all terribly depressing, and too awful to contemplate. He was in despair, he said. A man of his status could not be seen to be 'living in what was only one step up from a dosshouse'.

Amanda thought back to the rude girl on the desk at the dingy hotel, and the uncomfortable shock of finding herself sleeping in a bed in the hostel. She thought it was actually quite funny that her son had forgotten that she herself had taken this exact journey less than a week ago and that, when the same thing had happened to her, he had given her short shrift.

Amanda couldn't really remember who 'that bloody Jasmine' was. She supposed that must have been the girl who was moaning and whispering in the background when she had phoned him in London, asking for help.

Amanda continued reading – Mark was angry that, what with the family household bills to pay, he couldn't afford to stay in the kind of hotel which would make his life comfortable enough to continue working. Unless he found a decent place, he said, he would end up broke, and then his children, *her grandchildren*, would suffer, maybe even starve.

For some reason, despite his overdramatic tone, Mark's email made Amanda feel guilty. She didn't like the way he was somehow implying that it was all her fault he was in this mess. After all, he was the one who had deserted his family home, for this Jasmine woman. He only had himself to blame if he now had to pay for a household where he did not live as well as having to stump up for somewhere to rest his own adulterous head.

She still had both Patricia and Mark's bank details scribbled down on the desk jotter, ready to transfer the money left over from the sale of the old family home once the new flat was paid for. Perhaps if she forwarded him the cash right away ...

Amanda hesitated. It could only be disastrous if you tried to *buy* the goodwill of your own children. She would exchange that money only when she was feeling bright and cheerful and everything was looking good.

She stared glassy-eyed at the screen and suddenly realised she was still online. As she turned off the internet connection, to save the precious minutes, she saw that she had used up almost half of her paid-for internet package. Twenty-five dollars down the drain.

She flopped back on the bed.

The emails from her children had sucked the joy out of the evening.

Although she had intended to go back to the ball and enjoy herself, Amanda now felt utterly deflated. She was tempted to curl up and go to bed, but, what with the clocks having already gone backward one hour yesterday, as they were heading west, and due to rewind another hour tonight, she knew it was much, much too early for bed, not to mention too silly to give in to depression.

She would do her best to get on with her own life and leave others to deal with their own. She couldn't face the ballroom quite yet, so went up to the cafeteria.

It was bright and cheery in there. Only a few tables were taken. She recognised some of the dancers from last night's show, sitting with macs over their costumes, grabbing a bite between performances. Two members of the uniformed crew sat alone at a table in the corner, talking very earnestly.

Only a few guests, in evening dress and carrying their hats, were gobbling down plates of food, getting ready to go down and take to the floor again.

Amanda picked up a cup of tea and a slice of chocolate cake from the buffet and moved over to sit in a dark unlit alcove. She looked at the sea. Out there, everything was black.

Only now did she notice that the ship was rocking. The tea was slopping from side to side in the cup.

She bit into the cake, which seemed to be the most delicious slice of cake she had ever tasted.

Amanda realised that really she was glad it was impossible, without a king's ransom, to make phone calls. Anyway, she knew that if she had followed up those emails with phone calls the outcome would only have made her feel much, much worse.

From across the room the showgirls' laughter echoed round her alcove.

Laughter was the key. She had to live in the moment. You only live once.

It was strange that on this ship she felt so safe. The problems arose when she made contact with the world she had left behind, creating horrible worries which gnawed at her innards.

The funny little Italian magician in the ballroom had given her a fright, but that episode had really been stoked up by her own overactive imagination. The poor old man had been holding out a lucky rabbit's paw, like an amulet against evil. And when she thought about it, his looks were filled with fear, not hatred or even aggression.

Amanda was quite jealous of the magician's amulet, though, and fancied going back to her cabin and pointing something, a clove of garlic perhaps, at her laptop. She laughed and saw her reflection in the glass. She was still wearing the smart paper hat, only now it was rather bent. She thought she looked like a character out of a cartoon.

Dammit! She would go back and dance. Why not? It wasn't as though she could do anything else more serious while she was hundreds of miles from the shore. She would take a short walk along the deck to clear her head, then go and shake her booty!

She pushed through the double set of glass doors and ventured out on to the open deck.

As she emerged into the air, the loud hum of the engines, the crash of the waves and the howls of the wind mingled into a deafening cacophony.

A mighty gust of wind blew her paper hat clean away. It flew off her head and skittered along the glistening wooden deck. She ran after it, but the wind whipped it up high into the night air. Before she knew it, the hat wafted downwards then flew over the side, flapping off into the darkness, like a grey and red albatross.

She moved forward and clung on to the wooden rail, watching her hat grow smaller and smaller until it vanished. The ship's lights cast bright reflections on the black boiling water below. Apart from those glistening waves there was nothing to see – not a star, no moon, and no other ships, just a black blanket of nothing. Amanda had never seen darkness like it. She turned sideways and glanced up at the steep white walls of the ship. Its bright lights now seemed to summon up memories of all those films about the *Titanic*, and she felt completely vulnerable, as though she was in a small tub, bobbing up and down in an eternal swaying sea.

Still gripping the rail, she took one more deep breath of fresh air.

She was ready to face the music, literally.

Suddenly the horizon lit with an eerie purple glow, and, for a few seconds, a huge branch of lightning flickered. Amanda had never seen lightning like this and thought how like it was to those domes in science museums where you placed your hand down and caused a bright web of light. It glimmered for a while and was gone.

Amanda's clothing fluttered around her.

'Romantic, isn't it?' A man was standing beside her. His voice was deep and warm.

'Very.' Amanda didn't dare look around at him. She wanted to believe he was as handsome as Elvis, with a Clark Gable smile. She did not want to turn around and see a man resembling Michael Gove with acne.

So, instead, feeling like a character in a Noël Coward play, she focused on the flickers of lightning on the horizon and continued her conversation.

'I've always loved the sea,' she said. 'Since all those childhood day trips to Mudeford.'

'Mudeford!' The man laughed. 'Isn't that where all the millionaire footballers live these days? Near Sandbanks.'

'Not in those days. It was all "pay for your deckchair", penny-falls machines, calamine lotion and pots of cockles and winkles.'

'Good to know that you had a real childhood. None of this selfie and Facebook stuff.' He chuckled, then sighed and said, 'The sea, so beautiful. Keep your eyes peeled for dolphins. They're all over the place. Too dark now, of course.'

'I saw some this morning.'

'You're a very lucky woman. As well as a very good-looking one.'

Finally, Amanda turned to look at him.

The man was wearing an impeccable tuxedo and black silk dicky bow. His silver hair flapped in the wind. He was very good-looking, slim. What you might describe as a matinée idol.

'A pity you lost your hat,' he said. 'It was very stylish. I watched it disappear on its journey to Greenland.' He edged forward and stood beside her, leaning on the rail. 'I saw you earlier, in the ballroom, dancing with the mad magician. If you hadn't left after his little turn, I'd have come over and asked you to join me for a drink. It's lonely trying to get through a bottle of champagne on your own.'

'I'm going back there now,' said Amanda.

'You're right. It is rather cold out here,' he said. 'Can I join you?'

Amanda put out her elbow, then decided to be cheeky. 'And if the offer's still open I'd love to share a glass of bubbles.'

PART FOUR

The Faraday Fracture Zone

SUZY DECIDED TO grab a decent breakfast before class, so went up to the cafeteria, where she could also pocket a biscuit for later, when her class was finished.

She wandered around with her tray trying to find an empty table, but 9 a.m. was the most popular time. Eventually she found a window bay with one table free. She laid her things out, and pulled her notebooks from her bag so that she could glance over the plans for the class while she ate.

'Getting into the swing?'

It was Melanie, the social hostess, sitting at the next table, busily spreading marmalade on her toast. 'I'm just grabbing a coffee before I start "Forty Ways to Tie a Silk Scarf".'

Suzy laughed, then realised that Melanie was not making a joke.

'I thought it was napkin folding this morning?'

'Of course.' Melanie looked down at her folder and winced. 'You lose all sense of time once you're on the Atlantic. It's scarves tomorrow.'

'Any more calls from your stalker?'

Melanie looked puzzled.

'The pest, who keeps phoning the office.'

'Oh, him. Natch. He's been on this morning. Wanted to know if the "Art for Teens" class was open to everyone.'

'He's not a teen, is he?' Suzy smiled. 'I would have thought the title was self-explanatory.'

'Exactly.' Melanie tore open a wrap of sugar and emptied it into her coffee. 'Do you have problem customers in your world?'

Suzy mulled this over. 'We get silly things said to us by strangers in the street, I suppose. "I hated you in that" or "But it would have been so much better if Judi Dench had played your part". I had a woman once tell me she thought I was "way more wrinkled in real life than I was in *Dahlias*", a TV series which I did about thirty years ago!'

Melanie's face said it all. She stared at Suzy, open-mouthed, eyes popping.

'I had no idea!' She downed her coffee in one. 'You'd think actors only ever got people telling them they love them. I get people who know how to do things better than I do all the time, but apart from that …'

'I suppose we actors don't have very much direct communication with our customers. Sometimes our colleagues can be the problem, sometimes directors. Though I have to say they are mostly very sweet.'

'This fellow is an actor.'

'Which fellow?'

'The annoying one who keeps calling my office.'

'He's an actor?'

'That's what it says on his passport. I looked him up last night. It suddenly occurred to me he might be one of those secret agents sent by head office to test us, or perhaps a nasty journalist from one of those cruise magazines, trying to make trouble, checking me out in case I lost my cool.'

'But he's an actor?'

'That's right. An actor. Though personally his voice doesn't sound up to it. Weasely. I'd love to see him in the flesh, but I've only heard him down the phone.' Melanie stood up and laid all her dirty dishes on a tray. 'Name of Stanley K. Arbuthnot.'

Suzy had just raised a spoon full of cornflakes to her mouth. She put it down.

'Stanley Arbuthnot?'

'That's right.' Melanie blushed. 'Oh no. How embarrassing! You know him. He's probably your best friend or an ex-husband or something.'

'No, no. Stan Arbuthnot, you said?' Suzy's breath was quite taken away. Her heart pounded and her breathing became shallow. 'Where did he get on?'

'Southampton, of course. Only a very few people stayed onboard after the Med. Genoa to Southampton was only a repositioning cruise.'

Suzy's mind raced through all the events, starting at Zurich Airport. Barbara told them that Stan had left early that morning, on the same day that she and Jason had taken the train and gone down to Genoa to board the *Blue Mermaid*. There had been those few days at sea from Genoa to Southampton, then a day in Southampton … plenty of time for Stan to sort himself out and pack for a cruise.

'I hope I haven't upset you by telling you that. It was a spur-of-the-moment thing, I think. He booked on the day we sailed.'

Suzy's mind raced. Stan Arbuthnot! So it wasn't so batty to think that Jason and Stan were in cahoots.

Melanie looked rather panicked, as Suzy's wide-eyed silence led her to think that she had made a serious faux pas. 'I had no idea you were friends.'

Suzy wiped her mouth and got up.

'No. Sorry, Melanie. It's nothing like that at all. Really. It's just … just … I can't stand the man.' She took a quick swill of tea. 'I'm happy to be forewarned. Must rush. I need to speak to someone before my class starts, and I've just seen the time.'

Suzy could barely stop herself running as she rushed through the cafeteria, heading back to her cabin, which naturally was at the opposite end of the ship to where she was now, and then back to the ballroom, where her class would start in ten minutes.

Stan Arbuthnot! How absurd! She stabbed at the button for the lift, then impatiently decided she couldn't face waiting for it, so ran down the stairs instead. She turned the corner and marched into the entertainment quarters. She arrived at Jason's room and was about to knock when she remembered that Jason had a room-mate and that they had both been working till the early hours. However much she needed to speak to Jason she didn't want to upset his fellow ghost.

She looked at her watch. She was late for the class.

She ran into her own cabin and scribbled a hasty note. The message was simple:

> Jason. You should have told me. As you probably know, Stan Arbuthnot is aboard. If you can't explain yourself, I will have to go to the Captain and inform him. Find me after my class or asap. Suze.

She slipped the note under Jason's door, then she ran the entire length of the ship, taking the open deck which, at this time of day, was clogged with earnest joggers all doing laps in a clockwise direction. She felt like an Olympic sprinter as she whizzed past the more leisurely runners.

When she arrived, panting, in the ballroom, her students were already standing in a circle on the dance floor.

She ran down the ramp to join them.

'Pardon me. An unforgivable offence in the theatre, being late. It makes you very unpopular.' She flung her bag on to a seat and strode into the circle. 'Once upon a time, when I was young, believe it or not, actors were fined for being late. So now, let's get on with it! Yesterday we played the game of being seen. After our warm-up today we are going to play the opposite game: "The Art of Becoming Invisible".'

'Why would you ever need that?' enquired a keen stick-thin man wearing a T-shirt and shorts. 'Surely you want to be seen all the time.'

'No. There are scenes where it's necessary that no one notices you until you step forward and make some surprise announcement, for example. And another thing, which even some professionals don't ever grasp: for any play to work you have to give others their moments. For that you need to be able to fade in and out of a scene, without anyone noticing what you're doing.'

She looked up to where yesterday Jason had been sitting. Blake was there, regarding the class. He'd seen her come in late. He was not smiling.

'Will we be doing any textual work?' asked an earnest little girl with a very posh voice. 'I'm applying for drama school in January, and it would be very useful to go through my audition speeches.'

'Eventually.' Suzy really didn't want the class to be about one person. There was always one who simply thought the whole thing was about them. 'But we always start with exercises and games.'

'I just thought we would be doing scenes from plays.'

'Tomorrow morning I'll bring in some scenes for you all to work on.'

'Why can't I do my monologues? I've been working on them for weeks. But I need professional help.'

'We're all going to do some famous scenes. Together. In groups.'

From the corner of her eye Suzy saw Blake get up and leave the ballroom. No doubt he had taken a dim view of that little altercation, but what else could she do? You cannot give a group class and concentrate on one individual.

Suzy clapped her hands, turned to the others and said, 'Now let's get on with this morning's game.'

*

Amanda woke and lay in her bed, staring out at the grey clouds scudding by in an otherwise blue sky. She was warm and cosy, and feeling very happy after the surprise turn of events last night.

Despite losing her Tyger-made hat, she had gone back to the Ascot Ball and shared a table with her elegant new friend. She realised that she had not asked his name! Well, whatever he was called, he had been wonderful. He'd ordered champagne and they had talked as much as it was possible to when sitting so near the band. Mainly they discussed the ship and how comfortable it was, but he'd asked where she lived and she told him about her housing saga. He was very sympathetic and said that he was on the move himself. A far more major effort for him, moving from Europe to the USA. When he said goodnight, he had implied that they would meet again. Amanda had got out of the lift before he did. She presumed he must be staying in one of the fancy cabins on the upper floors.

Amanda sat up and read the ship's daily papers, then had a luxurious bath, dressed and walked slowly to breakfast. She hoped so much to meet her new friend in a corridor or perhaps in the lifts, or even in the cafeteria.

But no.

After eating breakfast, and dawdling with her coffee refill, Amanda decided to explore the library and bookshop, secretly hoping that her new friend might be in there. He certainly came over as the reading type.

Amanda was amazed how full the bookshop and library were. In the library not only could she not find an empty chair, but many of the people were fast asleep, which was very annoying. The window seats had a magnificent view over the prow of the ship and everyone sitting in them were slumped down and snoring! She wandered through the aisles of stacked books, looking for a novel which she could read in her cabin during the afternoons. She had turned a corner and inspected a whole shelf of books before she realised she was now beyond fiction and browsing the Natural World shelves: *Arctic Wildlife, A History of the Natural World, Animals – From Aaadvarks to Zebras ...*

Aardvark!

She still hadn't sorted the storage problem. Oh no! That would be another 24-hour top-rate extortionate bill.

She rushed from the library, down the stairs to her deck, then ran along the corridor. She was halfway down when she realised that she had lost her sense of direction and that she was on the wrong side of the ship. Hers was an odd-numbered cabin and all these were evens. She cut through, crossing one of the landings, marching past the lifts. One lift opened and a couple stepped out and stood still, deciding where to go. Amanda stopped and walked around them, and found herself colliding with a man who was running up the stairs in his gym clothes.

'Hey!' The gym-goer was her champagne pal from last night. He flicked his towel over his shoulders. 'Where are you off to in such a hurry? Must be something very exciting.'

Amanda laughed. Suddenly she could see how piddling were her domestic problems.

'It's silly really. As I told you, I've just sold my house, bought a flat, and all my stuff is in storage …' She stopped herself going on. 'But you don't want to hear this nonsense.'

'Storage can easily be sorted.'

'I know I'm being silly. At the same time my son is playing up. And …'

As she reeled off her problems the answer to everything dawned on her. Mark! Her son could be the solution to it all. If he could get to the solicitors' office to pick up the keys today, before they moved to Leicester, then go and get her furniture out of storage … Hey presto! He could have somewhere to stay – her flat. All her key and storage problems would be sorted. All their problems solved in one go.

'Amanda?'

The man stood beside her waiting for an answer.

Amanda realised she had not only failed to answer his question, she was so taken over by her own thoughts that she hadn't even heard it.

'I asked whether you might like me to talk to your son?' the man asked again. 'Man to man. When a stranger speaks, it is sometimes effective.'

'No, no,' said Amanda. 'I think I have a way to sort it all out. Look, I must rush now, but we could meet later. How about lunch or tea?'

'Tea!' The man wiped his towel against his cheek. 'I look forward to it.'

As Amanda dashed on along the corridor, she realised she had still not asked the mystery man's name. Though he, she noted, had rather flatteringly remembered hers.

Back in her cabin she wrote the necessary emails: first a note to the solicitors, advising them that her son Mark would come in and collect the keys; then a letter to Aardvark informing them that her son would arrive later to take away her things. While she was starting the long email to Mark, giving him the address of the lawyers' office, the details and key-pad number of the storage facility and a description of her new flat, she noticed that the solicitors had sent a reply. She popped down the current email and read it. They pointed out that before they could release the keys to her son they would need him to be carrying a passport or some other legally acknowledged identity papers, together with a signed letter of authority from her.

A signed letter of authority! How on earth could she get that to Mark? She was in the middle of the Atlantic Ocean, for God's sake.

To make matters worse she only had till close of business today to get it sorted. She glanced down at her computer clock which was now, strangely, coming up to 9 a.m. Surely it couldn't be that time? She had done so much already and had a lie-in this morning. She looked at her watch and turned on the small TV. She flicked around until she found the page devoted to sea conditions and charts and had an active analogue clock in the corner, which was always adjusted to ship's time.

But before she could click through the TV channels, passing from some old black and white film to a talk from the lady who ran the spa, in the corridor the tannoy sounded the daily bells. No need to find the time. The bells meant it was now noon. Amanda propped open the cabin door so that she could hear the Captain's announcement while she continued to write her email to Mark.

'Good afternoon, ladies and gentlemen. I hope you're enjoying your time onboard.' The Captain's voice was mellifluous and calming. She tried to imagine him sitting up in the bridge in his swanky uniform – not costume! 'Some of you will have noticed a little swell yesterday. We've skirted the main body of that storm, but we did catch a tiny effect of the tail end of it. Yesterday we took our normal track, sailing away from Bishop's Rock and across the Porcupine Abyssal Plain …'

In exchange for getting the keys and the furniture, she wrote to Mark, he would have somewhere comfortable to stay till she got home. Fitted kitchen, lovely bathroom, bedroom and large bright living room. Once he picked up the furniture he would also have two TVs, a double bed, sofa, desk, kitchen equipment like toasters, a kettle and cutlery, i.e. everything he needed to live a perfectly comfortable life, and it would cost him precisely nothing. (And, she thought, at the same time all her other worries at home would be solved. Howzat!)

She told Mark that he would need to bring a passport to the office, but then remembered the letter of authority. She realised that she had a good deal of time before the end of the working day.

Amanda slumped at her desk trying to think of a way she could get her signature to Mark within the next five hours. She wondered whether there existed a supersonic version of a carrier pigeon?

Through the corridor speakers, the Captain was still burbling on: 'Today we will continue our voyage along the great circle track, and pass over the Faraday Fracture Zone, an undersea range of volcanic mountains stretching from the Arctic to the tip of Africa, and which occasionally pops up above sea level forming, for example, St Helena and the archipelago of the Azores …'

Thinking about that brought her up short. Being so cut off, she could picture the ship, a tiny dot in the middle of a huge ocean. But now she had to factor in something more disturbing: the thought of the seabed under them.

'… Being mountains, it means the depth from the ship's hull to the sea floor today fluctuates from depths of over 3,500 metres, shoaling to only hundreds of metres. Make the most of the weather this afternoon, won't you, as tomorrow it looks as though we might be in for a bit of a choppy ride. And don't forget to change your clocks back one hour again tonight. I will now pass you over to our German hostess.'

Oh no! Amanda grabbed a pencil. She'd forgotten the time difference. During the night they'd put the clocks back twice since Southampton, so London would be what time now? If it was noon onboard would they be ahead or behind? Perhaps the UK was the time showing on her computer – 9 a.m. Why did the computer say 9 a.m. when it was noon? Was that UK time? Did you add or subtract? Her head was totally muddled; she felt herself go hot with panic. To make things harder, a metallic voice from the corridor speakers was now retelling the information that the Captain had just delivered, only this time in German.

Amanda grabbed a scrap of paper. New York, she knew, was five hours behind London. That would mean the ship was also behind London, so she wrote down the time and added the adjusted hours since Southampton then saw that the time in London must now be after 2 p.m. This meant that she had only three hours to work it out, and once you subtracted the time Mark would need to get to the office, that would be two.

How she wished she had not had the stupid idea of coming aboard this ship.

Everything would have been so easy if she'd just remained in London.

There must be a way that she could send a scanned signature to the UK, but it was obviously not something you could do sitting alone in a cabin.

There was only one thing for it – she would have to ask for help at the purser's office.

The queue at the desk was long, and by the time she reached the front it was almost one o'clock, ship's time. She had an hour.

*

After her morning class Suzy went back to listen outside Jason's cabin. All silent within. She returned to her own room to make sure he hadn't replied to her note, but nothing.

She felt really hungry and decided to grab an early lunch now, so that later, when she found Jason, there would be time for a serious talk before he went to work. She knew now that she had to find a real way to challenge him once more, and if his replies were as glib as they had been so far, she would have to take the information to the Captain who would deal with it his way and he could inform the police.

While picking the dishes from the hot display – tomato soup, poppy-seed roll and an apple pie – Suzy mulled over the dilemmas.

She still had no idea whether Jason had actually filched everyone's money, but it was possible. What other explanation was there? It had to be somebody in the company, and as it had affected everyone except Jason and perhaps Stan, it must be him. Probably both of them in concert. And if this actor Melanie was talking about really was Stan, she needed to quiz him too. Stan Arbuthnot! Of all people! Surely it couldn't be him? But as Equity didn't allow two performers to take the same name it had to be him. Maybe this man onboard was a non-union actor. There were so many of them these days. But that all seemed too pat. It was clearly their Stan.

And if Stan was onboard, it was too much of a coincidence. Perhaps, as Emily had feared, Jason and Stan were conspiring. Jason must have told Stan about the *Blue Mermaid* and then Stan had rushed down to Southampton to join him.

But Stan had left Zurich on the first plane. And she had been with Jason all that day and then they came aboard together that evening. He hadn't been out of her sight. How could Stan have known where Jason was?

She laid down her spoon.

Of course, he could know! The phones still had plenty of signal when they were near the coast of Europe. Jason could have phoned or emailed Stan many times between Genoa and Southampton.

Stan must have done all the bank transfers, then, flush with all their money, come aboard at Southampton to join his partner in crime.

On top of it all, Jason had admitted that Stan was there with him, at the producer's party in Zurich, where, in response to some unwanted sexual advances, Jason had done something so bad that, next morning, the show had been cancelled.

Taking everything into account, Suzy believed one thing was sure – Stan was working together with Jason.

She felt truly stupid. Why had she not thought things through before leaving the note in Jason's cabin? Now she had let Jason know that she knew, and, instead of being vulnerable to one person, she was in danger from two of them.

She slowly buttered her roll, and dipped it into her soup.

She wondered how she could have been so idiotic.

'Cutting it fine, darling!'

She looked up.

Jason stood before her, bearing a tray which he laid down on the table beside hers then sat beside her.

'So, sweetheart! Shove up and tell me all about Greasy Stan. But you'd better get a move on.'

'What do you mean, "move on"?'

Jason looked at his watch. 'You're on in forty minutes.'

'On?'

'Your lecture in the theatre … Oscar Wilde. Don't you check your *Programme* every day, my sweet?'

The lecture! 'Oh help!' Suzy took a huge bite of apple pie and wiped her mouth as she stood. 'I've got to get dressed up, and prepare myself.'

Jason grabbed his own roll and pieces of cheese from his tray and crammed them into his pockets. He followed, calling after her: 'Not without me, you don't.'

They both hurtled through the café and down the stairs next to the lifts.

'You were kidding me about Stan, I expect?' said Jason. 'Weren't you? Suzy? Trying to find a way for us to get together so that we could talk again?'

Suzy couldn't think straight. Her mind was now focusing on the imminent lecture, grabbing her notes and getting changed into something smart.

'No. No, I wasn't.' She clutched the handrail and spun round to go down the next flight. 'I didn't make it up.'

'What's his cabin number?'

Suzy realised she had no idea. Nothing but the name.

'It may not be him,' she said, hurtling down the next set of stairs. 'It may be another Stan Arbuthnot.'

Jason laughed aloud. 'Like that old John Gielgud gaffe to Athene Seyler, you mean? "Not you, Athene, I meant another Athene Seyler"?'

They had reached Suzy's cabin.

'Jason, I really have to go in and get ready,' she said, blocking the door.

'You're kidding me! You give me news like this and then leave me high and dry.'

'Later.'

Jason threw up his hands. 'By the time you've finished your lecture, I'll be doing my dance duty at afternoon tea. It's a tea dance today.'

'I've told you everything I know.' Suzy put her keycard into the lock and slipped into the cabin. 'Someone called Stan Arbuthnot came aboard this ship at Southampton. And I presumed you already knew about that, and that for some dreadful reason you've not told me.'

'How would I know anything about Stan?' Jason slammed his foot into the door gap before Suzy could shut it. 'Look, Suzy. When you say "someone called Stan Arbuthnot", do you mean any old bod of that name, or our own actor Stan, the actual Stan-the-greasy-Chasuble?'

'I have no idea. But he is an actor. An actor called Stan Arbuthnot.'

Suzy managed to slam the door shut, hastily pulled her smart suit from the wardrobe and, while climbing into it, fumbled about in the desk drawer for her lecture script.

'Suze!' Jason called through the door. 'If you like I could do that handbag scene with you, like we did coming out of Genoa.'

Jason's voice was so reasonable, Suzy felt dragged in by it, as though he was using the tempting tones of the snake in the Garden of Eden.

She stayed resolute. 'No thanks.'

While applying her mascara, Suzy glanced down at the script and realised that the first half was based on the handbag scene and from there into the play and then Wilde's life, and that, one way or another, she would have to do the scene, either with Jason or without. Doing it with him would certainly make much more sense to an audience.

Reluctantly she realised she would be mad not to accept his offer. After all, Jason would only be onstage with her for those few moments then he would have to hurtle, pell-mell, for the ballroom and the afternoon tea dance.

'All right, Jason,' she called through the door, while unscrewing her lipstick. 'We'll do the scene, as before.'

When she was ready, Suzy opened up. Jason, who had been sitting on the floor, scrambled to his feet.

'OK, gal. Spill. How did you find out that Stan was here with us?'

Suzy led the way, striding along the corridor, tossing comments over her shoulder.

'Someone on the crew simply mentioned his name and said he was an actor.'

'How can we find out where he is?' Jason scampered along at her side as they hurried down the stairs to the door leading backstage. 'Can we get our hands on a list of cabin numbers? How come we've not seen him anywhere?'

'It's a huge ship. There are thousands of people onboard. Look, Jason, let's talk later – I'll come down and dance with you at tea or something. But now, for goodness' sake, let's go over the lines for this performance.'

'Blah-blah-blah ...' said Jason, in his Earnest voice. '"Thank you, Lady Bracknell, I prefer standing."'

'"I feel bound to tell you that you are not down on my list of eligible young men,"' Suzy replied as they turned into the stage door and walked along the passageway leading to the wings.

'What's all this?' said Jason as they both had to squeeze past great painted wooden blocks and frames.

'Hi!' said Andy, the tech guy, stepping forward from the stage darkness. He held out Madonna-style radio mics. 'Be careful coming past all that stuff. It's the magician's equipment for the show tonight. We're teching it straight after your lecture ends.'

While Andy fastened their radio-transmitter boxes and slipped the wires down the backs of their jackets, Suzy and Jason stood behind the theatre curtain and continued muttering the words of the scene.

'You have quite a full house out there,' said Andy, when they had done. 'Good luck. I'll give you a light.' He romped off, squeezing through the gap at the side of the curtains.

'Look at all this amazing paraphernalia!' Jason took a step towards the magician's ornate structure, painted in garish circus-show colours: red, yellow, green, pink and gold.

Suzy cast her eye over the props. 'I can't believe that crazy little man can operate it all.'

'Do you think he saws women in half?' said Jason, turning back to face the reverse of the curtain, ready to go on. 'How can we find out where he is?'

'Arturo?'

'Stan, of course.' Jason spoke in a low intense voice. 'I have some unfinished business with that bastard.'

The warning light went red. Suzy walked forward and fumbled about in the curtains, searching with her fingers for the central gap. 'I don't know anything about him, Jason. Concentrate!'

'We've got to get a list of cabin numbers.'

Suzy was about to answer and remembered that they were miked up.

She pointed at her headset and put a finger to her lips.

'Later,' she said, as the light went from red to green.

She stepped through the curtains on to the floodlit stage and a wave of enthusiastic applause.

W HEN AMANDA joined the queue for tea, outside
the ballroom, she was fifteen minutes late. However,
she managed to find a table for two quite near the dance
floor.

She felt utterly puffed and befuddled, having spent the
whole afternoon writing out then typing her letter which was
then printed in the office. She signed the authority with one
of the ship's senior officers as a witness, and they had scanned
it and emailed it to her son.

In London now it was after five, so Mark may or may not
have managed to get the keys to her flat. She had no idea. But
she had done everything she could.

The waiters hovered, proffering silver trays laden with
sandwiches, and pots of tea. Amanda smiled and indicated
that she was waiting for someone.

A small dance band was onstage, playing the usual standard strict-tempo tunes. Amanda recognised the ship's male
escorts with whom she had previously danced. When they
approached, she shook her head. How wonderful that she
could do this. Today she was waiting for a real-life gentleman
to whisk her off her feet.

She waited for a while, trying not to look desperate while
leaning out to make sure he didn't miss her when he came
through the door.

She glanced at her watch. Twenty minutes late. And back
in England, Mark, she hoped, would have the keys by now,

and be on the way to Aardvark with a lorry to salvage her furniture from another extortionate day of storage.

After a while, the sandwich trays thinned out and more platters appeared, bearing scones and cakes. But no sight of the man whose name she had still not yet managed to discover.

Amanda had a sudden fear. What if there was another room where tea was served? She scrabbled around in her handbag and pulled out her *Daily Programme*. She pored over the small print looking for the words 'Afternoon Tea'. She felt cross when she realised that she had not only forgotten to attend the class this morning, given by that actress Suzy Marshall, but had also missed the talk this afternoon on Oscar Wilde.

Amanda put the *Programme* away, and suddenly saw her date. He was sitting at another table, on the other side of the dance floor, next to a group of teenage boys who were laughing loudly.

She waved. He noticed her and threw up his arms in a gesture which said: 'Oh dear!'

He then signalled that he would come to her and Amanda nodded in the direction of a pair of hovering waiters, one bearing a tray with a scant selection of sandwiches, the other scones with jam and cream pots.

As her date pulled out his seat, apologising, he indicated to one of the waiters to give him a scone, and cream.

'I knew this would happen,' he said. It was the first time Amanda had noticed that he had a slightly strange accent. Nothing you could pin a locality upon, but his English was almost too perfect and untouched, rather as though he had learned the language, rather than picking it up as a native child.

'I'm so sorry. I realise that I never caught your name?'

The man laughed and wiped his mouth with his linen napkin. 'My friends call me Karl.'

'And I'm Amanda.'

'I know. So your son is not joining us today?'

'I'm sorry?'

'I thought perhaps your son would be here and I could give him some advice. Weren't you telling me this morning that he …'

Amanda couldn't see how his wires had got so crossed.

'No. No. My son is in London. It's all very complicated because there was all this mix-up with my flat, and it's now empty and available, and, well, I'm stuck here in the middle of the ocean, and … it's all very boring. My son has suddenly found himself homeless, so I've been trying to arrange for him to get the keys from the solicitor and move all my stuff in so that he can stay there.'

'I see.' Karl cut into a scone and meticulously spread it with clotted cream. 'My mistake. What's his name?'

'Mark Bailey.'

'But you are Amanda Herbert?'

'I dropped my husband's name when we divorced.'

'Do you have many children?'

'Only the two,' she replied. 'My daughter Patricia is a head teacher.'

It occurred to Amanda that Karl was quizzing her about potential liabilities. No man wants to get lumbered with another's family. 'Do you have children yourself?'

Karl shook his head.

'I have never had the opportunity,' he said, picking up the milk jug and pouring some into the cups before topping up their tea. 'Which is a pity.'

'Do you live in London too?' asked Amanda.

'I used to.'

'But you're not from England?'

'No. I've lived everywhere, from Brazil to Brunei.'

'You're on your way to New York?'

'And onwards,' he said. 'To Seattle, on business.'

The band struck up a foxtrot.

'I have two left feet,' said Karl. 'But might you like to dance?'

Amanda nodded.

Karl took her elbow. As he steered her on to the dance floor Amanda noticed Liliane, who was taking tea with Myriam, only a few tables away from them.

'I feel a little nervous.' Amanda put her arm around Karl's back. 'Last time I tried to dance, there was a little incident.'

'I witnessed that, remember,' said Karl. 'The Italian entertainer is rather hysterical, no?'

'I think just rather superstitious. His pockets are crammed with lucky charms, I've been told. I only saw two of them.'

'Did he tell you what was upsetting him?'

'No. He suddenly went off into a state of high doh, rather like someone who'd been hypnotised in one of those 1960s brainwashing movies. It was silly really.' Amanda laughed and felt embarrassed that Karl had seen how she had reacted. 'I handled it very badly.'

'Not at all,' said Karl as he steered her masterfully around the floor. 'It would be shocking to be confronted by someone who went over the edge, especially when dancing cheek to cheek. But, luckily for us, he is not here now.'

For some minutes they danced without speaking. When the music ended and Karl led Amanda to their table he asked, 'Is your son keeping busy?'

'He will be today – he's moving into my new flat until I get home.'

Karl laughed.

'What about the young boy who's travelling with you on the *Blue Mermaid*?'

'Travelling with me?' Amanda had no idea what he was talking about.

'The boy who sits at your table, who goes to the cafeteria with you, who made your hat, etcetera.'

'Oh! You're talking about Tyger!' Amanda laughed. 'Oh no! He's not my … He's onboard with his aunt, Myriam, one of the ladies at our table. I have only the one son, who I told you about, who's moving into my new flat today, and a daughter. Both in London at the moment.'

Karl leaned forward.

'Would you say no to some more champagne to finish off the tea?'

*

When Suzy came offstage, after the lecture was done, she was shocked to find Jason still there, crouched behind the curtains, waiting in the dark.

'Shouldn't you be at the tea dance?' Suzy stepped towards the light spilling from the dressing-room door, and, turning off her mic, reached over her shoulder for the connecting wires.

'Let me ...' Jason stepped behind her and pulled the microphone wire up through the back of her jacket, as he unhooked her mic pack. 'I came off after our scene and decided to stay here and wait for you.' Jason wound the wires around the box and rested the kit on the stage manager's desk. 'You see, I need to talk to you about Stan.'

Suzy tried to sound casual. Did this mean he was about to make a confession? 'But your job at the tea dance? You'll be in trouble ...'

'Don't worry. I'll come up with some excuse.' Jason held the stage door open for Suzy. 'One of my migraines! Now, tell me, Suzy ... Stan ...'

'Yes? What about him?'

'It's obvious, isn't it? How are we going to find the bastard?'

They went through the stage door into the ship's main port gangway. People were sitting at tables playing cards, reading and knitting while gazing out at the waves.

'Let's not speak here.' Suzy put her fingers to her lips and they both remained silent as they walked the length of the corridor.

Suzy felt nervous of Jason, but could not at this minute see how she could avoid him.

They reached her cabin door before speaking again.

'You really should go down to the ballroom, Jason, and do your job.'

Jason followed Suzy into her cabin.

'Please, Jason. You must see that I have nothing to say to you.' Suzy proffered Jason the desk chair. 'Unless perhaps you'd like to explain yourself, the bank scam and your relationship with Stan.'

'Why are you being like this, Suzy?' Jason declined to sit. 'You know my relationship with Stan. It's much the same as yours. I despise the man. Only I hate him much, much more than you do, because I know so much more about him than you do. And please, don't look in my direction when you're throwing your accusations around. I was not responsible for stopping the run of *The Importance*, nor for taking anybody's money, and if you want to point fingers at anyone, the bastard at whom to direct your digit is Stan.'

'That's an easy out for you, isn't it, blaming him?' Suzy decided to test Jason. 'What does Stan think about it all?'

Jason threw his hands up. 'I haven't got a bloody clue what Stan thinks. In fact, Suzy, I would loathe to know what Stan thinks. The very thought of what goes through the mind of that lump of blubber which passes for a man, well, I …' He shrugged and shook his head. 'There are no words.'

Suzy thought that Jason sounded rather plausible. But she also knew that he was a good actor.

She said quietly, 'Can you prove you had nothing to do with the money thing?'

'No, Suzy, I can't prove anything. I can only give you my word. I can show you my passports, my French one in the name Jacques Scott – the same name as is on my English bank account – and take you online to show you my very modest balance. That's my real name of course, not Jason Scott, which might explain how I was not targeted, while being used as a scapegoat. I always use my stage name when filling in forms for the theatre, but for real life I stick to my real name. Jacques Scott.'

'I thought it was Jacques Barry?'

'Berry. But I told you, when my father buggered off, I changed it to my mother's maiden name – Scott.' Jason took a step forward and pulled two passports from his pocket.

'I didn't want to have to do this – prove myself to you, but ...' He opened them up at the details page. One was French, with the name Jacques Scott Berry; the other English, with the name Jason Scott.

'How was that allowed? They wouldn't just let you make up a name. This is a fake.'

'No. I had my Equity card, my mother's birth certificate, everything they needed. I'm an actor, Suzy, like you. I grub around for work and live on the edge, never knowing where the next penny will come from. I certainly don't have the kind of funds you need to open a Swiss bank account. And that brief twenty-four hours was the only time I've ever spent in Switzerland in my entire life. But that's all irrelevant, Suzy. Look. I can't argue with you any more on this subject. But one thing I can do is help you find Stan, who I know is a key player in the whole horrible Zurich disaster.'

'Rather than "find him", don't you really mean lead me to him right now?'

'For once and for all, Suzy. The last time I was in touch – if that is the word – with Stan Arbuthnot was at that horrible so-called producer's party. And it was because of Stan's vile antics that we were all doomed. If you find the fat slob, let me know. I really do want to talk to him. I thought I'd got the police on to them. But clearly he evaded that, like his pal, Appenzell. But, for God's sake, Suzy, please don't leave me alone with Stan because if you did I could not be held responsible for my actions.'

Jason was so impassioned that Suzy was inclined to believe him.

'Why do you want to talk to Stan in front of me, Jason? Have you both prepared a little scene for my benefit?'

Jason put his face in his hands. 'Sod it, Suzy. Be serious. I have to ask Stan a few things about that party. Last I heard of him he was doing his drama-queen thing and squealing like a stuck pig.' He ran a hand through his hair. 'Look, Suzy, I haven't told you the truth about what really happened. But there's a good reason. If that vile man is onboard this ship I *have* to find him. And, then, we should get the police on to him. Have them waiting to pick him up at the dock in New York and throw him somewhere dark and miserable where he won't be free for the rest of his sick, perverted life.'

This new turn took Suzy aback. She spoke slowly, knowing that she was near to reaching something new, something which could be the truth.

'Why would they pick him up, Jason? Filching money out of people's accounts? Wouldn't that incriminate you too?'

Jason took a step back. His lips tightened and he shook his head. His hand reached out and grabbed the back of the chair.

As Suzy leaned forward, she watched the colour drain from Jason's face. He became so pale she feared he might faint.

'What did Stan do, Jason?'

'We find him first. Get him to confess.'

'No, we don't.' Suzy stood up and faced Jason. 'First you will tell me everything you know. The whole truth this time. And you will tell me now.'

Jason bit his lip. 'I can't *prove* anything, Suzy. That's the problem. But I know what I saw.'

'What did you see?'

'Something very bad happened at that producer's party. It's why I left. And also why I ended up having the fight with Reg on the doorstep. Because when I tried to tell Reg he wouldn't believe me.'

'Why?'

'You tell me?' Jason shrugged. 'Maybe he's into the same thing. Maybe he was just so desperate to get the money out of that vile, disgusting alleged producer, Mr Appenzell, that he was willing to throw his conscience to the wind.'

'You're going off the subject, Jason.'

'No, I'm not. But we have to challenge Stan.'

'Challenge?'

'I need to see his reaction when I accuse him.'

'Accuse him of what, Jason? The bank thefts?'

Jason's knuckles showed white on his fists. He bashed one fist into his palm, and growled. Suzy took a step back. His intensity scared her.

'What is Stan supposed to have done, Jason?'

Jason put his face into his hands and sobbed.

'No "supposed" about it. Stan Arbuthnot,' he cried, '… is … is … a paedophile.'

*

After tea Amanda returned to her cabin to find a note under her door asking her to go as soon as possible to the purser's office. There she was handed a message from her son, asking for the code to get into her lock-up in Aardvark Storage. She looked at the time on the message and tried to work out how long ago it was sent. Might he still be there? Could she get a reply to him? If only texting worked from mid-Atlantic.

There was only one solution: she asked whether it was ever possible to make a phone call to the UK?

The steward behind the desk slid her a paper with a list of charges. Ship-to-shore satellite call $12 per minute.

What else could she do? She was taken behind the counter into a back office where she phoned Mark, who was sitting in the empty removal lorry, heading away from the storage facility. She gave him the number and, when he wanted to elongate the call with a string of abuse about the solicitors and the storage firm, she put her finger on the red button to cut the call. Why pay $12 a minute to listen to a tirade?

After this Amanda arrived late at the theatre for the magic show but her pals had managed to get there early enough to secure very good seats and they had saved one for her.

As she sank down into the red plush, she sighed with relief. What a day!

Tyger, Liliane and Myriam chatted eagerly about their own days onboard. Tyger had gone to an art class in the basement, while Liliane and Myriam braved the open decks to try their hands at shuffleboard.

'We found two ancient old geezers up there,' puffed Myriam. 'We tempted them into a game and fleeced them.'

'A pity we didn't 'ave money on the game,' said Liliane. '*Les pauvres!* Zey didn't 'ave a chance against us women.'

'We asked the old blighters to join us for tea, but, don't you know, they were so tired or doggone ashamed at being beat by us, that they turned us down.'

'When we were young we all played ze silly game of losing to men. Now not so much. Zey simply cannot adjust.'

Amanda laughed.

'What is it with men these days? No stamina.' Myriam let out a dramatic sigh. '*L'amour, l'amour!* It's not how it used to be in my younger day.' She turned towards Amanda, lowered her brow and pursed her lips. 'What is your secret to catching a man, Amanda? Your companion at tea was very illegible.'

Mercifully, at that moment, the house lights dimmed.

A ripple of excitement passed across the audience as a tight spotlight created a bright circle on the red velvet curtains.

Arturo the Luminoso stepped out on to the stage. His hair was slicked back, his features calm. He was dressed in immaculate white tie and tails with brightly polished patent shoes.

As he walked forward cards kept appearing from his clothing, from his sleeves and jacket pocket; he stooped to pull more which seemed to drop from the tails of his jacket.

Arturo made a very comical sight as he tried to catch all the cards, throwing some into the air so that he could grab each new batch which kept leaping from his clothing.

When the deluge of cards came to an end, and the whole black shiny stage was littered with them, Arturo stood still in the centre of the space, shrugged and said, 'So now you know why I don't work with cards!'

He looked suddenly shocked. His jaw dropped, his mouth opened, revealing an egg. He pulled this from his lips, as another instantly appeared. Three more eggs seemed to pop through his fingers. Egg after egg, until he had an armful.

'Eggs too can be a problem!'

He shuffled to the back of the stage. The curtains opened and he went through just as a huge brightly coloured box was wheeled on.

Holding a small leather lead which was attached to the box's side, Arturo strolled back into the main stage area.

'Here, boxy, boxy. Walkies!' he called, in a voice usually reserved for addressing dogs. 'And sit!'

The box came to a halt.

'Anyone here want to divide and rule?'

The audience was silent.

'I only want to chop you up into two. You don't mind, do you?'

He surveyed the rows of seats.

A few people put their hands up. Amanda turned to see that Myriam was one of them.

Arturo walked to the other side of the stage, then turned back, his finger pointing towards Amanda.

'Our dance was sadly interrupted. Would you like to waltz into the box and disappear?'

Amanda shook her head violently. She did not want to do anything onstage. In fact she felt very disturbed that a spotlight was illuminating her in her seat in the auditorium.

Arturo tilted his head.

'Your friend, perhaps?'

Amanda turned to Myriam, who was leaning out of her seat, desperate to be picked. But Arturo's finger was pointing to her other side, towards Liliane, who was making little finger gestures indicating no.

Arturo came to the corner of the stage, bent low in front of her and a large bouquet of flowers appeared in his hand.

'Madame, please do me the pleasure.' He smiled at Amanda and Myriam. 'I promise you I will bring your friend back to you in one piece.'

Blushing, Liliane stood up, took Arturo's hand and followed him on to the stage.

'Darn it,' sighed Myriam. 'I really wanted to try that.'

As she came on to the stage, Liliane winced back towards her friends.

'She can mug all she wants.' Myriam shrugged. 'It should have been me!'

'Ladies and gentlemen, lords and ladies,' said Arturo. 'I would like to introduce you to …?' He looked towards Liliane. 'Good lord, here I am about to make you vanish, and I don't even know your name. However would I call you back?'

He turned to the box and opened it up.

'A perfectly ordinary coffin – I'm sorry – I mean box. Though perhaps a little garish for some people's taste. But I am Italian, what care I for the taupe and beige of northern Europe style magazines. I am from the land of colour, heat and light. *Viva rosso, viva verdi, viva giallo, viva d'oro!*'

As Amanda watched she found it hard to equate this confident showman with the quivering wreck of a man who had dropped before her on the dance floor last night, waving his rabbit's foot. Maybe he was one of those people you read about who only really come to life when onstage.

Arturo guided Liliane up some steps.

'Now you have to go up into the box. It's not hard. Even a zombie could do it.'

Liliane pulled another grimace and the audience laughed.

'Have a little peek around. Comfy, eh?' As Liliane stood in the box, Arturo swirled it round. The whole equipment was clearly on castors, but by turning it a full circle everyone in the audience could see that there was no secret way out of the back.

'Pardon me, Signora. I have now to lock you inside. You do not suffer from claustrophobia, I hope?'

Liliane winced again, and shook her head.

With a sweeping gesture, Arturo closed the doors. He then strode across the stage and took a walking stick from someone sitting in the front row, with the quip: 'Don't worry, you'll get it back before the end.'

He used the stick to bar the front of the box, then pulled both knobs to demonstrate that the door could not be opened.

Again he swirled the box.

Then he reached into a large trunk and pulled out a sledge-hammer. He made much of lumbering over the stage, finding it too hard to carry in one hand.

'I am not a strong man,' he said, as he tied the sledgehammer to a chain. 'I usually exploit my brains rather than my brawn.' He turned back to the box. 'Are you all right in there, Signora?'

Liliane's voice, faint and muffled, said, 'Yes.'

'Good,' said Arturo, turning to the audience. 'And now I am going to do another trick in which I get the sledgehammer to transform itself into a feather duster.

Liliane could be heard inside the box crying, 'Please let me out now.'

Arturo pulled a magic wand from his pocket, and waved it in the direction of the box. 'Madame! You will now fall asleep and remember nothing.' He swirled the wand in the air, but meanwhile more magic wands kept on coming, multiplying and multiplying, wands seemingly appearing between his fingers, from his jacket, down his sleeves, until Arturo was grasping a whole armful of wands which spilled over on to the stage. He threw them all upwards and they rained down over the ground around him. Arturo now tried to walk forward but slipped and slithered on the treacherous bed of wands beneath his feet. He staggered backwards, and jerked forward, in the midst of which, as he landed flat on his backside, he somehow dislodged the sledgehammer.

From his seated position, Arturo's face registered shock. He tried to scramble to his feet, but remained like a cartoon character, his legs paddling, while he slid back and forth, all the while crying out, 'Watch out, Signora! *Attenzione!* Duck!'

But it was too late. The sledgehammer swung to the other side of the stage. It crashed into the proscenium arch, and, out of control, having picked up speed, it was heading directly for the coloured box.

Arturo was on his feet now, staggering and sliding on the slippery floor of wands, grabbing out to catch the swinging hammer.

Amanda found her mind racing.

Something had gone terribly wrong.

As the hammer hit, slamming into the side of the box with enormous force, the audience gasped.

The coloured box shattered and littered the stage with many shards of painted wood.

A woman behind Amanda actually screamed.

Amanda knew that Liliane had to be hurt. What would happen next? How could they get the poor woman to hospital? Were there enough medical staff onboard to deal with a catastrophe like this? Was there an operating theatre?

'It's never done that before!' said Arturo, his voice quite a few tones higher than it had been at the start of the act. He ran up the steps to where the box had once stood. He knelt on the floor and scraped around in the remains murmuring, 'Signora? Signora?'

Amanda couldn't breathe. The audience around her were now silent, leaning forward. No one dared blink.

The terrified silence was shattered by a loud snoring noise, coming from one of the audience seats, stage right.

Arturo jumped to his feet and ran to the side of the stage.

He stood at the edge of the platform, looking down, his hands on his hips.

'Now, Signora! Could you tell me how the devil you got there and, more importantly, how could you fall asleep during my act?'

A spotlight swung round, revealing Liliane, curled up in the featured seat, sleeping like a baby.

Arturo clicked his fingers and Liliane opened her eyes and stretched.

Amanda realised that she had been holding her breath for over a minute. She inhaled deeply and sat back in her chair as Liliane smiled and yawned, like a kitten waking from an afternoon nap.

13

WHEN JASON HAD gone off to work for the night, heading first to the head ghost to excuse his absence at the tea dance due to a blinding migraine, Suzy tried to digest everything he had told her. She was in shock.

Jason had made some startling revelations.

From what she knew of the characters involved, everything did add up. It could possibly be that everything he had said was some grand guignol creation, but her instincts told her not.

If the tale Jason had just told her was true, it was apocalyptic news.

Before making any decisions about how to take it further, Suzy decided to run the whole thing through in her head once more, looking for gaps in logic or practical reasons why the story Jason had told her might not be the truth.

She pulled off her shoes and sat at her desk.

According to Jason, their Zurich producer Herr Appenzell had asked Reg to bring the youngest boy he could lay his hands on to party in his private flat. Reg had commanded Jason to attend. Suzy had been there at the fondue house when the call came through.

For the sake of the whole acting company, the producer must be buttered up and cajoled, Reg had told Jason, because, as yet, the man hadn't coughed up any money at all, and until he did, no one would be paid.

Hearing this news about the unpaid fees had set alarm bells off with Jason. He knew that, back home, producers were obliged to deposit the wages money up front, even before rehearsals started. But he also knew that, when you worked on the fringes of the theatre, anything might be considered acceptable, including actors being expected to work for nothing. Usually when that happened, the lack of cash was put out in the open and agreed to by the actors beforehand.

In the case of *The Importance of Being Earnest* everyone had signed a contract which included being paid a full Equity wage, plus expenses. The plane tickets to and from Zurich would be provided by the management.

Like everyone else in the fondue house, Jason had not yet received his rehearsal pay, so his antennae were up.

What Reg told him did not sound good for *The Importance* company.

But if Reg thought Jason's presence at some silly party might save the day, naturally he would go.

Suzy herself had persuaded him to go.

Jason knew he had the gift of the gab, along with a great talent for flattery and being charming. So, of course, he believed that he could win the day. He did have an idea exactly what Reg had had him lined up for, but he believed that he could wiggle out of that, stay on for a drink or two and leave, and, by so doing, he would oblige Reg and hopefully help save the company from being cheated of their pay.

Still working through Jason's tale, Suzy moved over to lie on the bed. She glanced at her watch and realised it was now too late for her to take her place for formal dinner. She had spent hours going back over everything Jason had said this afternoon, rolling it around in her head, wondering what to do next.

Back in Zurich, Jason had arrived at the producer's party at around 10 p.m. The room was dimly lit. A few unattractive older men sat expectantly on leather sofas. Stan was one of them.

But when Jason had walked in, the guests seemed rather disappointed to see him.

From the look of the assembled company Jason had presumed that this was one of those meetings where people who put up money for a show were given a free drink and a chance to meet a few of the actors. At this point it didn't seem odd to him that there were no women present.

Jason accepted a glass of wine.

When no one seemed interested in talking to him, Jason had got bored. He decided to wait until Reg arrived then he would cut and run.

He wandered out on to the balcony and stood alone in the dark, admiring the lovely view over the lake, with its twinkling lights, small boats and ruffled wavelets. It was cold and the wind numbed him, so he didn't stay out there for long.

When he came back inside the atmosphere in the room had totally changed. There was a buzz of excitement. The men were standing now, chattering enthusiastically.

As he came further inside he saw that some other people had arrived. Standing nervously in the centre of the men were two teenage boys.

Jason instantly recognised one of the boys as April McNaughten's sixteen-year-old son, Declan. Declan's mother had been Jason's own friend and guardian when he was ten, filming *The Dangerous Season*.

Jason managed to get near enough to Declan to chat with him, asking him how his mother was doing.

'Hands off,' said one of the men. 'That one is marked for me.'

Jason didn't understand what was happening, but when he looked around, the other boy was out of sight. Then he saw that Declan's friend was chatting with Stan; he watched as Stan led him into another room. The door closed.

Jason asked Declan if the other boy knew Stan well. Declan shook his head. 'We've never seen him before in our lives. Isn't he one of the producers? Auditioning for this big shoot in Zurich?'

'No. He's an actor, working here with me on *The Importance*.'

'Are you trying to get into the movie too?'

'What movie?' Jason wondered whether there was going to be a screening.

'They're casting a huge movie. And all the producers are here tonight.'

Jason surveyed the room. One thing was certain. These men had nothing to do with the movie industry.

'How did you get here?' Jason asked.

'We're both in Zurich touring in *King and I*. We're playing the King of Siam's children,' said Declan. 'Well, two of them.'

'I mean here, to this event, tonight?'

'Oh. There was this man in the foyer of the hotel who told us if we came here with him there was a big movie going on which was looking for young actors. Are you up for it too?'

'Is that man here?'

'No. He was at our hotel. In the foyer.' The boy shrugged. 'He said he was working for my mum.'

'And your mum was with you?' Jason asked.

Declan said that his mother was in her hotel room rehearsing with the actor playing the King of Siam, and that he and Tim had grown bored watching TV and slipped out of their room to wander around in the hotel. They'd gone up to the roof bar but were chucked out for being underage, then they'd knocked on April's door and said they were going out to explore Zurich.

'She told us not to be long or wander too far,' said Declan. 'When we got down to the foyer this man was waiting by the lifts. He asked if we were part of *King and I*, and when we said yes he asked us if we wanted to be seen for this big movie which is shooting here.' Declan shifted from foot to foot. 'And he said he would give us a lift in his new sports car. I told him

209

I'd better tell my mum, and he said she already knew all about it.'

'He'd got permission from your mum?'

'He said she'd sent him to find us.' Declan looked at his feet. 'The man said it was Mum's idea. She's a movie star herself.'

Jason thought about this for a moment or two. He wondered if this really could be some odd kind of casting session. He'd done quite a few interviews in hotel rooms himself. Perhaps *The Importance* producer really was involved in a forthcoming movie. If so, Jason wanted to be seen. Maybe that was why they'd specifically asked for him to be here, after all. He had to make some enquiries.

'Don't go anywhere …' Jason strode across to Appenzell and asked him outright if he was producing a movie.

Appenzell leaned in and, smirking, whispered to Jason, 'It's a line which obviously worked to get them here! These tender peaches are not usually so easy to persuade.'

With a frisson of horror, Jason realised the truth of the situation. There was no movie. There was no casting. He suppressed his urge to tell Appenzell what he thought of him there and then. But the most important thing was to remove the two boys from the apartment as quickly as possible. So he smiled at Appenzell and walked calmly back to Declan.

'How old is Tim? Same age as you?'

Declan shook his head. 'Fifteen. But he pretends to be sixteen.'

'That's it. We're going.' Every warning light was now flagged up for Jason. 'Whatever happens, Declan, stay with me. I am serious. Do not leave my side,' he said, marching towards the door through which Stan had vanished with Tim.

He hammered on the door, calling Tim's name, instructing him to open up, now.

Appenzell crept up behind Jason and hissed in his ear, telling him not to be so greedy. There would be other 'tasty morsels', he said; boys even younger would be arriving soon.

Jason turned around and punched Appenzell in the face. Appenzell staggered backwards cupping his nose, just as the key turned and the bedroom door opened up.

Tim stood there, bewildered.

'Is the screen test over now?' he said. 'It's not a porno film, is it?'

Jason looked past him and saw that Stan had his trousers down round his ankles. Not being able to move his feet, together with the piles of exposed flab, prevented Stan from holding on to Tim or stopping him reaching the door.

'We're going, Tim. Now!' Jason grabbed Tim by the hand and steered him back into the main room, leaving Stan, underpants caught round his knees, squeaking like a fat, purple pig.

Despite the outraged attempts of Appenzell to snatch at them, Jason and the two boys ran down the stairs and out to the street, where they bumped into Reg, standing on the doorstep, ringing the bell.

Reg didn't believe what Jason told him was going on upstairs in Appenzell's apartment, and told him to go back up there and 'do his bit' for the company. 'They're sixteen, aren't they?' he asked. 'Age of consent.'

'No,' said Jason sharply. 'Tim is fifteen. And they've been brought here under false pretences.'

'Everyone's pay depends on this,' Reg reminded him. But when Reg added the trite phrase 'After all, boys will be boys', Jason saw red, and he hit Reg too, shoved him to the ground, strode into the middle of the road, hailed a taxi and took both boys back to April McNaughten's hotel.

Declan led Jason to April's room. At first delighted to see him, April was horrified when he told her how he had come upon Declan and Tim.

Jason had told her that he wanted to phone the police there and then, but April stated firmly that she would not have her own name or her child's dragged through police stations, or law courts, and would not let either of them endure the ensuing garish publicity. If that happened, she explained to Jason, Declan and Tim would live their whole lives being 'the kids who escaped from the Swiss paedophile's party'. She swore Jason to secrecy, for the children's sake. She reminded Jason that, when he had been assaulted by the actor playing the jolly innkeeper in *The Dangerous Season*, she had done the same thing with him, otherwise he would unfortunately be well-known only as the kid who had been molested by a now-reviled national treasure (a man incidentally currently serving time in Stafford Prison).

Suzy thought back to the innkeeper in *The Dangerous Season*. Wasn't it always the same? The nasty-looking actors playing Nazis were not the problem. The vile man who had tried fiddling with Jason was a sweet-looking, tubby and beloved comedian. A family favourite. Everyone's much-loved uncle.

Stan too gave the impression from afar of being a cuddly Friar Tuck figure. Suzy had seen him often on TV before meeting him, and he'd always come over as very jolly and utterly benign. Working with the man uncovered an alarmingly different side.

What a clever game Appenzell had played, Suzy realised. By becoming the producer of their tiny show for the Zurich Regal International Theatre, he got himself a certain credence. The theatre's name was so much grander than its reality, but by adding a classic play and a British company into the mix, he had scored a bingo. And, once he saw the posters up for *The King and I*, which were all over Zurich, Herr Appenzell would also have known that, in whichever hotel the company was staying, there would be children galore.

Suzy let her mind run back through the next events of Jason's night, while she was sleeping not so peacefully at the Zurich digs, dreaming of garden gnomes in boaters.

After he left April's hotel room, and despite her warning, Jason determined that he could not let the matter rest. So, before he went out of the hotel, giving scanty details, and not mentioning either his own name or the names of the children, Jason used the public phone in the foyer to make his anonymous call to the Zurich police. He gave the names of both Appenzell and Stan Arbuthnot, along with the address of the apartment. Jason told Suzy he had felt relieved to be taking action against the perpetrators. Something which he had been unable to do himself at the time with the jolly innkeeper.

As he walked out on to the street, Jason's phone rang. It was Reg, yelling at him, saying that Appenzell had not let him into the party, and, through the Entryphone, had informed him that never again would he mess with the theatre or theatre people and that Reg could say goodbye to his money and the show.

When Jason had tried to end the call, saying, 'See you tomorrow,' Reg had replied, 'Oh no you won't. The show's off. You're all going home. And I won't hesitate to let the others know that you're to blame.'

Jason had tried to emphasise to Reg what exactly had been going on in that flat. But Reg did not listen. He just continued shouting obscenities down the line, then hung up.

Walking back to his digs, well after midnight, Jason took a detour via Appenzell's apartment. He could see a light on inside the flat. And the shadows of two men, cast up on to the ceiling.

But there was no sign of the police.

Muffling his coat around him, Jason waited outside, sheltering under the canopy of a news-stand across the road, hoping that somebody would soon rally to his anonymous call and come here and catch Appenzell.

In the quiet between the noise from streams of traffic, held back at the lights further along the road, then all at once released, Jason could hear something which sounded like a row going on inside the flat. 'No! No! I will not leave!' He recognised Stan's high-pitched whine. 'You promised me, Herr Appenzell! I will not leave until you give me what you promised.'

Further talking, a low murmur which Jason knew must be Appenzell, though he couldn't make out what was said.

'I do not want my money back,' shrieked Stan. 'I paid in good faith. I will stay here and scream until I am satisfied.'

And then Stan let forth his siren call.

It was while Stan was in full vocal flight that a solitary police car pulled up. Two policemen got out and rang Appenzell's bell. The squealing got louder, then faded and stopped. A light went off in the apartment. A door slammed.

After a few minutes, a sleepy voice came on to the speaker-phone. Appenzell himself! A buzzer admitted the policemen.

Heart thundering, Jason waited in the shadow of the news-stand, never taking his eyes from the balcony and the windows of Appenzell's flat.

Two minutes later, the police came out again, got into their car and drove away.

And that was it.

Jason couldn't believe it. He wanted to run after the car and insist on accompanying them back inside.

He looked up at the flat and watched as Appenzell sauntered out on to the balcony. He was in a dressing gown and pyjamas. He stood there, in the dark of the night, watching the lights of the police car disappear along the road. He lit a cigarette, the flare from the match illuminating his face. It was definitely him. Cool, sophisticated, suave and sickeningly immaculate.

Taking a long drag on the cigarette, Appenzell turned and looked down at the dark place in the shadows where Jason stood.

It seemed as though Appenzell was staring straight at him, man to man, eye to eye.

Appenzell went on glaring until Jason could take no more. He flicked his collar up, quickly turned and strode away. He had felt so scared by Appenzell's fiery gaze that he decided not to go back to his digs that night, and instead to walk the streets till morning.

He spent some time pacing around the railway station. Just before dawn he made another anonymous call to the police, once more giving Appenzell's name and address, and saying that the man was a producer at the Zurich Regal International Theatre, and using that job title as a pretence to lure young boys.

Suzy remembered the rest – the lock-out at the theatre, the Swiss police arriving and enquiring of Appenzell, the phone calls, the airport, the journey to Genoa and boarding this ship.

If Jason's story was true, it would explain why he really needed to see Stan. At the same time, Stan would have every reason not to want to see Jason here, aboard the *Blue Mermaid*.

Suzy sat up.

She had to find Stan. Now. She had to get to Stan before Jason found him. Hear what Stan had to say about that party. Only then could she piece together the truth.

She pulled on her shoes and left the cabin.

Jason, she knew, was now busy whirling women round in the ballroom. He'd be at work until midnight or one in the morning. In the theatre, the big magic show was on. The dining rooms were full of people finishing their desserts; others might be in the bars or the casino.

As a result, the corridors of the ship were rather quiet.

Suzy would use the rest of the evening to conduct the search. She had no idea where to start – perhaps ask Melanie, though she doubted a social hostess would hand out such information – but somehow or other she would find Stan Arbuthnot.

And, when she had the man before her, she would sit him down and talk about Zurich, that party, and Mr Appenzell.

She would grill Stan, and, however much she instinctively disliked the man, get *his* side of the story.

*

After the magic show had ended, Amanda went with Myriam and Liliane to a cosy bar at the front of the ship and ordered a bottle of wine to share.

'You're so brave, Liliane.' Amanda sank back into her bucket chair. 'I could never offer myself up to something like that. Were you scared?'

'I thought you were a goner, Liliane. We all did. You should have felt my heart when that horrible big hammer hit the box,' laughed Myriam, whipping a fan from her handbag and flapping it. 'I was absolutely putrified!'

'But what did *you* feel, Liliane?' asked Amanda. 'Was it claustrophobic? Do you remember anything?'

'No.' Liliane shrugged her shoulders, then picked up her glass of wine. 'I got into ze box, next thing I woke up with ze audience laughing at me. It was rather disconcerting.' She waved her hand at a passing waiter. 'Pardon me, but could we 'ave some chips, olives or nuts, please?'

'What is this bar called?' asked Myriam. 'I've never been in here before, but it's lovely.'

'It's the Seahorse Lounge,' replied Amanda. 'Look, the name's on the drinks mats.'

'So, *this* is the place that dreadful woman has all her parties.'

'Which woman?' asked Amanda.

'You know, that awful Dorothy. Haven't you seen it in tomorrow's *Daily Programme* again? "Seahorse Lounge, 4.30 p.m., port side reserved for friends of Dorothy". As usual. So far it's been every single day.' Myriam clapped her hands on her knees and gave an exasperated splutter. 'That *damned* Dorothy. I can't bear that she has all these parties and doesn't invite *me*.'

Amanda said nothing.

'Anyway,' continued Myriam, '*whoever* she is, this Dorothy woman must be very rich. And I've been wondering how come she managed to get onboard at the same time as so many of her swanky friends? Did she buy them all a cabin so that they could spend every afternoon here in the Seahorse Lounge, partying like it was 1969?'

Amanda had seen the announcements for the meetings of 'Friends of Dorothy' and knew that Myriam had got quite the wrong end of the stick.

She was about to explain what the phrase 'Friends of Dorothy' actually meant, when she was interrupted.

'Ladies! Might I offer you a bottle of champagne?' Karl stood before them. 'I was sitting over in the corner when I noticed you here.'

'Oh, my word!' fluttered Myriam. 'Very grateful, I'm sure. I do love a glass of sparklers, deary. Amanda, darling, pull out the chaise lonzh for your friend.'

'I don't want to intrude, Mesdames, but your party seemed to radiate happiness. And I was feeling rather lonely in my solitary side seat.'

As Amanda adjusted a chair at the table next to theirs, turning it to join their circle, she noticed that Liliane shuffled her own chair back. It didn't seem to be so much a move to enable Karl to sit with them, rather an attempt to distance herself from him.

'Have you all had an interesting day?'

'You betcha!' Myriam rolled her eyes. 'We went to the magic show and the magician made Liliane vanish.'

'She appears to be here with us now,' said Karl with a saucy wink.

'We were all pretty scared,' said Amanda. 'It looked as though everything onstage was going wrong but it turns out that that is Arturo's act. Very convincing it was too.'

'Liliane was hypnotised! How about that!' Myriam leaned forward and adjusted her necklace. 'I've always wanted to be hypnotised.'

Karl turned towards Amanda. 'And did you sort out the problems about your flat in Pimlico, Amanda? Is your son settling in well?'

'Oh, Amanda, deary, moving to a new house is simply the end!' Myriam threw a hand out in an expression of exasperation. 'Don't they say that it's up there with all those stress-filled things you shouldn't do if you want to live a long life, like going out to work or marrying a poverty-stricken buffoon.' Myriam chortled and was about to carry on when the waiter arrived with a tray of snacks, an ice bucket, four glasses and a bottle of champagne. 'Lucky the hooch and canopies arrived,' she said as he laid everything out on the small circular table. 'I was about to start a long tedious antidote about the last millionaire I married! Saved by the bottle, eh!'

The waiter popped the cork.

Myriam sighed. 'I adore that smoke which comes out of the top, don't you?'

'It isn't smoke, actually,' said Karl, matter of fact. 'It's the condensation of water and ethanol vapour as the carbon-dioxide molecules expand with the dropping temperature.'

'Oh my, listen to that, dearies. He's swallowed a Lexington!'

'Are you a scientist?' asked Amanda, surprised at Karl's detailed reply.

Karl shook his head. 'I'm afraid not. I'm in computer finance.'

'Online banking?' Amanda nodded to the waiter as he filled her glass.

'That kind of thing.' Karl raised his glass. 'Now I think it's time for a toast.'

As the women clinked glasses, the ship lurched. Behind the bar, bottles shook and glasses rattled. At a nearby table a wine glass fell to the floor and shattered.

'What was that?' Amanda panicked. 'Did we hit something?'

'It felt like a large wave,' said Liliane. 'According to ze charts, tonight we are heading into quite a storm.'

Amanda was intrigued. 'Where are these charts? I'd love to see them.'

'On the landing, Staircase 3, right at the top, by the lifts. Deck 11 or 12. There is a little model of the ship which gets moved every day. But if it was to scale, the ship would be the size of Sicily.'

'It almost is,' laughed Myriam.

'Are we halfway across yet?' Amanda asked.

'Please, Amanda!' Still fiddling with her necklace with one hand, Myriam fluttered her fan with the other. 'Don't wish away our hours onboard, deary. Not when we're all having such a lovely time.'

'I'm just interested, Myriam,' said Amanda. 'And don't worry, I'm really loving being here on the *Blue Mermaid*. It's the familial storm which is happening at home that's the problem.' She nodded to Liliane, indicating that she must continue.

Liliane explained: 'Tomorrow we will get to a point where we will be slightly nearer ze American mainland than ze European one.' She speared an olive on a cocktail stick and popped it into her mouth. 'Halfway ship, so to speak. But the isobars are tightly packed, indicating some strong winds, and therefore high seas.'

The ship swayed again, and some champagne spilled over the lip of Amanda's glass.

'Is that usual?' She could feel herself panicking, especially after Liliane's information that in a few hours the ship would be the furthest from land of the whole voyage.

Liliane put out a pacifying hand. 'It feels worse because we are at ze bow of the ship, and on the highest deck. Here, every sensation will be multiplied. Zat's why I love zis bar. In the daytime, you can see for twenty or more miles. It's quite wonderful.'

Amanda saw that while she was talking to Liliane, Karl had edged his chair even nearer to Myriam and was now practically tête-à-tête with her. Myriam had her hand on her décolletage and was fluttering her eyelashes; Karl was smiling, and leaning in towards her.

Amanda realised, with another pang, that the sight made her feel rather jealous.

How absurd! First envious of people with the young dancing boy, and now Karl.

She'd only met the man for a few hours.

She reminded herself, she was not onboard the *Love Boat*.

*

Suzy started with the obvious routes. She went to the entertainment office, looking for Melanie intending to ask her straight for Stan's cabin number, but Melanie was not there. One of the entertainment team, just back in from hosting a pub quiz, explained that Melanie was on duty, dining at the Captain's table tonight, and wouldn't really be free till around midnight.

On the off-chance, Suzy asked the quiz host if he could tell her the cabin number of Stan Arbuthnot. He shook his head vigorously. 'Not allowed to give stuff like that out, I'm afraid. Do you know him?'

'Melanie was talking about him …' She could see that this was going nowhere, so she decided to lie. 'And er … He was at one of my classes. I was going to leave him a book.'

The quizmaster grinned. 'Simple. Just leave the book with me, and I'll make sure it gets to him.'

Suzy winced. Caught out!

'I didn't bring it down tonight. Didn't want to lug it around, just in case.'

She edged back towards the door.

'No worries,' said the quizmaster. 'Just drop it in and Melanie will get it to him tomorrow.'

Next Suzy went to the purser's office. Again she came up with a fudged story about wanting to talk to Stan Arbuthnot about the class tomorrow.

'If you write a note, I could make sure it gets to his cabin,' replied a tart little girl behind the counter, who was eyeing the long queue behind Suzy.

Suzy faffed a response. 'Not a problem,' she said. 'It can wait till morning, when my class resumes.'

The girl gave a smug laugh. 'I really doubt that. Don't you feel the ship? We're in for a bit of a rocky night. These people behind you will all be queuing to find out where to go to get the patch.'

'What's the patch?'

'Anti-seasick patch. You fix it behind your ear. Do you want the form?'

The girl held out a piece of paper headed *Dealing With Seasickness*. Suzy took it and moved away.

A Dixieland jazz band in the central lobby was playing a jaunty tune, and Suzy marched along to the rhythm. Where could she try next? She sat down for a moment, listening to the music, and toyed with staying here and waiting until Stan walked past. He must pass through the lobby eventually, at some point in the voyage – everyone came here on their way to the lifts or the dining rooms, or the ballroom or the cinema. Suzy settled back into the sofa.

But then, what if this Stan Arbuthnot wasn't their Stan but someone else of the same name?

She would be sitting here for nothing.

No.

This would not do.

The only way was to find the number of the cabin where Stan Arbuthnot slept, and stalk him from there until there was a suitable moment to challenge him.

Where else must it be possible to find room numbers? Whoever took cabin numbers after you first checked in? Suzy couldn't remember once having had to give her number.

She pulled a copy of the *Daily Programme* from the nearby table and flicked through the glossy pages. There was nothing, no activity she could see where giving out your room number was called for.

She threw the *Programme* on to the table and sat back, closing her eyes. She was getting nowhere.

Perhaps she should give up for now, and start again fresh in the morning.

Her stomach rumbled loudly. She realised she hadn't eaten since her early lunch and had to find some food.

She took a lift up to the cafeteria.

The usual late-night scene: dancers up from the ballroom, their smart attire now slightly awry; men with collars unbuttoned and bow ties askew, women with lipstick smudged or mere outlines remaining. Everyone bustled around the buffet, many of them grabbing a quick supper snack before heading back for more dancing at the late disco; others, exhausted from their evening spent waltzing and foxtrotting, grabbing a hot drink and a biscuit before heading for bed.

In the dark corners of the 'canteen' she could see some crew members huddled round a table, tucking into supper.

The ship was rolling quite heavily. People bearing trays were putting in fancy footwork as they zigzagged across the floor, trying to keep their hot drinks from spilling. As everyone had to counterbalance the same waves, they moved in similar directions at precisely the same moment. It looked like a segment from an avant-garde ballet.

Suzy served herself a fried egg, some baked beans and chips. Then she went to the hot-water urn and made herself a cup of strong tea.

She too moved to where it was darker and sat at an empty table and tucked in.

Halfway through her meal she wished she had stopped off at the bar and got herself a glass of wine to go with her snack. That was the downside of eating at the café. No alcohol.

She toyed with asking someone to keep an eye on her tray while she either dashed downstairs to the pub or nipped into the lift and went up to the Seahorse Lounge to grab a glass. Given the sway of the ship she realised it would be quite humorous trying to get it back here in one piece.

Then it struck her.

When you bought an alcoholic drink you *did* have to give your cabin number. It was the only time anyone ever asked for it, because drinks were the one thing for which you were charged. You signed a piece of paper and wrote down your number! Somewhere there must be a stack of small pieces of paper with Stan's signature and cabin number on them.

But that was only if he'd had a drink in a bar. And there were quite a few bars onboard. And they had been at sea for almost three days since Stan had apparently boarded. No doubt the bar bills would all be taken from their spikes regularly throughout the day and totted up in the hidden depths of the secure area of the finance offices behind the purser's office.

Suzy realised she was back to square one.

All this talk of drink had brought on a craving for a long gin and tonic, so, once she had eaten, she went up to the Seahorse Lounge, found an empty seat and ordered one. She kept her eyes scanning the people, looking for a fat, balding man with a purple complexion, probably bellowing tiresome theatrical stories, studded with outrageous name-dropping, to a small party of gullible fans. But no one in this bar came near the description of Stan.

When a very large wave rocked the ship everyone sitting around her let out a little gasp.

The storm they'd all been warned about had arrived.

Suzy had been so determined to find Stan, but sitting here she realised, short of plying Melanie with drink and subjecting her to the third degree, there was no way she could extract his cabin number from her. If she left a note, she would only prewarn him by letting him know she was onboard and give him time to prepare a story.

Mind you, if Stan read his *Daily Programme* he would soon know she was here. Her photo was in the latest edition.

A group of people asked if she minded them sitting at her table. They then proceeded to discuss Oscar Wilde with her, talking about productions and films they had seen, both filmed versions of his plays and biopics about his life and trial.

She knew that while she was in a public place she could not concentrate on finding Stan. So, after about a quarter of an hour, she finished her drink and, excusing herself, made her way back along the gangways and down the stairs to her cabin.

She chose the staircase nearest to the bar she had been in, at the bow of the ship. This was a mistake. With the rising and falling of the sea, the stairs seemed to fall away beneath your feet, then smash upwards, catching your feet mid-air. It reminded Suzy of a job, years ago, when she had played *Peter Pan*, and had to spend the whole show swinging about on wires high above the stage. Going down these stairs was just like theatrical flying. There were times during the perilous descent when she thought she must look like a cartoon character, paddling her feet in space while waiting for the ground to come up to meet them.

Once safely on her own deck, without having broken any bones, she turned into the entertainment quarters, passing Ong, her steward, who was squeezed into a corner, piling a trolley high with toiletries for the cabins.

'Good evening, Miss Marshall.'

'Good evening, Ong. Heading for bed now?'

'Getting things organised first.' The steward indicated the trolley. 'Tomorrow will be hard day. Many people sick.'

Suzy winced.

'Do you need a patch?'

'I've got a form, but I think I've got sea legs,' she said to Ong, crossing her fingers. 'Like you must have.' She put her keycard into the lock. 'Goodnight, Ong. Sleep well.'

'Goodnight, Miss Marshall.'

As Suzy pushed her door open she marvelled at how these stewards knew your name even though they usually only came into your cabin when you weren't there.

She went inside and threw her bag down on to the bed.

She was about to turn on the little TV, when it hit her.

Stan Arbuthnot must have a steward of his own. That steward would know both his name and his cabin number.

She grabbed her keycard and left the cabin. The trolley was all ready for the morning, stacked and secured, but Ong was gone.

She ran to the landing and saw him heading down the stairs. She clung to the rail and leaped down after him, calling his name.

After giving him a cock-and-bull tale about wanting to be able to present a surprise gift to a friend who didn't know she was aboard, she asked if maybe any of his steward friends knew a Mr Stanley Arbuthnot. And, if so, might she be able to talk to him? It was Mr Arbuthnot's steward, she pointed out, that she wished to speak to, not Mr Arbuthnot himself.

Ong gave her a bright smile and said he'd do what he could, then with a cheery wave he headed off downwards in the direction of the lower decks, the Digbeth Road and crew quarters.

Climbing back up the staircase was exhausting. Suzy felt as though her legs were made of lead, every step a mountain which suddenly pressed down like one of those machines in a gym.

She turned into the entertainment quarters.

Any minute now Jason would be heading back.

14

A MANDA FELT LIKE death.
She was up most of the night hanging over the toilet. Seasickness, she discovered, was relentless.

For several hours she lay on the bed in the darkness, wondering if this state of affairs would last all the way to New York. She hated the creaking noises as the ship rolled from side to side, which seemed to punctuate the waves of nausea which swept over her.

In her few lucid moments, she could hear the wind roaring past her balcony. She remembered some old saw she had been told in her youth: the secret method of combating seasickness was to keep your eyes on the horizon. This was all very well, but how did you do that on a pitch-black moonless night when there was no horizon to be seen?

She prayed for dawn, wishing with all her heart that she was back on solid ground. Even that lovely cosy dormitory in London, where the worst thing happening was the sound of seven other people snoring, would be preferable to this hell. At least she could run away from that. But there was no way to get off this ship or to escape the relentless rocking and rolling of the sea.

When she saw the first streaks of dawn lighting the sky, Amanda felt wildly relieved. Although her nausea was no better, at least she might be able to contact someone, try to find some medicine or something, anything to put a stop to this horrible feeling.

Some hours later there was a knock on the door. She felt too weak to shout. And when she failed to reply, her steward, thinking no one was inside, naturally enough let himself in.

He briefly entered, saw her on the bed, apologised and turned on his heels.

'So sorry, Mrs Herbert. I come back later.'

'I'm not well.' She waved her hand at him. 'I'm so sorry.'

The steward was obviously used to situations like this.

'Shall I get the doctor to come?' he asked. 'He can bring pills and patch.'

'Please!' Without a second thought, Amanda agreed.

When the steward had gone, she lay back, facing the windows, watching the horizon sway from side to side and heave up and down, until once more she found herself running for the bathroom.

The doctor eventually arrived, bearing a large grab-bag. By this time Amanda was back resting on the bed.

He gave her an injection, and explained how it was much easier to prevent motion sickness than cure it, so next time she should be sure to put on a patch at the start of the voyage. He also told her she'd probably feel drowsy, but, if she could manage it, to get up, dress, and order some room service – anything, but she really should eat. The jab, he advised, would take an hour or so to kick in, and, although it sounded like the worst thing to do, after that, she should get out of her cabin and spend the afternoon trying to do normal things.

Amanda wondered what was normal about being on a floating hotel in the middle of the ocean.

The doctor's parting shot was to tell Amanda that she should look for the bowls of ginger, which were laid out in the restaurants and in the spa. Keep your eye on the horizon until you feel better, he said, and nibble on pieces of ginger. That would do the trick.

Amanda felt rather wary about his advice but decided to follow it; after all, he was the professional.

She had a shower which did make her feel vaguely human. The very thought of food had her heaving again, but she determined to follow the doctor's instructions, so she phoned down to room service and ordered a bread roll, toast and a pot of tea.

While she waited, she went out on to the balcony but realised that this was a very bad idea. The wind was so strong that she feared she would be blown away, and fly off over the lifeboats to disappear beyond the horizon, a bit like a fat middle-aged Dorothy Gale, caught up in the twister.

When she came back in she had to rush once more to the bathroom.

A short time afterwards, a knock on the door and waiters came in and set up a table, complete with cloth and cutlery, for her feeble meal. She forced herself to take bites of bread roll, chewing it laboriously while breathing deeply. The tea she drank black but with a spoonful of sugar.

When this brought no bad effects, she lay down and within minutes was asleep. When she woke, she felt so much better that she left her cabin and made her way to the spa.

She hoped the whole ship would not be having the same idea. But there were very few people about, and along all the corridors of cabins she saw that many doors had 'Do Not Disturb' signs swinging from their handles.

She felt terribly weak, and wondered whether her friends, Myriam, Tyger and Liliane, were similarly afflicted.

Grabbing the rails, Amanda staggered down the stairs towards the spa, hoping that she would not bump into her new gentleman friend while she was feeling and no doubt looking so rough.

Her fears that she looked dreadful were confirmed by the cheery girl on the desk in the spa, who took one glance at her and gave a sympathetic sigh.

Amanda bought a two-day pass and was shown around. As she was ushered through the entrance she walked past a small metal basket piled high with crystallised ginger. Amanda took a piece and hastily chewed on it.

'It does work,' said the girl. 'Tasty too.'

They went through a pool area, with sauna and steam room, then along a dark corridor. 'These are the treatment rooms,' said the girl. 'You can book in for a massage, or many other treatments which you'll find described on the leaflets in your welcome pack.' She took a white towelling robe from a row of shelves laden with them and handed it to Amanda as they walked into a long room lined with loungers which faced a wall of windows and looked out on to the open deck. 'This is the relaxation lounge. You can lie here all day, or rest here between treatments.'

Amanda went to the dressing rooms, quickly changed into her underwear and robe and came back to lie on the day beds.

Soft music played, the kind of tuneless music you only ever heard in 'alternative' treatment centres. At the far end of the room, a woman in a towelling robe was sleeping. All the other beds were empty.

The spa girl was clearing away used towels from another bed.

'Can people not see us?' asked Amanda, looking out on to the open deck. 'All those windows!'

Two joggers, fighting against the wind, silently trotted by on the other side of the glass.

'Everyone asks that.' The girl laughed as she piled the towels into a basket at the end of the room. 'But you can't see in. From the outer deck no one would have a clue we are in here. Out there it looks like a large mirror.'

Amanda watched a couple stroll past, arm in arm, hunched together against the cold wind and spray. Amanda waved and smiled.

'Believe me. They can't see you!'

The woman on the outer deck turned and glanced towards Amanda. Then she froze, concentrating. She took a few steps towards the window.

Amanda was certain she was looking straight at her.

Then the woman on deck pouted her lips and started adjusting the hair within her hood.

'She sees a mirror and uses it. Giving herself the OK,' said the girl. 'She's looking at herself, not you.'

'I will certainly watch out for that mirror,' said Amanda, 'when I next take a stroll along the outside deck.'

'Make yourself comfortable. And there is always someone at the desk if you need assistance.'

Amanda settled herself on the nearest lounger.

'Could I get you a tea, madam?'

Amanda chose a ginger and lemon and lay down, keeping her eye on the horizon.

As the girl arrived with a steaming cup, Amanda started feeling very drowsy. She decided to follow doctor's orders, lie back and enjoy her spa afternoon.

*

Suzy was late again. She'd had a fitful night. Her cabin was near the prow of the ship where the movements were felt more violently. All night the clothes hangers in her wardrobe clattered back and forth. Whenever she drifted off to sleep, something smashed from a shelf in the bathroom, or a cupboard door opened and shut with a resonating slam. During her waking moments Suzy mulled over the conversation with Jason. Was it a desperate attempt to frighten her, or could Stan really be a paedophile? She fretted too about her missing savings, and the potential of finding enough work, once home, to get herself back on to an even keel financially. For an actress of her age there was never much work about. She wished that she could make this job on the ships into a regular thing. The money wasn't great but at least her bed and board were free.

So far she had done nothing to encourage Blake to think she deserved the job.

When, finally, she slept she was agitated by frenetic dreams in which she was chased around by Stan this time, who was wearing nothing but a straw hat and underpants. It was like some awful Benny Hill sketch in reverse.

Suzy awoke, saw the time, hastily washed, dressed and grabbed her notes. She then scurried along the corridors to the other side of the ship to take her morning class.

Along the way, she saw that the ship was much quieter than she had ever experienced. Corridors were deserted. Nor were many people in the cafeteria.

She bustled into the ballroom, and was disappointed to see that the girl in the purser's office had been right – no one was there for her class.

She dropped her bag on to a nearby table and walked to the centre of the dance floor, where she had a good stretch, then did a couple of tap steps to limber up.

'Oh goody!' said a voice from a large banquette in the corner. 'I was thinking the class must be cancelled.' A young woman sat up, emerging from behind a table. With a sinking heart, Suzy realised it was the girl who was planning to apply to drama school. She also understood that, unless someone else turned up soon, she had no excuse not to spend an hour-long, one-on-one session concentrating on the girl's audition pieces.

'I brought my speeches,' said the girl, rummaging in her bag. 'The prospectuses tell me that they'll want me to perform one classical and one modern speech. The classical is the tricky one, naturally, because I understand and speak in modern language. Do you think it's necessary to stick to Shakespeare, or should I try and be original and pick something from another classical play? What would you choose?'

Suzy pulled up a seat and slumped down at one of the tables. 'I believe that the whole point is to be yourself. And you must choose something which you love and believe in.'

'But I've never read any classical plays. Except for *Romeo and Juliet* which we did at school, but I wasn't interested in all that ye-olde-language stuff. Anyhow, you have more knowledge and experience, so you could show me something more interesting and original. A speech which would get me noticed, so that I can stick out and be memorable. So far I've only got a really boring one.'

'It really is the case that they want to see *you* – who you really are …'

'But my drama teacher at school thought that if I wear something outrageous and do something bizarre, they'd remember me and then I'd have more choice of schools.'

'Has your drama teacher ever worked in professional theatre?'

'No, but she knows such an awful lot about it. I really trust her opinions.'

Suzy looked at the girl in her beige cashmere sweater and stylish slacks and wondered what she might have in mind to wear to an audition.

'You wouldn't wear what you have on now? It looks quite smart to me.'

'No. I thought a T-shirt with a noticeable motif, ripped jeans …'

'I still say, be true to yourself …'

'But I'm positive my teacher is right. It's important to stand out.'

'You might find that everyone else attending usually wears clothes like the ones you're suggesting.'

'No, but they wouldn't.'

Suzy knew that whatever she was going to say would be followed up with a 'no' or a 'but', perhaps both. This girl knew that she was going to stick to doing what she wanted to do, and therefore Suzy could only sit back and agree with her.

'Let's get on.' Suzy resigned herself to the oncoming hour of torture. 'First, maybe, you should show me what you've prepared, and we can work on that?'

The girl walked on to the centre of the ballroom floor and hung her head, smoothing down her clothes with both hands as she took in a deep breath. Then she launched into her speech.

Portia from *Julius Caesar*.

'Is Brutus sick? and is it physical
To walk unbraced and suck up the humours
Of the dank morning? What, is Brutus sick ...'

For some reason the girl was shouting the speech rather angrily as though she was taking part in a bar-room brawl. Suzy held up her hand and said, 'Let's talk about this. You're in a garden, in the middle of the night, reasoning with your husband ...'

'With respect, Suzy, I do know what I'm doing, if you'd kindly let me continue before you put your two cents in.'

Suzy shrugged and rested back in her chair. This was going to be a very long hour.

*

Amanda awoke from a very refreshing sleep to find that the evening was drawing in. The horizon was a dark purple with a bright scarlet line running across it, the sea now a deep Prussian blue. The ship was still rolling about but Amanda felt fine, if exhausted. She glanced along the row of beds and saw that the woman who had been lying there before was gone but that, in the centre of the row, a couple were sitting up sipping teas.

'It's lovely to be away from the melee,' said the woman.

'I thought we'd never find a place to escape all those nasty people, don't you think, J? Not the class of person you'd expect to see onboard a fine ship like this. Table manners no better than pigs, most of them.'

'I quite like the ladies at our table, Chris,' Jennie replied meekly. 'They're nice.'

'Ladies, my eye, J! They're no better than brazen old slappers.'

Amanda pulled up the collar of her robe. She was in no mood to talk to anyone, least of all Chris and Jennie, though she did wonder whether they might have to retract their comments if they saw it was her – Amanda, one of the brazen old slappers! She rolled over on to her side, lay still and listened in.

'Don't you see the way they all slather over that greasy lounge lizard of theirs. In my opinion it's all just an unwholesome spectacle of lewdness. Women of their age should know better. And, anyhow, he looks more like a poofter to me. Velvet jackets and satin dickies on a real man? Not in my book, J. Not in my book.'

Oh lord! Amanda couldn't take any more of this. Before sitting up, she made sure that her back was towards the couple. She rose hastily and slipped away.

She was tempted to go straight back to the changing room and get dressed, but she'd paid for her day here, and why should she be driven out by those two vultures, with their horrible tight little minds?

She wanted to make the most of this place, to relax, to feel good again.

Dithering between two choices – Swedish sauna or Turkish steam room – Amanda settled on the latter.

Pushing open the door she was met by a thick, hot, eucalyptus-scented fog. Gingerly she entered, shutting the door behind her, and then felt her way to an empty seat.

'Oh yes, he was just OK when he was on *42nd Street*, but when he followed her into *Into the Woods*, that was the end.'

'Did she break it off?'

'Not before time.'

Amanda realised that there were at least two other women in the steam room, though she could only vaguely make out their shapes. From their voices she knew that they were from South London. But their conversation seemed very much like something you'd hear reported on the late-night TV show, *Forensic Investigators*.

'Was that before or after she did over *Little Mary Sunshine*?'

'Oh, before! And then she went on to murder Nancy.'

'Slaughtered her!'

Amanda dared not breathe. Did they know that there was another person in the room? Someone who could hear all the details of this grisly conversation?

'I'd have loved to have a go at Nancy but I only ever got as far as covering her. Never had a stab.'

'Where?'

'Alex.'

'Oh.'

Amanda now started to think that they must be talking in some odd code. Otherwise it must be something depraved.

'And meanwhile he was chucked out of *Saigon*.'

'Typical. What did he do that time?'

'Rubbed John Thomas up the wrong way. Then refused to wear the jacket at the call. That was the final straw ... out on his ear. But frankly by then we'd all had enough of him.'

'I didn't know you were in *Saigon*.'

'I was swing.'

To this point Amanda believed she had caught up. They were talking about someone who had got into trouble on a trip to Vietnam. Unfortunately, the last phrase threw her right off. 'I was swing'? She was back to thinking it was something immoral.

A heartfelt sigh reached her, through the warm fog.

'It was *Lion* finally did for him. Fell off his stilts during "The Morning Report" and never had a decent part since.'

'The Morning Report'! That was a song in *The Lion King*! Finally, Amanda caught on. While she had been suspecting all kinds of nefarious business, these girls were simply discussing theatre shows. She peered through the receding mist and could just make out the outlines of two attractive young girls who she presumed must be dancers from the variety show. One of them stretched and laughed.

'He's quite dishy, though, don't you think?'

'Mmmm. He looked quite hunky in *Kinky Boots*.'

*

When Suzy arrived back at her cabin Ong was inside, making up her bed.

'Oh, hello, Miss Marshall. My friend Jun tells me that he can see you whenever you like. He's looking after Mr Arbuthnot. I can take you when I finish your cabin.'

'Oh, thank you so much, Ong.' Suzy dropped her bag on the desk. 'I'll just pop into the bathroom and change into something better.' She was in the sporty clothes which she usually wore for rehearsing, and which she now put on each day for the morning class.

By the time she had changed and slapped on a bit of make-up, Ong was out in the corridor, adjusting his trolley.

They walked up the stairs together.

'Many people sick today,' he said as they passed a pair of cleaners striding along with a bucket and mop. 'People no have sea legs.'

'We're lucky, Ong.'

'Your friend is on Deck 8,' said Ong. 'Starboard quarter on stern. Near table-tennis room.'

Suzy hoped that these facts would remain in her memory long enough for her to write them down.

The pair strode along the starboard passage. In the distance, another steward saw them coming and waved.

As they approached he bowed slightly to Suzy. 'Mr Arbuthnot out to lunch now, madam.'

Suzy waited to see if she would get an indication of which of these cabins was his, but Jun's smile was inscrutable.

Ong excused himself and left Suzy alone with his friend.

'You want I leave note?'

Suzy shook her head. 'I really wanted to give him a bit of a surprise, Jun. We worked together recently and he doesn't know I'm aboard.'

'Oh, I think he know you aboard, Miss Marshall. He saw your photo in *Daily Programme*. He ask me if I know what cabin you staying!'

Suzy felt her chest constrict. That was not the way it had been meant to go.

'He did?' was all she managed to reply. Through the door at the end of the corridor the sound of ping-pong balls on a table kept up a steady rhythm.

'He is quite tidy man,' said Jun. 'Like everything so. It is easy for me to have tidy man.'

Suzy could not imagine Stan being a tidy person. But as she had never had much to do with him outside of the rehearsal room how would she know?

The ping-ponging stopped, followed by much laughter. Suzy realised she could not stand here all day, talking to Jun. And at least now she had narrowed the area down to a row of about twenty cabins which would be easy to find again, once she located the table-tennis room.

She thanked Jun and asked him please to keep the remains of her secret and not let Mr Arbuthnot know she was asking after him. Then she moved forwards and left the corridor through the door to the table-tennis room.

Inside the spacious games room there were two tables, with people playing at both, and teenagers chatting gaily while waiting on the benches lining the walls. In the corner were a pinball machine and a few large computer race-driving games.

When she looked around she could see that everyone in the room was a kid. Some must have been around nine, the oldest probably sixteen.

A door to the side led out to the open deck. She walked briskly through it and out into the elements. If Jason's story was true this became even more suspect. Had Stan booked his room with specific instructions that it should be near what amounted to the kids' playroom? She walked over to the mahogany rail and gripped it, gazing out on to the horizon as it swung up and down. The wind seemed to have calmed somewhat, but the swell was still strong and the ship was still lurching about in the water.

This new information about both Stan's cabin and its proximity to the games room made Suzy want to run to tell Jason, but she knew it would be better if she first had a chance to talk to Stan himself, alone. Though now that she knew about his proclivities she didn't think she would be able to bear being in his presence. He had sickened her enough in rehearsal, with his belches, his sweaty clothes, and the flabby cheeks flecked with crumbs and grease from the food he was constantly scoffing. Now the very thought of him made her feel physically sick.

She stood still, holding the rail, taking deep breaths.

'Seasick?'

It was Blake.

'Absolutely not,' she said. 'Just trying to take the air. Which is pretty hard at the moment.'

'If you were sick, you should never lean over the rails, you know. It's how people end up overboard. We wouldn't want that or there would be no one to take the morning drama classes.' Blake did a little rebalancing act to counteract the rolling ship. It consisted of a shuffle of tiny steps to the side and back again. Suzy had to bite her lip to avoid laughing out loud.

'Anyone turn up for your class this morning?' he asked.

'One girl.'

'Still able to do it?'

'Naturally.'

Every conversation with Blake felt like a test which she was failing.

'Anyhow, must get on,' he said. 'Best time to catch a quick game of tennis. No one wants to play when it's rocking about.'

'Table tennis?'

'Proper tennis.' He pointed in the direction of a large area enclosed in green netting.

'I had no idea there were tennis courts,' she said, just for something to say.

'Virtual golf too. And do you see those boxes?'

Suzy looked along to where Blake was indicating.

'Full of equipment for quoits, shuffleboard, Baggo. Old-fashioned deck games. We must have a match some day when the weather clears up.'

Suzy took a late lunch alone in the cafeteria, then went back to lurk near Stan's cabin. People came and people went, which meant that she could eliminate certain cabin numbers. When she saw Jun looming, preparing to start doing turn-downs and placing chocolates on pillows, Suzy made a hasty exit through the table-tennis room and returned to her cabin.

She checked her emails. Another from India telling Suzy that the police seemed to be tracking a small portion of her money. It was a long trail, covering many countries, and multiple accounts. They appeared to think that *The Importance* company were mere small fry who had accidentally led the fraud squad on to a vast financial operation. 'Small fry!' India declared. 'It's outrageous. How can they call tens of thousands of pounds small fry?'

Suzy laughed to herself. If India's tens of thousands was small fry, what on earth would the police be making of her few hundreds? But to Suzy it was a bloody fortune.

She moved to the next email: a reply from the bank, stating that they couldn't do anything by email instruction and would Suzy please put her request to stop the old account and open a new one in writing or call in at her local branch.

Oh yes. That was a jolly good idea! How much of her money would have disappeared by then? She spent a long while trying to open up a new account online, somewhere she could put her shipboard salary, but this was also to no avail. Did these people imagine that everyone was always sitting by a phone and a postbox? She sent off another impassioned email to the bank, explaining her circumstances and praying it would be read by a real person and not a robot, as the last one had obviously been.

She decided to go to the purser's office to try and sort things out.

While she stood in the queue, she wondered if Barbara had any more news about the investigation. Barbara did seem to be the one who held most knowledge about this whole horrible business. She would write to her later and let her know that Stan was here, aboard the *Blue Mermaid*.

Once Suzy reached the top of the queue, the girl behind the desk, not understanding that Suzy was on the entertainment staff, couldn't get to grips with her request that her pay must be held back until she could open a new bank account as her current London account was unsafe. Eventually a supervisor came out and Suzy was ushered into a back room, where she told the whole story once more. The supervisor wanted to know whether Suzy would like to contact the police. Suzy explained that they were already aware.

'Surely the money would be paid by *Blue Mermaid* directly to your agent?' said the supervisor. 'It's him you need to contact.'

Suzy felt an utter fool. Of course, the supervisor was right. It was Max she needed to tell to hold on to the money.

'That's what happens when you panic,' she said. 'I'm so sorry I wasted your time.'

'It's nothing, really. I'm glad to have reassured you.'

Suzy told her about the Zurich theatre company folding, and how it had unsettled her. She hesitated before disclosing the rest of the sordid story, but instead asked: 'If you find criminals onboard, do you lock them up? Do you have a prison? You seem to have everything else.'

The supervisor laughed. 'The Captain has power to lock criminals in their cabin and place a 24-hour guard outside. Then we wait until police can come aboard – either when we reach port or, in desperate circumstances, using the SBS.'

Suzy asked what that was and was told that it was the maritime version of the SAS. The Special Boat Service.

'On the US side of the ocean, of course, it wouldn't be the SBS, but the American equivalent, the Navy Seals, or, if we're heading into New York, the NY river police.' The supervisor scrutinised her. 'Do you know of a criminal aboard?'

Suzy wasn't sure what to say to this, as she had no proof of anything about Stan.

'I was just wondering,' she said. 'We actors! Vivid imagination, you know.'

As she walked away from the office she realised that the supervisor must think her slightly mad.

*

By dinnertime, Amanda was feeling not only better, and relaxed from her afternoon in the spa, but also very hungry.

She put on her best clothes and went along to the grand restaurant to join her friends. She could see that the ship was still swaying, but, now that she had had an injection, it didn't seem to matter.

On the way in she passed Myriam who was headed in the other direction.

'Amanda, honey, can't believe I'm going to miss you. I'm on my way to the cinema. There's a movie I've always wanted to see and it starts in ten minutes. How've you been?'

'A bit under the weather, but I'm fine now.'

'I wanted to pick your brains, my dear. I know you are a vast suppository of information. But I'd better get on. Perhaps see you later in the ballroom and we can gas till the early hours, while we dance the flamingo with those handsome hosts.'

'Maybe,' said Amanda, adding, just to be polite, 'and what film are you going to see?'

'*Tess of the Dormobiles*,' said Myriam, disappearing along the corridor in a cloud of wafting silk and the lingering scent of Arpège.

As Amanda, already feeling floaty on the mixture of hunger and drugs, tried to digest her third surreal conversation of the day, she saw that Liliane and Tyger were seated at the table, along with the magician, Arturo, who was bending down, pulling out a chair, ready to sit. When he saw Amanda approaching, he stood upright.

'I was just passing,' he said, 'and I recognised the lovely lady here, who I caused to vanish last night. I had to make sure she was all in one piece!' He bowed in Amanda's direction and moved away.

'Don't go on my account,' she called after him.

He waved back. 'I have my own place at my own table – over there.' He pointed to the other side of the room and headed off in that direction.

Amanda greeted the other two, and glanced at the remaining empty seats.

'No Chris and Jennie?'

After what she'd heard of their conversation that afternoon in the spa, she had been looking forward to talking to them.

'I don't think they like to come here when we have the darling boy with us,' said Liliane, smiling at Tyger. 'Which is a great relief. In show business, we are not used to encounter people with closed minds.'

Amanda looked at Liliane.

'I didn't know you were in show business.'

'When I was younger.' Liliane shrugged and waved the suggestion away. 'I was a singer at a bar in Paris.' She pulled up her menu and ran her finger down the list. 'Now, which delight shall I choose tonight?'

'You didn't fancy seeing the film, Tyger?' asked Amanda.

'No.'

'Are you having fun on the voyage?'

'I like the elegance in the evenings,' he replied. 'I should like to learn to dance well, like Jason. It's a good thing to have up your sleeve.'

He pulled a couple of toothpicks from the container in the centre of the table and fiddled with them.

Amanda wondered how she would have felt, and tried to imagine her son Mark when he was Tyger's age. It was a difficult comparison. There was something about Tyger, a mix of sophistication and naïvety, which made him unique.

'What do your parents do?'

'They're dead.' Tyger spoke in a matter-of-fact way. 'Car crash. When I was six. I live with my aunt.'

Amanda wished the floor would open up and swallow her. But it was Tyger who changed the subject.

'Which do people use more of on this ship, do you think? Teabags or toothpicks?'

Amanda had no idea but, seeing the little holder on every table, made her choice. 'Toothpicks, I suppose.'

'No. Passengers on this ship use almost three times as many teabags as toothpicks. It seems that these days no one cares much about picking their teeth.' Tyger dropped the broken toothpicks on to his side plate, while nodding proudly at his knowledge. 'Guess what? According to tomorrow's *Programme*, just after lunch we'll be passing over the final resting place of the *Titanic*. That'll be something.'

Not expecting a reply, he went back to his food.

'That gentleman friend of yours and Myriam's is quite a cool customer,' said Liliane quietly, out of nowhere, and, Amanda thought, with rather a sly air.

'Why do you say that?'

'Today, since you've been off the scene, he's lost no time becoming Myriam's best friend and most assiduous escort.' Liliane bent in towards Amanda and lowered her voice. 'I thought you should know. That I should warn you. Knowledge is power.'

Amanda felt a shock run through her: part disappointment, part jealousy and part anger that Liliane had taken it upon herself to share the information.

She paused before replying and tried to pull herself together. After all, only a few days ago, had she not dreaded the thought that this would turn out to be a real-life version of *The Love Boat*? She had not come aboard looking for love. This wasn't even a silly holiday romance. It was a dance or two and one episode of afternoon tea. If Myriam had won Karl's interest, then Amanda would leave things as they were. She had no intention of making a scene or fighting over a man she had barely known for a couple of days.

After dinner, Amanda felt very tired again and decided against returning to the ballroom.

Instead she went back to her cabin. She planned to spend tomorrow morning making the most of her spa pass, so tonight, before bed, she would catch up with life at home, via email.

She left the ones from her solicitors, as they were bound to be final statements of account or some things about the deeds. She went straight to a newsy email from Patricia, who was raving about the wonderful latest nanny and her own new job, which she said was both trying and rewarding. Mark, she wrote, was overjoyed at having the run of Amanda's new flat, which he thought excellently sited. It was so convenient, he'd told Patricia, that he no longer missed having a car (his own having been commandeered by the wife and kids).

Well, at least there was some good news. Amanda felt glad that everything had worked out so well.

Next, she tackled the solicitors' emails, which were exactly what she had expected.

The final email she thought must be spam as it was from no one she had heard of, and came with the heading URGENT PLEASE CONTACT SONIA.

At first, Amanda couldn't make it out.

Some woman called Sonia asking Amanda could she please phone her urgently. She claimed to be Mark's girlfriend.

Only three days ago Mark's girlfriend was called Jasmine, wasn't she? Was this a new one, or had Amanda got it all wrong?

Sonia wrote that she had moved in to Amanda's 'lovely new flat' yesterday ... Moved in? So, without a by-your-leave, Mark had invited some strange woman to move in to her new flat. Sometimes Amanda wanted to strangle Mark. Sonia continued, saying that they'd had one lovely day there, then she had just finished unpacking her things, and was curled up in bed with Mark, when the doorbell rang. At first they had ignored it, as the time was coming up for midnight. The bell went on ringing, so Mark opened up. Seconds later the bedroom was crammed with police officers, one reading Mark his rights, another putting handcuffs on him. They dragged him out of the flat into a police van, leaving her alone to sort it all out. She had only known Mark a few days and had no idea what to do next, but found Amanda's email on his laptop. Could Amanda help at all? Mark, she added, was now being held at the police station at Paddington Green.

*

Suzy was lying in her pyjamas reading when there was a knock on the cabin door. She knew it must be very late, so looked at the bedside clock.

12.29.

She sat up and asked quietly, 'Who is it?'

'It's me,' said Jason. 'I have to talk.'

Suzy opened up.

Jason looked exhausted. As he came in he undid his top button, loosened his bow tie and said, 'I know where Stan is.'

'You've seen him?'

'No. I haven't seen him … yet. I thought I'd wait for you.'

Suzy offered Jason a chair.

'I'm not staying. It's just that I've discovered his cabin number.'

Suzy thought through her various efforts and wondered how this could be true.

'I'm friends with one of the waiters. After I finished dancing, we met up and I got him to do a table search on the maître d's list. Stan's name came up pretty early. Lucky he's an A.'

Suzy felt cross that she hadn't tried this herself, but she knew no waiters, except for the one at her own table, and she'd eaten in the restaurant so rarely they had hardly struck up a rapport.

'If I get some kip in now I could join you in the morning, straight after your class, and we could try knocking on his door.'

Suzy was about to suggest they do it *before* her class but this she knew would be wrong on every level as it would mean knocking on Stan's door at 8 a.m. as well as dragging Jason out of bed cruelly early. After all, it was not as though Stan could actually go anywhere.

'OK. Let's do it.' She paused before adding: 'You know his room is right beside the place where the teenagers all gather to play games?'

'No. I didn't.' Jason visibly paled. 'You already knew his cabin number then? Why didn't you tell me, Suze? Have you been there already without me? Did you talk to him?'

'I only know which section he's in. Back end of the ship. Deck 8.'

'To be precise, 8127.' Jason turned and gripped the door handle.

'Goodnight, Jason.' Suzy pulled up the sheets. 'I'll be done by about eleven fifteen. Give me time to change then I'll come and knock you up.'

'Oooh-errr, missus!' Jason shut the door behind him and disappeared into the corridor. She heard him open the door to his cabin and close it behind him.

It was only after he had gone that Suzy remembered she had not written to Barbara. Before tomorrow's encounter with Stan, she wanted all the information she could get. So she got up and went back on to the laptop. Without saying exactly why, she asked Barbara for a clear indication of everything known so far about Zurich and the vanished money, with particular reference to Stan.

She worked out that in London it would be around 4 a.m. Hopefully Barbara would be an early riser and Suzy would wake to a detailed reply.

They had to get to the bottom of it all.

And the key to everything was Stan Arbuthnot.

*

Overnight, Amanda spent many hours down in the purser's office. She explained her predicament and was ushered once again through to a back room where she accepted the charges and was put on a satellite phone.

She talked to the Desk Officer at Paddington Green, who affirmed that her son had been arrested at her new address. The gruff-sounding man told Amanda that, as the owner of the property, they were also looking for her, so if she'd like to give herself up it would make life easier all round.

She told them that it would be impossible as she was now in the middle of the Atlantic. 'On what charge is my son being held?' she asked.

'I'm not at liberty to give you information like that over the phone, Mrs Herbert. But if you could just come into the station ...'

Again, Amanda tried to make it clear to the man that it was impossible, *at the moment*, for her to get anywhere.

She looked at the phone timer and realised she had clocked up almost $70 and yet got nowhere.

'If you'd like to give me your current address?' said the police officer.

Wishing she could thrust the receiver down his throat, she told him once more that he had her current address, but that at this time she was onboard a ship in the Atlantic Ocean. She was around 600 miles from the nearest land, which was probably Newfoundland or Nova Scotia.

'Where are you sleeping tonight?' he asked.

'In my cabin,' she replied.

'You don't have a more precise location?'

'I believe in a few hours we'll be sailing just above the *Titanic*,' she said.

'This is no time for joking, Mrs Herbert,' said the officer. 'Do you have a phone number we could reach you on? Preferably a mobile?'

Amanda gritted her teeth and repeated that if he needed to get hold of her he could use email or phone her, ship-to-shore, on the *Blue Mermaid* via the company's London office. In just over forty-eight hours, she informed him, the ship would dock in New York City. Then she hung up and signed for the extortionate call to be added to her room charge.

Once she was back in her cabin, she realised that after all that she had still not discovered on what charges her son was being held, nor what they wanted to talk to her about. In fact, she had just thrown away $120 on absolutely nothing.

She wrote impassioned emails to Patricia, and this girl, Sonia, then a more sensible one to her solicitors, asking if they could please try to make contact both with Mark and the officer at Paddington Green and get back to her, by email, with details, as soon as possible.

She looked at the bedside clock and saw that it was just after 2 a.m. Not long till morning and, hopefully, some information. Then she remembered that they had put the clocks back every night since leaving Southampton, including one hour ago, while she was in the purser's office. That meant that in London it was only 10 p.m. or 11 p.m. Or was it the other way? Perhaps in London it was now 6 a.m. Was it three or four hours? Back or forward? Did she have to include the hour that the ship was putting back, or was it forward, at this very moment? Her head was reeling from all this horological mathematics. All she could be sure of was that she was unlikely to hear anything from anyone back in London till the offices reopened, whenever that was.

How exasperating!

It wasn't something she'd usually do, but she went to the minibar, pulled out a small gin and tonic and drank it straight from the can. Then she lay on the bed in her clothes and stared at the ceiling.

Damn everything to hell and back.

Why wasn't she allowed to have a rest? What had Mark done to get himself in this trouble? She suspected it must be something like drugs. Maybe he was into puffing marijuana and someone had grassed on him. She laughed, realising her pun, then went to the fridge and took out a second gin and tonic. This one she poured into a glass and sipped sedately, standing by the window looking out into the darkness.

Paddington Green? Wasn't that where they took serious criminals like murderers, swindlers and IRA terrorists, back in the day? Surely, they couldn't suspect him of anything as grave as that …

Could they?

She took another quaff of gin.

Sod it all.
Sod everything.
She went to the bed, lay back and closed her eyes.
Blast it all.

PART FIVE

The Grand Banks

Suzy worked energetically through her class. She even coped with the audition girl, who now, in front of all the others, treated Suzy as her BFF.

When the session was over, Suzy ran the length of the ship, using the outer deck, loving the feel of the damp wind in her hair. The sea had calmed considerably since yesterday and was now like a sparkling grey rumpled sheet.

Back in the cabin she quickly changed, then spent a few moments checking her emails. She replied very quickly to Max, who hoped everything was going well for her. He would hold all income received for her till she got ashore and had a chance to sort out a new bank account. Suzy felt enormously relieved about this.

Just as she was about to disconnect, an email came in from India, with the subject line: LATEST!

Instinctively Suzy opened it, just as she cut off the internet counter.

You'll never guess what! It's simply AWFUL!

Suzy read on and caught her breath. As her eyes skimmed along the lines she felt her heart pounding. When she reached the end of the email she shut down the computer, immediately left the cabin and crossed the corridor to Jason's room.

She found herself hammering on the door, before remembering that it wasn't only Jason in there. George, the other ghost, might be asleep in the lower bunk.

Almost instantaneously Jason opened.

'Calm down, old girl. People are sleeping, you know.'

He stepped neatly out of the cabin and quietly clicked the door behind him.

'And now, off we go, in search of Greasy Stan, the man.'

Suzy caught his arm. She realised she was shaking so hard that when she spoke her voice came out really high and wobbly.

'Stan's dead,' she said.

'Dead? How the … he didn't jump overboard when he saw you, did he, Suze?'

'I'm not joking, Jason. I just got an email from India. She'd had Barbara on the phone.'

'How would India know? She's not onboard too, is she?'

'Stan died back in Zurich, Jason.'

'In Zurich!'

Someone popped their head out of a nearby cabin and whispered up the hallway: 'Keep it down could you, mates. Some of us have been on night-watch.'

Jason grabbed Suzy's elbow and silently steered her along and out of the entertainment and crew quarters. 'I think we'll have this conversation on the outer deck, shall we?'

Suzy nodded and in silence they both ran up several flights of steps.

Once out in the open, they found a less windy corner and sat, huddled together on one of the games boxes on the cold, dank top deck.

'Start at the beginning, Suze. Jesus. I can't believe this.' Jason wrapped his jacket tight around him and put his head in his hands while Suzy told him all she knew.

'Barbara phoned India this afternoon, London time, by which I think I mean less than an hour ago, as the Zurich police had contacted her. They wanted all the information they could get on Stan. Barbara phoned round, starting with India, wanting to know if she knew any more than Barbara did, and warned her that the Swiss police might well be in touch. As company manager, when the police asked, she had felt obliged to give out everyone's contact details. She's going to write to me by email, apparently. India just got in first.'

'I don't care about all that stuff. What the hell happened to Stan?'

'His body was found, half decomposed, in some flat by the lake. It was due to be serviced once a fortnight, but the woman was going away early for her Christmas break, so went in a few days early. When she came into the flat she was overpowered by the stench and then found Stan's body under the bed in the back room. She staggered out and called the police. They found Stan's credit cards and things in his jacket which was hung up on the back of the bedroom door.'

'I thought Barbara told you, when we were all at the airport, that Stan flew out first thing in the morning. Did he go to London then back to Zurich? I don't get it.' Jason stood up and took deep breaths. 'What the hell happened to him? How did he die? Did India say?'

Suzy shook her head. They stayed silent for some moments.

The ship was surprisingly steady in her forward passage. They could hear nothing but the steady rhythm of the engine. There were no waves. The sea was flat as a mirror, the horizon swathed in fine white mist.

'You don't think Stan died that night, do you, Suze, at that party? Oh God!'

Jason moved closer.

Suzy looked up. Before them a blanket of fog was rolling in. She looked down and saw dew forming on the sleeves of her jacket. She shivered.

'There's another burning question bothering me, Jason,' said Suzy. 'If Stan is dead, who is in Cabin 8127?'

Jason shrugged. 'Obviously has to be some other person called Stan Arbuthnot. Nothing to do with us. Our nerves were up. We were just barking up the wrong tree. It really *is* a case of another Athene Seyler.'

'No, Jason. I'm sure that it's more serious than that.'

'How can it be? It's just another person with the same name, Suze. And because we're here, in this strange cut-off world, we got ourselves into a state about it.'

'Look – the entertainment people let slip that this Stan Arbuthnot is an actor and, as you know, Equity doesn't allow more than one person to keep the same name.'

'So, he's an amateur who says he's an actor? There's enough of those around,' said Jason, pulling his collar up. 'Or he's in American or Australian Equity, or something. As I said – he's got nothing to do with us.'

'Jason! That wouldn't explain why Jun, who is the steward of Cabin 8127, told me that Mr Stan Arbuthnot, actor, who is onboard this ship at this minute, had recognised my photo from the *Daily Programme*, told Jun he knew me and asked where he might find *my* cabin number.'

'Jeez, Suze. That's horrible.' Jason stood up. 'Look at this fog. It's like a cloud rushing us.' He put out his hand and offered to help Suzy to her feet. 'Come on, Suze! Chop-chop!'

'Come on where?'

'We're going to take a look at exactly who *is* in that cabin.'

*

Amanda woke, still fully clothed in the formal wear she had put on for dinner last evening, just after 9 a.m.

She immediately went to the desk, turned on her laptop and checked her emails. Nothing.

She undressed, took a shower and put on casual clothes more suitable for the day ahead.

What should she do now?

There was nothing she could do, until someone replied to her.

She decided to book herself a massage in the spa, but first went down to take breakfast in the restaurant.

Myriam was there, alone at their table, tucking into a bowl of porridge.

'I adore Irish oatmeal, don't you, darling?' she cried as Amanda sat and unfolded her napkin. Amanda had always thought of porridge as being a Scottish thing, but said nothing.

Myriam put down her spoon and gazed at Amanda. 'You look all in, deary, if I may say. Are you all right?'

'I've had a bit of upsetting news from home,' Amanda replied. 'And there's nothing I can do about it.'

'Thank goodness for that!' Myriam laid her chubby hand on her chest. 'Oh, sweetie, no!' She held up her hands. 'I don't mean thank goodness you've had terrible news. For one awful moment, I thought you might be avoiding me and that I might have upset the apple tart. I hope nobody passed away?'

'My son has got himself into some trouble. He's been arrested. But no one will tell me what he's supposed to have done.'

Myriam stretched out her arm and patted the back of Amanda's hand.

'Oh, my, how terrible for yourself. I'm so sorry. Children can be such a worry.'

'He's thirty-four.'

'It doesn't matter if they're fifty-nine, sweetie-pie. To mothers, they're always their babies.' Myriam dabbed her mouth with her napkin and leaned in to Amanda. 'Now, darling, I don't want things to be awkward between us, so please may we address the pink elephant in the room?'

Amanda had no idea what Myriam was talking about, so smiled wanly and nodded.

'Karl!' announced Myriam. 'I hope you're not upset that he appears to have thrown his bonnet at me. I know that you were seeing a bit of him.'

Now that the subject had been broached, Amanda realised she couldn't care a fig if Myriam was being romanced by Karl. To be honest it was the last thing on her mind. If Myriam wanted the man she was welcome to him.

A waiter appeared at Amanda's shoulder. She wasn't in the slightest bit hungry but ordered Eggs Florentine and a pot of strong coffee.

'Long time, no see!' Chris stood opposite Amanda, pulling out a chair for Jennie, who obediently sat. 'We were wondering if you might have gone overboard,' he added, sitting down himself and picking up the menu. 'Tried swimming home to Blighty.'

'What have you two been up to?' asked Myriam. 'Making the most of the lovely ship?'

'I've splashed out on a morning's pampering for the lady-wife,' said Chris. 'She's getting the whole works: massage, facial, coiffure, the bloody lot. Nothing's too good for my little Jennie.'

Amanda waved a mental goodbye to spending her morning in the spa. She recalled the conversation she had overheard yesterday, and wondered whether Chris really hadn't seen her there lying a few beds away in the relaxation lounge.

'She's a strange one, that Froggy female, Lillian, isn't she? Never seen her down here for breakfast. If you ask me, Europeans are a bloody lazy lot. You had a near escape with the old Brexit, Amanda. Glad to say you Brits gave the foreign bastards the elbow. Good for you.'

Amanda didn't point out that she was a firm believer in the UK being part of Europe. Instead she gave a wan smile and filled her mouth with dry toast.

After finishing as much of the Eggs Florentine as she could manage, given the tension she was feeling, she excused herself and said she had to go up to the library to change a book. It was a lie, but once she said it she thought the library was as good a place as any to go and sit alone. There she could be sure she would be undisturbed.

She found a window seat and settled down to watch the ever-changing sea. The horizon was shrouded in mist.

When she awoke she realised it was after eleven thirty. She had done that thing which she hated others doing – hogged a seat with a great view and then fallen asleep. Feeling guilty, she vacated the chair and left the library.

She hadn't got very far when someone came up behind her and took her arm.

It was Karl.

'I've been worried about you, Amanda,' he said. 'You were unwell. Come and sit with me in the Port Lounge. No one's there. We can talk.'

He ushered her up the stairs and through into a small room which Amanda had never noticed before.

'If someone's booked it for a meeting or a wedding or something they'll throw us out, but in the meanwhile …' He pulled out a chair for Amanda to sit.

'Myriam tells me you've had a little trouble at home. I'm so sorry. If there's anything I could do to help …'

'No. Not really. I'm fine.' Amanda sat.

'You disappeared last night. I missed you. That woman does go on and on. I get the feeling she's after me.' Karl took a seat opposite Amanda. 'I prefer a little more dignity, myself. Should I order us some tea, perhaps?'

Amanda shook her head.

'It was lonely yesterday without you,' said Karl. 'I spent the day with Myriam, hoping all the time that you would recover, and come looking for us. Now that you are well again, I am your servant.'

Amanda's tension was greatly assuaged by the thought that she was not alone and could discuss her problems with someone sympathetic.

'It's the feeling of helplessness I can't stand. I have no idea what's gone on, and I'm stuck on this bloody boat and communications with land are such a horror …'

'You know that I'm a bit of a computer whizz? I could help you get around these limitations perhaps?'

'But you must be busy.'

'I'm on a cruise, Amanda! Remember, I work with computers for a living. I know how to do most things.'

Back in Amanda's cabin, Karl took charge of the laptop. With a few clicks he had got online.

'Can I just use this jotter to note down the password they give me?'

'Of course,' said Amanda, relieved someone was being so helpful.

He flipped the pad and then scribbled a few notes on the next page and tore it off.

'Voila!' He rose from the chair, offering it back to Amanda.

He had set up a way for her to call the solicitors directly using her computer.

'I don't suggest you do it for a long time,' he said. 'You'll still incur internet charges, and it will hitch up because the speed is tragically slow, but a quick voice call should make things much clearer than all those back and forth emails and Chinese whispers.'

He bowed slightly.

'I hope I will see you tonight in the ballroom, Amanda.' He scrunched up the piece of paper and put it in his pocket.

'You won't be needing this any more.' He moved back towards the door. 'Good luck with everything.' And he was gone.

Amanda got on to the solicitors straight away.

They told her that they were just writing her a detailed report. Mark was being held for fraud, theft and possessing indecent images of juveniles. These were serious charges and, if found guilty, he could be sent to prison.

'But that can't be true. Not Mark.' Amanda knew that her son was a bit of a womaniser, but fiddling with adolescents …? That was beyond belief.

'There's a matter of some dubious photographs and magazines hidden under the bath.'

Amanda shook her head. 'It can't be true. It just can't.' Mark was a philanderer, that was true. But not this.

And as for the other stuff, the bank fraud, Amanda knew that he simply didn't have the intelligence for it.

'They have irrefutable evidence, Mrs Herbert. USB sticks with incriminating bank-account details under various names were found in his possession. It doesn't look good.'

'But …'

'For the time being there is nothing you can do. You would be advised not to speak with the police again and, before doing anything, to wait until we contact you. Whatever you do, please do not try making further contact with your son.'

After the call was over, Amanda was so stunned she almost forgot to log off the internet.

She moved over to the bed and sat, speechless, looking out at the misty horizon.

Fraud, theft and indecent images!

What had her son turned into?

She didn't know what to do next.

She glanced at her watch. Just coming up to noon.

She recalled that the boy in the travel agent's had sold her this cruise as 'a totally relaxing, genuine break from the hustle and bustle of home'!

If only that were true. Home had pursued her like a demented Fury with a personal grudge. And being on a ship was certainly *not* relaxing during a crisis, particularly because communications were so expensive and nigh impossible.

Amanda leaned against the glass balcony door. She felt as though her life had spun totally out of control.

From the corridor, she heard the familiar bongs of the noon announcement. She pulled her door ajar, and listened. The Captain was telling those who were interested that within an hour the *Blue Mermaid* would be passing the final resting place of the RMS *Titanic*. Amanda had seen from her *Daily Programme* that there was some organisation of *Titanic* fans onboard. They were having daily talks in the Starboard Lounge, and presenting a small exhibition there about the ill-fated liner. They'd all be out there on the deck later with their cameras, taking photos of the sea, no doubt, despite the fact that those photos would look exactly the same as any taken of the sea since they had lost sight of shore.

Amanda decided that she couldn't bear to sit on her own in the cabin any longer, and hoped that Chris and Jennie must be out of the spa by now. She wondered if her blood pressure had gone through the roof. Her head was pounding and her heart thumping.

She'd go there and see whether she might get herself a massage to calm down.

*

Suzy and Jason had lurked in the corridor on the starboard side near the stern of Deck 8 for over an hour. Whenever anyone came along they took turns at walking up and down and going round the corner on to the landing where the lifts were, or going in and out of the table-tennis room, so that it wasn't quite so obvious that they were simply loitering with intent.

'How's your talk coming along for tomorrow then, Suzy?' Jason asked, as they lolled against the doorframe.

'Getting quite excited actually, Jason. Instead of focusing on me, I've got some very interesting titbits about actors through the ages. Did you know, for instance, that Ancient Greek actors had to eat a diet of only four things: lettuce, cheese, garlic and eels?'

'Delicious,' said Jason, wincing. 'Actually, they should bring that rule back. It would certainly get rid of all those silly wannabees.'

Suzy laughed, trying to imagine her drama-school girl being forced to live on that diet.

'I'd still do the job if I had to live on garlic and eels, wouldn't you, Suze?'

'Yes. I suppose I would. But hopefully they wouldn't have been able to see all the things I secretly ate at home.'

'No, Suze. Ancient Greece was famous for its CCTV cameras, which they kept perpetually trained on actors' homes.' Jason glanced at his watch. 'What time are you on next?'

'Tomorrow, 2 p.m. In the big theatre.'

'I'll be there, loudly cheering you on. Rent-a-claques are us.'

They stood in silence for a moment or two, then someone emerged from one of the lifts behind them and they both walked off in different directions, trying to look insouciant and everyday.

It was a woman in gym clothes. Suzy followed her as she turned along the corridor of cabins and, as she entered Cabin 8121, Suzy walked on to the table-tennis door then came back to join Jason near the lifts.

'Of course, he might be inside all the time,' said Suzy. 'Should we knock on the door and, if someone opens up, pretend we made a mistake?'

'Or be like kids, knock and run away, then peep around the corner to take a look?'

They both laughed nervously at the thought of being caught by whoever was going by the name Stan Arbuthnot.

Suzy said, 'Of course it might be one of those blokes who's out all day and only comes back to change for dinner.'

'You've hit it, dear Suzy!' Jason slapped his forehead in a theatrical gesture of mock surprise. 'We're wasting our time here. We should come back here at sixish. Everyone has to change for the evening. Come on. It'll give you time to do a bit more prep on your fabulous lecture.'

They both turned and walked back towards the lifts. Just after they left the corner they heard the door to the table-tennis room slam. They exchanged a look and spun around. Suzy took a peek.

'It's a bloke,' she hissed to Jason, who leaned in close behind her, his head touching hers.

Just as the man pulled out his keycard and put it into the lock of Cabin 8127, Suzy felt Jason's intake of breath. By the time she looked around to ask why, Jason had taken flight and had already disappeared down the first set of stairs. As Suzy followed him, galloping down through the decks, the tannoy bells rang and the Captain made an announcement about the final resting place of the *Titanic*.

Just what we need, thought Suzy, out of breath, as she turned into the entertainment quarters. The *Titanic*!

Jason was cowering outside her cabin. He was pale, and a slight sheen of sweat shone on his forehead. He looked as though he might faint.

'Are you OK, Jason?' Suzy whipped out her keycard and opened the door. Jason ran inside ahead of her, and lowered himself to sit, hunched up on the end of the bed.

'There's no escape,' he said quietly, putting his head into his hands. 'I have to get off this boat. Or I'm a dead man.'

'What are talking about, Jason? What just happened?' Suzy shut the door behind her, came in and sat at the dressing table. 'You look as though you just saw a ghost.'

'Worse than that,' said Jason. 'I saw *him*.'

'Him? Who's him?'

'The Devil himself. That was Mr Appenzell.'

Suzy took a second or two to understand him.

'*That* was Appenzell? Are you sure?'

'Certain. I will never forget him, or that last look he gave me from the balcony of that apartment.'

'Did he kill Stan, do you think?'

Jason sat silent for a second or two.

'Oh God, Suzy! It all adds up. I heard Stan saying "I'll scream until I am satisfied" and doing his squealing thing.

Then the police rang the bell. Next thing it went quiet. There was a little while, just enough for him to have stifled Stan. Then Appenzell came on to the Entryphone, sounding all drowsy. He must have wanted to shut Stan up, while the police were ringing at the door. Did India say how Stan died?'

'She just said he was dead. Perhaps there'll be more detailed info by now.' Suzy went to the laptop and turned it on. 'I'll check. I read her email so quickly and came immediately to find you.'

'Oh help!' Jason gave an agitated sigh. 'Why is Appenzell on this ship? He must have boarded at Southampton. But why? Did he know I was here? Is he chasing me?' Jason flung himself back and lay on the bed, staring up at the ceiling. 'He's come on this ship to finish me off. I know it. I'm terrified, Suzy.'

'How would he know you're here, Jason? No one knows.' Suzy scrolled through her emails. 'Things happened so quickly and I've never got round to telling anyone. The only people who know you're here are the crew, who never saw either of us before in their lives, me and Max. And Max has no connection with all that stuff. He just takes his twelve per cent. Appenzell *can't* have known you were onboard.'

Suzy opened India's email and read it through again. 'No, it doesn't say murdered. Just "found dead in an empty Zurich apartment".'

Jason groaned.

'I don't want the next email to be you writing to them: "Jason Scott was found dead on the *Blue Mermaid*."'

'"Stan had been lying there for about ten days."'

'Which means he *must* have died that night.' Jason covered his face with his hands and stifled another groan.

A knock on the cabin door caused Jason to jump bolt upright and run to the wardrobe. He climbed inside and shut it behind him.

Suzy went to the door.

'Who is it?'

'It's Ong, Miss Marshall, to do your room.'

'I don't really need it this morning, Ong.'

'I'll just empty your bins, then, and replace your toiletries.'

She stood in front of the wardrobe door and let Ong pass into the room.

'Did you find your friend?' he asked as he picked up the waste-paper basket and emptied the contents into a rubbish sack.

'Oh yes, thank you, Ong. It's not really a friend. Someone who had seen my talk and wanted my autograph,' she said, wondering how far this corresponded with what she had said about Stan earlier.

Ong went into the shower room and came out shaking his plastic sack.

A hanger clanged in the wardrobe behind her. Suzy feigned a sudden movement, as though she herself had caused the noise.

'I'll just quickly get the vacuum cleaner,' said Ong, passing her, heading for the corridor.

'No, don't bother, Ong. It's fine. Really.'

Ong nodded and left the cabin.

After a few seconds, Suzy pulled open the wardrobe and Jason stepped out.

'One thing is puzzling me,' he said quietly. 'Let's presume Appenzell left Zurich and then got onboard this ship in Southampton for whatever reason. Why on earth would he come aboard pretending to be Stan? Why not use his own name? And why take someone else's? And, of all people, why pretend to be Stan Arbuthnot?'

16

AMANDA LAY snoozing on the spa day beds. She had been in the sauna for a short while. She had ten minutes before her massage.

Pampering didn't make the anxiety go away. It hadn't even slightly assuaged the tension she had felt earlier. Three words kept running through her head: fraud, theft and pornography. She dreaded to think about the last one. Surely the police weren't going to pull you in if you had a few copies of *Playboy* stashed at the bottom of your wardrobe.

Amanda took a deep breath.

If there was nothing you could do, you had to stop worrying. Stop thinking about it! Stop worrying!

Boy, was that hard. It reminded her of sitting in traffic jams, tense and angry because you were late, but pointlessly letting your head almost burst with anxiety, instead of being a bit more Zen and humming along to soothing melodies on Radio 3. No amount of high blood pressure was going to dissolve the rows of static cars any more than getting stressed out would make things better for Mark.

As Amanda gazed out of the windows she watched the small gaggle of people, all wearing Titanic Club T-shirts, kagouls, caps and badges, chatting as they started to disperse. Two stragglers leaned against the rail. One threw a flower over the side and strolled away. Amanda wondered whether he had taken the flower from his table setting or ordered it specially from the onboard florists.

Now that the *Titanic*-watching gang had gone only one person was left. A lanky figure in a hoodie gazing down at the water below. He shrugged, then turned and pulled the hood down.

Amanda recognised Tyger. Typical thirteen-year-old, she thought. All teenagers seemed to have a fascination with the *Titanic*.

Tyger shook his hair and resumed his watch, seemingly riveted or hypnotised by the waves.

A jogger ran by, wearing only T-shirt and shorts. Amanda thought that it must be pretty cold today for such scanty attire, but presumably sporty activities like that warmed you up sufficiently for you not to notice.

It was lovely lying in the cosy, quiet warmth of the spa, looking out at the grey dull deck, with its ever-changing scene. Watching the world go by through the one-way mirrored windows reminded Amanda of watching those old late-night TV shows which displayed a log fire or the view from the front of a train engine chugging through the Alps.

The same jogger was back, trotting along in the other direction now. That was strange. It seemed to be an unwritten law among the joggers always to run round the deck in an anti-clockwise direction. As the man came past the spa he stopped, turned and looked in. She realised the jogger was Karl. How funny! He was adjusting his hair in the mirror. She waved to him, but of course he could not see her.

Karl turned and walked slowly towards the edge of the deck. He stood close to Tyger, leaning on the rail beside him. They seemed to chat for a little while, both looking down into the water.

Then Karl did something strange. Slowly, he brought his hand up and started stroking Tyger's back.

Tyger flinched and took a step away. After a brisk interchange, Tyger turned and bolted. Karl stayed where he was for a few moments, then, first brushing his hair back from his forehead, he resumed his jog, this time on the normal anti-clockwise track.

Amanda felt strange at having watched this little vignette through the two-way mirror. She felt dirty, almost as though she had been prying through a keyhole.

'Mrs Herbert?' A pretty Filipino girl stood at the end of Amanda's day bed. 'Would you like to come through now for your massage?'

*

Suzy looked at her watch and leaped up.

'Weren't you supposed to be at the tea dance?'

Jason shook his head. 'String quartet today. No dancing. Just tea. Not wanted.' He sighed again. Jason had been sighing for the last hour, as though his body could not get enough oxygen. 'I'm fearful for tonight, Suzy. What if he's there in the ballroom? Do you think he's seen me dancing there? He might lurk at the back every night, watching me.'

Suzy had been listening to Jason working up a state of increasing panic, but didn't know how to calm him down.

'Would you recognise him again, Suze?'

Suzy thought about it. Though she had only seen the man for a split second, before Jason ran off, she could recall his distinguished-looking appearance, the swept-back silvery hair, the chiselled features. Though she wouldn't trust her memory enough for a police line-up, she was pretty sure she would know his face again.

'Would you sit in on the dance tonight? You could be a lookout. I have to talk to the ladies I dance with. I can't spend the night looking over their shoulders. It would be as though I was rubber-necking to see if I could get a better date.'

'But if I saw him, what could I do?'

'You could warn me.'

'Then what?'

Jason shrugged. 'Not sure. We'd have to take it as it comes.'

'Should we go to the Captain?'

'And tell him what? That I was at a party with someone onboard who the police did not think was guilty of any misdemeanour?'

Suzy could see what Jason was saying.

'The police *were* looking for Appenzell that morning at the theatre.'

'Yes,' said Jason. 'But only because I had made that second anonymous phone call.' Jason perked up. 'They'd already gone to his apartment when I was outside watching and he had dispelled their worries. I made the second call, a little while later. They could only have gone to the theatre because there was no reply at his apartment. I did tell them he was backing our play.'

Suzy understood what Jason was implying. 'So you think that Appenzell was already out of the apartment before 7 a.m. when we were at the theatre.'

'Either he was hiding inside, not answering the door, or he was gone.' Jason ran his fingers through his hair. 'I really must have put the wind up him. He must have got out …'

'What about Stan?'

'Presumably Stan was lying dead, inside the flat.'

'But why didn't they find him for so long?'

Jason leaned forward. 'Don't you see, Suzy? The police don't knock your door down if you don't answer. And, after all, they were only responding to an anonymous tip-off from me. And they'd already spoken to him once and gone into his quiet, apparently empty, normal-looking flat. So they'd have just written it off as a nuisance call.'

'But Appenzell then left Zurich and made his way to Southampton.' Suzy shook her head. This was all too much. 'I can't get that link at all.'

'Me neither.' Jason shrugged. 'He can't have known we were onboard.'

'No one did.'

'But he did know that the heat was on …'

'And if Stan was there, lying dead …' Suzy tried to piece it together, attempting to put herself into someone else's mind. 'If the police were nosing about, but you had a dead body in your apartment, what would you do?'

'Try to get rid of the body, I suppose.'

'Stan's body? He was huge. Heavy, fat. Appenzell may be a fit man, but how on earth could he carry Stan? How could *anyone*? Especially if Stan was literally just a dead weight?'

'You're right, Suze. If Stan was lying dead inside that flat, which was on the fourth floor, there was no way he could have got him out. The flat was in the centre of a busy city. So, he had to have shoved Stan's corpse under a bed and then done a runner.'

'You remember when Barbara saw Stan's name on the flight list that morning? Maybe it was Appenzell on that plane. He may have had Stan's passport …'

'He'd hardly pass for Stan. They were as alike as Laurel and Hardy.'

'But look, Jason. Appenzell certainly knew the flight number, and all the ticket details. He could have printed them out.'

'Of course.' Jason tapped his fingers on the desk. 'After all, he bought our tickets. But the passport?'

'I don't know, Jason. Perhaps he has a way of changing photos or something.'

Suzy realised that they were starting to get somewhere. She was anxious to make notes. She grabbed a pen from her bedside table.

'Jeez, Jason, look at the time. I'd better get my glad rags on. You too.'

When Jason had gone to get smartened up, Suzy quickly logged on to the internet and sent emails to Barbara, India and Emily to ask what news they may have had since the one she picked up this morning. She tried to work out what the time was back in London and first thought it must be lunch-time, until she remembered that New York woke up later than London, so now it must still be night-time in England.

As though she knew what Suzy wanted, an email came in from Emily. It was crammed with detail.

Reg was being questioned by the police about his relation-ship to 'the money bloke', as Emily called Appenzell. Stan had, it seemed, died in the spare bedroom of a Zurich apart-ment, rented for that fortnight by a Mr Hamlyn. Reg had identified the flat as being the one in which Appenzell was holding a party on the night before the show was cancelled. No one knew why Stan was there. He had not gone back to his digs after the party, but the landlady had thought noth-ing of it as she was used to actors and their nocturnal ways. Though, after a few days, she had contacted the theatre to tell them she was worried. But the theatre simply told her the show was off and that Stan, along with the rest of the company, had gone back to London. The landlady waited a few days for a phone call from Stan, then gave the clothes and suitcase to charity, which, once his body was discov-ered, proved a great annoyance for the Zurich police. Stan had checked in for his flight, by computer somewhere in the vicinity of the flat where his body was later discovered, but had never arrived at the airport. Everyone, Emily wrote, believed that Jason was in league with Appenzell, and Reg was fuming about the whole thing.

As she read, Suzy started to feel very uncomfortable. She knew that she had to pass on the information that Jason was here with her, working onboard the *Blue Mermaid*, and that he had been here since the day they all left Zurich.

But knowing it was probable that Appenzell was also onboard was very worrying and made her hesitate. Finally, she came to the conclusion that honesty was the best policy. Maybe it was all true. Maybe Jason had somehow pulled off this enormous scam. She could not live with herself if she was protecting a felon. Suzy knew that the time had come and she had to let the police know Jason's whereabouts, and then they could deal with it as they thought fit. So she wrote a quick reply to Barbara, explaining that Jason was onboard the *Blue Mermaid*. They would be docking in New York the day after tomorrow, and, if the police wanted to question Jason, that was where they could find him. She added a PS that she had reason to think it was possible Herr Appenzell might also be aboard.

Once the email had left her outbox, another one came in, this from India.

India was out for Jason's blood, still believing that he had snatched all the money from her considerable allowance, dividends and savings. The police, she told Suzy, were on the verge of tracking Jason down, as they believed that he was in league with some bloke they had just picked up in London and were currently holding for petty larceny and possession of indecent images. India wrote that since he'd been back in London, Jason had been clever enough not to put in an appearance at his flat, but the police knew he *had* come back to the UK, because he had used his return ticket, as provided by the theatre, and had flown out of Zurich on the first flight to London at 6.50 a.m. on the very day when the rest of them had all been stranded, but before anyone else in the company knew a thing about the show being cancelled. Once back home, India continued, Jason had started lots of financial shenanigans with their money from somewhere near Victoria Station and, aided by this other bloke, he'd spent the subsequent three days moving money here, there and everywhere and leading the police a merry dance.

Suzy closed her internet connection and sat at the desk, putting on her make-up for the evening.

So the police believed that Jason had flown to London at 6.50 that morning and spent the next few days there!

But Suzy knew that Jason had done no such thing. Jason had been with her, and had travelled from Zurich to Genoa by train that morning, and then boarded the ship with her. There was no way Jason could have used his plane ticket to London. And that could only mean that someone else had used it.

Suzy herself was a witness to the fact that Jason had not been in London at all since Zurich, and that he had spent every day since Zurich with her, here, onboard ship, where escape or other alibis were simply not a possibility.

But now she had sent that email.

What had she done?

Suzy slipped on her dress, then applied her lipstick, turned off the lights and went out to pick up Jason.

She prayed that, thanks to her, when they reached New York, there would not be a posse of policemen waiting at the gate to arrest Jason.

From now on they really did have to stick together.

*

After her attempt at spending a relaxing time in the spa, Amanda returned to her cabin and went online. She picked up her emails, thereby destroying any benefits she might have accrued from her afternoon massage.

The solicitors' letter was not only bleak, but vaguely threatening. Amanda had believed that your own lawyers were meant to support you, but their tone was frosty and, worse than that, accusatory. Now, it seemed, just to make things worse, the fraud squad was busy tracking the stolen money and it had come from the Swiss bank account of one J. Scott, and been transferred to her *own* account. Today that money had been moved again, this time into her son, Mark Herbert's account. They implored Amanda to be truthful and not try to cover up for her own or her son's transgressions, which, they told her frostily, would invariably lead to her being arrested on her return to London, if not when she docked in New York. Putting stolen money into her son's account could lead to her having to face serious criminal charges. She would be tried as an accomplice, charged also with perverting the course of justice and, as a result, could be looking at a lengthy prison sentence. They wanted to know whether she or her son knew a man named Jason Scott.

By the time Amanda turned off the computer she was raging about the impotence of her situation. She knew nothing of any bank transfers. Why, she had not even thought of logging into her bank since they were docked at Southampton.

She cursed her son. How could he be so stupid? If he had received stolen money, why shove it into her account and thereby implicate her in his silly mess? He must know that by now the police would be watching his every move?

The name Jason Scott seemed vaguely familiar but she wasn't sure why. She considered getting into her nightie and lying in bed in the dark, feeling sorry for herself, but she also knew that that wasn't going to help.

In her present situation, she couldn't do anything until they docked at New York.

If she stayed fretting in the cabin she would only crawl up the walls with anxiety and nothing would be moved further on.

To hell with it. She decided that there was only one thing to do.

She would put on her glad rags, and go down to join her friends and get plastered.

Why not?

Yes, she would get dressed up, and enjoy the sophisticated and eccentric company of her friends at dinner. They might even be able to cheer her up. Then she would go dancing with her elegant gentleman friend, Karl.

After all, this was the last formal night onboard on this crossing.

Tomorrow, from early morning, suitcases would be packed and left in the corridor to be taken away by the porters, ready to be offloaded at dawn the following day, immediately after they docked.

It was not the first time that Mark had got into trouble. Of course, she would do everything to help her son, but at the moment she simply couldn't.

So, to hell with it, with him, with them and with the whole damned world.

She put on her red dress and went down for dinner.

She was walking through the central lobby, in the direction of the restaurant, when she bumped into Karl.

'I've been worrying about you all afternoon,' he said, leading her to one of the huge sofas in the central area. 'I hope things are settling down now for you at home. Did you hear any more news?'

'My son appears to have got into some money trouble and has now made it worse by implicating me,' she said, not really wanting to go into the wretched details again.

'Despite all your family troubles, Amanda, I have to say you're looking stunning,' he said.

She thought Karl looked pretty wonderful too, but she still had the disturbing image in her mind from this afternoon at the spa, of him out on the deck, in his shorts, stroking Tyger's back.

'I saw you out jogging this afternoon,' she said, fishing for a response.

'I like to keep fit,' he replied.

'You were with that young boy, Tyger.' She left it at that, to see how he would answer.

'Poor child,' said Karl. 'He was crying about the loss of life on the *Titanic*. I felt rather sorry for him. The young take these things very, very seriously.'

Amanda wondered why she hadn't realised that was what it was about. She had seen the *Titanic* enthusiasts on that same part of the deck only minutes before. She felt bad now for being suspicious of Karl's intentions and for seeing a picture without words and then writing her own macabre scenario to fit it.

'Shall I walk you into the dining room?' Karl stood and offered her his arm. 'I might come to your table for coffee, if that would be acceptable?'

In the dining room, it was a full table for Amanda. Myriam and Tyger, Liliane and the two tiresome Australians, Chris and Jennie, were all present.

'Anyone going to this magic show tonight?' Chris asked.

'We saw it the other night,' said Amanda, taking a swig of wine. 'It was very good.'

'Oh yes, Chris, we adored it, didn't we, girls? The magician made Liliane disappear in a box and wake up hypnotised,' said Myriam, fanning herself with her menu. 'It was enthralling!'

'I shall go to see it again tonight,' said Liliane with a laugh. 'After all, I missed most of it last time.'

'Speaking entirely for myself …' Myriam laid down her menu and looked Chris in the eye. 'I love a little lingerie-demain. I thought the Great Arturo's show was superb. *Asbsolutamento superba*, as the Italians would say! Talking of Neapolitans, deary,' Myriam leaned over the butter dish and patted Amanda's arm, 'I can highly recommend the special, *ce soir*, La Spaghetti Carabinieri with a sprinkle of partisan cheese and a dash of canine pepper. *Deliciosa*.'

Looking around, Amanda realised that Liliane, Myriam, Tyger, Chris and Jennie were already on dessert.

'I think he's a weird bastard, isn't he, that Eyetie fella who does it? But then IMO Italians are pretty much all nutters anyway. Ever been to Rome, anyone? All those blokes parading around the streets in their poncy clothes, hand in hand, manbags to the ready.' Chris gave a mock shudder.

Nobody at the table smiled, not even Jennie.

'If they don't speakah di English, frankly I don'ta have-ah di time for 'em,' said Chris, pouring custard all over his apple pie. '*Arrivederci Italia!* Anyways, it's well acknowledged that the English lingo is the language of the civilised world.'

'Actually,' said Tyger, 'English is only the third most spoken language. More people speak Spanish and Mandarin.'

'I said "civilised world", my boy, and Spain and China hardly qualify for that,' Chris snapped. 'And I wonder if you have any of those ridiculous facts of yours to add contradicting the fact that the Anglo-Saxons are the greatest race on the planet?'

In a feeble attempt to change the subject, Amanda refilled her glass and spoke across them, asking Tyger if he was feeling more cheerful now.

'More cheerful than what?' he asked.

'Earlier on this afternoon, Tyger. I heard you were upset over the *Titanic*.'

'Who would say that?' Tyger glared at her, his startling sea-green eyes lowering beneath his curved dark brows. 'Why should I be upset about a silly boat which sank over a century ago? I couldn't possibly know anyone onboard, even if they had been my great-grandparents.'

'But I thought …'

'Nor am I so raw that I think Leonardo DiCaprio and Kate Winslet were actually aboard. Frankly, I have no idea why the Captain made that announcement. I went out on deck to look, just because everyone else did. But what was the point of it? I stared and stared but all you could see was sea and more sea. It was so boring.'

'That's the trouble with these nippers. Got no sense of history.' Chris took a bite of his apple pie. 'Blimey. That pudding's as dry as a nun's nasty!'

He slid his plate away.

'Oh, do shut up,' said Amanda under her breath, as she allowed Liliane to top up her glass of wine. To be truthful, she hadn't noticed herself finish the others. But she took another quaff anyway.

Liliane stood.

'I'm sorry, ladies and gentlemen. If I am to get a decent seat at tonight's show I have to rush.'

Chris looked at his watch.

'Don't mind us, Lillian …'

'Liliane,' she corrected.

'Same difference, old bird. Don't bother to save us a place, will you, mate. The lady-wife and I prefer to sit somewhere at the back. Makes it easier to leave if the show's a total cock-up, eh, Lillian. Nothing worse than having to sit through a crock of shite performed by a loony old wop.'

Amanda turned on Chris. 'You go too far, Chris, with your ghastly opinions and your foul language. I think you should stop it. Now!'

Chris did a comic act of looking around himself.

'Who you speaking to, Mrs? If I was to state things frankly, I'd say you're five sheets to the wind, so you don't know what you're talking about. In my humble opinion, you lot of sad, desperate old scrags had better sit up and shut up. Talk about the three ugly witches cackling round the cauldron!'

'Oh my!' Myriam let out a whimper of indignation and dismay. Her lower lip started to quiver. 'I've never been called a witch before.'

'I think you should apologise to Liliane, Amanda and my aunt,' said Tyger.

'Who the hell are you to tell me what to do, you bloody little whippersnapper, poncing around in your swanky clothes like an old pooftah?'

Liliane held up her hands, backed away from the table, and swept towards the door.

'How dare you talk to Tyger like that?' Amanda swilled down the remains of her glass and turned to face Chris. 'Actually, how dare you talk to *anyone* like that?'

Chris pulled a face and wiggled his head from side to side, while clacking his fingers together to mimic a yacking person.

'You may think you're funny, Chris, but you're not. You're a rude, crude, insufferable, obnoxious pig with odious, if not illegal, opinions. And, by the way, your breath stinks.'

It was only after she stopped talking that Amanda realised she herself had spoken those words. She topped up her glass and took another gulp of wine.

'Come along, Jennie.' Chris rose from his seat and threw his napkin on to the table. 'We don't have to listen to claptrap from a sad hoary sow like old Fatso there.'

As Chris strutted off, dragging his wife behind him, Amanda raised her voice to shout: 'And I feel very, very sorry for poor Jennie, who clearly finds you as obnoxious as we do, but is too scared of you to say so.'

When Amanda turned back to the table Myriam and Tyger were laughing into their napkins.

'Oh! My! Deary!' Myriam sighed. 'That was the best goddamned spectacle I have seen since we boarded this ship.'

'Bravo, Amanda!' said Tyger. 'Thank you.'

Amanda poured more wine into her glass.

'I'm going dancing,' she said, offering the bottle around. 'Anyone want to join me?'

Myriam stretched out and once more patted the back of Amanda's hand.

'Do you really think you should, sweetie?'

Amanda pulled her hand back.

'I'm a free woman, Myriam. I'll do whatever I want.' Amanda wondered why everyone was suddenly turning against her. Didn't they know how hard things were? She stood up, pushing the chair back. It was odd how the ship was rocking again. She took a few steps across the dining room.

Next thing she knew, Tyger was at her side, linking arms.

'You're a sweet kid,' Amanda said to him. 'Thanks for helping an old lady.'

When they arrived in the ballroom, Tyger pulled out a chair at a table not too far from the door.

'This ship is in another storm, isn't it? Is it a force eight?' Amanda asked, sliding down into the seat. 'I can hardly keep my balance.' She looked around the ballroom. This wasn't right at all. Not the plan. 'I need to be nearer the dance floor,' she said, tugging at Tyger's sleeve. 'With the sea this rough I'll never get to dance. I'd fall down the stairs.'

Myriam was suddenly there, standing at Tyger's side.

They both helped Amanda down to a table nearer the dancers.

When they reached the table and tried to sit her down, Amanda pushed them away.

'Why are you two here, cramping my style?' she cried. 'I have a date. I'm going dancing.' She put up her hand and tried to summon a waiter. She took a few steps forward and fell into the arms of a stocky little man of her own age, with a well-trimmed military-style moustache.

'I can see you making eyes at Myriam.' She waved a finger at the man. 'But you're dancing with me now.'

'Of course, madam.' He held her and took a few steps on to the floor. 'But don't you think you would prefer to sit out for a little while? I can order you some coffee.'

'You're one of those gigolos, aren't you,' said Amanda, fingering his lapel. 'I want to dance with the handsome one. You know, the sharp boy, who looks like a young dashing Charlie Chaplin. He's got those enchanting black curls.'

'He's busy dancing with someone else right now. I'm sure you can get a dance with him later. Now let's sit you down and get you a coffee.'

Amanda was aware of this dancer making signals over her shoulder. She didn't like that. While these people were dancing with you they were supposed to concentrate on you and you alone. She grabbed him by the chin. 'You're not as good a dancer as him. We're practically standing still.'

'That's because I think you need to sit down for a little, madam.'

Amanda suddenly caught sight of the handsome young dancer. He was only a few yards away. 'I want to dance with him.' She thrust out her hand, pointing.

The gentleman host looked over his shoulder. 'That's Jason. Jason Scott. I'll get him for you when this tune is over, but, in the meanwhile, let's sit down, and have a little chat and some coffee.'

'I want to dance with Jason Scott!' Amanda flailed her arms around. 'What is wrong with this ship? Why is the dance floor rocking? It must be about gale force eight,' she said. 'I can barely stand upright.'

'It's like a millpond,' said her gentleman host. 'Misty out too. We could do with some wind to dispel it. Nasty for the sailing crew.'

Amanda couldn't understand how her legs appeared to be walking back to the table, when she thought she was standing still.

Next thing she knew she was sitting down.

'Thank you,' said Myriam to Amanda's dance partner. 'I think we can handle it now, ducky.'

'Perhaps somebody should take her back to her cabin.'

Amanda looked up. They were talking about her!

'I don't want to go to my cabin,' she said. 'I want to dance with Jason Scott.'

'He shares a cabin with me,' the gentleman host said to Myriam. 'I'll get him over.' He laughed. 'Everyone wants to dance with Jason! You can feel quite put out, when you're an old codger like myself.'

'You're all lovely,' said Myriam. 'What's your name?'

'I'm George.'

'Thank you, George,' said Myriam. 'It's so reassuring to have someone who really knows how to do the foxtrot and the rhomboid.'

The band played the final chord of the current dance.

Amanda wondered why everyone was standing above her, talking about her in hushed voices. It was like being on your deathbed. But she was here in the lovely ballroom of this gorgeous ship. What were they all looking at? She regarded the people, turning her head from side to side as each person spoke.

She couldn't do this. She wasn't a specimen for them to pick over.

Pressing her hands down on the arms of her chair, she managed to get back on her feet, but oh my, this ship was really swaying. She teetered forward and Jason was there to catch her.

Again, everyone pushed forward, hissing things at *him* now. George sloped off. That's right, she thought. No point staying where you weren't wanted.

Jason smiled that wonderful flashing smile of his.

'Shall we dance?' said Amanda, staggering into him. 'My word, this ship is lurching tonight.'

'I'm rather tired,' said Jason. 'Why don't we sit this one out and have a coffee together?'

'I want to dance!' Amanda didn't know why everyone wanted to stop her dancing. It was starting to make her feel rather cross. 'Why is everyone so mad about coffee, all of a sudden? I want to dance with Jason Scott.'

She thought that that name meant something, but couldn't put her finger on what it was.

'Aren't you friends with my son Mark?' she asked, leaning in on Jason, then losing her balance again. 'You're Jason Scott, aren't you?'

She pulled back and took another look at him.

'You're a lot younger than him. But you're in some scam with Mark. Mark Bailey? Name mean anything to you?'

She saw Myriam shake her head in Jason's direction and do a mime of holding a glass.

'I remember now. I know who you are. Jason Scott!' Amanda thrust her face right into his. 'You're a criminal. You've been putting stolen money into my son's bank and into mine. You're an embezzling little scumbag.'

Jason appeared to freeze where he stood.

'Got you there, didn't I, you little crook?' Amanda tumbled back into her seat.

'Ignore her,' said Myriam to Jason. 'We must get her back to her cabin.'

*

Suzy saw Jason get dragged over to deal with some woman who was clearly extremely inebriated. It was the same woman she had chatted with earlier on in the cruise. Amanda. Suzy didn't remember her as the type to get utterly plastered, but there she was staggering about looking as though any minute she'd arrive at that state of drunkenness where violence crept in.

Suzy was sitting at a table towards the front of the dance floor, with her back to the band. She scanned the room. From her seat, she could see the main entrance doors and the steps leading down from them. She could see everyone who came in and went out. Trouble was, she was by no means certain she would recognise Herr Appenzell again. After all she had only set eyes on him twice: once when she saw his back view at the far end of the rehearsal room, and this afternoon for two seconds as he let himself into Cabin 8127. Thus, every time a tallish, slim, silver fox entered, Suzy was on the alert. Only, on this cruise there did seem to be rather a lot of men who fitted that description.

Whenever a gaggle of guests poured through the double doors, Suzy stood up to get a better look. Her plan was that, whenever a possible subject came into view, she was to walk on to the dance floor and say to Jason and his partner of the moment, 'Nice footwork,' and move on in the direction of the suspect.

Jason had been busy on the floor since the band first struck up, whisking various ladies round to the rhumba, the foxtrot and the cha-cha-cha. Now he was helping to try and get the drunk woman to her feet. It looked like a very difficult situation.

Suzy swung her eyes back to the door and there was Appenzell. Even though she had only had those two short glimpses of him she felt certain it was him. He stood alone in the doorway, surveying the room. His clothing was impeccable: a black tuxedo with satin collar, black bow tie, white piqué dress shirt with pearl studs. His silver-grey hair was sleeked back.

He stayed there for a few seconds.

Suzy felt frightened that he would see her. She held up a drinks menu to cover her face, just in case she was the person he was looking for.

Still subtly glancing around, Appenzell took a few steps down the stairs. Suzy used the moment to lurch in Jason's direction.

Their agreed code was not going to work now, as Jason was sitting down, talking to the drunken woman.

Nonetheless Suzy swept past him and said it anyway: 'Nice footwork! Eleven o'clock. Right-hand door, down the steps.'

The band struck up a lively tango.

Amanda now grappled herself to her feet and started waving her arms above her head. 'Hello!' she called. 'Hello Karl! Karl!'

She was calling someone over to the table where Jason was sitting, and when Suzy turned to follow her gaze she could see that the man she was beckoning was Appenzell himself.

Suzy spun round and grabbed Jason, hauled him to his feet, and then steered him on to the dance floor. She whirled him across the room till they were both behind Appenzell.

'Look,' she said. 'That is him, isn't it?'

Jason peered over her shoulder then twisted her around in a sharp movement typical of a tango.

From their vantage point, at the far side of the floor, they could now watch Appenzell, without him seeing them.

'He's called Karl. How does that tally with the name Stanley Arbuthnot, do you think? Is Karl his real name?' asked Suzy.

Jason screwed up his mouth. 'I can't remember what his name was. Apart from Herr Appenzell.'

'Someone needs to warn that woman, Amanda. He must be after something from her.'

'That would have to be you, Suzy. I can't go back now. But she's as drunk as a skunk. She won't hear you.'

'I cannot stand by, though, Jason.'

A couple moved into the space between them and Appenzell, blocking their view of him. Jason performed a little swoop and positioned them in a better corner of the floor.

'It was very strange, Suzy. When she was trying to get me to dance with her just now, that drunk woman kept asking if I was a friend of her son, Mark, and she accused me of tampering with his and her own bank accounts.'

Suzy's hand tightened on Jason's shoulder. 'Tell me the exact words.'

'As I remember, she called me an embezzling little scumbag, and said I'd put money into her son's account and hers.'

'*Into* her account? Don't you mean took it *out* of her account?'

'No. She definitely said put it IN.' Jason engineered another perfect tango move to get a better view.

Suzy tried to put everything together – the Zurich theatre company being stranded at the airport, the actors having their bank accounts cleared out, the horrible paedophile party which Jason had witnessed, Stan being dead, Jason having apparently flown out of Zurich to London at the same time that he was actually with her at the airport, and Appenzell being onboard this ship with them, using Stan's name. And now Amanda was thinking that Jason was giving her money.

Nothing made sense.

'Appenzell is the only common denominator among all this stuff. He must somehow be involved in the embezzlement.'

'Perhaps he's using that woman and her son to move the attention from himself,' said Jason. 'Setting a false trail? There goes George to the rescue.'

Suzy looked across the room, and saw that Appenzell remained sitting, chatting with Amanda, Myriam and Tyger. George was standing nearby.

'What has that bastard got to do with the drunken woman, Suzy? Do you know? Do you think they're in on it together?'

'Oh no. I'm pretty sure she met him onboard. When I first encountered her, coming out of Genoa, she was definitely on her own.'

'Son's name is Mark Bailey. What is Appenzell to them? Unless he's using her as a way of getting close to that boy, Tyger.'

They both looked over again at the table where Amanda was now slumped, with George casting around for help, while Appenzell talked eagerly with Myriam and Tyger.

Next thing they knew, George and a waiter were helping Amanda to her feet, leaving Appenzell alone with Myriam and Tyger.

'That's it. He wants that boy Tyger. Look!'

'I'm going after Amanda. I have to warn her about Appenzell, tell her to keep her distance,' said Suzy. 'Should I tell her he's a paedophile too?'

'She's completely zonked, Suzy. I told you, she won't hear you.'

'I still want to have a try,' said Suzy.

'I'll keep my eye on him while you go, Suze.' Jason bowed as the tango came to an end. 'I'm going to have to move on now,' he said. 'They won't like it if I stay dancing with the same person, especially as you're in entertainment.'

Amanda was now being shuffled up the steps towards the port-side double doors. Suzy walked briskly across the floor and ran up the steps after her.

'Watch out,' she hissed into Amanda's ear. 'That man, Karl, is involved in some very dangerous things.'

'And who are you?' said Amanda, raising her head. 'Mind your own business. I have a date with a gentleman friend,' she said to George. 'Why are you abducting me from the ballroom?'

'Just getting you a bit of air,' he replied, as they steered her out and turned the corner into the lift lobby. 'We're OK here, thanks,' he said to Suzy, holding Amanda with one arm, using the other to press the lift call button.

Suzy turned and ran back into the ballroom.

She looked down at the table where Amanda had been sitting.

Myriam and Tyger were still there, but Appenzell was gone.

But, then, when she scanned the dance floor she couldn't see Jason either.

17

SUZY HAD WALKED back to her cabin along the open deck. The whole ship was shrouded in fog. Intermittently the ship's whistle gave a long sonorous blow.

It was impossible to see more than five foot ahead of yourself.

Suzy found it very eerie. It was also strangely warm for a December night in the Atlantic Ocean.

Back in her cabin she quickly got out all her paperwork, together with the notes for tomorrow's lecture, and sat down at the laptop to perfect it. She needed to get this out of the way. Later she would go down to the office and print it out, in large print to make it easier to read under the stage lighting.

The foghorn was still blowing regular blasts into the night.

At midnight there was a rap on her door.

'Who is it?' she asked.

'It's me,' said Jason.

Suzy opened up.

'Any developments?'

Jason flopped down on to the bed.

'As it happens – yes. George and the waiter were coming out of the lifts carrying Amanda Herbert back to her cabin when Appenzell suddenly emerged running up the stairs. I'd tried to follow him out of the ballroom, but got trapped by two very keen elderly ladies. George told me that Appenzell had taken care of her from the lift on.'

'They let him?'

'Why wouldn't they? He'd been sitting with her, and he was seemingly most assiduous, greasy almost.'

'I'm sure he was.' Suzy suddenly remembered to click save, so as not to lose her work. 'So what does Appenzell want with her?'

Jason shrugged. 'What does he want with any of us?'

'Do you think he's seen you yet?'

'I'm pretty sure he hasn't.' Jason leaned forward and peered at her laptop screen. 'What are you up to?'

'Tomorrow's talk. Still want to be part of it?'

'Rather. What do you need of me?'

'There are a number of blokes who sounded off about the theatre, mainly mad old Puritans. I think it would be fun if you could read those bits, plus other old geezers: the likes of Doctor Johnson. We'll see now when we read through on the computer, then I'll mark up the bits you'd like to do in red or bold, or whatever you'd like, and I'll print it out and leave it by your cabin when I've finished.'

'Sounds great.'

Jason moved to the edge of the bed, next to Suzy.

'Only one more day and we'll be in New York City.' He hunched himself up. 'I wonder if we'll make it.'

'What can he do, Jason?'

'He knows I'm on to him. Once he realises I'm here onboard, he won't be happy. I imagine, if he's travelling under an alibi, he'll want to get off quietly at New York without me pointing the finger and calling him a paedophile, or indicating that he can't be Stanley K. Arbuthnot, cos the man who genuinely owns that name was found dead several days ago in an apartment in Zurich.'

'But, Jason, why is Appenzell on the ship at all? What is he after? What about all this stuff with all our money? And Stan? Why assume his identity?' Suzy lowered the laptop lid. 'I know we've got to work, but all the time I'm trying to concentrate it's niggling away at the back of my brain. What do you think, Jason? Let's plot it out, episode by episode, and see whether we can get a pattern.'

'Let's do it.' Jason picked up a notepad.

'Start: Herr Appenzell is snared by Reg to finance a theatre company's production of *The Importance*,' said Suzy. 'We all roll up in Zurich, where he owns an apartment …'

'I don't think he owned it,' said Jason. 'It was like some rental. And you said he used the name Hamlyn.'

'One. We are all given apparently random airline tickets, which he, as producer, has purchased.'

Jason sat upright. 'For which he needed all our details: our passport numbers, dates and place of birth, everything.'

Suzy turned to Jason. 'You're right. And, in order to pay us …'

'Which he never did …'

'… he needed our bank details: the account numbers, branch addresses, sort code.'

'No. Surely he only needed our agents' details.'

'But I remember filling in my bank details, don't you? I thought it was for the per diems or something.'

'I didn't see the point so I left it blank.' Jason bit his lower lip. 'I wanted cash in hand. Isn't that the point of per diems? That you get some money paid to you in local currency?'

'So, Appenzell's sole purpose was to fleece us? It still doesn't make sense,' said Suzy. 'Actors are famously poor, especially if you're in the position of accepting something like a job in the English Theatre of Zurich. A two-bit company like that isn't going to be snaring any millionaire Hollywood stars or knights and dames, are they?'

Suzy watched as Jason scribbled an ornate doodle of a euro symbol.

They were getting nowhere.

'Mind you,' Suzy added, 'he did strike gold with India. It seems that she was loaded and he took the lot.'

The foghorn gave another long resonant boom.

'Nothing yet explains why Appenzell is on this ship. Presumably, the missing link is something to do with Stan Arbuthnot.'

Suzy moved to sit on the desk chair.

'What time is it now in the UK?'

Jason looked at his watch and totted up the hours. 'Must be about four or five in the morning.'

'I'm going to email Barbara.'

'He'd have been able to get refunds on all our airline tickets, too, once the show was off.' Jason sighed. 'But that's only getting his own money back. Not making a profit. He can't have gone to all that trouble just to clean out our meagre bank accounts. And why set up an account under my name?'

'Perhaps to get back at you for ruining his party?'

'That's true. But surely there must be easier ways of making that kind of pin money. And he wouldn't have needed to cancel the show.'

Suzy was writing the email, but she turned to face Jason.

'It all went wrong at that party. He must have thought, like so many people do, that the theatre is full of sex maniacs, like himself. Herr Appenzell's weakness for young boys is his Achilles heel. He could probably carry on ripping people off quite happily. I suppose you can make a tidy sum sitting at a computer and clearing out other people's bank accounts. But his vile predilection makes him vulnerable. He thought actors would be safe – but, Jason, you ruined that party, and, by summoning the police to his flat, rented or not, you put his little financial scheme in danger so he wanted out.'

'It still doesn't seem enough.'

'I know! There has to be something about Stan. That's why I wrote to Barbara. I want Stan's full name, for starters. And anything else she knows about him.'

The computer pinged.

'She's replied.'

'What's she doing up at this time?'

'Who cares?' Suzy opened up the email. 'Stanley Keith Arbuthnot. His body was found at Quai Olympique 49, Zurich.'

'That's it,' said Jason. 'That's definitely the address of the flat.'

'Stanley Keith Arbuthnot.' Suzy read on: 'Today they got the results of the autopsy … Stanley Keith Arbuthnot died of suffocation.'

'Suffocation! Blimey!'

'According to the post-mortem, he'd actually died sitting down, and his body was moved shortly after death.'

'That would take some doing.'

'You said that Stan was doing his Violet Elizabeth Bott thing when the police rang at the door?'

'Shrieking? Yes.'

'So, let's presume that Appenzell had got rid of everyone except Stan after you left with those two kids. But Stan refused to go. Appenzell must have known from your demeanour that you wouldn't leave it there. So when the doorbell rang, at that time of night, the person at the door must either be you, coming back for a fight, or the police.'

'Yes. I suppose he would have thought that.'

'So he had to stop Stan making a noise. How long before Appenzell spoke into the Entryphone?'

'Seemed an age.'

'Exactly. And had Stan shut up by then?'

Jason nodded.

'So, presumably Stan was sitting, squealing, arms folded, just like he was when he pulled the same trick in the rehearsal room. And Appenzell covered Stan's mouth, maybe used a cushion. For a man in Stan's state of health it would only take a minute to get him unconscious, wouldn't you think, Jason?'

'Now, when the police came in, Stan would have been sitting there, seemingly asleep. The flat quiet. Just Appenzell schmoozing them. He certainly put on a "just woken up" voice to answer. And, later, when he came out on to the balcony to give me the evil eye, he was wearing what looked like a maroon paisley silk dressing gown, so presumably he'd thrown that on while the police were coming up in the lift.'

'We're on to the right track here, Jason.'

'Perhaps Appenzell simply thought he'd knocked Stan unconscious. Left him there to sleep it off. Came out to glare at me. Went back in …'

'… And then, later on, couldn't rouse Stan, realised that he was dead, rolled him under the bed and, what next?'

'He had a dead body in his flat …'

'More than that, Jason. Because Appenzell knew that that body was supposed to be appearing next day in the *very* play he was producing; he knew that Stan would be missed quite early next morning when the dress rehearsal started …'

'And everyone would have gone searching after Stan, and they would have come to me to ask about him as Reg knew we'd both been at the party …'

'And you would certainly have pointed them to that flat.' Suzy clapped her hands. 'So, you see, he HAD to cancel the show.'

'And he also had to skedaddle,' said Jason. 'Using my airline ticket.'

'Jason!' Suzy gripped his arm. 'Talk about Tommy and Tuppence! We should be sleuths.'

'We should be asleep, you mean. And you've got to finish perfecting your script for the morning. Night-night, old girl.'

'Less of the old.'

As Jason left and Suzy went back to work, they felt as though they were starting to get somewhere. Their most pressing worry now was Amanda.

PART SIX

Cape Sable to New Jersey Bite

18

A MANDA WOKE slowly. Her head was pounding and her eyes glued together with sleep. She tried to look out of the window and saw nothing but a white sheet. She presumed it must be fog.

A long deep blast from the ship's whistle confirmed her suspicions.

She could remember little of last night.

Had she gone dancing?

She looked down. She was wearing a nightgown. If she was as drunk as she thought she must have been, how had that happened? She'd have expected to wake up fully clothed with her make-up smeared all over the pillow. Who had undressed her? Or had she had a sudden burst of sobriety before she got into bed?

Slowly, as she discovered that she was aching all over, she rolled back to face the main part of the cabin.

That was strange! Someone had tidied up her cabin too. The tops, which she had left cluttered, were empty. There was no make-up bag at the dressing table. The chair, which she had left draped with her day clothes, was bare.

Where was her suitcase? It was usually propped up in the corner. She twisted round to see the other bedside table.

Her laptop was gone too.

She pushed herself to a sitting position and surveyed the room.

Everything was gone. The cabin had been cleared of all her personal possessions.

But, apart from that, it did seem to be her cabin. She looked around for any distinguishing marks, but of course hadn't noticed anything to remember. Perhaps she was in another, similar cabin, not her own.

That was the only possible solution.

She pulled open the bedside drawer where she kept her underwear. The drawer was empty.

Amanda drew back the bedclothes and sat up.

Her head was still spinning.

She tried to remember last night, but only the vaguest flashes of memory returned. She recalled having a row with that odious man, Chris, at dinner. After that she knew she had probably gone dancing. That had certainly been her intention anyhow. But she could not remember being in the ballroom at all.

She tried to get to her feet but the room swam before her and she sank back on to the bed. She lay still for a while. The ship's foghorn let out a long deep blast, waking her from a momentary snooze.

She tried to get up again.

Her head was thumping. She staggered to the bathroom and took a few mouthfuls of water from her cupped hands. It was odd to her that there were no tooth mugs or glasses in the bathroom. There usually were.

She decided to take a tepid shower to try and get herself back on to an even keel. Afterwards, when she reached up for something with which to dry herself, she realised there were no towels, either on the rails or the racks.

Dripping wet, she came back into the cabin then dried herself by lying between the bed-sheets.

She pulled open the drawers, one by one, then opened the wardrobe. Nothing.

What was she to wear?

She put her nightie back on.

At that moment, there was a knock on the door.

'Who is it?' she asked.

'It's Karl.'

She started to get up to open the door but he had already let himself in. He was bearing a small breakfast tray. He came over and sat in the armchair by the balcony window, gesturing for her to join him.

Amanda had a sudden dreadful thought that last night he might have stripped her and put her in the nightgown. Maybe more had happened? 'You didn't undress me, did you?'

He laughed.

'No, no, no. I do know about a lady's propriety. I got a chambermaid in, and she prepared you for bed, with the help of a lady colleague.'

'But where are my clothes?'

Karl winced.

'I'm sorry to have to tell you that you had a little accident. So the girls took the clothes away to be cleaned. No doubt they'll bring them back later today, washed, pressed and better than new.' He pushed the tray towards her. 'Now, I think you should have a little porridge and the orange juice I brought you. It'll make you feel better.'

Amanda felt covered in shame. A little accident? What could that mean? Had she vomited? She was mortified. But she realised that Karl was right about eating. She needed to line her stomach. Her head still ached.

'I suppose you don't have any ibuprofen on you?'

Karl fumbled in his pockets.

'As it happens, I do.' He took out a tiny bottle from an inner pocket and emptied two little white tablets into the palm of his hand. 'I came fully prepared,' he said, dropping the pills on to the tray. 'I suggest that you wash them down with the orange juice. I suspect you'll need to rest here in your cabin today.'

'Did I really disgrace myself last night?'

'How much can you remember?'

'I remember having a quarrel over dinner. After that, not much.'

'You have no recollections at all of being in the ballroom?'

Amanda looked down into the lap of her nightie and, being so scantily clad, felt uncomfortably exposed. She had a fleeting memory of Myriam last night, sitting nearby and shaking her head at her.

'Did I do something awful?'

Karl laughed. 'Not as far as I know. You'd just had a little too much to drink after the upset of your son being arrested and all the trouble at home with your bank and the purchase of the new flat in Pimlico. Now that you're a little more sedate, perhaps you could tell me everything about what's going on, and I'll see if I can help. Remember that I work in finance.'

This statement brought another elusive image flashing into her head. Something to do with the money? Something to do with the email from her lawyers?

'Where are all my things? Why has my cabin been stripped?'

Karl looked around. 'Oh yes. I can see how that might have confused you. You're not actually in your own cabin. This is my cabin. I had no way to let you into yours. You didn't appear to have a key.'

'It was in my clutch bag.'

'Ah!' Karl sat back. 'You must have left that in the ballroom. I wouldn't worry. Myriam will have taken care of it.'

'I remember that she was there with me.' Amanda felt terrible. She now owed Karl such a huge debt of gratitude. 'I'm so sorry. Where did you sleep, Karl?'

'It was no problem. I'm a night owl. I wandered the decks for a while, played a little roulette, lost my shirt, then went up to the Seahorse Lounge. It was dark. The bar staff had gone off duty. So I curled up on one of those huge sofas and had a very comfortable night.'

'But your clothes …?'

'I let myself in, earlier on. You were out for the count. So I took all my stuff off in my suitcase and, after my morning gym session, I changed into what I'm wearing now.' He slid the bowl nearer to her. 'You really should eat.'

Amanda took a mouthful of porridge, and found it very comforting.

'I don't usually do things like this, you know. I can't remember the last time I got drunk.'

'You've been under great stress lately, Amanda. Moving home is a serious trauma, but then to discover that your son is in on some dreadful scam and trying to implicate you must be horrible. I can't imagine what it would be like.'

The mini-flashes of memory from last night suddenly merged into a pattern in Amanda's mind.

'Oh yes, Karl. I do remember something about the money thing from last night. Something very important.'

'You still haven't taken the pills,' said Karl.

'I'll save them for later,' she said.

'I think it's advisable to take them with food.'

Amanda moved the pills around on the tray. 'My solicitor sent me a nasty email telling me that my son was in league with some other man over the money thing. Jason Scott. That's his name. I don't trust him. Too good-looking.'

'Why would you know what he looks like, this Jason Scott?'

'I know Jason Scott.' Amanda took another mouthful of porridge. 'He's onboard this ship.'

Karl grew very still. When he next spoke it was with care. 'What do you mean, he's onboard this ship?'

'Jason Scott works for the ship.' Amanda swigged the orange juice. 'He's usually an actor, but was badly let down by a theatre company in Zurich, so he took this job to bail himself out. He's a very good-looking young man. But clearly also a crook.'

Karl appeared to be frozen in his seat. For some seconds he didn't even breathe, then he took one huge inhalation. 'What does he look like, this Jason Scott?'

'Dark curly hair, mid-twenties. Slim. Flashing teeth, oozing with charm, all that actory stuff.'

'And he works for the ship, you say. What does he do? Waiter? Barman?'

'No, he's one of those gigolos who dance with lone women. A gentleman host.'

Karl leaned forward and pushed the two tablets in Amanda's direction.

'I'm not leaving this cabin till you take those pills, Amanda.'

Amanda shrugged. 'You're probably right.' She picked up the two pills and placed them on her tongue and then took another gulp of orange juice to swill them down.

'There,' she said.

Karl sat back and stared at her.

She felt oddly disturbed by his attention. His look was sharp and intense, and he wouldn't take his eyes from hers.

'I was thinking I should perhaps report that Jason boy to the Captain, Karl. What do you think?' Amanda felt suddenly tired again. 'When I get back to my own cabin I will certainly write to my solicitors and tell them that Jason Scott is onboard.'

Karl leaned in and spoke urgently. 'You haven't told anyone yet, have you, about Jason Scott?'

Amanda shook her head. She wondered why this made her feel strange. Her vision was blurred, a dizziness spilling over her. 'Until last night I didn't realise he had anything to do with it. But last night I told him, all right. I told him.'

She found speech difficult. She couldn't seem to make her lips move. Everything she said sounded as though she was underwater.

'Are you feeling all right, Amanda?' Karl asked, standing now and walking around the table in the direction of her seat.

She tried to say no, she didn't feel all right at all, she felt strangely not all right, as though she was drunk again and worse, but no words would come out. She felt a warm trickle down her legs, and realised she had lost control of her bladder. Karl was lifting her up now, dragging her over to the bed, laying her down.

'I need to talk to the Captain,' Amanda tried to say, but realised no whole words came out, just an odd howling noise. 'I need to tell them about Jason Scott.'

'You're not talking to anyone about anything, Amanda,' said Karl, leaning over her and pulling at her eyelids. 'You'll lie here all day, until it gets dark. Then, dear Amanda, owner of my old flat in Pimlico, we will say farewell. For, during the pitch black of the early hours, you'll be accidentally falling overboard. And till then you'll keep quiet.' He looked at his watch. 'For the rest of the day you will sleep like a baby.'

Amanda lost consciousness.

*

Suzy clutched both her own and a spare script for Jason, just in case he forgot to bring his. She was all dressed up and ready, hovering in the wings. Andy had come down and fixed her microphone pack. Through the curtains, she could hear the murmur of the audience as they took their seats. She looked at her watch. Less than five minutes till curtain up. Where was Jason? He couldn't let her down now. Actors were usually early for everything. Jason knew how important this talk was going to be for Suzy. If she made a hit of it, she was hoping that the cruise line would renew her contract. There was so little work around for women of her age, and she was really getting into the swing of ship-board life.

Andy approached her.

'Do you want me to take away the other chair? It'll look odd having two if you're on your own.'

Suzy declined.

'With any luck, he'll arrive, panting, after I've begun. Let's leave it there. Just in case. I'm sure he'll turn up.'

Andy murmured through his headphones, then nodded at Suzy. 'We've got clearance. Off you go! Good luck!'

Suzy walked out through the curtains to the applause of a full theatre.

She launched into the talk with as much enthusiasm as she could, reading the men's roles with as much gusto as the women's. Although her mind was distracted by the thought that at any moment the curtains might part and Jason would dash through, leaping into his character, Suzy knew that the audience was with her. They were laughing at all the funny bits, and someone even booed when she read out the evidence of a Puritan campaigner who had succeeded in closing down all the theatres in England for nineteen years.

As Suzy turned the page, she took a moment to observe the audience. She was immediately drawn to a solitary well-dressed man sitting, arms folded, in the front row. She caught eyes with him. It was Appenzell.

Hastily she threw her full attention back into her script.

Why was he here? He was gazing up at her with a serene smile on his face. It was almost as though he was taunting her.

Her mind swung back to Mike Turner, collapsing in the audience during her first ever talk.

Just like on that day, someone in the auditorium coughed. Another echoed it, then a general shuffle around. She was losing the audience. She could hear them fidgeting. She knew she had to keep her focus.

She raised her eyes from Karl Appenzell, and hurled herself into the characterisations, telling the whole magnificent story of the English theatre from the Middle Ages to today with as much flare as she could radiate. There was a small clock on the lectern. She glanced at it from time to time. She was keeping the pace up, and making sure she was neither going too fast or too slow.

Once the talk ended, she was expected to do a ten-minute Q&A session.

She glimpsed at the clock when there were exactly ten minutes left. She read the final sentences, a quote from Shakespeare, and took a bow. As the applause dropped she stepped forward and asked for the house lights to be brought up.

She noticed that Appenzell was not clapping.

But that was his prerogative.

She took some questions from the floor, following the boy who scampered about the auditorium passing the microphone to people with their hands up. One man wanted to know if Suzy would be appearing in any plays coming up in the West End, as he'd love to see her in action in a great role. One woman actually asked if there was likely to be a revival of *Dahlias*. As the questions petered out Suzy checked the clock. It was almost winding-up time, when she must send the audience on their way.

She was very disappointed in Jason. He had let her down badly.

The lights flickered. Her cue to draw things to a close.

'One last question from the floor,' Suzy announced. 'And then you'll be in good time to rush off and claim your tables for afternoon tea.'

The audience laughed.

She had read them perfectly.

The boy with the microphone was running down the side aisle.

She watched him as he squeezed along the front row.

Then he stopped and thrust the microphone into the hands of Appenzell.

'I was wondering, Suzy,' he asked with a beaming smile, 'what can have happened to your partner in crime, Mr Jason

Scott? Was he not supposed to be reading with you? I noticed the spare chair right away.'

Suzy knew that he was throwing down a challenge.

She smiled, looked him in the eye and said, 'I believe that he was unexpectedly detained.'

'That sounds like a very accurate description, Suzy. And may I thank you for an excellent talk.'

As Suzy took a bow, the audience clapped again. Her heart was beating so fast she could barely breathe.

So Appenzell not only knew Jason was aboard, but there was no doubt in Suzy's mind that he was behind Jason's failure to appear this afternoon.

She took a final bow and walked back to exit through the curtains.

Andy was waiting, ready to relieve her of the microphone.

'Weird bloke, that last one,' he muttered under his breath as he removed the tape which stuck the microphone to Suzy's cheek. 'I've seen him round the place. Slimy customer.'

'You don't know the half of it.' Suzy pulled the bum-pack cable up through the back of her blouse. 'And now I'm very worried for both Amanda and Jason. That man has a grudge against him.'

Suzy went straight down to Jason's cabin and knocked at the door.

George opened up.

'Hello, Suzy. Did it go well?'

'Not really,' she said. 'I suppose you don't know why he didn't turn up?'

'I don't understand?'

'Jason.'

'Jason?' George raised his eyebrows. 'What do you mean? *Jason* didn't turn up? But this morning I couldn't shut him up about it, rehearsing, muttering away, underlining bits in the script you'd left. He was very keen to do it. In fact I got the idea he was exceedingly excited about doing your show.'

'When did you last see him, George?'

George rubbed his chin. 'At noon Jason was certainly in the cabin with me.' He nodded, as though agreeing with himself. 'Yes. When the Captain gave his talk about today's passage we were in here together. We were laughing about the name "Old Cape Cod", and wondering how it ever came to sound like a place romantic enough to get a song written about it. Then we wondered who Martha was and how she managed to choose such a dreary, foggy place to have her vineyard. Jason even asked if, maybe, when we were in New York, we might be able to find a bottle of Martha's wine.'

'What time did he finally head off for the theatre?'

'Probably about an hour after that, cos he went back to studying his script very intently for a while. We left together at lunchtime. I was heading up to the cafeteria, and I thought he was going straight down to wait for you back-stage, actually.'

'Was there anything else?'

'Not really. He was full of the show, and what fun it would be.'

Suzy turned away.

'Oh, there was one other thing,' said George, catching her attention. 'On our way out of the cabin Jason picked up a note from our letter rack. It was from that lad with the unlikely name of Tyger. Jason said he needed to go and find him; then, as far as I know, he was immediately going down to the theatre to join you.'

Suzy walked briskly round the decks scanning everywhere for Myriam and Tyger. She eventually tracked them down in the ballroom, where they were polishing off the remains of their final onboard afternoon tea.

'I was wondering if either of you have seen Jason today?' Suzy asked. 'He didn't turn up for my talk this afternoon.'

'You were giving a talk?' said Myriam. 'What a pity. I was bolivious of that.'

'He got your note, Tyger? Did you arrange to meet Jason somewhere?'

Tyger looked blank.

'What note?'

'You left a note for Jason this morning.'

'No, I didn't. Why would I send Jason a note? We've arranged to meet later on this afternoon on the top deck for a game of shuffleboard. I could tell him anything I wanted to say then.'

'You were going to play shuffleboard in the dark?'

'The decks are floodlit at dusk. It's more fun.'

'And you are certain that you sent him no note, and haven't seen him today?'

'Totally absolutely one hundred per cent certain.'

Suzy didn't know what to do next, so she headed back to her cabin.

'He was unexpectedly detained.' Appenzell's retort echoed around her brain. 'That sounds like a very accurate description, Suzy.'

As she turned towards her cabin, Ong handed her a sealed handwritten letter. 'My friend Jun gave this for you. He says it's urgent.'

Suzy ripped open the envelope and pulled out the note while she unlocked her door.

A careless scrawl: 'Trapped 8127. Bring help. J.'

Appenzell's room number. Jun was his steward. Jason was with Appenzell.

Appenzell had him.

Suzy considered heading straight to the cabin, but realised that it would be folly. She was a 60-year-old woman. Appenzell, male, younger and fitter, could easily overpower her.

That was if he opened the door when she knocked.

And Jason had explicitly asked her to bring help. So, help she would get. Without even entering her cabin she turned about and ran down the stairs, straight to the purser's office.

19

AMANDA FELT terribly groggy but, with enormous effort, opened her eyes. It was hard to keep them open. However much she wanted to wake up, her eyes seemed to shut again of their own accord.

She couldn't remember anything. Where was she? It was as though life was happening in slow motion. She could hear herself breathing. But she wasn't breathing normally at all. Each gasp was coming in a sharp loud snort.

She tried to move her body, but it felt as though she was paralysed.

She wiggled her toes.

But her back ached. It was a dull pain, as though something was pinning her down to the bed. Sluggishly, she twisted her head around and was startled to see a face lying on the pillow beside her.

Amanda blinked again, to be sure she wasn't dreaming.

No. There really was a face there. She was too close to make out the features but she could feel the breaths, coming from the nostrils, dampening the skin of her cheeks.

Whoever it was lying beside her was leaning heavily against her hip. She pulled her head back a bit to get a more focused look. Straight away she recognised the black curly hair, the slender male fingers draped across her rump.

It was that Jason Scott, the dancer.

But why did he have no mouth?

Amanda couldn't work it out. She blinked again and took another look. The lower part of Jason's face was bound with flesh-coloured tape.

More than that, when she looked down at his hands she could see tape tied around his wrists.

She pulled her own hands up and realised they too were strapped together. She reached around herself to nudge Jason.

When she tried to cry out she realised that her own mouth was taped shut too.

She shook the boy and poked her fingers in his face but got no response.

She could feel her heart beating strongly.

A vague memory flashed through her head of Karl, dragging her along the bed.

But how had Jason got here? And why was he gagged and bound, and lying beside her in Karl's cabin?

Her breast filled with a surge of terror. Something was terribly wrong.

They had to get out of here, to get help.

Amanda flung her hands out again, feeling the bedside table for the phone. But it was not there. She opened her eyes, and remembered the empty tops, all cleared and bare.

Until this moment, she had never even thought about the phone. Why had the phone been removed?

There was nothing she could use to call for help.

It was like waking to find yourself imprisoned in an asylum cell in a horror film.

She struggled for some minutes to move her legs, sitting up, using her hands to pull them out from under the dead weight of Jason Scott. Eventually she swung them down on the floor. Getting herself to a standing position was harder than she thought it would be. Using her bound hands to keep balance she groped her way around the bed, then, grabbing on to the walls and the wardrobe and drawer handles, she hauled herself towards the door.

To hell with the fact she was wearing nothing more than a skimpy nightgown. She would fling open the door and call out till somebody came and rescued them.

After what felt like an interminable effort, Amanda arrived at the door. She thrust her hands forward to grab the handle, but they swung straight down again to rest against her belly. She peered hard at the door. Momentarily she had forgotten where the handle was.

She bent down, scrutinising the door, fumbling at it with her fingertips. Eventually she came to the conclusion that there was no handle.

When had that happened?

Cabin doors always had a handle.

Another wave of panic flooded through her and she fell to her knees, sobbing.

How had it come to this?

On hands and knees, she crawled back to the end of the bed, then reached up to grab Jason's dangling foot. She shook it with all her might. She had to wake him. If she was left on her own, neither of them stood a chance. She had to wake Jason.

When she tried to shout through the tape covering her mouth nothing came out. Her vocal cords simply didn't work.

It was like being in a terrifying nightmare.

Perhaps none of this was true.

Maybe she really was still dreaming.

She lay back against the bed and shut her eyes.

That's right.

It was all a dream.

Best stop fighting now and let herself fall asleep again, and then when she woke up everything would be all right.

*

Suzy spent ten minutes trying to convince the pert little Irish girl behind the purser's desk that she was not drunk and that she really needed to talk to a senior crew member about a criminal onboard this ship who might have kidnapped one of the gentleman hosts.

Finally, and only, she suspected, because she was unsettling the other passengers in the queue, Suzy was ushered behind the desk and through a side door into a cramped little office, where a uniformed man sat typing at his computer.

'Miss Marshall!' He rose and held out his hand. 'I'm Robert, the Junior Third Officer. How can I be of assistance?'

Suzy started to explain everything: the Zurich job, the paedophile party, the death of Stan, the mysterious Appenzell. The more detail she told him, about everything, the more she realised that she sounded quite mad. It was obvious that, to this boy now sitting here in his uniform, she must look like some crazy old loony woman.

When, finally, her tale came to a halt, the officer put his head down, holding his hands together on his lap in a position of prayer.

Before replying to her long desperate rant, he took a deep breath.

'And what would you like me to do about this situation?'

'It's him, you see. The man onboard is called Appenzell. But he actually boarded as Stanley Arbuthnot. But Stan is dead, suffocated. In this very man Appenzell's apartment in Zurich.'

'And …?'

'Appenzell is holding my friend, Jason Scott, one of the gentleman hosts, as a hostage in his cabin. I think he didn't find out Jason was aboard till today. Jason, you see, was a witness to the paedophile party where Stanley was killed.'

Again, Suzy realised that she sounded lunatic.

'I need you to come with me to Room 8127, Officer. To his cabin …'

'Whose cabin?'

'Appenzell. I mean Stanley Arbuthnot.'

'And when we get there, what would you expect me to do, Miss Marshall?'

'Just get Appenzell to open up. I know he is holding Jason. There's no other reason Jason wouldn't turn up for my show.'

The Junior Third Officer gave Suzy another up and down look. She knew he was measuring her for psychological assessment.

'I believe Jason didn't show for one of the dance sessions, claiming a migraine. Perhaps he has another.'

'But where would he go? His room-mate, George, says Jason hasn't been seen since around one o'clock when he got the note from Tyger.'

'Tyger?'

Every time Suzy added anything she realised it made the whole story sound more and more absurd.

'So then, Miss Marshall, what would you like me to do about all this?'

'Go to Appenzell. I mean Stanley Arbuthnot. Ask to see Jason.'

'You simply want me to knock on the door of 8127 and ask Mr Arbuthnot if Mr Scott is there with him?'

Meekly, Suzy nodded.

'Have you tried doing this yourself?'

'I'm too scared of him. I believe Appenzell has killed some-one already.'

The officer nodded slowly. Suzy thought he looked like a silly toy dog in the back of a car window.

'Please,' she cried. 'I have to help Jason. Please! I beg you. Please come with me. When we find Jason is inside, we can take it from there and decide what to do next. But I have to check it out.'

The Junior Third Officer rose and took his peaked cap from the hatstand.

'Let's go,' he said.

Timidly, Suzy followed him out of the office.

They stood together in silence as the lift ascended to the eighth deck.

On the landing they took a sharp right and strode briskly along the corridor, passing rows of suitcases waiting to be taken away to the bowels of the ship for offloading in the morning. At one stage they both had to stop and wait as a large, fully laden trolley swept across their path, heading towards the lifts.

Since leaving his desk the officer had not spoken a word.

They reached Cabin 8127.

The Junior Third Officer adjusted his cap and rapped gently on the door.

Silence.

They waited.

'I know he's in there,' said Suzy. 'Knock again.'

The officer ignored her.

They waited some more.

The officer was on the verge of knocking a second time when they heard a shuffling noise.

The door opened a crack.

Appenzell's head appeared.

He looked surprised.

'Can I help you, Officer? I was just taking an evening nap.'

'Open the door,' cried Suzy. 'I know you've got Jason trapped inside. Open up and let us see.'

Appenzell shrugged and exchanged a man-to-man look with the Junior Third Officer.

'Are you feeling quite well, Miss Marshall?' said Appenzell calmly. 'I have to tell you, Officer, Miss Marshall acquitted herself very bravely this afternoon in the theatre when her colleague failed to put in an appearance. I was very impressed.'

Suzy knew all about his smooth talk. She also knew how he'd pulled this act once before, and there was a man behind him who was dying or dead. In Zurich it had been Stanley. Perhaps Jason was lying smothered on the bed.

'You seem anxious to look inside, Miss Marshall.' Appenzell opened the door wide. He stood before them, wearing a maroon paisley silk dressing gown and fancy embroidered velvet slippers. 'Please do come in.'

Suzy rushed in. The room seemed utterly normal. A library book was lying face down on the coffee table.

'Agatha Christie,' said Appenzell. 'She never fails, does she?'

Suzy looked around her.

The cabin was too tidy, too perfect.

'I'm so sorry to have disturbed you, Mr Arbuthnot.'

'Absolutely no problem, Officer.'

The officer reached out to take Suzy's arm, but she pushed past him and hauled open the balcony doors.

'I'm so sorry, Mr Arbuthnot,' said the officer, under his breath.

'Poor thing.' Appenzell shook his head. 'If it'll keep her quiet …'

Suzy caught the interchange and realised it was one of those condescending moments shared by men when patronising older women. Also she noticed how Appenzell was barefacedly answering to the name Arbuthnot.

But Suzy was not to be put off by their smug attitudes.

Appenzell had Jason hidden somewhere. She knew he had him. She had to find Jason.

'We'll be on our way, Mr Arbuthnot,' said the officer.

'No,' cried Suzy. 'You can't. We have to …'

But the officer spoke over her.

'Might I offer you a complimentary bottle of wine, sir, as compensation for this unfortunate disturbance?'

A reward for his suave ability to lie and make pretence? Suzy was appalled.

She darted swiftly back towards the door, pulling open the wardrobe and sweeping her hand through the clothes, bending down to check the racks at the bottom.

'He must be in the bathroom then,' she cried, stepping briskly inside. She tore at the shower curtain which was pulled tightly closed around the bath.

But the bath was empty.

Frustrated, angry and desperate, Suzy started to shout. 'Murderer! Embezzler! Paedophile! Where have you hidden him? You bastard! BASTARD!'

The Junior Third Officer grabbed Suzy round the waist and steered her sharply out of Appenzell's cabin.

'I'm sorry, Miss Marshall, but I am going to accompany you down to the Medical Centre, so that a doctor can take a look at you.'

As Appenzell clicked the door shut on them, the officer let go of Suzy. His voice took on a wheedling tone. The kind of voice you would use to a child holding a gun. 'I believe, Miss Marshall, that you are not feeling quite yourself.'

Suzy looked into the young man's eyes. He actually appeared frightened. Frightened of her!

Suzy wanted to scream.

'I'm sure that if the doctor can give you a little something to relax you, you'll feel better in a whizz. Let's go down there together, shall we?'

He was tiptoeing stealthily towards her, as though she was a wild animal: a tiger or a wild dog on the loose.

'You have to believe me,' she howled, backing away from him along the corridor. 'There is something very wrong going on here.'

The Junior Third Officer had hold of her again now, and however hard she struggled she could not free herself.

20

Amanda kept shaking Jason, prodding him, pinching and slapping him, in the hope that he would wake up.

She herself was feeling much less frail and powerless. This meant that the drugs must be wearing off, but she feared that would also mean the imminent return of Karl to come and give her more.

She had an idea. She threw herself back on to the floor, crawled to the fridge, and rooted about for cold things, which she tossed back on to the bed with her conjoined hands. She felt like a performing seal. She then pulled off Jason's shoes and socks and rubbed the soles of his feet with the icy cans and bottles.

She felt him stir. He also let out a stifled groan.

She crawled back to the other end of the bed and shook his shoulders. He blinked a few times, then his eyes opened wide, shocked.

He made a burbling noise, which she realised was him attempting to speak.

She moved closer to him and clawed at the end of the tape with her fingernails. At first, she couldn't get a grip, but eventually a small corner came loose. She tugged with all her might and managed to get it half off.

She made out his words: 'Where are we?'

All she managed to say by return was 'Karl'.

Jason nodded, his head flat against the pillow. He had understood her.

He summoned her to sit back up on the bed.

Then, using his teeth, he tore at the pair of tights which bound her wrists.

As he gnawed she got more and more purchase and was able to press hard enough to slip one hand out.

Once freed she tore at the tape on Jason's mouth.

'He'll be back soon,' slurred Jason. 'He'll know exactly how long those drugs work.'

While Amanda tugged at her own gag, Jason lifted his head, then immediately flopped back on to the pillow.

'Where are we?'

'In his cabin.'

'We have to get out.'

'The phone's gone,' said Amanda. 'And there is no handle on the door.'

Jason looked at her intensely.

'I know why he has me locked in here, Amanda, but what did you ever do to upset him?'

'It's something to do with the row I had with you, last night. My son, Mark, who's staying in my new flat in Pimlico, was picked up for embezzling money with you.' As Amanda spoke a vague memory gnawed at her. Something to do with the flat. She couldn't grasp it.

Jason nodded his head towards the balcony. 'Let's try that as a way out.'

Amanda rolled off the bed and crawled over towards the sliding glass doors. She pulled with all her might, but realised she first needed to release the latch. Using a nearby chair, she hauled herself up, and sat on it, then reached forwards and pulled the handle out. She heard it click.

Leaning against the frame, Amanda pushed the edge of the front window, then yanked it.

She turned back to Jason for help.

'It won't budge,' she said. Flopping like a fish, Jason rolled himself across the bed on to the floor. Amanda now ripped at the tape binding his wrists and ankles.

'It's hard to move, isn't it, even without the tape? I feel as though I'm made of lead,' he said. 'Sorry if I'm not being very effective.'

He tugged and shoved at the glass door.

He stopped and shook his head. 'He's blocked it somehow.' Stretching out his fingers, he felt along the guiderail.

'There we are,' he said, his fingers pinching at something. 'He's used the curtain rod to stop it. Help me get it out. Your nails are longer.'

On their knees, the pair of them worked together, using their nails to gouge around the white shiny rod, until they had a grip. First time they got it up a quarter of an inch then lost purchase and it dropped straight back into the gap. Second time they fumbled more but still lost hold. Third time, Jason jammed his thumb under the rod as it came up and they lifted it out.

Using the chair again, they helped one another to stand upright, then heaved the door half open.

They both staggered over the raised bottom step, a protection against incoming water, and found themselves outside on the balcony. Leaning against the rail, they looked down at the row of orange lifeboats hanging below, and beneath them the open deck.

They could see people jogging, running, taking an evening stroll.

Both tried shouting, but the fog, the ship's movement and their own feebleness meant that no one below heard anything at all.

Amanda could see that Jason was barely conscious. After every effort, he slumped back into a semi-sleep, his body going floppy and limp. He seemed to need tremendous force to open his eyes. He rocked forward, a rag doll pressing against her.

'We don't have much time, Amanda. If you help me to climb up these rails, I could get myself around that partition and jump down on to the next balcony. We must just hope someone's in there, and they can help us.'

He tried pulling himself up the guardrails, but each time his grip would go and he slithered back to the floor.

Amanda realised in his present state it would be highly dangerous to let Jason go ahead. If he lost his hold for a second he would hurtle down thirty feet and smash on to the hard deck below.

'Jason. You must help *me* get up,' she said. 'I've been alert longer than you. I'm less likely to fall.'

'But ...' Jason shook his head. 'You can't, Amanda. It's too dangerous for you.'

Amanda raised her foot on to the lower rung and hauled herself up, grabbing hold of the edge of the white metal partition, shielding them from the next cabin's balcony. She found herself hanging back into the empty space. Jason lolloped forward and caught her. 'Careful!' he cried. 'Swing your leg round. I've got you.'

Amanda managed to sit astride the balcony rail, a leg either side of the partition. She held on to the freezing-cold metal panel. It was slippery with dew and very hard to keep a grip.

'One last thrust,' said Jason. 'Remember to put all your balance forward in the direction of the other balcony's floor. Hold on. Now, on the count of three.'

Amanda's heart was thumping, her fingers were numb. Her flimsy nightgown was sodden with damp.

She seized Jason's hand and took a deep breath.

'One ...

'Two ...

'Three!'

Amanda lurched forward. As she twisted around the side of the partition she scraped her thigh against a rusty joint. She felt the warmth of blood as her leg caught against the edges of the round metal screws. Disregarding the pain, she used all her strength to fling herself down on to the other balcony.

She landed with a thump. Winded and shivering with fright, Amanda lay still for a moment or two, feeling like a beached whale. She took deep breaths. When her heart calmed a bit, she felt strong enough to start getting to her feet. She raised her knees.

'Are you all right?' she heard Jason hiss under the partition.

'Yes,' she replied. Her voice came out as a feeble croak. She slid her hands to her side, pressing down with all her strength, trying to sit up. A memory flashed. Hadn't Karl said to her, just as she was slipping under, that he was the previous owner of her new flat? Karl was the Swiss banker, the man who had messed her about. He'd even said her address out loud. How else would he know it?

Amanda rolled over and hauled herself up on to her knees, using the wooden deck lounger as a prop to steady herself.

She looked up.

Although the curtains were drawn, Amanda could see that there was a light on inside. A yellowish glow seeped through the gaps at the top and sides of the curtains. She hoped that it meant somebody was in the cabin, getting dressed perhaps for dinner.

Amanda tried to stand tall and appear decent. She looked down at herself. She was wearing nothing but a ripped, blood-stained nightie.

It would not look good.

When she felt composed, she raised her fist and knocked against the glass.

She heard movement in the cabin.

Someone was coming.

What a relief.

She heard the clack of the handle.

She did her best to smile.

She so needed help.

The curtain drew back and the glass door slid open.

'Amanda!' said Karl, otherwise known as Appenzell. 'I wondered what all the noise was about. I watched you come round the great divide. Thought I'd let you have a moment to contain yourself. In you come.'

Amanda tried to stagger back out on to the balcony again, but Karl had hold of her, grappling her waist with his strong arms.

'I really must have miscalculated the time on those drugs. Next time I'll double the dose.'

He dragged her inside, then slammed the balcony door shut behind her.

SUZY HAD BEEN marched down to the Medical Centre. Once the Junior Third Officer had gone and she was alone with the doctor, Suzy had deliberately curbed her behaviour, telling him that everything was a terrible misunderstanding. She talked lucidly about simply trying to look for a friend who seemed to have disappeared, and excused the disappearance by talking about it being a silly temper tantrum. It was after all such a very big ship, with so many places to go and so many decks, etcetera, and she had got so frustrated she had reached the end of her tether. Eventually the doctor relented and said she could go. He nodded sagely and told her that if she felt any more panic attacks or semi-psychotic episodes coming on she should return to see him at once.

Suzy was appalled that, before he let her go, she had to swipe her keycard and allow him to charge her for a consultation.

But anything to get herself back upstairs and on to the trail of Jason.

She returned immediately to her cabin to have a think. She shared her thoughts by email with Barbara, telling her everything she knew about Jason, Stan and the erstwhile producer of their show, Herr Appenzell, who was now passing himself off as Stanley K. Arbuthnot. Only for Appenzell the K stood for Karl, not Keith. 'No one believes me about any of this,' she wrote. 'Jason challenged the man and has now gone missing. We're about a hundred miles off Long Island, coming into New York Harbour before dawn, docking tomorrow at seven.'

She left the cabin and made her way back up to the purser's office. Perhaps she could attract someone else's attention. With any luck, there would have been a change of staff by now and she could start afresh.

Once she reached the front of the queue, she came up with a new idea.

'I think that a man has gone overboard,' she said firmly.

'I see.' The girl gave her a piercing look. 'Did you witness this episode?'

'I can see no other reason why he would not have turned up for the show or apologised afterwards. It is now a matter of hours since anyone saw him.' Suzy decided to take the risk of continuing. 'I also believe that there is someone onboard, a known criminal, who had a very good reason to get rid of him. His name is Karl Appenzell but he is passing himself off as a dead man – Stanley Arbuthnot.'

Behind her she heard a scoffing laugh. She turned to see a man, who said out of the corner of his mouth to the woman standing beside him, 'Didn't I tell you these Pommie actresses are all as mad as March hares, Jennie?'

'I think you had better go back down to the Medical Centre,' said the girl at the purser's desk in a steady, threatening tone.

Suzy looked round and saw two members of staff heading in her direction, but at this moment the elegant Frenchwoman, Liliane, stepped forward and grabbed Suzy's hand.

'It's all right, everyone. Suzy is coming with me. She's preparing for a dramatic role. We theatre folk, "mad as March hares" as our Australian friends back zere in the queue say.'

Liliane marched Suzy along.

Suzy tried to shake her off. 'You don't understand. We don't have much time. For all we know, Jason went overboard this afternoon or is lying dead somewhere.'

'Hush,' said Liliane, stabbing at the lift button. 'Come with me.'

They went up and got out at the same floor as Suzy's cabin but at the lifts took a right rather than a left.

Suzy realised she was being frogmarched into the starboard side of the entertainment quarters.

Liliane used her keycard and ushered Suzy into a large cabin, where Arturo the Luminoso sat reading.

He pulled his spectacles down his nose and said briskly, 'Ah, Suzy Marshall, I wondered how long it would take you to find us out.'

'Find you out?'

'We are an item, Arturo and I,' said Liliane rapidly. 'Professionally and personally, but, for theatrical reasons, obviously whilst onboard we have to keep a distance and pretend to be strangers.' She turned to Arturo. 'Suzy has had a desperate encounter with Karl, or as you call him, the Devil, and needs our help.'

'My God! I knew he could not last the whole voyage without breaking out of his diabolic shell.' Arturo rose instantly from his chair and rolled up his sleeves. 'What can we do? I can sense your anxiety, Suzy.' He ran his fingers through his hair, and squeezed his temples with the palms of his hands. 'I know we don't have much time.' He pulled a rabbit's foot from his pocket, kissed it and put it back. 'You realise, I am sure, that this soi-disant Karl is a very dangerous man? I felt his wicked vibrations even before we boarded. He sat in the departure lounge holding himself with such tranquil authority that it had to be a lie. I could feel that behind that suave, urbane façade he was exceedingly nervous, and therefore I knew that he must recently have done something very wicked.'

'He's doing something right now,' said Suzy, proffering the note she had received from Jason. Almost gabbling, she told how she had taken the Junior Third Officer up to Karl's cabin, where she felt sure Jason was being held, only to find

Appenzell sitting there, cool as a cucumber, in his silk dressing gown and velvet slippers, making her look like a hysteric.

'You are sure this note was written by your friend?' Arturo held it up. 'Is it in his hand?'

Suzy took a close look.

'Would you recognise Jason's hand?'

Suzy peered at the neat row of script.

'Oh, what a fool! I was so frightened I didn't really look closely.'

'It's not Jason's writing?'

'His is similar, but not nearly so neat. Much more of a spidery scrawl.' She felt like crying. She could see that she had been deliberately lured to Appenzell's cabin to make a fool of herself in front of the crew.

She had fallen into Appenzell's trap.

'I don't know what I can do,' she appealed to Arturo. 'I have to find Jason. What if he's been thrown overboard?'

'It is very difficult to throw a person over,' said Liliane. She paused before continuing. 'Difficult, but not impossible, especially in this dense fog.'

'No one could be found in the water on a day like this,' said Arturo. 'Especially if you say he's been missing for …' he glanced at his pocket watch '… over six hours.'

'It's seven already? Oh God!' Suzy felt desolate. Outside she could see it was now both foggy and dark.

'Tell us everything you know,' said Liliane, sitting Suzy down on the sofa. 'Let's put it all together. Something may emerge.'

'Lili is right,' said Arturo. 'For us to better understand you must tell us everything you know.'

Suzy told the whole tale from Zurich right up to today. Liliane added what she and Arturo already knew of Karl Appenzell. 'From the moment he came aboard zat man has been homing in on Amanda,' she said. 'I have even seen him following her, watching, when she was unaware. He has some unknown interest in zat woman. It's as though he knew her from before.'

'It's nothing to do with romance?' asked Arturo.

'No. No. He is targeting her.' Liliane sighed. 'Zere was a small diversion when he directed his attention towards Myriam, but we all know what *zat* is about …'

'Her nephew, Tyger,' said Suzy.

'Exactly.' Arturo clapped his hands together. 'That is his weak spot.'

'I worry about Amanda,' said Liliane. 'She is a decent woman. Ze reason she got so drunk last night was because her son had been arrested, something to do with an apartment in London which she had recently purchased. There was also talk of embezzlement. The name Jason Scott came up.'

'Jason?' Suzy looked up. 'Could that be because Amanda danced with him?'

'No.' Liliane was emphatic. 'Something to do with bank accounts and theft.'

'Jason and I have been caught up in a similar thing,' said Suzy. 'To do with the Zurich theatre company we were both in.'

'Really?' Liliane exchanged a look with her husband.

'We need to talk to Amanda.' Arturo stood up. 'We have to find her. She is the key. Find Amanda and we will discover Jason.'

'I don't know her cabin number,' said Suzy.

'I do.' Liliane reached over to her dressing table and pulled up a piece of paper. 'On the first night out of Southampton the ladies of our table swapped numbers. Here it is.'

'Let's go,' said Suzy, taking Liliane by the hand.

Arturo patted his pockets, grabbed a sturdy walking stick and followed them.

They took the lift to Deck 8. As they came out they passed Myriam coming down the stairs from the upper decks.

'I was just heading along to meet Tyger in the ping-pong room,' she said. 'Do you know what? Tyger says it's really called whiff-whaff. I think he's making it up. What do you think?'

'We need you, Myriam. You can play ping-pong later.' Liliane grabbed Myriam's hand. 'Ze more ze merrier,' she said. 'Come help us, Myriam.'

The four ran along the odd-numbered corridor, counting cabins as they stumbled past suitcases and trunks waiting for collection.

'That's his.' Suzy pointed to 8127.

'Amanda is next door,' said Liliane.

'*Next door?*' Suzy was shocked.

'It's too bad,' said Arturo, flicking at the DO NOT DISTURB signs which dangled from both 8125 and 8127.

Suzy rapped on 8125. After her recent experience in Appenzell's cabin she dared not call out.

'Amanda!' called Arturo.

'Amanda! Amanda!' echoed Liliane and Myriam.

Arturo held up a finger and asked them to hush.

'Someone is in there,' he said. 'I hear scratching.' He bent down and put his ear to the door. 'Someone lying on the floor …' Arturo got on to his hands and knees, pulled a small mother-of-pearl horn from his pocket and held it up to listen. 'Who's there?' He pressed his finger to his lips and listened intently. 'They sound very feeble.'

All three women now banged on both doors, pounding with their fists, kicking with their shoes.

Attracted by the noise, a flurry of porters and stewards arrived, running down the corridor.

'Mesdames!' said one. 'Do stop! People are resting.'

'Someone inside is in grave danger,' said Suzy. 'We need to open up.'

A cabin boy scuttled along. 'I cannot let you in,' he said. 'I saw you here before. I shall have to call an officer to restrain you.'

'You won't restrain *me*, though,' said Arturo, raising his stick and bringing it down hard on the door.

'Please desist,' ordered one of the stewards. 'You must not knock. Not when the DO NOT DISTURB signs are up.'

Suzy grabbed both signs, ripped them off the doors and flung them over her head.

'Now have a go. Open up!'

Wincing with apprehension, the cabin boy held up his passkey, which swung from a chain round his waist. Arturo snatched it from his hands and dragged the boy forward, then used the card to open Amanda's door.

Inside, sprawled on the carpet between the wardrobe and the door, lay Jason, prostrate but on the verge of consciousness.

'Oh, my word!' cried Myriam, running inside. 'It's that handsome giggler.'

'Phone for help, Myriam,' shouted Suzy, who was kneeling just inside the door, loosening Jason's clothes.

'The phone is gone!' Myriam, flustered, looked around on the tops, pulling open the drawers. 'There IS no phone.'

'Call for a doctor,' Suzy shouted back to a steward, who stood gaping in the corridor. 'This is an emergency.'

The steward turned to run off.

'But where is Amanda?' Myriam was trying to pull open the balcony doors.

As Suzy jumped to her feet, Liliane and Arturo stooped to take care of Jason.

'No! Come back!' Suzy shouted after the steward. 'First you must open that other door.'

She pointed at 8127.

The steward shrank back.

'He frightening man,' he said, cowering. 'Too much. No. I cannot.'

'Hear my voice.' Arturo leaped up and blocked the steward's way. He pulled a small blue stone on a gold chain from his pocket and dangled it in front of the boy's eyes. 'Watch the stone. Do as I say. When I click my fingers, you will freeze.'

Arturo clicked his fingers. The boy stood transfixed.

'Now open the door to 8127,' said Arturo, softly but deliberately. As though in a trance, the steward pulled the chain from his waist, went straight to the door and slid in his universal keycard.

Together Arturo and Suzy pushed the door open.

Arturo clicked again and the steward stood still, bemused.

'Off you go!' said Arturo. 'Get help.'

The steward ran off.

Suzy dashed into the cabin.

Amanda lay inert on the bed, her face in the pillow. She was wearing a bloodstained torn nightgown. A gentleman's tie was knotted round her neck.

Suzy climbed up on to the bed and rolled Amanda over. Her face was swollen, her tongue protruding.

'Help!' Suzy struggled to loosen the tie. 'Help!'

Arturo pulled a penknife from his pocket and cut the tie.

Amanda's fingers were twitching. As Suzy knelt upright, Amanda took a sudden massive intake of breath.

'We need water,' said Arturo.

Myriam ran round the side of the bed and telephoned down to the Medical Centre. 'This is an emergency! Come to Cabin 8125 and 8127. Bring oxygen.'

Suzy jumped off the bed and flung open the bathroom door. She stood by the basin, took a tooth mug and ran the tap.

Then she froze.

The shower curtain had moved a fraction, giving out a little plastic crackle.

Suzy knew that Karl Appenzell must be standing in the bath.

'Where's that water, Suzy?' shouted Arturo.

Suzy rested the mug on the basin, turned and ripped open the shower curtain.

330

Karl Appenzell fell upon her with all his force. He had a long length of dental floss, wound round and round both hands into a fine but strong string. He drew this around Suzy's neck, gripping both ends. Suzy struggled. She could not cry out. She tried to pull away but it caused the floss to cut into her skin. Appenzell tightened his grip. She managed to slip one finger under the floss and wriggled it, trying to get herself loose. She could hardly breathe. The pain from garrotte was beyond anything she had ever known.

Suzy tried to shout but she could not even manage a whisper. Her tongue was being squeezed out of her mouth.

She knew she could only last a minute or two of this torture.

'Suzy, what are you doing, we need the water!' Liliane appeared in the doorway. Suzy grasped an arm out in her direction.

Liliane froze and screamed out to Arturo. 'Help! Now!'

Then Liliane turned away. Suzy couldn't believe it. Liliane was going to leave her here.

Suddenly Liliane stepped backwards and, gripping the towel rails with all her force, shoved her bottom into Suzy's stomach, thrusting her against Karl until he lost his balance and reeled back into the bath, losing grip of the garrotte.

Suzy bent forward, gasping for breath, and staggered out of the bathroom.

At that moment, Tyger appeared in the cabin doorway.

'I heard all the noise right from the table-tennis room,' he said. 'What's going on?'

Suzy was on all fours. She rocked towards Tyger, trying to push him out of the way.

But she was too late.

Karl jumped out of the bath, shoved Suzy and Liliane out of his path, and ran towards the corridor.

He grabbed hold of Tyger and sprinted away.

Suzy, still bent double, teetered forward, trying to chase after Karl. She opened her mouth to scream, but her voice was gone.

In the distance, along the corridor, she could see the doctor and some uniformed men running in their direction.

She turned and lurched in the other direction, following Karl, who had slammed out through the door into the table-tennis room.

When Suzy came into the games room, the ping-pong players were all gathered, cowering, in a corner. One of them pointed towards the door to the open deck.

'They went that way,' called the kid.

Suzy hobbled after Karl and Tyger. She stepped outside and was met by a cold damp blanket of fog. Light from the deck lamps pooled in fuzzy white balls, suspended in mid-air.

She looked around in every direction, listening. But although she could feel the muffled vibrations of the ship's engines, she could hear nothing but the sheering water being repulsed from the ship's beam.

There was no sound of footsteps.

She stood still, straining to hear. She had no idea which way Karl Appenzell and the boy had gone. The deck was at this point both wide and long.

To run in the wrong direction now would be a disaster.

A sudden deep blast from the foghorn shocked Suzy into taking a few tiny steps to keep her balance.

She realised that she was nearly at the stern of the ship. Surely Karl would have headed towards the bow, which gave him so many more options: more doors in, more stretches of open deck, more places like tennis courts to hide.

She spun round and ran forward into the patchy mist, stopping every few moments to listen. After about twenty yards she found herself standing next to one of the large games boxes. She knew these were full of heavy shuffleboard discs and deck quoits. If she opened one up it would at least provide her with something of a weapon.

She pulled out a rubber deck quoit, then, moving on, unhooked a shuffleboard stick from its clip on the wall.

The foghorn once more blared out its warning. Suzy wondered why the two blasts were so near to one another. Usually the interval was longer. Was the ship running into some obstacle? Or was the Captain warning another ship it was in their path?

She moved stealthily along, always scanning the mist for movement.

A distant sound. Whirring growing louder. Then a helicopter flew above the ship and away. Under cover of the engine noise Suzy ran forward quickly. She managed to cover some distance, certain no one could have heard her footsteps.

About twenty yards further on there was a sudden break in the haze and Suzy saw them. Karl had his arms around Tyger. He was gripping the boy, bending him back over the rail. Tyger was grappling, trying to push himself away. Doing her best to remain silent Suzy darted forward.

She wished she could call out for help, but did not want to warn Appenzell that she was so close. She stood very still, pushing herself back against the damp white metal walls. She estimated the distance, then threw the hard rubber quoit high into the air.

It rose in a steep arc, disappeared for a few moments into the mist then landed with a loud thud, hitting the deck just behind the spot where Appenzell was standing.

Appenzell jumped back in surprise.

Tyger pulled away.

Appenzell looked around.

He caught eyes with Suzy, then turned and ran.

Suzy dashed after him, running like she never had run before.

But he was gone again, disappeared into the fog.

Suzy halted. She remained motionless, once more listening for footsteps. She could hear nothing but the pulsing of the ship's engine.

She tiptoed forward once more. She could see yellow haze flooding through a door. Just beside this was a metal ladder, rising perpendicular up the ship's side.

With a holler, Appenzell leaped down from above, landing upon her, flinging her on to the deck.

Suzy fought to knock him off her but he grabbed her wrists and pinned them to the slippery wooden planks, his own weight preventing her from moving.

'That friend of yours, Jason, deserved what he got,' he hissed into her ear. 'He ruined everything for all of you.'

The dampness in the air made it hard for Appenzell to get a purchase on Suzy's wet skin and she slid her hands free. They wrestled on the decking.

'I never wanted you in that Zurich theatre company, you bitch. The actress I wanted pulled out. She was a real woman. She had kids. When you joined the show it turned my whole plan into a pointless exercise.'

Suzy groaned. This appalling man thought that running a theatre company would be an easy way to procure the company of other people's children.

'You revolt me,' said Suzy.

Appenzell shoved her, then rolled her over. He pressed her head down. She brought her knee up, but failed to hurt him. Appenzell flipped her over again, holding her down, pressing her arms against the wooden deck.

She felt a distant sound, a kind of dull clang.

'You killed Stanley,' she said.

Appenzell looked up; at the same time Suzy lurched forward and bit into his cheek, gripping his flesh between her teeth, until he yanked his head back.

She rapidly rolled away from him, backing up until she hit the ship's cold metal side. Here she could grasp her way to an upright position.

Once she was standing she stooped to grab the shuffle-board stick, which she had dropped when Appenzell had jumped her.

A sudden flurry and she saw him scuttling in her direction. She shunted the stick forward, bumping at his feet, knocking him off-balance.

Once he was down Suzy jumped, landing with all her force on his back.

Winded, Appenzell gasped, still grabbing out behind himself to snatch at her ankle.

In the distance she heard Tyger shouting. 'This way! This way!'

'Stanley was a fat useless waste of space,' hissed Appenzell. 'I wish I'd never set eyes on him.'

Suzy spat into his face.

'You bitch,' Appenzell jeered. 'You and that crazy woman, Amanda.'

He toppled Suzy back down on to the deck, her cheek hitting the floor with a crack. He pushed her head down, pressing her ear into the wet wood.

She could hear a pounding sound, like a battery of drums. What was it? Could it be the sound of her own heart?

Appenzell stayed on top of her, bashing at Suzy with his fists. She lifted one hand and pressed the side of it against Appenzell's Adam's apple.

She was aware of black shadows gathering around her.

She feared she was losing consciousness until, with three shouted words, the black shadows, moving as one, descended on her and Karl.

'Go! Go! Go!'

Karl was lifted from her body.

Three men in black wetsuits stepped forward.

'You OK, ma'am?' asked one.

Suzy nodded.

'We got him,' one of the men in black said into a walkie-talkie.

They helped Suzy to her feet.

'You put up a great fight there, ma'am. Now we need to get you inside, get some warm clothing on you, and let the doctor take a look at you.'

He gave a hand signal to another man. They carried Suzy through the main doors into the warmth and safety of the ship.

She smiled.

PART SEVEN

The Hudson River

A T 4 A.M. AMANDA was wide awake.
    Since her ordeal last night, she had been handled so kindly by the ship's staff. The doctor and nurses had treated her cuts and bruises. While the nurse took her blood pressure and temperature, and thoroughly checked her over, Amanda had learned a lot.

Appenzell had convinced her, while tied up, that she was lying in his cabin, when in fact she had really been lying tied up in her own, which he had methodically stripped down, removing all her personal possessions along with the phone, the tooth mugs and the door handle.

Once the doctor declared her to be fine, she was told she could go back to the upper ship, but that she should take care in case she had a sudden moment of post-traumatic shock.

Her own clothes had been taken away by the New York police as evidence so some ladies from the purser's office brought down fresh new clothing from the onboard shops. She was told it was being provided free of charge by the ship.

Everything she possessed onboard had been discovered bundled up inside one of Karl Appenzell's own suitcases, stashed away in his cabin. This was also deemed to be evidence, so now she had nothing whatsoever to call her own.

Once dressed, Amanda had been taken in a wheelchair (though she could perfectly well have walked) to a luxurious cabin on the top deck where, at the door, the Captain himself had welcomed her.

'Considering everything you've been through,' he said, 'I have to say you're looking pretty lovely, Mrs Herbert.'

'I feel such a fool,' she said, as he took control of the wheelchair and steered her inside.

'I can only apologise for the appalling behaviour of one of our passengers,' he said, pushing her towards the window.

The fog had lifted now that they were in the river, and outside Amanda could see the black water, sparkling under a bright full moon.

'I really don't understand why he chose me to torment,' said Amanda. 'Do you know why, Captain?'

'It appears that Karl Appenzell was the previous owner of your new flat in Pimlico.' The Captain pulled a chair forward so that he could sit close beside her. 'Do you mind?'

Amanda shook her head. She found the Captain's presence immensely calming. He removed his cap and sat down.

'But how can selling me a flat be an excuse for all these horrible shenanigans?' Amanda could vaguely remember the wretched man hissing something about her flat, as she fell into the drugged stupor. 'Really. It still does not answer the question why?'

'I gather that Europol had been pursuing this man for some time.'

'But why?' asked Amanda, realising that it was becoming her standard question. Why, why why?

'Appenzell was a fraudster, on a large scale,' explained the Captain. 'For months he had been siphoning off vast amounts of money from the bank accounts of some of the richest people in Europe. And when I say vast, I am talking millions of pounds.'

'And the police waited until a week after he got onboard a ship before coming to arrest him?'

'To be fair, the man went by so many assumed names that they had had trouble pinning him down,' he said. 'I gather that the police had got wind, from their colleagues in New

York, that he was planning imminently to cash in his illegally gained fortune and then to fly out to Brunei, which has no extradition arrangement.'

'I still don't get it,' said Amanda. 'What have I to do with any of that? I feel so stupid.'

'You mustn't think that anything was your responsibility. This man was clearly a psychopath.' The Captain took out a notepad. 'If you give me your home number I could phone your husband, or …'

'I'm a widow,' she said. 'And it's probably best to leave *me* to speak to my children. Despite being old enough to have kids of their own, they can get very panicky.'

'I understand,' he said, putting the notebook away. 'I'm in much the same position myself. Widower. Children flew the coop many a year ago. It's a lonely old life …' His voice trailed off. He put on his cap and stood up. 'I'd better go now, and let you have some rest.'

'Please, don't go, Captain,' said Amanda. 'I know it sounds absurd, but I need to go on talking about it all, learning everything you might know about how this all came to pass. Every titbit.'

'I believe that the police are down in the Medical Centre with Suzy Marshall and Jason Scott, getting evidence from them. I'm afraid I don't know that much more. I can only tell you what the London police told me.'

*

Battered and bruised, Suzy sat up in bed, talking to the New York detective. She had given him all the evidence he needed but now she wanted some answers for herself.

'Why us?' she asked.

'Yeah, he's some guy, that Appenzell. But seems it took a couple of limeys to knock him off his high horse.' The detective leaned back in his seat, took one of the grapes off the nightstand and tossed it into his open mouth. 'Hoofers! Really! You couldn't make it up.'

'None of us could understand why he was meddling in our world in the first place,' said Suzy. 'It's well known, in Europe anyhow, that it's a rare man who makes money out of backing little companies like the English Theatre of Zurich.'

'True,' said the detective. 'What we think is that he imagined you'd all be a lot more naïve than you actually are, and that he could use your details, names, passport numbers and all, to set up a whole new set of identities for himself when he went on the run. He really didn't have to put up much money, considering what he was getting in return.'

'And do you have any idea how events rolled out after that?'

'We've been talking to your colleague, Mr Scott, or Monsewer Berry as he is legally known. And between us we got a pretty good picture of it all.'

'We both realised that Appenzell was using his new role as a theatre producer to attract the boys to his nasty little soirée.'

'Oh, yeah. The posters for *The King and I* had been up in Zurich for months, and *even I know* that that show is positively crammed with kids. So the plan was that this Appenzell fella was going to have his sex party, and already intended to run off to London and leave you all high and dry, but not until after your little show opened. He'd already prepared all the passports he needed, using the identities of the male members of the company. So he thought he'd attend the first-night performance, swan around very visibly in his velvet tuxedo and dicky bow at the after-party, then hotfoot it straight to the airport and back to his apartment in London, England. None of you would have missed his presence, I presume, for a few days after that.'

'If at all. Maybe by the weekend we'd realise we'd not been paid, then we'd probably have gone looking for him.'

'But the party went wrong, and the fat man died.'

'And with Stanley missing … everything would have had to come to a head that morning, before opening night. And with the police knocking at Appenzell's door …' Suzy could understand that the events during that party would have necessitated a quick change of plan on Appenzell's part. 'He'd have had to do some pretty quick thinking.'

'That's right. So he moved his whole plan a day forward. We estimate Herr Karl Appenzell got rid of the party guests from his apartment, with the exception of Mr Stanley Arbuthnot – gee, you go in for some pretty weird names on the other side of the pond – at about midnight. Anyhoo, this Stanley fella was making a bit of a fuss about leaving, then the Zurich police came knocking. He silenced the Stanley fella, but it had all got too hot for him. So he made up his mind to get out. He checked into his flight, having decided previously that he would exit Switzerland using the passport he had already made up in Mr Arbuthnot's name. A kind of act of spite, I suppose. Appenzell checked in on a computer in that apartment just after 1 a.m., a short while after the police had gone.'

'I know what happened next,' said Suzy. 'That's when he murdered Stanley.'

'I'd hesitate to use the term murder. We know that he was trying to keep the man quiet. He just went a little too far, is all. But after the visit from the police it was all change again. He discovered that he had *actually killed* Mr Arbuthnot, and knew he had to split from that apartment real quick. And by now he also had some mighty big axe to grind with your friend Jason. We presume he also got squeamish about using the passport of a dead man.'

'So he changed his mind and used a faked-up version of Jason's passport and his ticket to get away from Zurich that morning.'

The detective nodded.

'From computer records, we think Appenzell left the apartment pretty early for the airport and sat in the departure lounge working on his laptop. That was where he had the idea to use all of you actors to set a trail of what they call on TV mysteries "red herrings". He created a subsidiary Swiss account, as you might have an account called "Household" or "Income", only he called this one "Jason Scott". Herr Appenzell didn't like Scott, he blamed him for causing all his troubles, and he couldn't steal money from him as he didn't have his bank details, so, instead, he planned to drop Jason Scott right in the middle of everyone's suspicions by putting some of the theatrical company's stolen money *into* it. In Jason Scott he found a perfect scapegoat.'

'Yes. I can see that Jason had wrecked his whole plan and ruined it for him in many ways and that he wanted revenge. But why target us?'

'Why not? It was always his plan to use you all, your identities anyway. Why not move your money around, create a false trail? While he was at it, why not fleece you all? He truly believed that you had all cheated *him*. In his head it was plain and simple payback.'

Blake popped his head around the curtain. 'Suzy. Could I have a brief word?'

The detective stood and looked at his watch. 'We've been gassing way too long.' He tapped his notebook. 'I'll see you around, Miss Marshall … or not.'

*

'So you're telling me that Karl arrived in London all of a sudden, and went to the flat he was already selling to me.'

Amanda still sat in her wheelchair, sipping hot sweet tea. The Captain had sent down for a tray of tea and biscuits, then proceeded patiently to explain everything he knew about Appenzell's targeting of her.

'Yes. His original plan was to stay in the London flat for two days. But, after the unforeseen events in Zurich, he now had three days in London. He had already booked his flight to New York. For reasons of his own, he needed to arrange for the sale of the London property to go very quickly, so that he'd have that money to hand before he left town. He phoned his solicitor, only to find that everyone of importance was out attending some big court case. Appenzell was fobbed off with the old "we'll call you back" line. And that's when he decided to get onboard this ship.'

'But isn't it an enormous coincidence?' asked Amanda. 'That the very same man from whom I bought my flat should suddenly decide to get on to this ship, which I just happened already to be aboard?'

The Captain smiled. 'No coincidence about it, I'm afraid. He knew you were here. I'd say you gave him the idea.'

'Me? But I had never had any contact with the man before meeting on this ship.'

'When a man like Appenzell is in a hurry, he likes to speed things along, so, feeling rebuffed by his own solicitors, he ignored etiquette, and phoned your solicitors' office. However, when the girl on the switchboard realised that his call was about you, Mrs Herbert, she told him how there was no longer any rush on your part as you were away on a cruise, and then she excitedly told him every gory detail – the name of the ship, and all the ports of call.'

Amanda thought back to her own conversation with the receptionist and realised how easily that could have happened.

'Till that phone call, Appenzell had been intending to fly out of London the next afternoon, using the same alias he had used when he flew in from Zurich, Jason Scott. He'd even checked himself on to next morning's New York flight. But after the switchboard girl told him how this ship would be putting into Southampton at dawn and later in the day would sail out, non-stop, to New York, arriving after a week of glorious, uncontactable solitude, it gave him a wonderful new idea.'

Amanda groaned.

345

'You got it! Appenzell believed that he could have some fun with you. He already knew so many of your details – your address, your full name, date of birth, status, occupation. He hoped that once aboard he would be able to get into your life, on to your computer, fiddle a few passwords, take your savings and throw that money into the distracting mix, and then use your bank account to cover his own tracks. So as soon as he realised he was going to be able to come in direct contact with you, he planted incriminating materials around the flat: indecent photographs, some USB sticks with bank-account details of the acting company from whom he had been stealing. Then you let him know that your son was in the flat, giving him a wonderful new stooge. Once Appenzell came aboard, he checked you out and stalked you, till you gave him all the information he needed to instigate a police raid on your flat and get your son arrested.'

'I told that man everything. His name, I described Mark.' Amanda put her face into her hands. 'I even had Mark's bank details on the jotter on my desk when he came into my cabin. It's all my fault. How stupid I am.'

'Not stupid, Mrs Herbert. You were a sitting duck.'

It all still seemed strange to Amanda.

She had so many more questions.

'Tell me, Captain, wasn't it dicing with danger for a wanted man to spend so long in one place?' Amanda thought back to her first meeting with Appenzell on the deck, when he had been so suave and cool, and so convincing. He did not seem like a man who was being pursued by the police. 'Surely, if time was of the essence, he could have got away quicker by taking that plane?' she said.

'His plan was to hide in plain sight. Appenzell reckoned that if he sashayed around openly on a ship it would be far less "hot" for him. He wasn't using his own name. Why would anyone suspect Stanley K. Arbuthnot, a man with impeccable manners, a man who always dressed perfectly for the occasion, a man who never made a fuss or drew attention to himself?'

Amanda brewed this over.

Again she could see how Appenzell's plan just might have worked.

'One more thing: there are hundreds of cabins on this ship. How did he come to be in the one next door to mine?'

'He wanted to keep track of you and to make the most of his knowledge of you. He knew so much about you. Had googled you and found your photo …'

'Oh God. That silly column I used to write.' Amanda could see how easy it would have been for him.

'Once onboard, Appenzell made a point of finding out where you were, and asked to be moved to that corner of the ship. I gather he followed you around quite often without your noticing.'

'He did appear to have an uncanny ability to bump into me.' Amanda thought back to the meeting on the deck and shivered to think that it had been a set-up.

'It's quite usual for passengers to ask to be moved to a different part of the ship. In fact, Herr Appenzell took a downgrade. The previous holders of his new cabin were only too excited to be bumped up a class. Appenzell had, rather cleverly, bought his ticket and come aboard using one of his stolen aliases, Stanley Arbuthnot. And he was quite certain that this man would not by any chance put in an appearance, as he was – unknown to anyone but Appenzell – lying dead in Appenzell's Zurich apartment.'

Amanda recoiled. 'Oh, how horrible.'

'But it was the problem of disembarking which came to be the undoing of the man. His original plan was to get off the ship using the same alias he used to get onboard. He had only brought three of his passports with him, one genuine, two fakes.'

'Only three!'

'He had around fifty. But thinking he was due to be flying out of London, he had already couriered the others from Zurich to an address in New York. No one having a random Customs check wants the authorities to discover a stash of forty or so passports in their suitcase. Three is just about manageable. One in the jacket pocket, another in the computer case, the third in an inside pocket of your overcoat. But yesterday, Mr Appenzell found out that Stanley Arbuthnot's body had been discovered, four days earlier than he had anticipated.'

'How on earth did he find that out while on this ship?'

'Apparently he followed all the local newspapers in Zurich from his laptop,' said the Captain. 'I suppose if you've killed somebody, it would rather weigh on your mind, and in his position you'd certainly want to know when that body was found. But of course once it was discovered, Mr Appenzell knew he couldn't use Arbuthnot's identity to disembark. As it was a flat he had been associated with, he was also feeling apprehensive about using the passport which was in his real name. So he got out that *third* false passport, and, after dinner last night, he applied for his ESTA, using the one he had made in the name Jason Scott.'

'I see.' When the penny dropped, Amanda could almost hear its clatter. Everything suddenly seemed so clear.

'But then I told him that Jason Scott was onboard this ship.' She took a deep breath, realising that she had been to blame for Appenzell going after Jason. 'And he knew that Jason would *also* be disembarking at New York.'

The Captain nodded. 'Exactly.'

Amanda felt desolate. To think that she had caused this whole debacle by getting drunk and blabbing.

The Captain continued calmly: 'Appenzell had no choice left him. He *had* to use the fake passport he held in Jason Scott's name. But when he discovered Jason was actually here onboard, Appenzell realised he was cornered. He could not disembark. So he went into overdrive. He knew that if he didn't prevent Jason Scott getting off the ship, he was done for. The game was up.'

'But why did he need to silence me?'

'He certainly didn't want you coming to me, making a fuss about a man called Jason Scott fiddling with your bank account. He didn't want anybody drawing attention to Jason. Plus, he is a very vengeful person. It was you who had, in his mind, *lured* him on to this ship in the first place. And so, he needed to get rid of you, or at least to hold you, along with Jason, until he had safely disembarked and boarded that flight to Brunei.'

'And he so very nearly got away with it all,' said Amanda. 'We have both been very lucky.'

The Captain got up.

'And now that you know the full story, I'm sure you'd like to get some sleep.'

The Captain popped on his cap. He strode to the door, where he turned. 'Just one more thing, Mrs Herbert. If you wish to disembark today and fly home, we will understand and will willingly refund your return trip and pick up the bill for your flight. No decisions necessary straight away, but ...'

Amanda nodded. She had so much to think about.

'Oh, and, by the way, we'll be coming into New York Harbour very soon. There is a lounge reserved for you and your friends, if you'd care to sit in the comfort and warmth to see the sights.'

B LAKE ARRIVED AT Suzy's bedside with the offer of a first-class cabin for what remained of the night. He had also said that, in light of the circumstances, he would happily let her leave the ship when they reached New York, along with Jason, and the two could fly back to London together.

She chose to take up his offer and, once she was given pain-killers and her wounds had been re-dressed, she went up to her new cabin on the upper decks to sleep away the last few hours of the voyage.

After a short nap in her luxurious new bedroom, Suzy woke. She felt oddly depressed.

The adventure had come to an end. She wondered to herself what she had done wrong. It seemed as though she had failed, failed in every possible way.

It was just after 4.30 a.m. and the ship was already steaming past Sandy Hook, heading towards the Hudson River. The Captain had sent a message, letting her know about a private lounge which was reserved for her and her friends.

Suzy was keen to watch the ship go under the Verrazano-Narrows Bridge and pass in front of the Statue of Liberty. How could she eschew this once-in-a-lifetime experience?

The effects of last night's horrors were still there, but she didn't want to be on her own. She wanted to be up with the others, celebrating their triumph over evil. She needed to be with Jason and Amanda, and also wanted to see Tyger, Arturo, Liliane and Myriam once more, before they all disembarked.

It might be that they all felt differently and wished to remain in bed until the ship docked, but, come what may, Suzy was going to sit in that private lounge.

She got up and hastily dressed.

Her throat still ached.

She pulled down the bandage and looked in the mirror. There was a horrible red ring left around her throat from Appenzell's makeshift garrotte. Examining the unsightly mark, she now wished that she had attended Melanie's class on fifty ways to tie a silk scarf.

Suzy grabbed her own scarf and threw it carelessly round her neck.

When she emerged from her new cabin, as it was so early in the morning, Suzy expected the ship to be quiet. Instead, the corridors and cafeteria were alive with excited chattering people, grasping cups of coffee, heading for the outer decks to watch the ship's arrival into New York.

She pushed through them and made her way to the top deck.

Up in the private lounge, Suzy found Jason, who greeted her with a bear hug.

'I'm so sorry I let you down, Suze,' he whispered. 'But I was out for the count.'

Poor boy! Seeing him made Suzy forget her own worries.

He looked quite awful. His eyes were puffy and his speech was slower than normal.

He pulled out an armchair for her, and she sat down.

'Oh, Suze,' he said. 'Considering everything, you do brush up well!' His flashing smile remained undimmed.

Jason flopped down into the chair beside hers and pointed a finger at a huge ice bucket filled with a magnum of champagne, surrounded by a circle of champagne flutes. 'Bit too early to pop that cork, do you think?'

'Oh God!' Suzy reached out and grabbed Jason's hand. 'We got him, Jason. We got the bastard.'

The door opened and in came the steward who, under Arturo's spell, had helped them get into Appenzell's cabin. He pushed a wheelchair bearing Amanda.

'Don't worry,' said Amanda firmly. 'I am quite able to walk unaided, but the doctor insisted.'

Once positioned beside them both, Amanda spoke. 'Thank you, you two. Thank you, thank you, thank you, thank you!'

'We're all going to be thanking one another for a long time,' said Suzy.

'Why are we gathered in the middle of the room?' Jason stood. 'If we want to see anything we need to be by the windows.

He wheeled Amanda's chair to a spot where she'd have a better view. He then pushed two more chairs either side so that he, Suzy and Amanda could sit together.

'We'll have the best view on the ship from here,' said Suzy. 'What a trip! We were an unwitting team. All three of us unintentionally connected with that vile man.'

'What happened to *him*? Does anybody know?' asked Amanda.

'They winched him off the ship,' said Jason. 'He's been taken straight to some penitentiary in New York for questioning by Interpol.'

'Good riddance,' said Suzy. 'I hope they bang him up for a very long time.'

'What is that land mass?' asked Amanda, pointing through the window to rows of orange lights.

'That'll be Staten Island.' Suzy found the sight of the first onshore lights they had seen since passing Land's End strangely unsettling. 'Look beyond, you can see the planes circling over Newark Airport.'

'Which means we're about to sail under the Verrazano-Narrows Bridge, everyone,' cried Jason, cupping his hands to peer through the glass. 'Quick! Look up!'

They all gazed at the red and white lights of the massive bridge. They could hear cars and lorries hooting, welcoming the huge ship into the harbour.

They watched the ship's funnel seem to skim under the wide span, appearing to miss it by a mere few inches.

'Welcome to New York!' Jason raised an empty glass. 'We must open that bottle.'

After a few moments' silence Amanda put out her hand to touch the large arrangement of roses, lilies and gypsophila on a console table near her chair. 'Look at those gorgeous flowers! One of the marvellous things about this ship is their constant use of beautiful floral displays. I've never worked out how they manage to keep them all so fresh.'

'Barbara sent me a bouquet, Suze,' Jason said quietly.

'Yes. Me too. Thank God for her.' Suzy turned towards Amanda. 'Barbara was our stage manager in Zurich,' she explained. 'She is the last link in the chain. It was Barbara who alerted the police. She had received an email from me. But it was Barbara who put two and two together and phoned Scotland Yard. Then the boys in blue sent for the New York City harbour police to board the ship.'

'You'd think they might have waited those few hours till we dock,' said Jason.

'I supposed they feared that, unless they picked up that swine Appenzell straight away, by the time we reached dry land there might be a few more dead bodies onboard,' suggested Amanda.

'There nearly were.' Suzy fought back tears as she reached out once more to hold hands with Amanda and Jason. 'Oh, for goodness' sake, Jason. Arise from your semi-recumbent position and pop that bloody bottle. We need to celebrate.'

There was a knock on the door and Liliane peeped inside. 'Do you mind if we join you? Ze Captain invited us.'

She entered, tailed by Arturo, Myriam and Tyger.

353

'I'll look after that,' said Arturo, taking the champagne bottle from Jason, who had removed the foil and the cage. He held the bottle aloft in one hand. Then he glared at the bottle and clicked the fingers of his other hand.

The cork flew up and hit the ceiling.

He handed the open bottle back to Jason.

'Please do the honours, Mr Scott.'

While Jason poured, the door opened again and Melanie, the social hostess, came in bearing a large tray of sandwiches.

'You poor things. You've all been through so much,' she said, then turned to Jason and Suzy. 'And as your talks on *The Importance of Being Earnest* were so well-received, I thought a tray of these might be just the thing.'

Amanda, Jason and Suzy took a finger sandwich each.

'Cucumber,' said Suzy.

'Cucumber sandwiches?' said Jason. '"Why such reckless extravagance in one so young?"'

Despite their attempts to lighten the atmosphere, there was still a pall of depression over the room.

Myriam piped up. 'I forgot to tell you! I finally went to that ghastly Dorothy's party. I just turned up uninvited in the Seahorse Lounge after tea, wearing my best party dress, and do you know what? The woman was a no-show! At her own party! However, I made so many new friends. Such *nice* young men. Extremely funny, and all so very beautifully turned out.'

No one said anything.

After a brief lull, Melanie asked Suzy, 'Will you be leaving us today?'

'I think so,' Suzy replied. 'Blake didn't seem to want to keep me on. So yes, I'll be leaving.'

'Really?' Melanie gave Suzy a puzzled look. 'I'm sorry to hear that. Anyway – goodbye, then, in case we don't bump into one another again.'

She left the room.

'Thinking about Appenzell …' said Jason, staring down at his sandwich.

'Must we?' Arturo hissed and held his fingers up in his familiar protective gesture against the evil eye.

'It simply occurred to me that we had the vital clue in *The Importance of Being Earnest*,' said Jason. 'Appenzell was a Bunburyist. In order to get his own way, and deceive others, he lived under multiple aliases.'

'He was a Bunburyist in the most dangerous fashion,' added Suzy.

'He was a monster!' Myriam took a sandwich and a napkin, with which she fanned herself as she sank sedately on to the sofa. 'And please don't think that man took me in for one moment. I always knew he was simply a wolf in cheap clothing.' She turned to Tyger who was taking a full glass of champagne from Jason. 'Tyger, you're too young to drink liquor on *either* side of the Atlantic. But … well, just one small glass.'

Tyger picked up the wire cage from the floor. 'This is called a muselet. It's the French word for muzzle.'

Liliane laughed. 'Pity we did not 'ave a real muselet for that diabolical man.'

Amanda gazed out at the New Jersey coastline. Everything was resolved. Mark had been released with no charge. She was shaken but fine. But she couldn't help feeling blue. She could see planes taking off, their lights throwing long beams into the black sky. She imagined herself getting off the ship in a few hours and flying home to London.

Then what?

Where would she go?

Her only possible home would be the flat where Appenzell had run his nasty operations and got up to God knows what else. Despite being in this room full of people, she felt alone and very dejected. Sitting in the wheelchair as the doctor had suggested wasn't making her feel better. Quite the opposite. She called across to Jason.

'Would you be a sweetheart?' she asked him. 'I hate this damned chair. Please get me out of it.'

Jason and Suzy stood either side of Amanda, their arms around her waist, and helped her to her feet.

The three, linked together, stared out of the window.

'Well, we have certainly had a time of it, wouldn't you say?' Suzy sighed. She wasn't sure whether they were experiencing some syndrome or other, but she felt emotionally bound to Amanda and Jason, and wanted to remain in their company, united against a common evil.

Suzy also felt desolate that the job had come to such an abrupt end, and that she had failed. Clearly, as far as Blake was concerned, nothing she had done onboard had been good enough. He was obviously glad to see the back of her. She felt like crying.

There was a knock on the door, and the Captain entered with Blake and another man. After a few pleasantries, they excused themselves to the others and went across to Jason, Amanda and Suzy.

The Captain introduced the third man as the ship's hotel manager, Rob Ritchie.

'I know I said we would provide you all with a flight home today, but my colleague, Mr Ritchie, has just suggested another proposition.' The Captain paused, and left the hotel manager to continue.

Rob spoke with a charming Scottish burr. 'First, we completely understand if you want to leave the ship in New York,' he said. 'But if any of you would like to remain onboard, we'd be delighted to offer the three of you the same cabins you are now in, along with first-class dining, for the journey back to England.'

'Compliments of the company.' The Captain turned and spoke directly to Amanda. 'You've probably had quite enough of us and want to get back, but I just thought I'd offer you the choice.'

'Could I add something, sir?' Blake interrupted. 'Suzy, I apologise if I gave you a false impression. You see, we have all been more than happy with your classes and talks, and particularly with the way you coped during innumerable unforeseen onstage disasters. So, if you would like to stay on the team, giving your talks and classes all the way up the coast and back to Southampton, I would love it.' Blake smiled at Jason. 'You too, Jason, have acquitted yourself admirably, always doing more than you were asked, never being seen on the decks without a smile on your face. But, as you know, you are way too young to qualify for the position of a gentleman host.'

Suzy's heart plunged as she realised Jason was about to be booted off the team.

'I wondered,' Blake went on, 'whether you would be interested in taking on some entertainment duties, hosting quizzes, helping Suzy in the acting classes and lectures, and also staying with us, travelling back to the UK?'

The Captain surveyed the group. 'I'll leave you all a little time to think about it.'

'I don't need to think about it, Captain,' Amanda blurted out. 'I'm going to instruct an estate agent to sell that awful man's flat. And in the meanwhile, it would be lovely to have somewhere to stay, if only for the ten days back to England. And I love this boat.'

'Ship,' corrected the Captain, closing one eye tight. 'Aaargh!'

Amanda laughed.

Suzy felt the way actors felt after a first night – exhausted but exhilarated and hyped up with adrenalin. She didn't want to climb on a plane home in a couple of hours. Back to dreary London in December, with nothing to do, and no one to do it with. The ship was bright, cheery and busy and offered her everything that she loved. Work, company and glamour.

'Please can I stay aboard too?' Suzy asked. 'In spite of everything, I love this ship.'

'Don't leave me out of this,' said Jason. 'If they're staying, I have to stay as well.' He paused and asked, 'I do get the fancy-cabin offer too, don't I?'

'Of course,' replied the hotel manager.

'Let's do it!' Jason turned to Suzy and Amanda. 'I won't be an official dancing partner any more, but I hope you'll both still join me for the odd cha-cha-cha.'

Suzy, Amanda and Jason clinked their glasses together.

'Happy to hear it,' said the Captain. 'I shall look forward to seeing you all one night at my table. Oh, and Melanie, we could do with another couple of bottles of champagne. Could you please phone down?'

'Quick! Quick! Everybody!' Myriam, face pressed to the port-side window, waved her hands up and down. 'Look! Come, come, come! Quickly, quickly, quickly!'

The Captain, who knew perfectly well what had caught Myriam's eye, took the moment to slip away, leaving Amanda, Suzy and Jason to join the gaggle gathered at the window.

'Lady Liberty!' said Suzy, looking out at the floodlit Statue of Liberty standing proudly on Liberty Island in a golden haze, her lamp and crown glowing orange in the morning mist. 'What a beauty she is.'

'"Send these, the homeless, tempest-tost to me, I lift my lamp beside the golden door!"' recited Amanda. '"The home-less, tempest-tost." That's us all right.'

'I don't know about lifting my lamp,' said Suzy. 'But, if we're talking about lifting our glasses, I could do with a top-up.'

'You get the wish!' Arturo poured the last of the champagne into Suzy's glass.

Suzy closed her eyes as she made that wish.

'We've come a long way since those auditions in Palmers Green. Haven't we, Jason.'

'Not to mention since the grim rehearsals next door to that cemetery!' Jason put his arm around her waist. 'Thank you,

Suze.' He shrugged and smiled. 'Thank you for being such a sport, for saving my life, for everything.'

He looked across at the others, all staring out at the Statue of Liberty.

'What more do you want?' he asked, gesturing towards Eiffel's famous copper-green statue. 'Liberty enlightening the world.'

'Oscar said it better,' said Suzy. '"The good ended happily, and the bad unhappily ..."' Once more she quoted from *The Importance of Being Earnest*.

'"That is what Fiction means,"' she added, as Jason spoke in unison with her.

'And that is, hopefully, what real life means too!'

Suzy raised her glass.

ACKNOWLEDGEMENTS

Thank you:

To the commodores, captains, hotel managers, entertainment managers, social hostesses, waiters, gentleman hosts, dancers, singers, musicians, entertainers, lecturers, technical teams, stewards and crew who have always given me such a good time while crossing the Atlantic in their magnificent ship, the *Queen Mary 2* – which bears only the slightest resemblance to the *Blue Mermaid*! In particular, thanks to Bernard, Kevin, Christopher, Jamie, David, Robbie, Paul, Jo, Cat, Amanda, Tommi and Cheryl for making me laugh, come hell AND high water!

    I still say it's the ONLY way to travel.

To my friends at La Civette, Le Safari and Les Jardins du Capitole: JF, Sebastien, Charles, Raymond, Gilbert, Daniel, Fabrizio and Gianni. *Issa Nissa! Allez Nice!*

To Lina, *merci tellement*.

To Alexandra, Robert, for encouraging me to write this book.

To all my pals at the Regal Cinema Club for our jolly afternoons watching those camp and wonderful films. 'Hey! That horse looked at the camera!'

To Fidelis, who first coaxed me on to the *Queen Mary 2*, and whose research into the world of cruising and sea travel, and enthusiasm for and knowledge of the sea and transatlantic liners, really helped this book take shape. Ahoy there – Cap'n M!

A NOTE ON THE AUTHOR

Celia Imrie is an Olivier award-winning and Screen Actors Guild-nominated actress. She is known for her film roles in *The Best Exotic Marigold Hotel*, *The Second Best Exotic Marigold Hotel*, *Calendar Girls* and *Nanny McPhee*. Celia has recently starred in the major films *Bridget Jones's Baby*, *Absolutely Fabulous: The Movie*, *Year by the Sea* and *A Cure for Wellness*. In 2016 she also appeared in FX's new comedy series *Better Things*, and returned to the stage in *King Lear* at The Old Vic. She will co-star with Imelda Staunton, Timothy Spall and Joanna Lumley in the upcoming *Finding Your Feet*. Celia Imrie is also the author of an autobiography, *The Happy Hoofer*, and two top ten *Sunday Times* bestselling novels, *Not Quite Nice* and *Nice Work (If You Can Get It)*.

www.celiaimrie.info
@CeliaImrie

A NOTE ON THE TYPE

The text of this book is set in Adobe Caslon, named after the English punch-cutter and type-founder William Caslon I (1692–1766). Caslon's rather old-fashioned types were modelled on seventeenth-century Dutch designs, but found wide acceptance throughout the English-speaking world for much of the eighteenth century until replaced by newer types towards the end of the century. Used in 1776 to print the Declaration of Independence, they were revived in the nineteenth century and have been popular ever since, particularly amongst fine printers. There are several digital versions, of which Carol Twombly's Adobe Caslon is one.